Praise for Gallagher Gray's Hubbert & Lil mysteries

PARTNERS IN CRIME

"Deftly plotted and well-paced . . . Two wonderful sleuths make their debut."
—*The San Francisco Chronicle*

"Weaves a wondrous web of work relationships shrouded by ghosts of a long-ago scandal . . . In the classic British cozy tradition right down to the body with the antique dagger in its chest."
—*The Drood Review of Mystery*

A CAST OF KILLERS

"With a fond eye for the eccentric, Gray gives the streets of Hell's Kitchen the air of a gritty English village."
—*Publishers Weekly*

"Gray has the rare talent of being able to combine humor with sensitivity, and high comedy with realistic portrayals of genuine people."
—*The Virginian-Pilot & The Ledger-Star*

By Gallagher Gray
Published by Ivy Books:

HUBBERT & LIL: PARTNERS IN CRIME
A CAST OF KILLERS
DEATH OF A DREAM MAKER
A MOTIVE FOR MURDER

A MOTIVE FOR MURDER

Gallagher Gray

IVY BOOKS • NEW YORK

Ivy Books
Published by Ballantine Books
Copyright © 1996 by Gallagher Gray

Library of Congress Catalog Card Number: 95-95081

ISBN 0-8041-1248-7

Manufactured in the United States of America

First Edition: April 1996

10 9 8 7 6 5 4 3 2 1

CHAPTER ONE

1. The phone rang just as the New York Giants neared the end of a hard-won ninety-two-yard march. It was third down and goal to go at the Redskins' three-yard line. The crowd was roaring with enthusiasm. T.S. wasn't sure what all the excitement was about because this was the first football game he had ever watched. But the announcer sounded like he was being strangled, so T.S. was pretty sure that the Giants were doing well. He leaned closer to the television, hoping to decipher why the quarterback kept shouting numbers at his teammates and what that information might mean. Perhaps he was identifying the jersey numbers of opposing players that should be hit on the next play. In the background, T.S. noted the mechanical click of his answering machine as it picked up the call.

"Theodore. Are you rotting your brain again?" Auntie Lil's voice cut through his apartment, rising easily above the televised noise. It nearly shook the answering machine off the desk. Brenda and Eddie shifted in their feline sleep, no doubt dreaming of the booming loudspeakers at the ASPCA, where T.S. had brought them for neutering.

He ignored Auntie Lil with a vengeance. She was the reason why he was sitting in front of the idiot box in the first place, desperately clutching a can of beer in one hand and the remote control in the other. He had never in his life watched a football game or swigged beer straight from the can. But he had, that very morning, felt an overwhelming desire to touch base with the untapped resources of his

1

middle-class, middle-aged soul by joining America in watching football. And it was all Auntie Lil's fault.

Any man would have crumbled. For the past few weeks, without respite, she had dragged him to one avant-garde dance performance after another. Last night had been the proverbial last straw. He had given up his favorite true-crime television show to accompany her to a premiere at the Joyce Dance Theater. There, surrounded by women who looked like men and men who dressed like women, T.S. had endured two hours of thumping atonal music and the unappetizing sight of twelve dancers—clad only in boxer shorts and black combat boots—stomping about a set that resembled a mental asylum for dangerous prisoners. Muscular men and women shrieked at each other, threw themselves against the fake brick walls that lined the stage, rattled plastic bars like actors in a bad B movie, and did no dancing at all that T.S. could discern. By the end of this night, his head was pounding and he never wanted to see another energetic movement in his life. He'd rather move into a retirement community for overweight couch potatoes first.

The worst was yet to come. Later, he dreamed he was incarcerated on Riker's Island with a pink-tutued Hell's Angel devotee for a cellmate. This hulking vision kept demonstrating a series of intricate ballet steps over and over while threatening to beat T.S. if he did not memorize the sequence perfectly. T.S. woke in a sweat and declared a moratorium on dance. He then dashed out to the corner deli and surprised the clerk by requesting a six-pack of Rolling Rock beer instead of his usual roll of chewable antacids. He was sure that a few sessions watching sports and swigging beer would restore him to normalcy.

Unfortunately, the choreography on the field made no more sense to him than what he'd seen the night before. A player had broken through the human wall before him on the last play and was prancing around the end of the field, wiggling his butt at his opponents while waving the ball at a riotous crowd. If you put him center stage at the Joyce Dance Theater, he'd get a standing ovation.

"Theodore, I know you hated last night's performance," Auntie Lil announced over his phone machine. "And I also know you hold me personally responsible. But you simply must pick up. This is a matter of life and death." She paused dramatically. "I am talking about the ballet!"

The field was in turmoil. The players were piled in a jumbled heap on top of a Giant who had tried to kick the ball. The two men in striped shirts were blowing their whistles wildly. Reluctantly, T.S. took his eyes from the screen and stared at the telephone. The ballet? Then he remembered: Auntie Lil had mentioned a board meeting for the Metropolitan Ballet today.

The Metro Ballet was a fixture of life in New York City and one of the few charitable projects undertaken by Auntie Lil that T.S. endorsed. Ever since she had inherited a great deal of money, his obstinate but beloved aunt had suffered from an acute case of dance fever. She had endowed scholarships to budding Isadora Duncan reincarnations all over the United States. But she had also rescued an ailing Metro Ballet, effusing it with enough money to finish last year's season and, quite literally, saving a dozen or more careers. She had been rewarded with a coveted seat on the ballet's board of directors, thanks, in part, to the influence of their mutual friend, the wealthy and well-bred Lilah Cheswick.

The thought of Lilah made T.S. forget about football. His heart skipped a beat as he pictured the silver-haired object of his self-conscious attention. She would be at the Metro's board meeting. His hand inched toward the phone.

"If you don't pick up the phone, I will inform Lilah that you are deliberately ignoring me," Auntie Lil announced with uncanny accuracy. "Despite the fact that I am your closest living relative."

She was merciless. She was also capable of carrying out her threat.

"What is it?" T.S. demanded, trying to sound busy. "You've called at a bad time. The Giants are only minutes away from scoring the winning basket."

"Impossible," she retorted. "Giants are football. Football players make touchdowns. This is more important."

"What is it?" he asked warily.

"You must call Margo McGregor immediately and get her down to Lincoln Center. There is a disaster in the making, Theodore."

"What kind of disaster?" he asked faintly, knowing that, somehow, Auntie Lil was involved. Disaster was her maiden name and Chaos was her middle.

"That pompous Lane Rogers and her weaselly cohorts are trying to vote Fatima Jones out of *The Nutcracker*," Auntie Lil said, enraged. "Theodore, that Rogers woman is wearing a Chanel suit two sizes too small. It's a travesty."

T.S. was not interested in this fashion faux pas. "What?" he asked. "Get rid of Fatima? They can't do that." Fatima Jones was a young ballerina who had emerged from the hopeful ranks of Auntie Lil's inner-city scholarship program as a potential star.

"They can and they will if we don't stop them. Hurry." She hung up without saying good-bye, a move T.S. anticipated. With satisfaction, he beat her to the punch.

Football game forgotten, T.S. set to work dialing the offices of *New York Newsday*, beginning a long search for the whereabouts of columnist Margo McGregor. Auntie Lil was right. It was a disaster. Maybe Margo could help.

2. "We have no business interfering in artistic decisions," Auntie Lil said crisply. "That should be left to the artistic director." She folded her hands primly in front of her, a difficult move to pull off since they clenched into fists every time she looked at board chairman Lane Rogers. Lane was an unpleasant, hulking woman who invariably dressed in shades of plum and brown.

"It is our responsibility to protect the ballet," Lane countered piously. "We have a fiscal duty to make difficult decisions such as this." Her voice was peppered with dropped *r*'s to emulate a New England accent, one of her many affectations. The truth of the matter was that Lane Rogers was really Lani Kaufman from Yonkers—and Auntie Lil knew it because she had worked with four of Lane's uncles years ago in the garment industry.

The Kaufman brothers had been the finest cutting team on Seventh Avenue. All four had followed their niece's social journey to Manhattan's Upper East Side—via a name change and Seven Sisters school—with merciless and scornful enthusiasm. "Sol's shiksa-in-training," they called her, referring to their deceased brother Solomon, who had worked himself to death selling pocketbooks to put his beloved daughter through the college of her choice. Hiram Kaufman, the only brother left alive, still called Auntie Lil every year on the first day of the spring season to cluck over the year's collections and to catch up on family gossip. Not only did Auntie Lil know that Lane Rogers had spent two weeks every summer for the last twenty years at a fat farm desperately sweating off excess poundage, she also knew Lane had been one of the first women in New York City to sign up for liposuction and that the entry sutures had gotten hideously infected. It gave Auntie Lil great satisfaction to hoard these details and never repeat them. But Lane still sensed that Auntie Lil knew she was a phony—and she hated Auntie Lil for it.

"It's our duty," echoed Ruth Beretsky when Lane concluded her fiscal responsibility spiel. Ruth was a mousy board member who quivered fearfully whenever she spoke, as if an invisible stun gun were hovering about her body at all times. Or perhaps she lived in fear that Lane Rogers would start beating her about the arms and legs without warning. Auntie Lil would not have been surprised to see this occur. Scrawny Ruth was the perfect sidekick to Lane's hulking presence. The omnipresent cloth bow that bloomed at the base of her turkeylike neck made her an even more obsequious target for Lane's constant bullying authority. Why they were friends, Auntie Lil could not fathom, but she didn't understand a lot of other things either, particularly the current fad for body piercing. Surely all those rings snagged on clothing and jewelry. She'd tried to ask a young man about it down on St. Mark's Place just the week before, but he had walked right past as if he didn't hear. When you were eighty-four years old, this happened a lot. But not usually to Auntie Lil.

"I fail to see how removing the most talented ballerina to come along in two decades will help our box-office receipts," Lilah Cheswick pointed out. "Fatima Jones has natural talent, flawless timing, and a classic frame." Lilah was the wealthy widow of a former Wall Street wizard and no slouch herself when it came to business matters. She had informally inherited a dozen seats on corporate and charitable boards when her husband died unexpectedly—and proved to be a far more capable and creative director than he had ever been.

"She is certainly talented," Artistic Director Raoul Martinez agreed in his dramatic basso. "And I must concur with Miss Hubbert that it is inappropriate for the board to interfere with my artistic vision. After all, auditions have been held, the students expect results to be released tomorrow, and we are competing with two other versions of *The Nutcracker* for the holiday crowds. I must be allowed to take chances, to paint new vistas—"

"There he goes again," Lane Rogers interrupted, rolling her protuberant eyes. "Mr. Artistic Vision himself." The coterie of prominent wives who rounded out the board twittered dutifully at this witticism. They reminded Auntie Lil of a flock of terns whenever they made noise, so uniformly small and delicate were they.

"Let me tell you what we should do," board member Hans Glick interrupted in his clipped Swiss accent. A collective groan rose as the assembled group hunkered down for another lecture by Glick. Not a proposal was set forth, not a document typed, not a luncheon served, and not a ballet presented that Hans Glick could not improve on with his wisdom. He was pigheaded, long-winded, indecisive, occasionally right, and—most important of all—president of the

Metro Ballet's largest corporate sponsor, Swiss International United. "We should lay out the pros and cons of what we are facing and then our decision will be easy. I will show you."

He stood with a barely perceptible click of his heels and marched briskly to a wheeled chalkboard that stood near a window overlooking Lincoln Center. Auntie Lil gazed wistfully out at the twinkling lights of the early winter evening and wished that she was sipping drinks in the Rainbow Room, waiting for Herbert Wong to join her for a tango.

Glick dragged the portable chalkboard to the head of the long conference table, frowning at the squeak emitted by its wheels. The slightest deviation from perfection, as defined by himself, could distract Glick to the point of incoherence. He chose a fat wedge of chalk and held it above the chalkboard, but paused in his impending lecture to pick up the telephone. He knew the extension by memory. "Send someone up to Conference Room 224 immediately," he demanded. "Tell him to bring a can of WD-40 and a Phillips head screwdriver. I will tell him how to fix the problem once he arrives."

He placed the phone back in the cradle and wiped his hands clean with a handkerchief before addressing the waiting board members. He began by drawing a huge dollar sign in the center of the board. "This is our objective," he announced crisply, "and these are our options." He drew thick chalk lines to the right and left of the dollar sign, labeling one side "A" and the other "B." Under the letter A, he drew a tall box then sketched in small squares arranged in rows within its parameters.

"What is that, please?" Artistic Director Martinez thundered, looking confused.

Glick was offended. "That is obviously a New York City apartment house."

"Why?" Martinez demanded loudly.

Glick ignored him and continued. "If we let Fatima Jones dance in the role of Clara, we will gain some publicity due to her unusual background," he said. "But the demographics are not as profitable as Option B." He drew the stick figure of a young boy under the B heading, then added several rows of dollar signs at the boy's feet. "Mikey Morgan is a box-office star. His movies brought in more than two hundred eighty-seven million dollars to his studio last year. His fan club numbers over eight hundred thousand young people in the U.S. alone."

"The only drawback being that he can't dance," Auntie Lil interjected.

Several of the more silent board members looked aghast, as if she had violated an unspoken code of conduct. Auntie Lil hoped fervently that she had.

Raoul Martinez was thoughtful. "It is true that he is not inordinately talented," the artistic director conceded. "But he is coachable. When he was a student here, I spotted his promise."

"How odd," Lilah Cheswick remarked, her well-bred Connecticut smile never faltering. "Just last week I read an amusing interview with Mikey Morgan that appeared in the Sunday *Times* magazine. He related several stories of being suspended and eventually thrown out of the Metro's school. 'Thrown out on my butt by this aging old greaser in tights' I believe were the exact words he used. He seemed to find it amusing from his current perch as a box-office star. I wonder why he wants to dance the role at all. I don't feel comfortable with his stated motives."

Martinez shrugged dramatically. "I am an excellent teacher. I have confidence he can dance the role."

"Don't forget that another young man's career is at stake here," Auntie Lil said. "If we vote no on Fatima Jones and Mikey Morgan steps into the role of the Prince, then what will become of Rudy Vladimir? He won the role of the Prince fairly."

"Rudy can easily dance a lesser role," Martinez offered.

"Of course he can easily dance a lesser role," Auntie Lil said. "He could easily dance *all* the roles, for that matter.

At fourteen years of age, he makes the rest of your company look like a tired troupe of vaudeville hoofers."

"Really, Miss Hubbert, I hardly believe you are qualified to comment," Martinez retorted in a low voice that had tamed many an unpredictable dancer. On Auntie Lil, it didn't even make a dent.

"I cannot believe that we are even considering bumping these two young dancers from the show," she said. "It is outrageous."

"We do not 'bump' our dancers," Martinez said grimly. "And we are not putting on a 'show' in some barn like those cheap Mickey Mouse and Judy Garland movies."

"Maybe you had Mickey Mouse down in Mexico, but here in America it was Mickey *Rooney*," Auntie Lil pointed out.

"I am from *Spain*," the artistic director explained grimly. "My family is of impeccable Hibernian descent."

Auntie Lil sniffed skeptically.

Lane Rogers attempted to regain control. "The ideal choice, of course, would be to have both Mikey Morgan and Fatima Jones. Unfortunately that is not possible."

"You mean that, unfortunately, we are being extorted by the young man's manager father to get rid of Fatima," Auntie Lil said. "And we demean ourselves by giving in."

"Now, now," Hans Glick argued smoothly. "It is not extortion but a legitimate concern. If Fatima Jones were to dance, much of the publicity would be focused on her, taking away from the attention paid to his son. It is his duty as the boy's manager to ensure his client's career. We must not forget the young lady's background." He tapped his crudely drawn tenement building with the piece of chalk. "It will attract attention. The press love such stories these days."

Auntie Lil lost her temper. She stood and propped her sturdy frame on the table, leaning forward until her purple scarf fluttered in Lane Rogers's face. A white curl escaped from beneath her matching hat and dangled between her large dark eyes. Her strong German face flushed a dangerous red as her wide mouth struggled to hold back intemperate words. "Will you stop referring euphemistically to 'her background,' " she demanded of Glick. "It is a bit ridiculous for you to deny that your real problem is that Fatima Jones is rather obviously black."

In the silence that followed, the door to the conference room opened and a maintenance man the color of motor oil strode into the room. He held a spray can of WD-40 in one hand and a yellow cloth in the other. He was middle-aged and well built, his shoulders straining at his gray uniform. The silence that greeted his arrival did not throw him off at all. He simply said calmly, "Someone called about a problem?"

Auntie Lil sat abruptly and watched as Hans Glick described exactly where and how the maintenance man should minister to the squeaking chalkboard. Oblivious to this interference, the maintenance man efficiently banished the squeak, tightened a few bolts, and marched quietly from the room.

"He *heard* you," Lane Rogers hissed as the door closed behind him. She glared at Auntie Lil.

"So you see," Glick continued quickly, "it's rather obvious, isn't it? If Mikey Morgan will not dance on the same stage with Fatima Jones, he must dance with some other lucky young lady." He drew a circle of chalk around the stick figure of the boy then pointed proudly to the nonsensical chart, as if he had just deciphered the hieroglyphic secrets of a lost pharaoh's tomb.

"I call a vote," Lane said firmly. "So we can go on to other business. Mikey Morgan is a very talented young man and deserves this chance. I intend to vote yes."

"If you vote Fatima Jones out, the press will eat us alive," Auntie Lil warned. "They're sure to find out."

"However would they find out?" Lane asked, her gaze warning the assembled crowd. "Board business is confidential—or else."

Despite this veiled threat, the vote was quick and overwhelming. Fatima Jones was out. Child star Mikey Morgan was in. And Rudy Vladimir was not even mentioned. *Nutcracker* rehearsals would begin the next day. Only Lilah Cheswick and, at the very last minute, the unpredictable Artistic Director Martinez joined Auntie Lil in voting to retain Fatima Jones.

"You should all be ashamed of yourselves," Auntie Lil said as the votes were recounted for the record. "Compromising the careers of talented young dancers to satisfy the greedy needs of a power-hungry stage father."

It was an insult worthy of Dickens, but Lane Rogers easily ignored it. "That's settled," she said crisply, consulting the agenda meticulously typed by the cooperative Ruth Beretsky. She decided on the next item of importance. "Let's move on to the pending business of our opening night benefit," she said. "Let me begin by saying that I cannot agree with Miss Hubbert that it would 'be fun' to make it a casino night."

3. "Where were you?" Auntie Lil demanded when she spotted T.S. waiting for her in the hallway after the meeting.

"I could hardly burst into the meeting," T.S. protested, firmly removing her grip from his arm. "I am not a board member."

"Why are you alone? Where is Margo McGregor?"

"They couldn't find her," T.S. explained. "She's out on assignment somewhere. I left a message telling her to get in touch. What happened?"

Auntie Lil nodded toward the other end of the hallway, where board members stood clustered around a satisfied-looking Bobby Morgan. They were listening as he painted a Hollywood-star saturated premiere of *The Nutcracker* starring his son. "See that man?" she asked.

"He's hard to miss," T.S. admitted.

Bobby Morgan stood out in distinct contrast to the grimly thin New York socialites surrounding him. He was in his mid-thirties and of average height, but had the look of a man who has recently packed on excess weight and whose self-image and skin have not quite caught up to the change. Not even a deep golden tan could disguise the pallor of too many overindulgent late nights. He wore expensive designer clothing, no socks, and a pair of loafers that T.S. knew had cost him close to a grand. He had a thick mane of brown hair slightly grayed at the temples that was pulled back off his face into the requisite small ponytail currently in vogue with aging creative types. His features were oddly delicate given the chubbiness of his face, particularly his narrow, ruler-straight nose. He gesticulated grandly as he entertained the rapt crowd. His remarks were punctuated by the occasional metallic glimmers the overhead lights sent spiraling from his abundant jewelry.

"Let me take a wild guess," T.S. ventured. "He's from Los Angeles."

"He's the father of some child star named Mikey Morgan," Auntie Lil explained.

"Never heard of him," T.S admitted.

"That's to your credit, dear." Auntie Lil patted his hand. "A few days ago, the Metro's artistic director got a call from him. His name is Bobby Morgan. He offered his son as the lead in our upcoming production of *The Nutcracker*. But he made one stipulation: Fatima Jones could not dance opposite his son."

"Why?" T.S. asked. "Fatima is terrific. Even I can tell that and I don't know a leaper from a leper."

"She is terrific, but because she's black, Morgan is afraid the publicity over her participation will take away attention from his son. Since he acts as his son's agent and manager, what he says goes."

"That sounds incredibly selfish," T.S. said. "Why does the kid want to do the part anyway if he's a Hollywood hotshot?"

Auntie Lil shrugged. "Lilah asked the same thing. Morgan says it's because his son needs some legitimate stage credits and that he wants to prove to his old teachers at the Metro that he can do it. The boy was a student here a few years ago before the father took him to California. Not a very good one, either."

"And the board agreed?" T.S. asked.

"Almost unanimously," Auntie Lil said grimly. "Thanks to that human slug Lane Rogers."

On cue, Lane sailed past with Ruth Beretsky dutifully trailing after her. She paused at the edge of the group surrounding Morgan and waited to be recognized. When this tactic did not work, she extended a hand through the crowd, skillfully pushing aside less hefty members and planting herself firmly in Morgan's line of vision.

"Hello, Bobby," she thundered. "It's so very lovely to see you again. We're delighted to have your son with us this season. Of course, you'll join me at the head table during the benefit dinner?" She laughed girlishly and T.S. realized, with some horror, that she was attempting to be coquettish.

Morgan's smile was automatic and completely plastic. "Of course, Mrs. Rogers. I'd be delighted," he cooed, taking her limp hand and holding it as if it were a sock he had just found on the floor.

"That's Miss," she corrected him. "And please call me Lane."

"Call me nauseated," T.S. muttered as Morgan beamed brightly back at her.

"This is disgusting," Auntie Lil decided. "Sucking up to people because they have poolside drinks near other people who star in bad television shows. What ever happened to culture? I'm going to blow the lid right off this disgraceful decision when I see Margo."

"Maybe not," T.S. said firmly. "I think we need to discuss this in private." He steered her down the hallway toward the elevators. "Where's Lilah?" he remembered, peering into the conference room.

"She had to leave early for another board meeting," Auntie Lil explained. "She has quite a few, you know."

An anxious twinge took root in the base of his stomach. Was it his imagination or had Lilah been attending constant meetings for the past few months? He wondered if she . . . but then, no. She would tell him if there was someone else. And yet . . . would she? T.S. knew little about women, despite his fifty-five years. He should have worked less and played more, but what could he do now? He could only try to make up for lost time.

"Theodore?" Auntie Lil asked. "What are you gooning about?"

"Sorry," he said, escorting her into the elevator. He had no intention of telling Aunt Lil the truth. She pestered him enough about Lilah as it was. "It's about this plan of yours to 'blow the lid off,' as you put it," he said. "In this case, I think discretion really is the better part of valor. You could seriously harm the Metro with a story like this. I can understand using the press as a deterrent to head off the vote, but if they've already voted, maybe we would be better off trying to help Fatima find another role rather than trying to hurt the company."

Auntie Lil did not reply, and in her silence, he could sense her stubbornness rising like a beast from the depths. "Aunt Lil," he warned, "I am very serious about this. I will take you to dinner and we will discuss it."

"Dinner?" she repeated hopefully. Food was the one sure way to get her attention. "Do I get to pick the place?"

"Of course," he agreed, knowing that, whether he liked it or not, she always chose their restaurants—and chose them well.

"I'll listen to what you have to say on one condition," she decided.

"What?" he asked warily.

"You must accompany me and Herbert to *The Nutcracker* premiere next month and look properly outraged at how poorly this child star creature dances. You must complain loudly about it at both intermissions."

"Agreed," T.S. said quickly as they reached the lobby. The outer doors opened on the spectacular sight of the Lincoln Center fountain shooting plumes of water high into the sky. The streams of liquid shimmered like gold against the New York City skyline. "I'd be glad to come with you and

Herbert," he added, smiling. T.S. was no fool. Lilah would surely be there, too. With any luck, he'd wind up as her date.

CHAPTER TWO

1. Auntie Lil may not have alerted the press about Fatima Jones, but someone else most certainly had. The day before the Metro Ballet's premiere of their annual production of *The Nutcracker*, Margo McGregor's biweekly column was devoted entirely to the subject.

Auntie Lil knew she would be blamed. Her remarks at the board meeting almost guaranteed it. Yet she had followed T.S.'s advice and avoided Margo McGregor's eventual call back. She pondered the best way to deal with the situation as she sat at the dining-room table in T.S.'s apartment high above York Avenue on Manhattan's Upper East Side. She had consumed her customary hearty breakfast and was now in the process of eating her nephew's while she waited for him to model his rental tuxedo. It had been altered for him at the store, but Auntie Lil did not trust their tailor. She intended to perfect the fit herself and had lugged over several pounds of supplies in anticipation of correcting a shoddy job. Now greater problems demanded her attention.

"Oh dear," she muttered, absently finishing the plate of Danish as she scanned the long article. Margo had included details of audition results that only an insider would have known. Who had leaked the incident and why?

"What do you think?" T.S. entered the dining nook resplendent in his evening wear.

"I think we're in for trouble tomorrow night," she muttered back, rereading the article anxiously.

"What happened to the sweet rolls?" T.S. asked, noticing the empty plate.

"You don't need any sweet rolls," she said quickly, hoping to head off his protests. "You are starting to fill out a bit, I notice." Much to her chagrin, the tuxedo fit T.S. perfectly. The tailor had done a good job.

"I am not filling out," T.S. said, nonetheless checking his reflection in the glass doors that led to his balcony. He patted his tummy. He thought he looked rather trim in his tuxedo. He weighed the same as he had at thirty-five, thanks to sane eating and regular exercise. It would never have occurred to him to abuse his body. Everyone knew that the Hubberts were blessed with stout constitutions—and that they took no chances with their good luck.

"Stop admiring yourself and come take a look at this." Auntie Lil spread the paper out on the dining room table. SO NO ONE KNOWS WHAT GOES ON BEHIND CLOSED DOORS? asked the headline. Worse yet was the opening sentence. Auntie Lil read it out loud: " 'Was it old-fashioned racism or simply a contagious case of Hollywood fever? You be the judge. Regardless, the behavior of the Metropolitan Ballet board of directors in the matter of Fatima Jones can only be called misguided.' " She looked at T.S. from over her reading glasses. "Not exactly the publicity the board had in mind."

T.S. locked eyes with his aunt grimly. His big night out with Lilah as his date had just taken a turn for the worse.

2.   The turn for the worse turned out to be more like a headlong dive off a high cliff. The next evening, as they approached Lincoln Center in Lilah's limousine, they could hear angry shouting from a block away.

"Trouble ahead," Grady the chauffeur informed them. "Shall I go on?"

"What in the world?" Lilah murmured. She was dressed in a simple gown of black that draped in soft folds from a diamond clip pinned over one of her shoulders. Her upswept silver hair complemented her healthy complexion. Her face gave off the well-weathered glow of a woman who spent a lot of time with her horses. T.S. thought her stunning and much preferred her naturally aged beauty to the artificial youth of many of the women in her moneyed circle.

Auntie Lil slouched down in guilt, gathering her purple chiffon concoction over her knees. She tugged the voluminous folds of her gown around her ever-present matching trousers. Auntie Lil wore the world's most elegant pant suits but seldom touched a dress—unless she was creating it, of course.

T.S. averted his eyes from Lilah and stared out the window. He had a good idea of what might lie ahead. Margo McGregor's column could only have stirred up trouble; he was sure the angry voices were about Fatima.

Only Herbert Wong—as oblivious as Lilah to the article published the day before—addressed himself to the problem. He rolled down his window and stuck his head out for a better look. "There is a large gathering of some sort at the entrance to the theater," he announced. "I am reminded of the 1968 Democratic Convention."

"Slow down, Grady," Lilah requested. "We'll walk from here." Unsure of the protesters' politics, Lilah was wise enough to know that emerging from a limousine into an angry crowd was as foolhardy as walking into a herd of migrating wildebeests.

They approached Lincoln Center on foot, surrounded by the usual chaos of the cultural center near curtain time: cabs honked impatiently; buses roared by; frantic musicians clutching strangely shaped instrument cases dashed past, looking stricken; and well-dressed people laughed in groups, cheerful from pretheater drinks and giddy with the anticipation of beauty. This well-choreographed chaos took place against a backdrop of headlights streaming past and the twinkling lights of the center's well-lit atrium.

The noise was even more cacophonous than usual thanks to a parade of fifty protesters marching in a large circle in front of the entrance to the State Theater. They jostled placards and shouted slogans as if they had been beamed down into New York City from another, more political era. Elegantly dressed patrons huddled in their minks and scurried fearfully on their way to the Metro's premiere through the chanters. News cameras were being hastily set up to one side, triggering a flurry of related activity. As Auntie Lil and her entourage drew near it became obvious that the protesters were being led by a beefy black man in a snug blue suit whose white hair stood straight up from his head as if he had stuck his finger in a light socket.

"Ben Hampton," Auntie Lil whispered to T.S. "And they're going to blame me for it."

The Reverend Ben Hampton was rapidly becoming as familiar a fixture in New York City as the Statue of Liberty. And, to some New Yorkers, he represented many of the same ideals. Using media savvy and a dubious diploma from a third-rate law school as his credentials, Ben Hampton had earned a colorful reputation as the leader of numerous (and not always wisely chosen) protests against social injustice. He did not always check his facts first and had been embarrassed in the past by staged scandals. But he weighed in often enough on the side of the angels—and uttered so many good sound bites—that many of New York's poorer residents saw him as their champion, as a man they could go to when the system turned against them. In the past few years Hampton had organized successful protests against the closing of a swimming pool in Harlem and several parks in the Bronx; unequal funding of neighborhood schools; a handful of alleged incidents of police brutality; and one spectacular case of statutory rape against a city-council member that turned out to be false and nearly cost him a lawsuit for libel. He was a fixture on the local news and a frequent guest on national television programs. Whether he was truly a reverend or had merely adopted the title was a matter of lively debate. The walls of his small office were papered in certificates from numerous organizations and a handful of churches, but few people had ever heard of any of them. Some politicians made the mistake of thinking he was harmless; others made the even bigger mistake of combating him in the press. No one could deflect a charge and turn it against an opponent better than the Reverend Ben Hampton. His emotional and thunderous countercharges seldom made sense, but they sure sounded good—and that's what counted when you had all of fifteen seconds to capture the attention of the public.

"It's that man with the strange hair again," Lilah said, echoing the sentiments of New York's truly wealthy about Ben Hampton. He mostly perplexed them: they could not understand his pulpit histrionics and they rather wished he would just go away.

Herbert was beginning to catch on that Auntie Lil might have had something to do with the commotion. He gazed back and forth between the protesters and Auntie Lil, trying to puzzle out the connection. He was a patient man, however, and held his tongue. He knew Lillian would tell him when she was ready.

Auntie Lil eyed the protesters nervously, though it was not outsiders she feared. She was sure Lane Rogers would come charging around the corner at any moment and accuse her of having leaked the vote details to the press.

"Let's just get inside," T.S. suggested. He and Herbert flanked their companions and waded through the crowd, ignoring the shouts of "Justice for Fatima!" that rang in their ears. As they neared the entrance doors they could hear applause behind them. They turned and watched as Ben Hampton hoisted his plump frame onto the ledge surrounding Lincoln Center's magnificent fountain. It was a well-chosen pose. Sparkling lights thrown off the water plumes blazed behind him like a biblical endorsement, framing him in reflected glory. Flashbulbs popped and news cameras began to roll as he held aloft a large photograph of Fatima Jones posed en pointe and looking ethereal as she held a classic arabesque pose, one long leg extended out behind her.

"She had a dream!" Ben Hampton thundered, shaking her photograph at the crowd. "Yes, she had a dream and she worked toward that dream. But they have destroyed her dream!" He pointed to the Metro's theater with an accusatory finger. Hundreds of gathered protesters and curious onlookers joined the crews of four local television stations in turning to where he pointed.

His timing was impeccable. Auntie Lil and her companions were pinned in the glare of television lights right in the middle of the main doors to the theater. The next day a photograph of the four of them would appear on the bottom of page one of two local tabloids, their mouths agape and incredibly guilty expressions plastered across their faces. Only Herbert Wong would emerge looking dignified, his bland expression in the line of fire making him appear like a particularly dapper modern Buddha.

"What is going on?" Lilah asked in horror as a security guard appeared belatedly and escorted them inside to the lobby.

"The press found out about Fatima Jones," Auntie Lil explained miserably.

"You didn't . . . did you?" Lilah asked, knowing Auntie Lil.

"No, I did not," she promised emphatically.

The mob scene inside the theater rivaled the one outside. The long walk to their seats involved wading through an overexcited crowd and a huge sea of noise. They were seated in the third row and had to battle their way to the front. As usual, Auntie Lil had insisted they obtain seats as close as possible to the stage. She had even declined the offer extended to all board members to observe opening night from backstage. She liked to see the dancers sweat, she explained. It made their talent that much more amazing to behold. T.S.—who had wiped the perspiration off his face from far too many talented dancers at far too many performances—had protested in vain. If he leaned forward, T.S. reflected, he risked being poked in the eye by the conductor's baton.

Once seated, they turned for a better look at the noisy crowd behind them. The audience was in a state of pandemonium, not because of the protest but because it consisted chiefly of adolescent girls and their overwrought mothers.

"Tickets were a hundred dollars apiece for the premiere," Auntie Lil said. "How can these young people afford it?"

"They didn't pay," Lilah pointed out. "Their parents did."

Someone had paid, that was for sure. Beyond the first twenty center rows—which were largely occupied by Metro patrons and their guests—the opulent auditorium was a sea of raging female hormones. Girls whispered, squealed, wiggled, and elbowed each other as they waited in breathless anticipation for the emergence of Mikey Morgan. Chewing gum popped anonymously all around them in a maddeningly uneven rhythm. T.S. felt like he was trapped in a giant bag of popping corn.

"That had better stop immediately," Auntie Lil said grimly. "Or I shall have to insist on an announcement." She began looking around for a microphone—Auntie Lil said very few things in jest—but when she noticed Lane Rogers at the far right edge of the main curtain, peering out from backstage, she sank lower in her seat and took a great interest in the hem of one of her trouser legs instead.

T.S. sat stunned by the difference between the world churning outside the theater and the world percolating inside it. The well-dressed, pampered preteen crowd seemed oblivious to issues of race, talent, or culture. They, instead, had focused to the point of hysteria on one single burning goal: to catch a glimpse in the flesh of someone they recognized from the silver screen, to be able to say that they had seen Mikey Morgan in person. T.S. wasn't sure what it all meant for the future of the world, but he knew clearly what it meant to him: despite the presence of Lilah, he really should have followed his better instincts and just stayed home in bed.

"I wonder what Martinez has in store for us tonight," Lilah asked T.S., referring to the Metro's temperamental artistic director.

This was a very good question. *The Nutcracker* had as many interpretations as it had productions. In an effort to attract an audience and captivate new generations, ballet companies all over the world had put their own spin on the rather macabre traditional Christmas story of a young girl gifted with a wooden nutcracker and her subsequent dreams of toy soldiers, a Mouse King and his troops, the Sugar Plum Fairy, and other exotic creatures. Versions ranged from the classical, featuring rich turn-of-the-century costumes, to the romantic, with their long flowing gowns and nearly lawless improvisations. The world of modern dance had even weighed in with one particularly memorable version by Mark Morris called *Hard Nut*, which featured a sixties-era American setting, complete with stoned party guests, undertones of adultery, and a stage full of bell-bottomed dancers doing the bump. How Martinez intended to top these versions and draw an audience in the fiercely competitive New York City area remained to be seen.

"I think his 'vision,' as he calls it, is going to be along the lines of 'more is more,'" Auntie Lil confided. "I was able to sneak into one rehearsal and they were practicing the toy-soldiers-versus-the-mice battle scene. There were enough dancing rodents on stage to make me queasy. It was an infestation more than anything else."

Flooding the stage with dancers was not, at first glance, a bad move on the artistic director's part. The more students he could use from the Metro's ballet school, the more tickets he could sell to proud relatives. And perhaps even score some points for pageantry along the way.

Or perhaps not. As the curtain rose on the main set it was obvious that Auntie Lil had been right. Martinez was going for quantity over quality. He chose to begin the ballet with a meaningless preface staged on the proscenium in front of a painted backdrop depicting the stately home where the central story would unfold. Buckets of snow fell from the rafters above, wafting over the orchestra and causing the French horn player to look up in alarm. T.S. expected Nanook of the North to come pirouetting by at any second accompanied by a team of prancing huskies. Instead, a troop of children emerged out of this flurry of plastic flakes and headed for center stage like well-trained lemmings. There, they executed a dizzying array of leaps and turns before entering a front door cut into the simulated house front. Scores of adult dancers depicting their parents scurried across the stage and followed them inside the door, each stopping first to exhibit their poise and control with a determined ferociousness that turned the scene into a dance contest that would have made even Dick Clark nervous.

As the backdrop rose out of sight an ostentatiously furnished parlor set was revealed. Perhaps Clara and her family were bunking down at the Trump Plaza. The usual Christmas tree was curiously missing from the stage. But the excess space was easily filled with dancers pantomiming roles as excited children and their parents at a Christmas party. Auntie Lil searched through the crowd for a dark face, but she did not really expect to see Fatima Jones. She had heard that the young girl had declined an offer to dance a lesser role, and had rather admired her spunk.

The party scene quickly deteriorated into a turn-of-the-century Woodstock with waves of dancers whirling and parting and forming again, taking turns dominating the stage. How anyone could find their mark given the crowded conditions, Auntie Lil could not fathom.

The young lady who had replaced Fatima Jones as Clara—Julie Perkins, according to the program—was not bad, but she had no sparkle. Her body was certainly a perfect example of the long and lean frame favored in American ballet, but her dancing lacked passion. Good ballet, Auntie Lil believed, combined skilled movement with real emotion. Julie Perkins possessed one of these traits quite admirably, but completely lacked the other. Her blond hair had been carefully wound at the nape of her neck in an older style than most Claras wore. The reason why became obvious when Herr Drosselmeyer entered the party. Martinez was playing up a romantic relationship between Clara and this mysterious friend of her family.

He'd done this for a very good reason. As promised, Martinez had combined the parts of Drosselmeyer and the Prince, awarding both to Mikey Morgan. In this manner, the young teen idol would be onstage for a maximum amount of time, delighting the audience and, if one stretched a point, playing two romantic roles. Not coincidentally, he could also dance part of his first-act role cloaked in a black, floor-length cape, thus disguising his ineptitude.

But not even the cape could mask Mikey Morgan's melodramatic sense of emotion. Making the leap from screen back to stage had apparently triggered a histrionic reflex in the young film star. He interpreted the admittedly creepy Drosselmeyer as if he were the greedy landlord in an old vaudeville play. He stalked around the stage, leered at Clara, waved the toy nutcracker around like it was a bomb, and frequently whipped his cape in the face of the other dancers. All that was missing was a twirly black mustache. None of this dampened the enthusiasm of his audience, however, since squeals and sighs continued to rise from the darkened rows with religious fervor.

In one particularly ill-chosen pas de trois, Drosselmeyer demonstrated a series of steps to Clara and her little brother. This had the unfortunate effect of directly comparing Mikey Morgan's lack of technique with the talents of far better dancers. There would be no need for either Auntie Lil or T.S. to loudly complain about his lack of finesse at intermission. It would be obvious to anyone that the years spent in Hollywood had eradicated any discipline or ballet aptitude that the young man might once have possessed.

This inescapable fact was confirmed when Morgan shed his cloak for a pas de deux with Clara a few moments later. The grace of this classic ballet partnership was ruined when he hoisted her into the air as if she weighed five times more than he and then set her down like he was planting fence posts. Worse still, his appearance in tights made it obvious that he was not in top physical condition, and toward the end of the passage, Julie Perkins began to favor her right foot as if she had been injured by all the manhandling.

As the party scene progressed it became clear that this particular interpretation of *The Nutcracker* would go down in history for all the wrong reasons. At one point, the boys separated from the girls and mounted wooden hobby horses for what was intended as a charming showcase for the talents of the corps de ballet. Unfortunately, so many young male dancers occupied the stage that they stampeded across like Custer's charge, with equally ill-fated results. Then, during a Punch-and-Judy segment where puppets entertain the party guests, Martinez let so many young dancers ad-lib unmercifully that it triggered an instant dislike for child dancers in those many audience members who had, until then, convinced themselves that child dancers were at least a cut above child actors.

The one bright spot in the confusion was the debut of Rudy Vladimir as the Nutcracker. If the young man was upset at being bumped from the lead role, he did not show it. Instead, his love for dance shone through. As Clara unwrapped her oversized gift Rudy burst from the box onto center stage with the assurance and mastery of dancers twice his age. As if out of respect, the cluttered corps stepped back to give him more room. He used every inch of available space as he whirled, leaped, and bounced his way through a two-minute solo that came close to bringing the curtain down. Every movement was breathtaking yet reined in just enough to convey the feeling that he was, indeed, a wooden creature. Even the starstruck girls in the audience burst into wild applause when he was done.

"Fancy bit of footwork, there," T.S. whispered hopefully to Auntie Lil, painfully aware that his vocabulary as a critic lacked finesse.

"It only makes the rest of them look worse," she whispered back. "This is a catastrophe."

But the real catastrophe still waited in the wings. As the act drew to a close it became obvious why the Christmas tree had been missing from the set. There was no room at the inn. Martinez had chosen to make the tree so huge and the corps de ballet so large that physics forbade their occupying the stage at the same time. Instead, he had reserved the appearance of the tree as a kind of climax for the Act I curtain. Members of the corps began to melt off to the side, leaving Clara and her family alone on the stage, where they clustered, bidding Drosselmeyer good night. Suddenly lights appeared behind a transparent scrim that masked a rear series of simulated windows. The window frames appeared in stark relief and the shadows of departing guests could be seen crossing in front of the windows. A gasp rose from the audience as a twenty-foot, brightly lit Christmas tree began to descend from above the stage, framed by the backlit windows. The base of the tree inched downward majestically in time to the music. The dancers froze in tableau as if awestruck—and they were not the only ones. The tree continued its dramatic descent, but when it reached halfway, true disaster struck.

The supporting weight controlling its descent apparently snapped, sending the tree crashing to the stage floor in a frightening explosion of breaking lights and crashing limbs. The dancers jumped back, startled, and the well-lit windows looked suddenly barren at center stage. Out of nowhere, the shadow of a man hanging from the neck by a rope swung in silhouette behind the windows. It was grotesquely realistic, sweeping in from stage right in a full arc before swinging back again. Worse, it grew and shrank in size as it swung, thanks to a spotlight set front right.

This is really going too far, T.S. thought to himself. This is supposed to be a children's show.

The audience murmured uneasily when the dancers onstage continued to stare at the shadow. Suddenly the young dancer playing Clara's little brother screamed and pointed up toward stage right. As if he had summoned its presence, the body of a man hanging from a thick brown rope swung into view, this time in front of the windows, hurtling across the stage until its feet touched the fallen Christmas tree and the body swung back.

The audience held its breath and the dancers stepped back in unison, crowding together like frightened sheep. When Mikey Morgan broke free of the group and dashed off stage left, a buzz ran through the audience. What was this? The body was swinging slowly to a stop, barely visible at the edge of the stage-right curtain. The dancer playing Clara's father approached the body slowly and laid a fingertip of his right hand on the cheek of the hanging man. The dancer paused then began to shout, waving his hands frantically to someone backstage. Chaos broke out onstage. Julie Perkins abandoned her Clara facade and began to scream. Two older dancers dragged offstage. A stagehand streaked across the set to the hanging figure, followed by a group of younger dancers still dressed as party guests. They crept toward the body and several began to cry, causing a group of older dancers to scurry out from backstage to collect them. The stagehand gesticulated wildly to an unseen cohort and the curtain began to fall. A young girl in the audience screamed, and like a town full of dogs picking up the cry at twilight, young girls all over the vast auditorium echoed her sound. "Lights!" someone shouted, and the adults took up the cry, adding to the pandemonium. "Lights! Lights! Lights!"

Abruptly, the houselights blazed and T.S. blinked in the glare, confused by what he had seen. "What is this?" he asked Herbert.

Herbert turned to him, eyes wide. "Lillian is gone," he said.

Auntie Lil had insisted she sit on the aisle and now the aisle seat was most assuredly empty.

"Something's wrong," Lilah whispered. "This doesn't seem right."

"I'll say," T.S. agreed.

3. Auntie Lil found the side steps easily in the darkness; she had planned to mount them before the show if the obnoxious gum cracking continued. Scurrying up, she slipped behind the heavy velvet side curtains and followed the sound of anxious voices.

"Cut him down!" someone was insisting. "He may still be alive." Others argued to leave him as he was until the police arrived.

Auntie Lil brushed past another layer of curtain and came abruptly on a macabre tableau. Costumed dancers crowded in a circle around the crumbled figure of a man slumped on the floor, his head bent back grotesquely. A thick rope encircled his neck, and coiled on the floor beside him lay the ragged end where it had been hastily sawed seconds before.

"He's dead," a male dancer announced, removing his fingers from the man's throat. "Very dead."

Auntie Lil pushed through the crowd and knelt beside the body, taking care not to touch anything. Her eyes were drawn first to the man's neck. The knot cut savagely into the neck just below the windpipe. She adjusted her reading glasses and bent so close that some in the crowd thought she was attempting to revive the victim. There, caught in the fibers of the deadly rope, were minute wisps of a fluffy white substance that looked like cotton. Finally, she looked up to confirm who was so very much hated that he should be killed in such a public manner.

Just as she had suspected when the body first swung into view, the murdered man was none other than Bobby Morgan, agent—and very much deceased father—of Hollywood's biggest child star.

CHAPTER THREE

1. There was little else Auntie Lil could uncover before the police arrived. Wisely, she had slipped out a side stage door and made her getaway before she was detained for questioning. If any of the dancers had reported her presence backstage to the detectives, they had not caught up with her yet. On the other hand, she had very little information to go on when it came to the identity of the killer. Only that someone had fashioned a very professional-looking noose around the neck of Bobby Morgan without being noticed in the middle of a busy backstage—and then given him a few good shoves to send him swinging when it became obvious he was only going to hover on the sidelines without help. She was nearly certain that he could not have swept across such a spectacular portion of the stage without a deliberate push.

When a call came early the next morning announcing an emergency meeting of the Metropolitan Ballet Board that afternoon, she readily agreed to be there. Perhaps she could pick up more information on Bobby Morgan's death.

The conference room was strangely quiet when she arrived. Board members sat glum and silent, exhausted after battling their way through the phalanx of reporters and film crews camped out in front. Lane Rogers did not even bother to glare at Auntie Lil. She simply sat at the head of the long conference table gazing down at her notes. Her face was drawn and white. Either dozens of new wrinkles had appeared around her reddened eyes overnight or she had been too upset to follow her usual makeup regime.

"Let's get started," Lane said abruptly. "Someone lock the door." Ruth Beretsky scurried to do her bidding.

"Lock the door?" Lilah asked. "Are we in danger?"

"In danger of being overheard," Lane answered ominously. Many of the assembled group turned to stare at Auntie Lil, correctly interpreting the accusation for what it was.

"I did not inform the press about the Fatima Jones decision," Auntie Lil said firmly. "And I most certainly did not murder Bobby Morgan."

"Indeed," Hans Glick added. "The matter of Fatima Jones seems to me to be a moot point. Have you seen the newspaper today?" He held up a handful of lurid headlines. "We have gone overnight from being a respected institution to being a 'hotbed of intrigue' as one despicable rag called us." His outrage was genuine. Any event out of Glick's control enraged him. "We must do something to regain our respectability."

"We can try to repair the damage," Lilah pointed out. "But if the murderer turns out to be someone in the organization, then we will be right back where we started."

"Someone in the organization?" Raoul Martinez bellowed. "We are artists, not murderers! Are you implying one of my dancers is at fault?"

"It was someone backstage," Lilah answered calmly. "I should think that is obvious."

"Anyone had access to backstage," Martinez countered. "The outer doors are not locked during performances and the security is laughable. I have been saying for months that too many unauthorized individuals are allowed where they don't belong."

"You have been trying for months to have board members banned from backstage," Lane corrected him. Her eyes slid involuntarily to Hans Glick. "I can understand your desire to keep interference to a minimum, but we do, after all, guide the Metropolitan."

"So what we are saying is that the murderer is most probably a member of the company or the crew," Auntie Lil said brightly. "Or a member of the board." Every face turned to her in horror. "It certainly seems logical to me. Of course, I am a bit more experienced than the rest of you in such matters. You think none of us are capable of murder because we live in nice homes and have money in the bank." She folded her hands neatly in front of her. "My dears, we are each and every one of us capable of murder."

Silence greeted her. Hans Glick was, of course, the one to break it. "I will tell you what we should do," he said. "We must hire a private investigator for a great deal of money to get to the bottom of this. We will leak our hiring him to the press and it will seem as if we are very serious about determining the culprit, regardless of their position."

"I thought we *were* very serious about determining the culprit," Lilah said dryly. Glick looked at her without expression.

Auntie Lil stood and walked to the chalkboard Glick was so fond of using, unable to resist the impulse. "Nonsense," she said. "We are not paying anyone anything. I intend to solve this mystery for free." She drew a large question mark in the middle of the board and a large dollar sign beside it. She tapped the question mark. "Who is best qualified to determine the killer? That's obvious. I am. I have done it before, I am part of the organization, and"—she drew a heavy circle around the question mark—"I am happily devoid of any preconceptions as to the guilt or innocence of *anyone* I meet, believe me. However, our responsibility for controlling this mess must not stop with helping to solve this murder." She tapped the dollar sign, then dramatically erased it as if it were an obscenity. "Some of you may believe that the matter of Fatima Jones will go away, but I can promise you it will not." She locked eyes with Lane Rogers. "For one thing, the two matters could very well be related." She walked back to the table in the shocked silence that followed this remark. "Until that is determined, I think it would be wise to correct the error of our ways as soon as possible. Fatima Jones should be given the role she deserves. As Mikey Morgan will surely not wish to continue dancing now that his father has died onstage, as it were, he should not be a problem—if he was the problem in the first place."

"But think of the crowds," Hans Glick pleaded. "Granted this publicity is regrettable, but we sold out for the entire run this morning. People will be expecting him to perform. If we replace him, we may find ourselves with a flood of refund requests."

"If you are suggesting that we keep Mikey Morgan in the role so that thrill-seeking ghouls can sit there and stare at him, you are very much mistaken," Lilah said quietly. "I will not allow it. It is unseemly, it is inappropriate, and it will not go over very well in civilized circles. I can guarantee you that I will resign from the board. I will withdraw my funding. And I will make sure my friends do the same."

Auntie Lil was astonished. Ultimatums were not in Lilah's repertoire. Yet she sounded as if she meant every word she said.

"I mean it," Lilah added firmly, meeting Auntie Lil's eyes. "Children should be children and this young man is not going to continue dancing given the circumstances."

"Rudy Vladimir will step into the Drosselmeyer and Prince roles," Martinez said quickly, visions of his salary being cut in half flashing through his mind. Lilah was one board member who believed that artists should be paid enough to live well. "That leaves the way open for Fatima Jones to dance Clara. I can move Julie Perkins to a lesser role. She injured her foot last night anyway. That can be my excuse."

"What about our legal exposure?" Lane Rogers brought up. "We have a contract with Mikey Morgan."

Glick cleared his throat uncomfortably. "Actually, the contract has not yet been signed. There had been some problems." He blinked and one corner of his mouth twitched. "I had not yet reached an understanding with the young man's father as to the exact percentage of the gate that he would be entitled to."

"What?" Lane asked sharply. "We don't give dancers a

percentage of the receipts. Who authorized you to pursue such an arrangement?"

"I am the board member in charge of business affairs," he said with dignity. "It is certainly within the realm of my authority."

"You better be damn glad you didn't sign that contract," Lane snapped back, a hint of her Yonkers accent returning.

Auntie Lil was in a hurry to find the killer and in no mood for a political debate. "Good. It's settled," she said, heading off a power struggle. "Fatima Jones takes over as Clara, and Rudy will dance the roles of Drosselmeyer and the Prince. And I will be the board's official representative in the matter of Bobby Morgan's death."

"And I will assist you," Glick added.

"No, you will not," Auntie Lil corrected him. "How can we expect to appear impartial if one of the suspects assists in the investigation?"

"See here," Glick protested. "Why am I a suspect and you are not?"

"Because I was sitting right up front in full view of three thousand people when Bobby Morgan was killed," Auntie Lil explained logically. "I am sure there are many witnesses in this very room who saw me."

A murmur of assent rose from the back of the room. It was true: Auntie Lil had been pretty hard to miss in that getup she'd had on.

"I protest," Lane said firmly. "You have no right to such power."

"Oh, let her," a woman suggested from the back of the room. "It will get her out of our hair."

Ruth Beretsky cleared her throat and the entire board turned to stare. She shrank from the scrutiny but gathered her courage to speak. "I don't see why we can't accept Miss Hubbert's offer," Ruth pointed out. "She isn't asking for money. She has experience. And a man *is* dead, after all. I think it's rather generous of her to offer, myself. . . ." Her voice trailed off as the full impact of Lane's glare sank in, but Ruth still managed to hold her chin defiantly high and refused to reverse her opinion.

"Yes, let's vote and go home," someone suggested. "This place gives me the creeps."

"I'll not have her interfering," Lane began, but was overruled by other voices calling for a vote.

Before Lane knew what had happened, the vote had been taken. Auntie Lil's plan was approved and the meeting was adjourned. "Wait!" the chairman cried as board members streamed for the door, eager to get back to their murderless lives. "What about the leak? Someone here is a spy. Someone is talking to the press. I demand we find out who!"

Her words were in vain. The board members had scattered. Not even Ruth Beretsky stayed behind to agree.

2. Despite her seeming indifference, Auntie Lil was just as eager as Lane Rogers to determine Margo McGregor's source. After all, she thought it could relate to Bobby Morgan's murder. So she took the direct approach. She arrived at the Manhattan offices of *New York Newsday* and refused to leave the waiting room until the newspaper located Margo. Jimmy Breslin spent a few minutes hovering behind a potted palm evaluating Auntie Lil as potential fodder for his own Runyonesque column, but when she seized the opportunity to take a catnap, he slunk away in disappointment.

The harried receptionist finally located Margo in a third-floor snack area. "Why didn't you return my calls last month?" the petite columnist asked as she hurried out to greet Auntie Lil. "First your nephew calls me and leaves a dozen urgent messages and then I don't even get a call back from either one of you?"

Margo McGregor was pint-sized but she carried a lot of weight in city press circles. It was rumored that the mayor sent her a dozen roses each week just to stay on her good side. His strategy was hopelessly old-fashioned and seldom worked, but the poor man kept trying. Roses did not dissuade Margo McGregor. Not even a Scud missile would cause her to miss a beat. She was a human wolverine. Her deceptively friendly face twinkled out at readers complete with button nose, friendly eyes, and an innocuous schoolgirl flip to her short brown hair. But she was one of the most sarcastic—and skilled—investigative columnists on any of New York City's dailies. She had brought down much bigger organizations than the Metropolitan Ballet and would not hesitate to use her wit and wiles against the pope if she felt he deserved public exposure for some betrayal of ethics or trust.

"Let's go somewhere for coffee," Auntie Lil suggested, certain that the single best place in the world to be over-heard was probably a newspaper waiting room.

"Sure. What's on your mind?" Margo did not hurry Auntie Lil. She knew from experience that the best way to get information from a source was to let them take their time and work out their fears at their own pace.

"I'll tell you when we're alone," Auntie Lil promised as they made their way into the hordes of busy strangers clog-ging Forty-second Street. "No problem," Margo agreed. She wholeheartedly supported Auntie Lil's paranoia.

"I did have T.S. call you about the Fatima Jones matter last month," Auntie Lil admitted once they had settled in a crowded coffee bar near Times Square. The seats were metal and uncomfortable because, as usual, groups of youn-ger people already occupied the few plush, living-room-style arrangements dotting the room. Manhattan had lately sprouted numerous such coffee bars, ostensibly as havens for the hurried and weary. In reality, more tempers were irked than soothed by the jockeying for good seats that went on in these java joints.

"What happened?" Margo asked. "Why the change of mind?"

"I chickened out once the vote was taken. My nephew convinced me that it would be better to let it go, that it might harm the Metropolitan more than I intended."

"It probably will," Margo agreed. "But from what I un-derstand, it will not be your fault. You voted against it."

"You're well-informed. And I need to know who told you about the vote," Auntie Lil said. "Your source may well be connected to the murder of Bobby Morgan last night."

"I wondered," the columnist admitted, pulling a small notebook from her backpack. "Tell me what you know about the murder."

Auntie Lil shook her head firmly. "Tell me your source first."

Margo gazed at Auntie Lil from above the rim of her coffee cup, her eyes an innocent blue. "Miss Hubbert, you know that there is no way that I am going to give you the name of one source. That is my livelihood. All I have is my word when it comes to building trust with people. I wouldn't give the name to the Supreme Court itself and I am certainly not giving it to you."

Auntie Lil considered herself more important than the Supreme Court, but knew better than to argue. She had a more roundabout method in mind. She sighed heavily, as if the burdens of the world were just too much for her. Taking a handkerchief from the depths of her enormous pocket-book, she patted her brow daintily. "It's very distressing, this entire matter. I am merely attempting to help the Metro board out of a tight spot and do the right thing."

Margo McGregor was not in the least bit fooled. She had seen Auntie Lil in action. "What's the deal?" she demanded. "What's the trade?"

Auntie Lil stuffed her hankie out of sight and pulled out her own notebook. Pen poised above a clean page, she began firing questions. "Can you tell me some facts that weren't in the paper about the Fatima Jones incident? Could you help me out without divulging your source? Do you know who on the board approached the Morgans about Mikey dancing or was it really the other way around? Tell me what you know and I will tell you what I know about the death of Bobby Morgan."

Margo thought it over while she sipped her coffee. Auntie Lil was content with her latte, a concoction of coffee and steamed milk. She had long ago discovered that the only difference between a latte and a cappuccino was a lot of hot air. Quite naturally, she avoided the hot air. "Well?" she finally asked, impatient as always.

Margo shook her head. "I am a fool to do this," she admitted. "But just in case you come up with something good, here goes. But I get to hear it first if you uncover anything about the murder, no matter who is involved. Deal?"

"Deal."

Margo flipped back to some well-worn pages near the front of her notebook. Auntie Lil tried without success to read the writing upside down in hopes of finding a clue to her source's identity. Margo, well aware of Auntie Lil's tricks, pulled the notes closer to her chest and smiled. "Bobby Morgan approached the board," she told Auntie Lil sweetly. "Hans Glick specifically. It was Morgan's idea to put his son in the role and he said it was because his son was at that awkward stage between child star and adolescent. He thought legitimate stage credits and a little seasoning would help him make the transition more smoothly. He was adamant about no Fatima Jones from the start, but no one seems to know how he knew about her in the first place." She looked up at Auntie Lil. "What you have to remember about Bobby Morgan is that he had his own agenda here. He was a student himself at the Metro thirty years ago and didn't do very well. When he was plucked from the student ranks to audition for a new sitcom back in the sixties, he was one of two Metro students to get a part. The other had stage experience as well. Bobby Morgan left dancing far behind to try to become a child star. For a while he succeeded. His sitcom ran for a good eight years and he became a very big television star in his own right during the late sixties and early seventies. Until he turned eighteen."

"What happened then?" Auntie Lil asked.

"Talk about an awkward age. He was hit with everything most adolescents go through at age twelve. Height gain. Pimples. A month's worth of bad hair days at a stretch. Mood swings, all that stuff. Delayed adolescence had helped prolong his appeal for many years, but when it hit, his career was over. He wasn't cute anymore and the show had gone stale. Both his looks and the show disappeared, almost overnight. I don't know what happened to him in the years in between, but by the time he arrived back on the scene a few years ago, this time as manager to his son, there were a lot of people who felt that the father was using the son to settle some old scores."

"So Bobby Morgan was a child star, too?" Auntie Lil said. "Like father, like son?"

Margo nodded. "In a manner of speaking. He was nowhere near as successful as Mikey has been, but that's in part because he didn't make the move into film and he didn't have a good manager when he was Mikey's age. I understand his parents blew most of his earnings and he didn't have much left by the time his show was canceled. He's been living pretty well off his son's earnings for the last couple of years. Twenty percent of twelve million a year is not too shoddy."

"And he sent Mikey to the Metro Ballet School to follow in his footsteps?"

Margo nodded. "A lot of stage parents do that, at least at first. Ballet teaches a child grace and stage presence. They also learn to work like dogs and the constant rejection of auditions is good for them. Toughens them up."

"Sounds like they're breeding pit bulls," Auntie Lil said.

"Believe me, some of them are."

"Where is the child's mother?" Auntie Lil asked. "Why has no one heard of her?"

"That's an interesting story," Margo admitted. She checked her watch and began to speak even faster. "The mother and father divorced a few years ago, apparently over the future of their oldest son and biggest asset— Mikey. It seems that Mom was not keen on nonstop exploitation of Mikey and was worried about the effect of all the attention on his younger brothers and sister. But Dad was adamant on cashing in while the cashing in was good. So they split. There were a few other reasons, too, I understand."

"A few other very female reasons?" Auntie Lil guessed.

Margo rolled her eyes. "Some women go for the ponytail-and-gold-jewelry look. Me? I like wrinkled Irish faces and scraggly beards."

"Why did you run the story on Fatima Jones when you did?" Auntie Lil asked. "So close to opening night?"

"I didn't know about it until then," Margo explained. "When my source came to me, they let me know that Ben Hampton knew about it. I knew the good Reverend would make a big deal out of it. I also knew that it would be a real coup for me if I could get my column out first, making it look like Hampton had responded to my story. It doesn't hurt to look like you have a lot of influence, even if you don't." She smiled modestly, although she was fully aware of the very real clout she wielded. "So now it's your turn," she told Auntie Lil. "What do you know that you're not telling?"

Auntie Lil described the murder and the way the body had swung first behind the set windows and then in front. "I am convinced that he was killed earlier in the show, perhaps strangled manually by the extra rope attached to the Christmas tree's counterbalance. The killer made a noose out of this rope, figuring that once the tree started to descend, he could cut the counterbalance free and the rapid fall of the tree would jerk Morgan's body onto the stage. It worked, but not well enough for the killer. I think he or she was waiting in the wings and, during the confusion of the Christmas-tree lights exploding, grabbed the hanging body and gave it a good shove to send it center stage."

Margo stared at Auntie Lil. "That's a pretty dramatic gesture," she said. "Not to mention risky if you want to stay anonymous."

Auntie Lil nodded. "I know. Someone wanted this to be a very public murder."

"What else?" Margo demanded.

Auntie Lil shrugged apologetically. She was not about to let Margo know about the tufts of cotton worked into the rope fibers. "Just that anyone could have found their way backstage. There are at least four fire-door exits opening on to separate sides and back alleys and none of them are locked during a performance. Any one of the fifty or so protesters could have slipped inside and done it. Or anybody backstage. Or a tourist passing by, for that matter."

"Hell of a New York City souvenir," Margo remarked. "You'll give me more when you get it?"

Auntie Lil nodded. "And you'll call me with the same?"

"Agreed." The tiny columnist rose, her five-foot frame giving off a power that exceeded her physical limitations. "Be careful," she warned Auntie Lil. "You remember what happened last time?"

Yes, Auntie Lil still remembered the sharp point of a knife twisted cruelly in her side the last time she and Margo had found themselves on the same case. "I'll be careful," she promised. Auntie Lil left the coffee bar knowing a lot more about Bobby Morgan but very little about the possible identity of Margo McGregor's source.

But what was it the columnist had said about having to run the story because she knew that Ben Hampton had been alerted as well? If someone had leaked the news to the Reverend Hampton, it didn't guarantee that the informer was black, but it did indicate that the possibility was worth pursuing. Besides, using the chalkboard at the emergency board meeting earlier that day had reminded her of someone easily overlooked. She remembered the placid face of the maintenance man and the timing of his entrance at the acrimonious vote meeting. Had he been listening at the door?

Lincoln Center was no more than a four-dollar cab ride away. She decided to ask him for herself.

3. Auntie Lil camped out at the service entrance to the State Theater and shanghaied the man she had discovered was named Calvin Swanson. He was in a hurry to get home after a long day. But the maintenance man did not seem surprised to see her. "Evening," he said, tipping his hat back on his head.

"I'm Lillian Hubbert. I'm on the Metro's board of directors. May I talk to you privately?" she said without preamble, figuring correctly that he was a man who wasted neither words nor actions.

"About what?" he said carefully, his eyes searching Amsterdam Avenue for a bus he could take home to the Bronx.

"Look, I'll treat you to a cab ride home if you'll just agree to talk to me for a few minutes about Fatima Jones and the vote to replace her in *The Nutcracker*."

"Fatima?" He sang her name like he was at a gospel meeting. "What do I know about that girl except that she's a fine dancer?"

"Oh, come on, Calvin," Auntie Lil insisted as she managed to block a frantic executive with her hip and flagged a passing cab to a screeching halt with a well-practiced wave. Calvin opened the door with supreme satisfaction and a polite nod to the apoplectic businessman. Auntie Lil climbed inside first and waited for Calvin to give his address to the irate driver. Cabbies liked to stop for little old ladies in New York City; they did not like to stop for large black men. The driver, highly suspicious of his passengers, slammed the plastic divider between the front and back seats shut in defiance, leaving Auntie Lil and Calvin to exchange a knowing glance.

"Nice change to be taking a cab," Calvin said.

"I'll bet," Auntie Lil agreed dryly.

Calvin decided he liked the old lady's attitude. "Miss Hubbert, I can't help you. I have merely watched the girl practice. But what could I tell you about Fatima Jones that you don't already know? Just because we're both black doesn't mean we're related."

"I know that." Auntie Lil paused. "Someone leaked the details of the board's vote to oust her to the press. I think it might have been you." She stared at Calvin's face carefully as she spoke, hoping to read new information there.

His face remained blank and he shook his head. "Not me. I admit I heard what you were talking about that day." He shrugged apologetically. "Could hardly help it. If you don't mind my saying so, you do talk very loud."

Auntie Lil nodded. She was famous for her booming voice.

"I may even have listened in a bit at the door afterward. I can't say I agreed with the decision," Calvin added. "But I wasn't surprised. And I certainly didn't call the press."

"But surely you know something," Auntie Lil asked. "You work throughout the building every day. People may not notice you because you're so familiar. They might have talked while you were around."

"They might have," he agreed. "But just because they don't know how to keep their mouths shut doesn't mean I don't."

"Please, Mr. Swanson," Auntie Lil pleaded. "I worked hard to stop them from doing that to that young girl and now I'm working hard to find a killer. The two events may be related. Don't you know anything that might help?"

"Like what?" Calvin settled back for the unexpected luxury of passing over the Harlem River by car. Even its sluggish murkiness seemed to sparkle in the reflection of the arriving sunset.

"Have you seen anyone talking to the press?" Auntie Lil asked. "Did you notice any board members leaving the meeting and running right for the pay phone?" She knew this last scenario was absurd, since no one would be so obvious. Of course, she had *wanted* to be that obvious, but Theodore had stopped her.

"By the press, you mean that columnist who broke the story?" Calvin asked. "Or do you mean any press at all?"

"Anything!" Auntie Lil declared in desperation.

Calvin rubbed his hands on his well-worn jeans. "I guess if I were you," he finally said. "I would talk to that lady who runs the rehearsals."

"Paulette Puccinni?" Auntie Lil asked.

"That's the one. And maybe that fellow who plays the piano for her. The one she likes so much. The one losing his hair."

"You saw them talking to someone?" Auntie Lil asked.

"Not exactly. But I've been seeing them huddled together in the hall a lot, kind of whispering and looking guilty. I would say they know something and it's not good."

Auntie Lil thought it over. "How would I approach them?" she asked.

Calvin shrugged. "I guess you'll just have to wait until Tuesday," he said. "I know they don't come in tomorrow because both of them teach dance classes over at that Dance Center on Broadway." He laughed. "Sure am glad I didn't want to be a dancer when I grew up. I make more money than both of them. They teach classes over there to make some extra cash; at least that's what I heard."

"The Dance Center?" she asked.

"That's it," he replied. "I thought about taking a few classes there myself, you know. They were advertising ballet classes for older people, saying it was a good way to keep your joints stretched and all. My back hurt from some heavy lifting and I thought about giving it a try. After watching so many ballet classes and all, I guess maybe I caught a touch of the bug myself. But I ended up taking yoga instead, because when I went over to the Dance Center to take my sample class and sign up, I found out that the classes were for *really* old people. You know—even people as old as you." He realized what he had said and ducked his head. "No offense meant, of course," he said.

"No problem," Auntie Lil assured him. "It's no secret that I'm old." She stared out the window and watched the high-rise apartments of Riverdale as their cab sped past. Ballet classes for old people led by Paulette Puccinni?

Auntie Lil knew exactly what her next step would be.

CHAPTER FOUR

1. Later that evening a quick telephone call to an acquaintance in the corps de ballet gave Auntie Lil the information she needed: Paulette Puccinni's favorite accompanist was a fifty-five-year-old man named Jerry Vanderbilt who had been with the company for the past four years. The two were as close as twin kangaroos in the pouch, but "not in that way, if you know what I mean. Jerry's on the other team." Both, her source confided, were suspicious of others in the company, gossiped a great deal between themselves, and while they were respected, were also considered a bit antisocial. And yes, both did teach senior ballet classes at the Dance Center. Because these classes were so rough on the instructors—old people could be far more stubborn than children—Jerry and Paulette earned double the going rate for their services. After a few moments of commiseration with her source over the low salaries paid to artists these days, Auntie Lil rang off to consider her strategy.

If Paulette Puccinni and Jerry Vanderbilt were that close, Auntie Lil wondered if directly questioning them would work. Even if one opened up to her, the other's suspicions could soon prove contagious. She'd be better off choosing a more circuitous route to winning their trust. Besides, it would be more fun that way.

She rose early the next morning and called Theodore with an appropriate cover story: she was taking an exercise class. She felt guilty about misleading him, but he was, as expected, tiresome and pedantic about her extracurricular activities. When she told him she had been elected the board's official spokesperson in the matter of Bobby

Morgan's death, he had reacted with the usual warnings not to interfere. She justified her lying by deciding that she needed to put Theodore off her scent for a while, until she made some progress.

Next, she called Herbert Wong, knowing he would be the perfect companion for her undertaking. He readily agreed to meet her on Broadway with exercise clothes in hand. He did not even ask why—a wonderful trait in a friend. She hung up and pawed through her bureau drawer for suitable attire. Auntie Lil was incapable of appearing anywhere without what she deemed the perfect outfit. Her idea of the perfect outfit was admittedly unconventional at times, but she still felt the confidence that comes from knowing one is dressed for an occasion. Unfortunately, nothing in her current wardrobe would do. She hated synthetic fibers and it was tough to find tights in 100 percent cotton. In the end, she stopped off at a lovely boutique near the subway and found exactly what she wanted: a raspberry leotard and matching tights.

The young man at the front desk of the Dance Center was alarmingly cooperative. Of course, they could take a sample class. There was one starting in just a few minutes, in fact, and if they were interested in an entire series of classes ... He launched into a sales pitch that left them dizzy and wondering about the financial footing of the place. Promising to return and discuss their bargain lifetime plan for multiple classes later, Auntie Lil and Herbert embarked on their latest subterfuge.

Herbert was well-dressed for the occasion. He emerged from the locker room of the Dance Center clad in sleek black biking shorts. His ebony knit top had cut-off sleeves, just like a professional dancer. He wore black Chinese slippers that made Auntie Lil wish she had thought of them first; her own clunky white tennis shoes spoiled the effect of her ensemble.

The sales spiel had taken so long that they were late for class and apparently interrupted at a bad time. About a dozen elderly people lined the mirrored room, their faces reflecting the polished glow of a gleaming hardwood floor.

They were leaning against the barre—a long wooden rod that rimmed the room just above waist height. Their eyes were fixed eagerly on an argument that had broken out at the piano. A spry old lady no more than five feet tall stood nose to chest with the accompanist, Jerry Vanderbilt. A plump woman dressed in a diaphanous caftan was attempting to referee. Auntie Lil correctly inferred that this was Paulette Puccinni, maître de ballet—or head of the Metro's corps de ballet—when she was not instructing retirees on their form.

"I do *not* play too loud," Jerry Vanderbilt was shouting. "How dare you insinuate I am deaf." He was of medium height, with well-muscled shoulders. He was extraordinarily strong-looking, in fact, and Auntie Lil wondered if the physical demands of playing the piano for a living could account for his stature alone. Maybe he lifted weights. Vanderbilt had a chiseled, almost craggy face with a proud nose, wide eyes, and generous mouth. A German face, Auntie Lil thought, or perhaps Austrian, with maybe a touch of Eastern Europe in his prominent chin. His reddish brown hair was receding rapidly from a high forehead that was, at this particular moment, flushed an angry red.

The accompanist's strength did not intimidate his current opponent. The tiny old lady scowled at his denial, then produced a small plastic box from the pocket of her tunic. She carefully extracted two wax earplugs from the box and dramatically inserted them into her ears, screwing each into place as if she were securing electrical fuses. "You sound like a herd of thundering elephants!" she snarled for emphasis.

Jerry glowered. "How appropriate. Since you dance like one."

"Please, please, please!" Paulette Puccinni pleaded, sweeping her caftan into the air as if taking flight. "You are upsetting the artistic air of the room. It is true all dance is based on emotion, but this is not the mood we are attempting to create." She patted her student on the back, made soothing noises under her breath, and steered the old woman back to the barre. When she returned to the piano,

Auntie Lil distinctly heard her hiss, "I'd like to rip her shriveled old ears off," to Jerry through clenched teeth.

Jerry smiled thinly and began a dignified adagio beat, but stopped abruptly when he noticed Auntie Lil and Herbert standing by the door. "Newbies," he said, sighing in exasperation.

"I'm so sorry we're late," Auntie Lil apologized. "The young man out front kept us. Are we intruding?"

"No, no, no," Paulette insisted, confirming that she got paid by the pupil. "You simply must come in and join our little gathering." Her caftan flapped about her like uncoordinated wings as she moved her arms in emphasis.

They crept to the center of the room, self-conscious in their dancing attire. Auntie Lil was acutely aware that she resembled an oversized M&M in her leotard, especially compared with the other students—who were astonishingly sleek for their age. The other women in the class eyed her covertly as they stretched and bent at the barre. The four men in the room were less critical. They looked as if they felt vaguely foolish at being there in the first place and one of them even wiggled his eyebrows at Herbert.

"We're rank beginners," Auntie Lil explained. "With emphasis on the 'rank.'"

"No matter, no matter," Paulette gushed, escorting her to the barre. "Today we are working on musical interpretation. It will give you just a taste of how soaring to the soul ballet can be. Good for your body tone, too, of course." She patted Auntie Lil's fanny in a conspiratorial way and it was all Auntie Lil could do to resist demanding that Paulette strip off her camouflaging caftan and let it all hang out with the rest of them.

Herbert was as comfortable as a duck in water. He seemed to glide effortlessly toward the barre, accepted the space the other students made for him with a graceful nod, and began to stretch. Auntie Lil watched enviously.

Herbert was of indeterminate age. The best she could guess was older than seventy and younger than eighty. But he was also undeniably fit. His small frame was compact and muscled, upheld by a pair of deceptively thin legs. She already knew his strength and endurance were that of a man several decades younger. More than once she had been forced to call it quits on the dance floor when he had been willing to continue. Herbert also had wonderful equipoise. She suspected he practiced martial arts in private, some sort of balancing-the-harmony-of-the-body-with-the-harmony-of-the-world type thing, but she hadn't the energy to ask. His agility and balance would serve him well today.

Auntie Lil was another story. She was a stout woman, certainly not fat, but no one would ever call her willowy. She had not changed shape or gained weight in forty years. Her body had found its equilibrium and, despite her fondness of food and Bloody Marys, had stayed at its most comfortable. Unfortunately, her optimum physical shape was nowhere near that sought after in ballet. American ballet dancers were tall. Auntie Lil was medium height, at best. Ballerinas had small breasts and long, slender arms that could arc above their heads in graceful positions de bras. But Auntie Lil had developed large square shoulders and impressive biceps during her career as an assistant fashion designer. She still carried much of her bulk up high, giving her an awkward center of gravity. Finally, most dancers also had long, lean legs; Auntie Lil's were like muscular sausages. Despite these obstacles, she was grimly determined to prove to herself that she could be a ballet dancer.

Too bad Paulette Puccinni didn't want to help. "Face the barre," she ordered the class. "Grasp it firmly. And listen carefully as we work on posture. It sounds simple, but it is not. Ready? Go!" She began to bark out orders as if she were a gunnery sergeant training a new crew. "Bend your body over the front third of your foot. Knee up and straight in back. Thighs out. Let me see those inner thighs. Lift up the abdominal muscles. Up, up, up. Lift the rib cage. Up, up, up. Relax the shoulders. Stretch the neck. Head erect." She clapped her hands sharply on each command, the echoing sound in counterpoint to the improvised tune her accompanist contributed.

Auntie Lil tried to do as she was told, but with each sharp clap and each barked command, she felt her body rebelling as it was pulled farther and farther away from its natural center of balance. She ended up hunched over the barre, teetering precariously, with all of her muscles clenched desperately inward.

"No, no, no, no, no! Exactly *wrong*. I told you it would not be easy." Paulette made a beeline for Auntie Lil. "What is your name, dear?"

"Lillian Hubbert."

"Class, watch as I help Lillian attain the proper posture."

"Please," Auntie Lil murmured. "You may call me Miss Hubbert."

Paulette retaliated by pulling Auntie Lil's shoulders back. "I said shoulders back," the instructor demanded.

Auntie Lil obeyed, but every time Paulette pulled one of her body parts, the corresponding muscles on the other side of her body quite naturally followed. Auntie Lil felt she could be given credit for flexibility, but Paulette disagreed. After tugging Auntie Lil this way and that, the former ballerina finally gave up. "The fundamental problem, Miss Hubbert," she said, "is that your head is simply too big for ballet. It destroys your balance. But do carry on. Trying is better than nothing. At least you are getting some physical exercise." With this parting shot, her eyes sought out a fresh victim. She steamed toward Herbert Wong, then stopped short in surprise.

"Excellent! Excellent," she cried, clapping her hands together like a trained seal who smells herring on the wind. "Class, we have here a true natural. Look at that balance, note his regal carriage, note the straight line from the nape of his neck all the way down to the base of the spinal column. Bravo! Bravo!"

The class burst into spontaneous applause while Herbert posed like a dignified crane. Auntie Lil checked out her own contorted frame in the mirror and hoped the class would be over soon. She'd had enough time to evaluate Paulette Puccinni and Jerry Vanderbilt. She planned to show them no mercy and was anxious to get started.

The interpretive dance portion of the class was a little better. It also gave Auntie Lil an opportunity to observe Paulette up close. Swooping her way to the front of the long line of students swaying obediently behind their teacher, Auntie Lil evaluated Paulette's physical conditioning. She knew that years ago, Paulette had been a prima ballerina who had studied under George Balanchine. Rumor had it that she had walked away from the American Ballet Theater during one of his temperamental fits. She had then thrown herself into a yearlong sulk, compounded by excessive drinking and overeating. Eventually, she had been offered a new job training the corps at the newly founded Metropolitan Ballet. But by then, her aging body and rusty technique were incapable of recovering from the months of abuse. Her dancing days were over. Some said she did not take the transition well. She was still quite strong, however, as Auntie Lil realized when Paulette single-handedly moved the piano back several feet to make room for a group interpretation of cattails waving in the wind. She pondered whether this fact was significant as she bent to the left and right, doing her best to convey the essence of cattailhood.

"Thank God that's over!" Auntie Lil whispered to Herbert a half hour later in the reception area. They had showered and studied the upcoming class schedule while they waited for Paulette and Jerry to finish with a private lesson in the studio.

"I enjoyed myself," Herbert admitted. "I have always admired the deceptively effortless grace of ballet." For emphasis, he bent his knees out and dipped low in a grand plié. Auntie Lil ignored him.

"Here she comes," she muttered, nodding toward the studio door. A frightened-looking student scurried from the room and Paulette emerged soon after, her caftan billowing in a blast of air-conditioning.

"Miss Puccinni," Auntie Lil said, stepping out to block her exit.

"Yes?" she asked suspiciously, staring at Auntie Lil as if her street clothes completely obscured her identity.

"I am Lillian Hubbert. We just met in class."

"I remember. Don't feel bad, dear. You tried your best." She patted Auntie Lil's shoulder. "Some people just aren't built for ballet."

"I am not here to discuss my balletic abilities," Auntie Lil answered quickly. "I am a board member of the Metropolitan and I am inquiring in an official capacity into the death of Bobby Morgan three nights ago. You remember, I presume?"

Paulette froze just as Jerry Vanderbilt came charging through the door behind her. He crashed into her and stopped in surprise.

"She's on the board," Paulette explained tersely. "She wants to ask us questions about Morgan."

"I didn't say that specifically," Auntie Lil said. "But now that you mention it . . ."

The pair exchanged a glance. "Better be nice," Jerry grudgingly advised Paulette. "She pays the bills."

"What exactly do you want?" Paulette asked, drawing herself up to her full height. Her eyes blazed and Auntie Lil caught a hint of the fiery presence that had been her hallmark during her prima ballerina days.

"I do want to ask you a few questions. In a very friendly way. Over lunch," Auntie Lil admitted.

"I never eat lunch, but all right," Paulette agreed. "I can make an exception. But you'll have to be quick. We have another class in two hours."

Auntie Lil doubted that Paulette's stout frame had missed too many lunches lately, but she played along. "Fine," she agreed. "You must join Herbert and me for a salad. Perhaps you can be wicked and order the consommé."

2.   It was like eating lunch with a malevolent Abbott and Costello. Paulette and Jerry had the ability to finish each other's sentences with extrasensory spite.

"Raoul Martinez was never a great dancer," Paulette said when Auntie Lil asked her about the Metro's artistic director. "Perhaps not even a very good one. He just rode the craze for dark, brooding men in the seventies. He was more of a—"

"Poor man's dancing Errol Flynn," Jerry finished. "Even starred in some Grade-C flicks back in Spain wearing tights and waving a sword."

"He seems an excellent artistic director," Auntie Lil said mildly. She was waiting for her foot-long chili dog with melted cheese and onions. It was a little much, even for Auntie Lil, but she still had the urge to get even with Paulette for her earlier humiliations and she had a hunch this was one way to do so. The former dancer had rather wistfully ordered a large garden salad.

"He can control the company all right," Jerry said enigmatically. "It's the ones who are closer to home that he has trouble with."

This was hardly a discreet reference. The whole dance world knew that Raoul Martinez was married to the Metro's aging prima ballerina, a temperamental woman named Lisette Casanova-Martinez. Their stormy relationship and public fights were legendary in ballet circles and had even ended up on the gossip pages of New York's tabloids on several occasions.

"Yes, I've heard," Auntie Lil murmured. The waiter approached their table with a well-filled tray. Her lunch smelled exquisite. The huge hot dog steamed with the delightful odor of a fair's midway, causing Paulette's nose to twitch in envy. She stared at the enormous platter of cholesterol-inducing goo with undisguised envy as it was set in front of Auntie Lil. Herbert had confined himself, as usual, to broiled fish and a salad. Only Jerry had joined Auntie Lil in enthusiastic gluttony—after all, he wasn't paying—and was about to dive into a plate heaped high with fried seafood.

"Jerry can eat anything and never gains an ounce," Paulette said, staring at the golden battered shrimp like a gull might eye the fried shrimp's more alive brethren.

"Metabolism," Jerry explained, crunching in contentment. The free lunch was putting him in a good mood. "If you're really digging for the dirt on Morgan's death, you ought to talk to Martinez," he said helpfully.

"Among others," Paulette added.

"Oh yes?" Auntie Lil waited to hear more. The synchronistic effect she had feared might work against her was working for her instead. Paulette and Jerry seemed to be in a race to cast aspersions on as many other people as possible.

"You mean the fight?" Paulette asked Jerry, raising her eyebrows. He nodded back mysteriously.

"What fight?" Auntie Lil demanded.

Herbert remained silent, watching his companions. In this way, he could pick up nearly as much useful information as Auntie Lil could with her mouth going.

"With Paulette here," Jerry offered with a wicked smile.

Paulette looked grim. "I wasn't talking about the fight with me. That was just a small misunderstanding. Besides, I wasn't the only one he fought with during the six weeks of rehearsal," she retorted, eyeing Jerry back.

The accompanist countered by thoroughly confusing the issue. "True," he admitted. "Morgan did have a knock-down-drag-out with Martinez about the interpretation of the play and the demands he was making on his son, after he fought with Paulette here over driving his son too hard in rehearsal."

"His son is not a dancer," Paulette offered. "Never has been."

"And he fought with that know-it-all board member," Jerry finished. "The one who is always lurking around the halls trying to run everything."

"True," Paulette agreed. "I thought he was the president at some bank somewhere. Doesn't he ever actually go there and work?"

"Hans Glick?" Auntie Lil said. "Fought over what?"

Jerry and Paulette shrugged simultaneously, and Paulette spoke first. "Everything, I'd say. They argued all the time. Some ongoing thing. They'd meet in the halls outside the rehearsal rooms while I was trying to improve the poor boy's technique. We could hear them arguing outside the door."

"I play rather quietly," Jerry explained. "Helps the mood, you see. They were arguing over contract negotiations. Couldn't really hear the details, though God knows I tried." He gave a bright smile and popped another shrimp into his mouth.

"I see." Auntie Lil bit into her gooey hot dog, sending a waterfall of pungent chili tumbling off the other end. Paulette groaned and licked her lips as she watched Auntie Lil eat, unaware that she had moaned out loud.

"So he argued with Glick over the contract terms and with Martinez about the demands of his son's role," Auntie Lil said. "Was that all he argued about with either man?"

"What else?" Paulette answered too quickly and Auntie Lil knew she was lying. Especially when she exchanged a glance with Jerry. A signal was sent and received.

"That's all?" Auntie Lil repeated.

"What else?" Jerry echoed with a shrug.

"How badly did you argue with Morgan?" Auntie Lil asked Paulette.

Paulette flushed lightly. "We had harsh words a few times. He claimed I was trying to cripple his son."

"But you convinced him it was the best thing for Mikey?"

"Hah!" Jerry shoveled a forkful of crispy clams in his mouth and munched with divine satisfaction. "She backed down when he threatened to have her canned."

"Jerry!" Paulette glowered at him and her thin smile faded to an ominous frown. Her eyes gleamed as if she were searching her brain for equally incriminating information on him.

"Who do you think could have killed Morgan?" Auntie Lil asked quickly. If they began to fight, all of their energy would go into the battle. She needed their attention for a few minutes more.

"A lot of people," Paulette and Jerry answered almost simultaneously. They burst into what they considered to be wicked laughter. To Auntie Lil and Herbert it sounded more like nasty cackles. The pair took mutual delight in the misfortune of others—and were none too kind with each other, either.

"A lot of people at the Metro?" Auntie Lil prompted.

Paulette nodded. "He had a colossal ego and he used his son to feed it. He's made quite a few enemies in a few short weeks."

Jerry nodded agreement. "But how's this for a darkhorse-killer candidate?" He relished the nervous expression that crossed Paulette's face. "Surely you've noticed that Madame Chairman had the unreciprocated hots for our murder victim?" He raised an eyebrow for emphasis.

Auntie Lil's mouth dropped open at a most unfortunate time, considering she was eating a chili dog. "Lane Rogers took a romantic interest in Bobby Morgan?"

"I don't know how romantic it was," Jerry admitted with a sly giggle. "It was certainly interesting."

"I think when a woman reaches a certain age she should put such things behind her," Paulette added, wrapping her caftan around her as if no man, by God, was going to gawk at her body.

Auntie Lil could not have disagreed more. She thought people should go on falling foolishly in love for as long as their breath held out. But she did not say anything except, "How could you tell her affections were not returned?"

"How could we tell?" Jerry asked. "Just look at her! The only person who would look at Madame Chairman's body with any interest might be the defensive coach of the New York Giants!" He and Paulette shared a laugh.

"There must be more to it than that," Auntie Lil insisted. "How did you know she was interested in him?"

"She followed him around," Paulette offered. "Through the halls, trapping him in corners, saying she needed to discuss all sorts of trivial things. It was humiliating, really. I could hardly bear to watch."

Auntie Lil knew full well that Paulette Puccinni could hardly have borne *not* to watch, but she held her tongue. "And you knew her affections were not returned because of . . . ?"

"The way he would run into the men's room and hide when he saw her coming was a dead giveaway," Jerry explained, deadpan.

It was hard to argue with that reasoning. "Why didn't Martinez bar Morgan from the rehearsal areas?" Auntie Lil asked, switching tracks. "He seems to have caused quite a bit of chaos."

"Not enough guts," Paulette explained. "None of us want to be unemployed by next season and it seemed obvious to us all that Bobby Morgan had an awful lot of influence with the board. After all"—this time it was her turn to stare at Auntie Lil—"he managed to have one of our finest dancers to come along in decades removed from her role."

Auntie Lil was surprised at the honest indignation in Paulette's voice. It seemed the first true ring of emotion she had heard from the woman. "You taught Fatima Jones?" she asked.

Paulette nodded. "I inherited her from the New School of Ballet. She came out of their public-school program. She already had her own style, but her technique lacked polish. I taught her everything I know. She'll go further than I ever went." She sighed involuntarily.

"You had quite a distinguished career," Herbert offered gallantly. "It is praise indeed to predict the young girl will surpass it."

"Paulette is right. Fatima is better than any of our young dancers and already better than most of the principals." Jerry shot a glance toward Paulette and an unspoken message was once again received. "Especially Lisette."

"Lisette is way past her prime," Paulette agreed. "If she had any pride, she'd hang up her shoes and go on to other activities."

"And I bet she has a few in mind," Jerry added with his by-now-familiar knack of not actually revealing the entire story yet managing to besmirch his subject with accusations unspoken.

Auntie Lil pondered this latest slur. She remembered that fidelity had been long rumored to be a problem in the

Martinez marriage. She had always assumed it was Raoul who was the cause. Now she was not so sure.

"I'd talk to Emili Vladimir if I were you," Paulette offered suddenly.

"Who in the world is that?" Auntie Lil asked.

"Rudy Vladimir's mother," Jerry explained. "The young boy who got bounced from his role so Mikey Morgan could take over."

"I know Rudy," Auntie Lil admitted. "One can hardly fail to notice him at rehearsals. He stands out, wouldn't you say?"

"As nice as he is talented," Paulette admitted in an uncharacteristic burst of generosity toward a fellow human being. "Obedient, very hardworking, very respectful of my authority and abilities."

"Too bad you can't say the same about his mother," Jerry said, smiling innocently.

Paulette glared at him.

"What?" Auntie Lil demanded.

"Jerry is under the misconception that I am jealous of Rudy's mother," Paulette said coolly. "That was all many years ago."

"Hah!" Jerry demolished his fried flounder with unrestrained glee, spreading an inch of tartar sauce on top of it first.

"How do you know her?" Auntie Lil asked, hoping to get at the truth somehow.

"She defected to the States in the late seventies when the Kirov Ballet was touring Canada," Jerry explained helpfully, ignoring his companion's warning stare. "Baryshnikov did the same thing. She didn't make such a big splash, of course. She wasn't that big of a star. But she did manage to displace a few well-known American dancers when Balanchine took her under his wing."

"Because he was infatuated with her!" Paulette spit out. "It was always the same story with him."

In other words, Auntie Lil surmised, the legendary tiff with Balanchine had probably been over his decision to replace Paulette Puccinni in some role with a relatively unknown Russian ballerina named Emili Vladimir.

"What happened to her?" Auntie Lil asked. "Why haven't we heard more about her?"

Jerry shrugged. "She was a purist about the Kirov's ballet techniques. Refused to adapt to ABT's quicker style. Opened her own school downtown. After she had the kid."

"The kid?" Auntie Lil said.

"Rudy," Paulette explained. "She was pregnant when she defected." She smiled in remembered satisfaction. "Old George only got a few months' worth of dancing out of her. After the baby, she drifted into modern dance. One of *those*."

"Her husband's death may have had something to do with it," Jerry added. "He was supposed to join them here in America. I don't know what happened." He shrugged. "He got killed by the KGB or disappeared into Siberia or something. He was a dancer, too. Some people say she never had the heart to dance a pas de deux after he died."

"Romantic nonsense," Paulette countered. "Having a baby ruined her body, that's all."

Auntie Lil fervently hoped that Herbert was listening carefully. These two collected grudges the way other people collected stamps. "But you didn't actually see anyone suspicious or anything odd the night Morgan was killed?" Auntie Lil asked. "Nothing that could help us?"

"I wasn't even there," Jerry said. "I prefer playing at rehearsal rather than performances." In other words, he had not been chosen as principal pianist for this run of *The Nutcracker*.

"I was too busy trying to supervise all those damn children," Paulette said with a sigh. "I don't know what possessed Raoul this time around. I didn't have time to see anything. Besides, Morgan was on the opposite side of the stage from me. Not many dancers are on that side at that point in the performance. Most have just exited stage left. There are just a handful of technical crew stage right, actually, at the Act One break."

"If you talk to the tech staff, be careful," Jerry offered.

He pantomimed taking a slug from an imaginary bottle. "If you know what I mean."

Auntie Lil stared first at him and then Paulette. "No, I do not know what you mean," she said firmly.

"They drink," Paulette explained. "Our tech crew is wetter than the Mississippi. Someone could have dissected Morgan under their noses and they wouldn't have noticed unless the killer had called for a spotlight. Too busy trying to hit their cues while under the influence."

3. "They incriminated everyone but Mother Teresa," Auntie Lil explained when she reached T.S. by phone an hour later. "And that's only because she was in Calcutta the night Bobby Morgan was killed."

"I am sorry I missed seeing you in tights," T.S. told her. "You said exercise class, not ballet."

"Same thing," she said, changing the subject. "Meet me and Herbert in midtown. I need your help."

"Where?" T.S. had spent the last few days reviewing back issues of *Sports Illustrated* and was no closer to understanding America's fascination with sports than he had been to understanding downtown's fascination with modern dance. He was getting bored and ready to toss prudence to the winds. He suspected Auntie Lil was out somewhere in New York City having fun and now he wanted a piece of the action.

"Meet me at the Museum of Radio and Television Broadcasting," she said. "We're going to take a trip down Memory Lane."

4. "There are over one hundred episodes of *Mike and Me*," Auntie Lil explained. "I can't possibly watch them all."

"Why are we watching them in the first place?" T.S. asked, rather sensibly, he thought.

"I can't quite explain it," Auntie Lil admitted. They were waiting at the counter of the museum's archives while the clerk located the requested tapes. "It's the way Morgan was pushed center stage after being killed. It was such a mocking gesture. I thought perhaps we might get a clue to his character if we looked at the tapes."

"If you want a clue to Bobby Morgan's character," T.S. said, "consider the fact that he named his son after his own fictional character. I think that's creepy. Think of the pressure that went with the name."

"Yes," Auntie Lil agreed. "That's why everything begins with this. It formed the basis for Bobby Morgan's personality for the rest of his life. Besides, I don't know what else to do. We can't question anyone else at the Metro today. There's no one there."

T.S. nodded agreeably. This would be better than football, at any rate. "Talked to Lilah about the murder?" he asked casually.

"No, dear. I told you, she's been busy in meetings."

The old familiar doubt gnawed at the edge of his stomach. How could one person have so many meetings? Was she avoiding him? He looked up to find Herbert watching him quietly, as if he could read his mind.

"I have a plan," he whispered to T.S. "I will tell you later."

T.S. nodded, mystified.

"Here you go—six years of *Mike and Me*. Enjoy." The clerk pushed a stack of videotapes over the counter and nodded to a bank of carrels against one wall, each equipped with a combination television and VCR. Auntie Lil divided the stack and they headed off to review their assigned episodes.

Compared to his son, Bobby Morgan had been an unlikely-looking child star. Part of this may have been due to his career's time period. The early seventies had been an odd time for American style. In episode after episode, Bobby Morgan had been plagued alternately with a shag haircut, bushy Afro, improbable sideburns, and, finally, a disco do that made him look positively ludicrous. His clothes were even less attractive, though no different from his cast mates': bell bottoms, tight knit shirts, circus stripes, suspenders, floppy hats, and platform shoes. But not all of his awkward appearance could be attributed to the costuming. Bobby Morgan had evolved undeniably from an appealing child in the very early episodes into a gawky, acne-plagued teenager desperately trying to be cute by the final shows. It was easy to see why his popularity had faded. It was even possible to feel sorry for him and to sympathize with his attempts to relive his child-star days through his son.

The plots were no different from those offered by more modern sitcoms. Bobby Morgan's character had been called Mike, the later inspiration for his real son's name. The fictional Mike lived in a modest middle-class home in Brooklyn with his Irish-butcher father, ditzy Italian mother, bullying older brother, and adorable little sister. Each week the show was told from a different character's viewpoint, using a voice-over technique to explore that character's relationship with Mike. Most of the shows revolved around Mike's propensity to get into trouble: Mike tying his scoutmaster to a chair while trying out knots during a Boy Scout meeting then accidentally locking him in a closet as a fire broke out; Mike sneaking into the circus because he had no money for a ticket and inadvertently being swept into center ring with the clowns during a routine; Mike pretending to drive his family's parked car and releasing the parking brake, triggering a preposterous ride downhill through what seemed to be nearly all of Brooklyn.

Everyone watching the well-preserved tapes had different reactions to these situations. Auntie Lil was irritated by the canned laughter and renewed her vow never to watch television. T.S. was annoyed by the precociousness of all three child actors and embarrassed because he had actually dressed in pants approaching bell-bottoms during those same years. Herbert was scientific about his observations and scrutinized the interplay between the fictional family members in an attempt to pick up clues about Bobby Morgan's real personality. In the end, no one had the stomach even to contemplate watching all of the episodes in order.

They fast-forwarded through many of them and, after four hours of nonstop watching, finally threw in the towel.

"Anything interesting?" T.S. asked, bleary-eyed, as they rode the elevator down to Broadway.

"The actor who played his older brother on the show looks familiar," Herbert offered. "Andrew Perkins. Did he go on to movies?"

T.S. shook his head. "I didn't recognize him."

"I did," Auntie Lil agreed. "He must have grown up to be someone."

"Unlike Bobby Morgan," T.S. offered.

Auntie Lil nodded in agreement. "He looks nothing at all like his son Mikey," she said. "The boy must take after his mother."

"Good point," T.S. said. "And where is this mother anyway?"

"The funeral is Wednesday," Auntie Lil explained. "She'll be there with her children, I am sure."

"That's a whole day and a half away," T.S. joked. "What are you going to do until then?"

"Go see Myron Silverstein," Auntie Lil explained promptly.

"Who is Myron Silverstein?" T.S. asked, knowing he was taking the bait.

"Bobby Morgan's old agent," Auntie Lil explained. "The one who got him the job on that wretched show. While you were fast-forwarding, I was reading the credits. I am not content to let bygones be bygones just yet."

CHAPTER FIVE

1. The next morning, Auntie Lil could rouse neither Theodore nor Herbert by telephone, an unusual situation that triggered a suspicion that they were up to something. But she pushed this thought aside in favor of finding Bobby Morgan's former agent. Six phone calls later, she located the right Myron Silverstein. His office was on Fifty-seventh Street around the corner from the Stage Deli.

The address sounded better than it looked. Myron Silverstein may have made a fortune off Bobby Morgan in his gravy days, but he was coping with hard times now. His office was barely bigger than a pantry and smelled of bourbon and kitty litter.

Silverstein was only slightly more uplifting. He was a pudgy man, well into his sixties, with the desperately weary air of someone who has not yet begun to save for retirement—or even his quarterly estimated tax payments. His few remaining strands of gray hair were combed across his mottled scalp in an ineffectual attempt to hide massive baldness. He wore a blue suit and a green tie that featured an embroidered version of a moth-eaten Oscar statuette. The top of the statue's head was ragged where he had rubbed it. Small threads of gold sprouted from its scalp like a cowlick, making the icon look more like Alfalfa than Oscar.

"What can I do for you?" he asked Auntie Lil in a gravelly voice, eyeing her as if she were an actress at an audition. "I handle mostly kids, you know."

She carefully averted her eye from a mangled cigar that poked from the ashtray like an enormous leech. "I understand you used to handle Bobby Morgan," she said, after explaining who she was and why she was there.

"That was a long time ago," Silverstein explained. "He was my last big meal ticket, if it isn't obvious from this dump I'm in."

"It's very cozy," Auntie Lil said, fooling neither one of them with her bravado. "You heard the details about his murder?"

The old man nodded. "Sure. Didn't everyone? Talk about going out in style. Sad ending, to what would have been an entire sad story. Except for all the money he made off his kid, of course. Would have liked to have had a piece of that action." He fiddled despondently with a pencil, daydreaming of more successful days.

"How long were you his agent, Mr. Silverstein?" Auntie Lil asked.

His face scrunched into a ball, as if the concentration required to think back that far in time was excruciating. "About four years," he finally said. "I discovered him back in 1968, in some crappy production the Metro was giving. We found a lot of our kids in the performing arts in those days. It's still a good training ground for a professional career, though the parents don't have the patience to let their kids wait that long anymore. They drag them in my office at two years old these days. Can't talk, can't read, can't hardly walk, but they're gonna be a star. At least the parents think so." He shook his head in disgust. "Bobby Morgan wasn't as good-looking as your typical kid star, but he had confidence. Plus it turned out that he could learn lines just by looking at them. Photographic memory—the real thing. Amazing, really. He didn't get the part right away. Almost lost it to another kid. In the end, they gave him the part because he was easier to work with and they decided the other kid was too old. Wrote the other kid in as the older brother instead."

"That was Andrew Perkins?" Auntie Lil asked.

Silverstein nodded. "Yeah. Came out of the Metro School, too. I tried to sign him along with Bobby, but that bastard Cy Cohen beat me to it. He'd represented the kid in some other minor roles. I lost out again about four years later when Morgan wouldn't renew his contract with me. His parents decided to manage him themselves. Spent all his money, is what I heard. By the time the kid left the show, he didn't have much left. Enough to get through college is all. Violated the law, but what are you going to do? Throw your own parents in jail? They died a couple years later anyway. Car wreck."

"Yet Morgan turned around and did the same thing to his own son," Auntie Lil pointed out. "Took over managing his career."

Myron Silverstein stared at her. "I definitely would *not* say that Bobby Morgan did the same thing. His parents may have robbed him blind, but Bobby Morgan was a *great* agent for his own kid. Listen, I know what they say in the press. That Morgan was greedy, that he was reliving his career through Mikey, that he was a real . . . uh, backbreaker. Producers hated him. Directors hated him. Everyone hated him. That's mostly true. But he was a damn fine agent and a smart manager of his kid's career. Mikey Morgan gets more per picture than any other child star in the history of Tinseltown. And why shouldn't he? He's a living, breathing gold mine for the studios. If his father hadn't been related to him or been labeled a failed child star himself, people would be singing his praises and lining up to be his other clients. I can't fault Bobby professionally." He leaned forward and examined the cigar. Auntie Lil fervently hoped that he would not actually put the soggy lump in his mouth. "He was pretty good as a kid actor, too," Silverstein added. "He made that sitcom stand out from the other crap on television. It's a shame he grew up to be so awkward, but that happens, you know. All part of the business."

"How did he take it when the sitcom got dropped?" Auntie Lil asked. "It was a long time ago, but it could be relevant to his murder."

Silverstein shrugged. "Not good. He knew his acting days were over. Hollywood and television are pretty cruel to child stars who've outgrown their cuteness. But he knew it was coming. Same thing had happened to Perkins, the kid who played his older brother. He'd been written out of the show a couple years before. And the same thing happened to the girl who played his little sister once the show was canned. She made one unsuccessful movie, then developed these huge kazankas for her age. And her career as a kid actor was over."

"Do you know what he did between the time his show was dropped and he became known as his son's manager?" Auntie Lil asked. The missing pieces of Bobby Morgan's life intrigued her. She wondered if the clue to his murder lay somewhere in those forgotten years.

Silverstein shook his head. "Not really. Lived in California for a while, I heard. Married a girl when he was too young. Didn't work out. Tried to get some acting jobs. No dice. Tried producing. Tubed out. Married again. That broke up a couple of years ago. Every now and then he'd call the kid who played his little sister and touch base. I tried for years to get her another acting job and she'd let me know whenever she heard from Bobby."

"What about Perkins? Did they keep in touch?"

The agent shrugged. "Doubt it. They didn't get along. Perkins never got over not getting the lead."

"Does he live in California now, too?"

Silverstein shook his head. "Naw. I think he lives here in New York somewhere. Heard he became a broker or a banker or some sort of Wall Street exec. He got married and divorced same as Morgan. No surprise there. Professional casualties, that's what I call old child stars. Life never gets easier once you're done as a celebrity. Marriages fail, people forget you, they get angry that you've changed, dreams die out. . . ." His voice trailed off sadly and Auntie Lil was struck by what seemed to be genuine compassion in his voice for his former clients. "Some of 'em can't take it. They end it early, know what I mean?"

Auntie Lil nodded, though she felt strongly that Bobby Morgan had not hanged himself in mid-*Nutcracker*. "Can you think of anyone who might have wanted to kill Bobby Morgan?" she asked Silverstein.

His mouth dropped open again. "You're kidding, right?

Because that particular A list would be a long one. Start with the heads of all three major studios, throw in a couple of producers, a financial jerk or two." He stopped and raised his eyebrows thoughtfully. "But you might look into a guy named Gene Levitt. Morgan pulled his kid from a movie Levitt was making after the contracts had been signed. This was about two months ago. Without Mikey Morgan, Levitt lost his backing. And his shirt. Word is that his company is going under. He lost millions in preproduction expenses because of Morgan. I'd say that's a pretty damn good motive for murder."

"How could Morgan pull his son out of a movie after the contracts had been signed? Isn't that illegal?"

"Sure." Silverstein's snort was sympathetic. "But what is Levitt going to do? Sue? He hasn't got a dime left. No lawyer will touch him because there's a good chance they'll never get paid. Morgan had millions to fight him in court. And they always come up with some reason they can point to as legitimate for breaking the contract."

"But that's not fair!" Auntie Lil said indignantly.

"Hey, it's a shark pit out there. Kill or be killed."

"Well, someone took that advice a little too literally for my tastes," Auntie Lil informed him. She rose and extended a white-gloved hand. "Thank you so much for your time, Mr. Silverstein. You've been most helpful."

"My pleasure." He smiled, revealing yellowed teeth as he reached toward the bloated cigar remnant.

Auntie Lil fled the office quickly. The smell of kitty litter and bourbon chased her all the way to the dingy elevator.

2. As she stood gazing at the menu in the window of the Stage Deli—trying to decide which of the eatery's famous enormous sandwiches she should eat—she remembered something Silverstein had said: Andrew Perkins had been Bobby Morgan's costar twenty years before. And the name of the ballerina who originally replaced Fatima Jones was Julie Perkins. Could they be related? She thought this possibility over. Why would Bobby Morgan do his old rival

a favor by making it possible for Perkins's daughter to dance the lead? And if Morgan had cleared the way for Julie Perkins to take center stage, why would the girl's father kill him in retaliation? No, it didn't make sense. Yet Silverstein said that the Metro School was still considered an excellent training ground for a performing career. And if Andrew Perkins was anything like Bobby Morgan, perhaps he harbored dreams for his progeny as well—and sent his daughter to Metro for the training.

There was only one way to find out. She'd have the chopped chicken liver, bacon, and egg-salad combination on whole wheat and then, refreshed and resolved, march right up to Perkins's front door and ask.

After lunch, she had to pull rank in the Metropolitan Ballet's business office in order to obtain Julie Perkins's address. But pulling rank had never bothered Auntie Lil. In fact, it was one of the few times when she was capable of subtlety. While the young secretary scurried to find the proper records for the obviously important board member, Auntie Lil appropriated her phone and called T.S. He answered on the first ring.

"Where have you been?" she demanded.

"Been?" he answered innocently. "Did you call?"

"This morning. Three times."

"I was sleeping late," he explained, although the truth was that Herbert had been teaching him ballroom dancing.

"Nonsense, Theodore. You haven't slept past eight o'clock since you had the measles in 1951."

T.S. resisted the urge to point out that she was the main cause for that, but he held his tongue. "I am retired and entitled to sleep in," he said.

She let this pass but filed it away for future reference. Now she was certain that he was up to something that excluded her, which positively rankled. Auntie Lil was of the opinion that everything was her business, especially when it involved her beloved Theodore.

"I may have a lead," she explained. "But I am a little uneasy about going it alone."

"Is this really Lillian Hubbert?" T.S. asked with mock seriousness.

"Well, I *am* uneasy," she said defensively. It wouldn't hurt to have Theodore along in case she ran into trouble, a thought that occurred to her more and more often in her . . . well, more advanced years. But he didn't have to rub it in.

"What particular brand of trouble are you contemplating?" he asked.

The secretary returned with Julie Perkins's enrollment card and handed it to Auntie Lil with an uneasy glance at the telephone. Surely the old woman wasn't making long-distance calls? The young girl left nervously and hovered on the other side of the office, wondering when Auntie Lil would leave her alone.

Auntie Lil examined the card carefully. "Remember Bobby Morgan's costar in *Mike and Me*? The one named Andrew Perkins?"

"You and Herbert remembered him. I didn't."

"Julie Perkins has an 'Andrew Perkins' listed as the person to contact in case of emergency on her Metropolitan Ballet School enrollment card." Auntie Lil turned the card over and read further. "That's odd," she added. "No mother is listed."

"You think it's the same Andrew Perkins?" T.S. asked.

"Of course it is," Auntie Lil said. "And I'm going to go talk to him."

"Why?"

"Why not?" she replied. "Come with me?"

T.S. sighed. He could not, in good conscience, refuse. And if he admitted the truth—that his feet hurt too much—she'd ferret out his ballroom-dancing efforts. "I'll meet you there," he promised. "Don't try anything on your own."

"Of course not," she murmured sweetly. Getting her own way always put Auntie Lil in a good mood.

Andrew and Julie Perkins lived in an expensive high rise co-op a few blocks from Lincoln Center. It was one of a dozen or so brick buildings that had risen around the cultural area in the seventies and eighties. Purchase prices and rents were exorbitant. As Auntie Lil waited in the lobby for

T.S. to arrive, she surveyed the marble floors and the squad of doormen, then decided that Andrew Perkins must be doing pretty well to afford such a home.

"Nice digs," T.S. said, meeting her by the miniature lobby waterfall. "I guess he revived his acting career pretty successfully."

"He doesn't act anymore," Auntie Lil explained. "According to Morgan's former agent, he works on Wall Street now."

"I should have known," T.S. said piously, conveniently ignoring the fact that he had spent thirty years on Wall Street before retiring early at age fifty-five and leaving all of the backbiting and obsession with profits behind.

Auntie Lil asked the doorman to ring the Perkins apartment. She was willing to settle for either Perkins, but was expecting the daughter or, perhaps, the unlisted mother. After all, it was the middle of a Tuesday afternoon and she was sure Andrew Perkins would be on the job. But, surprisingly, he was the only one home.

At first, he wouldn't let them up. But when Auntie Lil grabbed the house phone from the startled concierge and explained her position on the Metro's board, Perkins gave the okay to show his visitors upstairs.

"Upstairs" was an understatement. The Perkins lived on the forty-fourth floor and enjoyed a breathtaking view of the Hudson River. A long plate-glass window ran along the side of a large sunken living-room area. If Andrew Perkins had not been standing in front of the window with an unhappy scowl on his face, it would have been a lovely vista.

"What do you want?" he asked, waving reluctantly toward a low seating arrangement that bordered the living room on two sides. He remained standing, his gaunt figure made ghostlike by the glare from the afternoon sun behind him. He was a tall man, yet lacking in the grace that acceptance of his height would have provided. He stooped, as if permanently tired. His blond hair was thinning and brushed carelessly back from his forehead; the ends were in need of a trim. His features did not match: his nose was too broad for his thin lips and his small eyes looked lost in his pale face. Yet his daughter, Julie, was beautiful.

T.S. noted that the apartment was as sparse and orderly as his own. Hardwood floors gleamed beneath white rugs, the furniture was modern with clean lines, and not a single magazine marred the coffee table's glossy surface. No ashtrays either. This was a no-smoking home. All together, T.S. approved.

"I have been asked by the board to look into the matter of Bobby Morgan's death," Auntie Lil explained.

"Why?" Perkins demanded, pacing in front of the window and reaching for his short pocket, before stopping abruptly. T.S. knew at once that the absence of ashtrays was probably part of the man's desperate attempts to stop smoking. "Can't the police do a good enough job on their own?"

Auntie Lil let a moment of silence pass. Just because she had barged in unannounced was no reason to be curt. "I am sure the police are making plenty of progress," she explained.

"Are they?" Perkins interrupted. "What have they found out?"

"I don't know," Auntie Lil admitted, exasperated. "It's just that the board felt we should make an extra effort to demonstrate our determination to get to the bottom of this unfortunate occurrence. So they elected me."

Perkins stopped pacing and stared at Auntie Lil. "In other words, they realize how much bad publicity they've gotten over the past few months and they want to cut their losses?"

"Well, yes," T.S. interrupted. "I might summarize the situation that way myself." Auntie Lil glared at him, but T.S. ignored her. He was starting to enjoy himself. He was used to dealing with men like Perkins from his old Wall Street days, impatient men who felt their business alone took priority. They could not fathom why anyone else should think that what they had to do could possibly be as important.

"Do you have an objection to the board attempting to find out the truth?" T.S. asked Perkins calmly. T.S. had learned that rephrasing a person's comments into a challenging question was a good way to put them on the defensive.

Perkins scrutinized T.S. and patted down his pockets absently. "Of course I don't have an objection. Why would I?"

T.S. shrugged. "Then you wouldn't mind answering a few questions from my aunt here?"

"Fire away," Perkins agreed. Then, as if obeying his own command, he walked over to a black enamel sideboard and opened a small bottom drawer. Reaching to the very back of the compartment, he produced a pack of cigarettes and quickly lit one up, tapping the ashes into the base of a potted ficus tree nearby. T.S. wondered how many hours he had managed to go without the nicotine.

"You are the Andrew Perkins who costarred with Morgan in *Mike and Me*, aren't you?" Auntie Lil asked.

Perkins shrugged again. "So what? It's no secret. He came up to me in front of three dozen people and made a big deal about seeing me again. Everyone knew we had acted together as kids. If you're suggesting I killed him out of jealousy because he got the lead in *Mike and Me* twenty-five years ago and I didn't, you couldn't be more wrong. I enjoyed every bit as much success as him. I got just as much fan mail and, when it was all over, just as many offers for more work: zero, zippo, absolutely nothing."

"Were you surprised to see him?" Auntie Lil asked, ignoring his outburst. "You had nothing to do with his returning to New York and offering his son for the role?"

Perkins shook his head vehemently. "I didn't invite him, if that's what you mean. I'd just as soon he'd stayed in L.A." He walked over to the window and stared out. A tugboat was moving up the Hudson far below and he watched its slow progress intently.

"My aunt asked if you had anything to do with his returning to New York," T.S. pointed out. "Not whether you invited him."

Perkins stared at T.S. "Bobby may have come back to the Metro just to piss me off," he finally said. "If that's what you're getting at. He was like that. Might have wanted to rub my face in how well his kid was doing, compared to mine. Bobby always had to win more than anyone else. But I doubt that's why he showed up on the Metro's doorstep. I doubt I'm important enough for the great Bobby Morgan to really give a crap about, to be perfectly honest." He stopped and stared at T.S. again. "Have we met before?" he asked abruptly.

"It's possible," T.S. said. "I understand you work on Wall Street. I worked at Sterling & Sterling for twenty-seven years. As personnel manager."

Perkins nodded. "I interviewed there once for a job. Didn't get it. Went on to Salomon. I was their top bond producer for three years in a row. In the eighties. Made a pile of dough. Who needed acting?"

"Congratulations," T.S. said dryly. "How are things going in the bond world now that we're in the nineties?" T.S. knew full well that the bottom had dropped out of the bond market and that everyone's top producers were struggling these days.

"I quit," Perkins said. He ground out his cigarette and lit another. "Time to move on."

The man sounded suddenly as if he did not have a care in the world. T.S. was intrigued by his combination of arrogance and defensiveness. The oddest references seemed to set him off. Perhaps T.S. had turned Perkins down for the job and he still harbored a grudge. T.S. could not remember for sure, but it was possible. He had turned many people down over the years.

Auntie Lil had been watching T.S. question Perkins and her eyes glittered with a dangerous curiosity. She sensed the undercurrents in the room and was intent on uncovering their meaning. "What do you do now?" she asked Perkins. "Manage your daughter's career?"

Perkins perched on the edge of the low-slung sofa. "My daughter can manage her own career," he said. "She's sixteen years old, going on thirty-five. I don't know what I intend to do next. I am sure I will think of something."

Better make it quick, T.S. thought silently to himself, calculating the probable mortgage and maintenance charges on such an opulent apartment, not to mention the tuition for Perkins's daughter at the Metropolitan and all the expenses that went along with a professional dancing career.

"Your daughter lives with you?" Auntie Lil asked.

"Yes. Why do you ask?" Perkins answered.

Auntie Lil shrugged. "I was just thinking of how fortunate she is to have such a nice apartment so close to the school. Many of the other children aren't so lucky. They live at the YMCA or as boarders with other families."

"And many of the other children aren't so fortunate as to be given a role they don't deserve," Perkins added suddenly.

"I didn't say that," Auntie Lil said. "I saw her as Clara the night of Morgan's death. She did a very capable job."

"My daughter was not ready to dance that role," Perkins said. "I was against it. It's too soon. She needs time to develop, time to gain enough confidence in her technique to expand her interpretation. She may have the body of a young woman, but she is still a child in many ways. She needs seasoning. Didn't you see the reviews? They will harm her career."

"Then why did you allow it?" Auntie Lil asked.

Perkins laughed. "Allow it? You obviously have not yet met my daughter. My opinion is of no consequence to her."

"What does her mother think about it?" Auntie Lil asked.

Perkins inhaled deeply and blew a long stream of smoke from his mouth, his eyes narrowing. "I wouldn't know. Neither would Julie. We haven't seen her in several years. Not since she packed up and left when Julie was up in Sarasota with the company one summer. To be perfectly frank, it was no great loss."

"That must have been hard on Julie," Auntie Lil remarked.

"Nothing is hard on Julie," Perkins said. "Unless it's about dance. That's all that matters to her."

"Then she, at least, must have been delighted to have performed the lead," Auntie Lil said.

"I'm sure she was." He stood up with a sudden jerk. "What more do you want to know? I don't really see how

I can be of help. Whoever killed Bobby Morgan probably had a good reason to do it. He was that kind of a guy."

"How do you know?" Auntie Lil asked. "I thought you hadn't seen him in years."

"I hadn't," Perkins replied. He stared out the window again. "I've been following his career as an agent. He couldn't have picked a better occupation, given his talents." His laugh was short and bitter. "Bobby Morgan, big man about town, on top again, twisting the strings, torturing the people who tortured him, getting even for his bad skin and tendency to bloat. Ah, revenge."

"You think he became an agent just to get revenge for the way he had been treated?" T.S. asked.

"Of course not." Perkins strode to the ficus tree and ground out his second cigarette with one swift gesture. "He became an agent so he could make millions. And he did. He got one screwed-up kid out of the bargain, but hey— what did he care? He became a millionaire."

"You consider Mikey Morgan a troubled child?" Auntie Lil asked.

"I don't consider him a child at all," Perkins said. "I consider him an abomination."

"Is there anyone in particular who you think might have wanted to see Bobby Morgan dead?" T.S. asked.

"I can think of a dozen people without ever moving east of L.A. But I don't have a shred of evidence that any of them did it, so I refuse to give you any names." He produced yet another cigarette, then gazed sadly into the now empty pack. He would soon be facing the big decision of whether to break down and buy a new pack or try to quit again.

"Where were you the night he was murdered?" Auntie Lil asked.

"I beg your pardon?" Perkins said, standing up straight and staring at Auntie Lil.

"I presume you were at the performance," Auntie Lil answered, "watching your daughter enjoy her big moment."

"Of course I was there," Perkins said, looking at his watch. "She may be ungrateful and stubborn, but she's still my daughter. Why? Want to see my ticket stub?" His tone and subsequent laugh were both sarcastic, an attitude that Auntie Lil despised. T.S. was suddenly glad he might have turned Perkins down for employment years ago. He hoped he'd been rude about it.

"Well, we won't trouble you anymore," Auntie Lil said suddenly. "May I use the ladies' room first?"

"Down the hall," Perkins said, nodding toward the back of the apartment.

Auntie Lil was like a camel, capable of going without water or a bathroom break for days, if need be. T.S. knew this and had a feeling she was up to something. In such situations, his time-honored role was to distract. "So, you worked at Salomon?" he asked Perkins easily. "Which bond desk? I know a few good men over there still."

As T.S. began to name acquaintances—receiving desultory replies from an unenthusiastic Perkins—Auntie Lil scurried down the hall. The first bedroom was clearly Perkins's. It was as neat and sparse as the rest of the apartment. But the second room had to be his daughter's. It had all the telltale signs of a young dancer's abode. Leotards were flung over chairs and heaped on the floor, discarded toe shoes hung from nails on the wall, posters of Baryshnikov and Nureyev decorated the doors where other young girls might pin images of rock stars. Sweatpants with the legs cut off at midthigh were tossed across the bed and assorted trim and discarded ribbons from various costumes littered the pale pink carpet. Auntie Lil crept inside the room and peeked into the closet. There were few street clothes hanging inside. She opened the drawers of the pink dresser, her innate nosiness taking over. Many of the drawers held only a few articles of clothing, often hastily pushed to one side as if someone had searched through there before her. Two of the drawers were completely empty. Auntie Lil identified the probable compartments for underwear, socks, shirts, pajamas and pants. That meant the empty drawers had probably contained dance apparel such as more leotards, cutoff sweatshirts, and leggings. That was odd. She checked around the room for the ubiquitous oversized tote bag that no dancer could afford to be without. Nothing. She examined the dresser top and the adjoining bathroom for makeup. Again, nothing—an unheard of situation for a sixteen-year-old female dancer. She then examined the discarded clothing more carefully, even going so far as to handle the texture of the fabric and sniff delicately at its surface. Auntie Lil hadn't checked up on how well the models treated her clothes during runway shows for decades and learned nothing. The clothing was stiff with longdried old sweat and no overt smell remained. Auntie Lil was sure that the clothing had been flung there at least a few days before and then left exactly as it was. Julie Perkins did not live in this room or in this apartment anymore. Why had her father lied?

When she returned to the living room, Perkins was still standing by the window, looking bored. T.S. was looking determinedly cheerful.

"Ready to go," she announced brightly as a wave of relief swept over both men's faces. "Thank you so much for your time."

"No problem," Perkins replied, suddenly friendly.

His mood changes were constant. As they walked back toward the brass elevator both Auntie Lil and T.S. found themselves wondering if maybe the man wasn't on some sort of medication. They shared their concern on the way down.

"Something was odd," Auntie Lil agreed. "He seemed to resent the most innocuous questions. And he was up and down like a rabbit."

"Yes, he was touchy about such innocent questions. Like where he worked," T.S. decided. "I'm going to call my friend Victor over at Salomon and see what I can find out about Andrew Perkins."

"Victor?" Auntie Lil said as they emerged into the lobby. "Isn't that the tiny little man with the gorgeous six-foot wife? The one who loves fishing?"

T.S. shook his head in admiration. She might be getting on in years, but his Aunt Lil seldom forgot a detail about people she met.

3. Auntie Lil was not ready to call it a day. First she suggested a walk through Central Park, an option that T.S.'s feet could not afford. So when he spotted a theater near Columbus Circle that was showing Mikey Morgan's latest escapade, he suggested a movie instead. They were just in time for the late matinee before the evening rush and snagged plum seats in the middle of a center row.

"The last movie I saw was in 1966," Auntie Lil confided. "That one about fashion. *Blow-Up*, I think it was called. They got all the little details wrong. Maybe it didn't bother some people, but it bothered me."

"Movies have come a long way since then," T.S. lied. "You aren't going to talk all the way through this one, are you?"

"I'll try not to," Auntie Lil promised.

The movie was a typical big-studio offering. Loud—very loud—and too quickly edited. Both Auntie Lil and T.S. felt they were on a runaway train. The plot involved a group of boys who are mistakenly sent to a summer boot camp for problem children by uncaring wealthy parents who think, instead, that their precious sons are attending a plush resort in the Poconos. Because no phone calls or outside contact with the world is allowed, the boys are trapped with a cast of marinelike counselors for six weeks and transformed from little monsters into young men. The plot was utterly preposterous, the dialogue puerile, and Mikey Morgan hardly more appealing than he had been during *The Nutcracker*. But he was adorable, that was undeniable. The movie had obviously been filmed more than a year earlier, before Mikey's latest growth spurt. He had a long face and a mop of blond hair that hung over his eyes. His nose was straight and his mischievous eyes sparkled intensely. His smile was his trademark and Mikey flashed it often while onscreen, the wide grin splitting his face with impish confidence. Not a freckle, much less a pimple, marred his smooth skin.

"He's a much better actor than he is a dancer, don't you think?" Auntie Lil whispered loudly at one point. "Given the ridiculous plot, of course." Several people near the front glanced back at them irritably. People in Manhattan tended to go to matinees to escape the ever-present talkers that evening shows attracted.

"Not bad," T.S. agreed, eyes glued to the screen.

Shushing Auntie Lil became unnecessary as the plot took a bizarre and ironic twist: the boys in the movie—led by Mikey Morgan's character—had slipped away during a five-mile camp run and were circling back toward the waterfront. There, Mikey crawled under the foundation of a small shack and emerged with a thick rope. The boys ran back to the head counselor's cabin and invaded the private bathroom, fashioning an elaborate slipknot noose around the edge of the metal shower's floor rim before running the end of the rope out a window and over a nearby tree limb. Their intent was to snare the instructor in midlather, stringing him up like an animal trapped in an African safari movie.

"Are you watching what I'm watching?" Auntie Lil whispered loudly.

"Of course I am," T.S. whispered back as indignant *sssshhh*s echoed at them from all sides.

Sure enough, in the middle of the night, as the boys waited breathlessly outside, the counselor entered the shower stall and began loudly singing as he soaped up in the buff, unaware of the rope coiled around his feet. The boys banded together outside the window and, at an opportune time, grabbed the end of the rope and pulled. In a flurry of Hollywood editing, the rope uncoiled and tightened around the counselor's feet, flipping him upside down and leaving him hanging from the ceiling like a well-dressed gazelle. The shower was, in reality, too small for such a move, but this was Hollywood and the miracle of editing made anything possible. The few children in the audience giggled hysterically at the sight of a bare butt, but Auntie Lil and T.S. were left speechless at the implications.

"That was bizarre," T.S. said after the show. "Positively creepy."

"Yes," Auntie Lil agreed, "more than a little macabre. And I think we know where the killer got his technique. All we need now is a motive."

CHAPTER SIX

1. Bobby Morgan's funeral was scheduled for 2:00 P.M., a time that he would probably have endorsed, as it gave him maximum newspaper and television coverage. Legions of reporters hovered on the edges of the well-dressed crowd and a dozen media vans blocked the streets nearby, littering the sidewalks with thick black cables.

Auntie Lil, T.S., Herbert, and Lilah arrived an hour early and positioned themselves on the front steps, where they could watch the well-dressed mourners who had shown up to pay their respects and, possibly, cut a few deals within the hallowed walls of St. Paul's Church. Auntie Lil insisted on waiting for the appointed hour before entering because she wanted to sit in back to observe the crowd better. They settled into a pew of their own near the rear. Auntie Lil immediately fumbled in the depths of her enormous pocketbook in search of her glasses. She located them next to a paperback she had been missing for weeks and a theater program from a show she had seen in 1986. As the priest entered from the rear of the church and raised his arms for the benediction, she adjusted the glasses carefully on her nose and scrutinized the room for familiar faces.

Most of the other board members were present, including a conspicuously sobbing Lane Rogers. Her mascara trickled down her cheeks as she heaved great sobs into a ragged tissue, her linebacker shoulders shaking with the effort. She was flanked by the ever-present Ruth Beretsky, who held a small pack of Kleenex obediently at the ready for her friend. Hans Glick sat stiffly in the aisle seat next to Ruth, his back ramrod straight and his eyes fixed on the profusion of flower arrangements with a disapproving frown. He was no doubt mentally calculating how to arrange the blooms in a more logical fashion.

Mikey Morgan sat in a front row, inadvertently framed by a gigantic wreath of carnations dominating the altar. He was wearing a custom-cut black suit with boxy shoulders and pipe-stem legs that made him look years older. His somber face added to the impression. Auntie Lil was struck by how much he had aged since he had starred in the movie they had seen the day before. His mother sat next to him. She was a petite woman with close-cropped brown hair and a triangular face. She wore a simple navy suit, a string of pearls, and matching earrings. Her arm was draped protectively over the back of the pew behind her older son. She was remarkably thin, given that she was the mother of four children. The rest of her brood sat in descending order to her right. Auntie Lil knew that Bobby Morgan had moved to Los Angeles two years before, following his divorce, and taken only Mikey with him. Though the younger children had presumably not seen him much since, their rigid posture and stunned expressions belied their disbelief that their father—however distant—had died. The row of tiny faces, crumpled in bewilderment, triggered the first pangs of true regret in more than one mourner's heart.

Many of the pews were jammed with fashionably thin colleagues whose almost bizarrely deep tans, frosted or feathered hair, and loosely constructed designer clothing marked them as members of the Los Angeles entertainment community. There was more makeup per square inch of skin than at a Mary Kay cosmetics convention. Interspersed among these glowing humans sat the paler and more diverse New Yorkers, their faces grim. Unlike the uniformly fit West Coast contingent, the New Yorkers ranged in size from the emaciated to the downright obese. Among the emaciated were many members of the corps de ballet, who had turned out to pay their respects to the man whose death they had witnessed. They dotted the room with their own brand of brightly colored, free-flowing fashion.

Artistic Director Raoul Martinez sat in a third-row pew,

his mane of glossy black hair gleaming with multicolored reflections from a nearby stained-glass window. His wife, Lisette, sat regally beside him, her long neck swaying slightly to the organ music floating in on waves of flower-scented air. She was an exotic figure, dressed in austere black that highlighted the extreme angles of her sculptured cheekbones. Her hair was pulled back in so severe a knot that Auntie Lil wondered if her grimace was due to her hairstyle. Tears glistened prettily on her eyelashes as the priest began the opening prayer.

Many of the couples in the crowd held hands or draped arms around each other for support. Raoul and Lisette Martinez were an exception. They sat side by side without acknowledging each other's presence.

They were joined in their row by a subdued Paulette Puccinni, wearing a black caftan, and Jerry Vanderbilt, whose face was respectfully somber. Although the crowd represented numerous opportunities for comment and gossip, neither Paulette nor Jerry looked up to the task. In fact, they both seemed queasy at their proximity to death.

Andrew Perkins sat in the opposite pew, next to a willowy teenager whose sullen frown proved she was his daughter much more than the fact that she was a plainer version of the self-possessed dancer of a few nights before. Julie Perkins looked younger without makeup, though still much older than her years. Her blond hair was combed to midback and anchored with a wide black velvet ribbon. The simple style suited her delicate, deerlike features. She had the preternatural bearing of a well-trained dancer, which gave her a grace that was eerie in so young a child. Her hands did not simply turn the pages of the prayer book; they posed and fluttered in a delicate progression. As the service began she inched farther and farther away from her father until she had opened the space of another body between them. Several other young dancers, possibly from her class, sat quietly on her other side. As the atmosphere inside the church grew increasingly stuffy and the music louder, they began to weep as only teenagers can weep: with wide eyes, flowing tears, and an enthusiastically morbid realization that death could happen to them as well at any time. Julie Perkins wept with the same ritualized style she had used to ignore her father: her shoulders moved in delicate rhythm to the organ, her hands spread out like paper fans over her face, her head held at a becoming angle.

"Who are those people?" T.S. whispered to Auntie Lil when a pew of gray-haired, plainly dressed people caught his eye. Two men and three women, all in their late sixties or early seventies, sat in the second row. Their faces were stamped honestly with their age; no artifice or surgery had been used to mask the wear and tear of passing years. The men had stiff crew cuts of a style long gone from favor. The women had white hair swept and lacquered into obedient mounds. Though clad appropriately in dark suits and dresses, their dated attire looked curiously new, as if their clothes had hung unused for decades between funerals. When the coffin was brought down the center aisle, all three women produced handkerchiefs and began to cry in unison, like an elderly Greek chorus.

"That's his family," a woman behind them whispered in response to T.S.'s question. When she leaned forward, a cloud of perfume preceded her, choking his nostrils. Thank God Lilah didn't fumigate herself like that, he thought. She smelled of soap and fresh air.

"They're his uncles and aunts," the woman continued, as if savoring her grasp of inside information. "They're straight out of *On the Waterfront*. Can you believe it? I could cast them as extras tomorrow."

T.S. glanced behind him and caught a glimpse of a woman so thin that her arms protruded from her black linen dress like a child's mistakenly grafted onto an adult body. Her face was deep bronze, the skin stretched tight and the hair relentlessly feathered in too casual spikes. He turned quickly back around and calmed himself with a peek at Lilah. Lilah seemed so more vibrant and human, with her delicate wrinkles and silver hair. Were these the people Bobby Morgan wheeled and dealed with? They were like well-dressed Halloween ghouls.

The service itself was curiously devoid of emotion.

People wept, but with the exception of the teenagers, they shed their tears sparingly and surreptitiously repaired the damage to their makeup when they were done. They were playing out a script, reacting on cue, producing appropriate rather than true feelings. Few seemed genuinely sorry that Bobby Morgan was dead.

"He shows no emotion whatsoever," Auntie Lil whispered as the service drew to a close. She nodded toward Mikey Morgan. He sat stone-faced next to his mother, staring at his father's coffin. Not a muscle twitched. He could have been in a trance.

The doors of the church were heavy and soundproofed. As two men in suits opened the heavy slabs for the pallbearers who would lift the coffin into the waiting hearse, a wall of sound invaded the church like the roar of a terrifying beast: people shouting, horns honking, engines racing. It was more than typical New York City chaos. As one of the first people to follow the casket outside, Auntie Lil soon found out what the commotion was all about: the Reverend Ben Hampton was back. He had chosen to stage a demonstration at Bobby Morgan's funeral. Though a tasteless occasion for protest, she had to admire his sense of drama. Ben Hampton was dressed like a preacher at an old-time Southern revival and held a black Bible aloft from his perch on a makeshift platform set up on the church steps. Dozens of reporters and television announcers elbowed each other for room before him. They competed with Hampton's regular protestors, who were dressed in black and held a small coffin labeled RACIAL EQUALITY on their shoulders.

The Reverend's words were inaudible to few beyond the immediate crowd, but whatever he was saying must have made for good copy. Not a single reporter reacted to the real coffin being carried down the church's front steps. In a perfect example of the fickle interests of the American public, Bobby Morgan had been replaced by a fresher story before his own had even drawn to an end.

Suddenly a squad of patrol cars swarmed to a halt behind the television vans. A sleek black limousine eased in behind them like a shark gliding silently toward its prey. A silver-haired man dressed in Armani strode from the car holding handcuffs aloft. He was followed by a pack of faithful flacks in slightly less expensive suits.

"The police commissioner," Lilah told them. "What's he doing here?"

As cameras clicked and whirred, the commissioner pushed his way through the crowd behind a wedge of uniformed officers. Climbing up the church steps until he reached the Reverend Ben Hampton, he held the handcuffs up for the cameras and proclaimed, "Benjamin Hampton, you're under arrest for the premeditated murder of Robert K. Morgan, with malice aforethought. You have the right to remain silent. . . ."

Many cautious NYC precincts had recorded prior Miranda warnings on film. But it was doubtful that any Miranda warning had ever been immortalized by so many cameras before. By that evening, the Reverend Ben Hampton's arrest and the meticulous upholding of his constitutional rights had been beamed into over 80 percent of all American households, courtesy of modern technology.

2. Auntie Lil did not like to rise before 10:00 A.M. and usually consumed four cups of strong black coffee before she attempted communication with other human beings. Thus she was annoyed the following morning when her doorbell rang at eleven. She had not even finished her third cup of coffee and should have been busy slathering a bagel with cream cheese. A visitor would disrupt her routine. Even worse, she might have to share.

"Who is it?" she shouted into the intercom. Auntie Lil did not trust telecommunications devices. She bellowed into any receiver, no matter how state-of-the-art.

"Mattie Jones," a modulated voice replied. "Fatima Jones is my niece."

Auntie Lil admired the economy of the answer. She was also curious as to why the aunt of the Metro's most promising young ballerina would want to see her. She knew that

Fatima's mother had been missing on the streets for years and that the identity of her father had never been clear. But despite the fact that she had helped underwrite Fatima Jones's dance scholarship, Auntie Lil had never met the woman responsible for Fatima's upbringing. She buzzed her in eagerly.

When she opened the door, a stout black woman with hair cut close to her rounded head stood before her. She was wearing a neatly pressed red suit that Auntie Lil's practiced eye pegged as home-sewn. It was a good job, too. The finishing work was beautiful and the tailored lines took pounds off the woman's frame. Mattie Jones held a black pocketbook in front of her nervously, as if shielding herself from possible violence. Auntie Lil noted with approval that Mattie wore sensible black flats instead of the crippling high heels that sillier women preferred. She noted with even more approval that Mattie Jones also held a bakery bag in her hands.

"Thank you for agreeing to see me," the visitor said politely, holding out the white paper bag. "I brought us some fresh doughnuts so we could talk over coffee. That is, if you'd care to invite me in." She had a clear, rich voice. Auntie Lil wondered if she was a singer.

"Of course," Auntie Lil said. "I would be delighted. I have followed Fatima's career carefully over the past few years. You have done a beautiful job of raising the child."

"Fatima raised herself," Mattie said, trundling her big frame into Auntie Lil's apartment. She stopped in astonishment at the cluttered glory of what lay before her: rooms full of fabrics, furniture, mementos, photographs, and the cherished debris of eight decades of robust living. "My goodness," she said with admiration. "What a colorful home you have."

Auntie Lil thought the comment remarkably tactful. She couldn't have put it better herself.

"My nephew Theodore thinks I'm messy," Auntie Lil explained as she swept two contrasting bolts of cloth from the white sofa and dumped a pile of remnants into a chair. "But

I know where everything is. I can put my hands on anything within seconds. Just ask."

"How about putting your hands on some coffee?" Mattie suggested with a musical laugh. When she smiled, she revealed a gap between her two front teeth that made her look jolly and benign. But Auntie Lil knew that anyone capable of successfully rescuing a parentless child in New York City could not possibly be benign.

Auntie Lil fetched a fresh pot of coffee and considered offering her guest one of her trademark Bloody Marys. But since it wasn't even noon, a rare burst of discretion won out and she settled for coffee alone.

"First of all, I would like to thank you for what you have done for Fatima," Mattie said. She slipped her shoes off with a groan and wiggled her toes as she munched on a cinnamon-cake doughnut. Auntie Lil could not decide between white powdered sugar or coconut. She compromised by choosing both, holding one in each hand and taking alternate bites as she listened.

"You're quite welcome," Auntie Lil replied. "I'm sure the friend who bequeathed me his fortune would be delighted to see how much of his money's worth he has gotten out of Fatima."

"She's a special child," Mattie agreed. "But I didn't just mean the scholarship money. I also want to thank you for standing up for Fatima at the board meeting and for making sure she got the role after all."

"Who told you I stood up for Fatima?" Auntie Lil asked.

Mattie hesitated, her discomfort obvious.

"I am not a big believer in board confidentiality," Auntie Lil promised. "I won't tell anyone and I don't really care. I'm just curious."

"Calvin Swanson," Mattie admitted. "He's a maintenance man at the theater."

"Yes, we shared a cab uptown one night. He's a nice man." Auntie Lil did not add that Calvin had denied knowing Fatima Jones and her aunt. She understood why he had been cautious. But she did wonder if he had lied about anything else.

"Calvin keeps an eye on Fatima for me," Mattie explained. "We go to the same church. Church of the Good Shepherd up on a Hundred Twenty-fifth and Broadway. Our gospel choir is famous."

"Yes, I know the church," Auntie Lil said. "You attract quite a lot of Scandinavian and German tourists each Sunday."

Mattie nodded. "More blondes than you'd find in Sweden, it seems like some weeks." She laughed and the musical notes filled the living room.

"What made you come to see me today?" Auntie Lil asked. "Fatima is doing well in rehearsal, isn't she? I understand she takes over the role of Clara starting tomorrow."

"Yes, she knew the role already," Mattie said. "Played it last year in Philadelphia for a special NAACP performance. It's just a matter of adapting to Mr. Martinez's style. She's doing just fine. There's been a lot of excitement about her, I know. People protesting and calling other people names." She bobbed her head apologetically. "It's not the way I like to do things, but people feel strongly about what they believe in and I think folks have a right to stand up for what they care about."

"I couldn't agree more," Auntie Lil said.

"But I'm not here about Fatima. She is just as calm as a baby sleeping through a storm about all this. I'm here about another friend of mine."

"Oh?" Auntie Lil stopped with a chocolate-covered doughnut inches from her lips.

"The Reverend Ben Hampton," Mattie explained. "He's been arrested by the police."

"You and the Reverend Hampton are friends?" Auntie Lil asked. "Is he the pastor of Good Shepherd?"

Mattie shook her head. "No. He has his own church and it's a little too *too* for me, if you know what I mean. But I know him from my work with schoolchildren in Harlem. I help tutor and his people work with the kids, too. He's a good man, Miss Hubbert. I know he hollers a lot for the cameras and says some things that white people don't want to hear. But he's no fool and he's not a man who believes in violence. He didn't kill that boy's father. They say they have proof, but I have the proof he didn't right here." She tapped a fist over her heart and scrutinized Auntie Lil. "He has no one to help him. That's the funny thing about this all. If anyone else had been arrested unfairly, the Reverend would be out on the streets making sure justice was done. But he can't be out on the streets because they have locked him up and they want an awful lot of money for his bail. An awful lot."

"What's an awful lot?" Auntie Lil asked.

"It's a million dollars, but the bail bondsman needs just one hundred thousand to take it on. Ben's church is trying, but they don't have that kind of money. Their building is already mortgaged. And he needs a good lawyer, too. He keeps spouting about how he's going to represent himself, but you know what they say."

"A man who represents himself has a fool for a client and an idiot for a lawyer?" Auntie Lil said.

Mattie nodded. "He wouldn't do the right things to protect himself," she explained. "He'd be making a speech when he ought to be making a motion. He's been arrested lots of times, mostly for disturbing the peace, when running his mouth didn't harm him much. But this is murder."

"I understand," Auntie Lil said. "And you want me to put up the money for this?"

Mattie nodded. "I know it's a lot to ask. And I can't give you much more than my word that you won't lose any of it in the end."

Auntie Lil needed to think about it for only a moment. A woman who had raised a discarded child, kept her from drugs, nurtured a dream, and then made that dream possible was a woman who could be trusted. Still, it might look bad given her position on the board. And Theodore would throw a fit.

"I wouldn't expect you to do it if there wasn't something in it for you," Mattie added, as if she could sense Auntie Lil's hesitation.

"Indeed?" Auntie Lil asked.

"Calvin told me you were looking into who murdered that boy's father," Mattie explained. "If you help bail out the Reverend and can find him a good lawyer, I promise you that he will talk to you about the murder. He knows things, he says."

"What things?" Auntie Lil asked.

"Things he won't tell the police," Mattie said. "He doesn't like the police. He's hardheaded that way. Doesn't understand that they have their jobs to do."

"But he'll talk to me?" Auntie Lil was skeptical.

"He says he will."

That made the decision easy. She had plenty of money. But only one opportunity to talk to the Reverend Ben Hampton.

3.   It took nearly twenty-four hours to get Ben Hampton released from custody. Not even Auntie Lil's high-priced lawyer, Hamilton Prescott, could make the wheels turn faster. At first Prescott had been reluctant to take on the high-profile case, but when Auntie Lil appealed to his sense of fair play—and promised to find another lawyer should the case come to trial—he agreed to oversee obtaining Hampton's release on bail.

Given his initial resistance, Auntie Lil was bemused to see her reticent lawyer beaming in front of television cameras the next day, his hand on Ben Hampton's elbow as he steered him through the courtroom's hallways to freedom. The phone call she had been expecting came two hours later.

"Miss Hubbert?" Mattie Jones said in her flawless voice. "We can send someone to pick you up now if you're ready to talk to Ben."

"I'm ready," Auntie Lil told her. Theodore would be angry she had left him out of the loop, but it served him right. Once again he had disappeared for half a day—as had Herbert—and she was irritated at being excluded from their plans. She was wearing a bright red pants suit for the meeting with Hampton. The color had been chosen carefully. Red made her feel powerful and she would need considerable self-confidence to match wits with the Reverend Ben Hampton.

It did not surprise her that the Reverend had a chauffered limousine at his beck and call. Nor did it surprise her when the car drew up in front of a magnificent restored mansion in the section of Harlem known as Sugar Hill. At the turn of the century, the street had been home to New York City's finest houses, stately homes that fell into disrepair decades later. The real-estate boom in the seventies had brought many back to life when affluent blacks repaired them to their former grandeur. Ben Hampton's was one of the finest examples of Victorian architecture she had ever seen. She passed through the elaborate wrought-iron gate and up wide wooden stairs to a massive oak door inset with a huge fan-shaped wedge of stained glass. Perhaps his church actually owned the home, she thought to herself. This was almost too much for a man who claimed to be of the cloth.

A neatly dressed teenage girl ushered Auntie Lil into a high-ceilinged parlor with red velvet drapes exactly the color of her suit. Ben Hampton sat in a leather armchair pulled up next to a small fire. To her surprise, Hamilton Prescott sat beside him. The men—so different in race, temperament, and dress—were sharing a smoke and glasses of brandy. The show of brotherhood was touching but not touching enough to stop Auntie Lil from pointedly glaring at the cigars. Both men obediently ground out their stogies and rose to their feet.

"My thanks for your financial support," Hampton said smoothly, with a formal bow. He extended a huge hand and grasped hers firmly. He was so physically immense that she wondered if he had been a prizefighter or football player in his youth. Up close, his shock of pure white hair looked even more startling. It rose straight from his scalp like a patch of albino lawn left too long in the sun.

"I trust Mr. Prescott has been of service to you?" Auntie Lil said, casting an amused glance at her straitlaced lawyer. Prescott paused with the brandy glass halfway to his lips, as if he had been caught by a teacher doing something naughty.

"It's a most interesting case," Prescott said defensively. "Far more interesting than my usual. Except for you, Lillian, my clients can be downright boring."

"I can imagine." She settled herself on a brocade sofa the color of autumn leaves and accepted Hampton's offer of a drink. The man who brought her an extra spicy Bloody Mary at Hampton's request was dressed casually in sports slacks and a neatly pressed golf shirt. His manner was polite without being the least bit deferential. Hampton's casual thanks to the man told her that he was not a servant but, more likely, a member of the congregation helping to guard him.

"I thought it might be best to stay," Prescott explained. "What the Reverend has to tell you impacts on his defense. I'd like to hear it again. If you don't mind, of course."

"No. I don't mind at all," Auntie Lil said, turning to her host. "Mattie Jones told me you had evidence you didn't want to share with the police?"

Ben Hampton laughed with a snorting glee that sounded like a buffalo sneezing. "It's not that I didn't try to explain it to them," he said. "It's that they don't believe me. You see, what I have to tell them sounds like excuses because they have already made up their minds about me. But I know what the truth is, and the truth is that I did not kill that boy's father. But I might have seen who did."

"Can you explain?" Auntie Lil sipped her Bloody Mary. It was perfect. She sighed in contentment. Her drink was strong, her life interesting and her health remarkably good. What more could anyone ask?

"I can, but first I want your word that you will agree to stand by me when I hold a press conference later today about the injustice of my arrest." The reverend settled back in his arm chair and folded his elegant hands over his ample tummy, waiting for her reply.

"I can't possibly do that," Auntie Lil said firmly. "I do not believe that this condition was part of our original deal."

"Miss Jones may have failed to mention it," Hampton said smoothly, "since she is not as experienced as I am in these things. But your presence as a member of the Metro's board would certainly add credibility and help erase part of the stain of shame the board created when it refused to let that most talented young lady, Fatima Jones, dance." He gazed confidently at Auntie Lil.

But Auntie Lil was not a pushover and she particularly disliked last-minute surprises. Especially when she had just spent $150,000 of her own money on bail and a legal retainer in keeping up her end of the bargain. "Mr. Hampton," she said quietly, "you must forgive me. I am an old lady and certainly I am not as experienced as you at using the media to my advantage. But I do hope you will acknowledge a few facts before you insist on this last-minute condition."

Hamilton Prescott squirmed uneasily in his leather chair. Unlike Ben Hampton, he knew Auntie Lil.

"Number one," she said, "I put a great deal of my own money on the line on the proviso that you would talk to me. But I did not agree to put up either my name or my face. Number two, as a board member of the Metropolitan Ballet, I can neither endorse your innocence nor proclaim your guilt at this time. Especially since I have been asked by the board to look into the murder in an official capacity. Number three, I underwrite over five hundred thousand dollars' worth of minority scholarships in this city each year and I will not be made to feel guilty about my contributions to racial equality. I am perfectly satisfied with my soul. It is yours I have come to evaluate."

The Reverend's eyes grew wider during this speech, but his expression did not change. When she was done, he threw his head back and roared with laughter. He wiped his eyes and took a sip of brandy, shaking his head. "I can see I will put nothing over on you," he admitted. "I may as well not try."

"You would be wise to make me your ally," Auntie Lil agreed, "if I choose to make you mine. I can help you gain much badly needed legitimacy if what you are interested in is a long-term career in city government."

The Reverend cocked his head and scrutinized her. "You're offering me a spot on the Metropolitan's board?" he guessed.

Auntie Lil shook her head. "That is not within my power. But certainly, if I so choose, I can propose your candidacy in the future. This would underscore our intention to address the concerns of minority artists within the company. That is, if I leave today convinced that you are a man of your word, a man of honor."

The Reverend tapped the floor with a foot as he considered how best to proceed. "Okay. I'll keep my end of the original bargain."

"How delightful," Auntie Lil murmured, sipping her drink.

"The police believe I murdered Bobby Morgan for several reasons," Hampton explained. "As near as I can tell from the not-so-subtle hints of the detectives who questioned me, the rear doors to backstage are left unlocked during performances because of fire regulations. Both doors lead into an alley not twenty feet away from where I was standing with my protesters. The protest dispersed about an hour after the performance started, once the media had left."

Of course, Auntie Lil thought to herself. Why bother protesting if it didn't translate into a couple inches on the front page?

Hampton continued. "Most of my people left right away. They have families, jobs that start early in the morning, children who need their homework supervised, mouths to feed, long subway rides. You understand?"

"Certainly," she said. "The working class. I was a member of it myself for sixty years, my good man. I inherited this money only last year."

"I apologize," the Reverend offered. "I assumed you had been born into wealth."

Hamilton Prescott—who had been born into wealth and wondered why these two felt it necessary to apologize about it—wiggled uneasily. But he was transfixed by the colorful character before him and the tabloid nature of Hampton's personality. Just the same, he wanted them to hurry up and get to the point so he could go home and scan the local television stations to see if he had made it onto the early-evening news.

"Your followers dispersed quickly?" Auntie Lil reminded Hampton.

"Yes." He nodded his massive head. "In the confusion of the crowd, I was separated from my usual companions and bodyguards. I have four of them because of death threats. All part of the price I pay."

It wasn't anyone's fault but the Reverend's that his mug was plastered on half the newspapers in the tristate area every week. But Auntie Lil kept this opinion to herself.

"My people are honest. When the police came to them afterward, asking about my whereabouts, they admitted that I had not been with them between nine and nine-thirty. I would not expect them to tell anything but the truth."

"Where were you?" Auntie Lil demanded.

The Reverend hesitated, opened his mouth, shut it, stopped dangling his leg, and adjusted both pants cuffs.

"Come on," Auntie Lil said. "Let's have it."

"I met a young lady," the Reverend explained with as much dignity as he could muster. "We took a stroll there in the park at the rear of the Lincoln Center complex."

Auntie Lil had not been a New Yorker for eighty-four years with her eyes closed. She immediately pegged this feeble excuse for what it was: a cover story to account for the fact that the Reverend Ben Hampton had nipped over to Tenth Avenue and engaged a young lady of the evening for some recreation.

"You told the police that?" she asked.

"Of course not. It would only be misconstrued."

You bet your white clerical collar it would be misconstrued, she thought to herself. The media would love it.

"Thus they find it hard to believe that I would simply be enjoying a stroll through the complex for the half hour in which this man was killed."

"There's more," Hamilton Prescott interrupted. "Go ahead and tell her. *She's* been accused of worse before. She'll understand."

Hampton looked impressed. This little old lady accused of murder? Perhaps she did know how it felt. "They discovered my fingerprints on the back fire-exit doors," he explained. "They took that as a sign that I had entered and exited through those doors in order to kill Bobby Morgan."

"Why were your fingerprints on the doors?" Auntie Lil demanded. She asked obvious questions without apology.

"I admit that I did enter and exit through those doors," the Reverend explained. "But that was earlier. Around seven o'clock. Some parents of the children were leaving backstage and I caught hold of each open door and just peeked inside, getting the lay of the land."

"In other words, you were considering storming the stage with your troupe of protesters and wanted to know how easy the access would be?" Auntie Lil guessed.

"Precisely. But I grasped at once that such a scheme presented too many problems."

"You'd be caught long before you got to the stage?" Auntie Lil said.

The Reverend nodded. "Or not be noticed at all! The backstage was filled with people. Instead, I went with the traditional march in front of the entrance doors."

"Lucky for me," Auntie Lil said dryly. "I might not have ended up on the front page of two tabloids otherwise, my mouth hanging open as if I were a murderer caught red-handed at the scene."

The Reverend was nonplussed. "An unfortunate pose, I do admit. But the press is just doing its job."

Auntie Lil exchanged a skeptical glance with her lawyer and took another healthy gulp of Bloody Mary.

"So they have a time frame, and your fingerprints on an entrance and exit route," Auntie Lil said. "What about means and a motive?"

"The motive is obviously my anger at seeing Fatima Jones bounced from her leading role. Since Morgan was ultimately responsible."

"How did you know about that, by the way?" Auntie Lil asked.

The Reverend shook his head slowly, a grin breaking out. "Now, Miss Hubbert, you know I can't reveal my sources."

"Why not?" she demanded. "This is not Watergate."

"Miss Hubbert, I have a network of injustice fighters all over this city. They can be found in every agency, all levels of government, and most of the important organizations. Their access to information depends on their anonymity. I can't compromise that freedom."

"So the motive was revenge," Auntie Lil said. "What about the means? How are you linked to the rope?"

"I'm strong enough to have done it," he explained. "And I know a lot about ropes."

"Know a lot about ropes?" she asked. "What in heaven's name does that mean?"

"I supervise several Boy Scout troops up in Harlem and often teach the knot-tying classes myself."

"Surely you jest," she said. "What kind of skill is that to teach a young urban man these days? In preparation for what? Shimmying down roofs and breaking into high-rises?"

"Miss Hubbert," he informed her with dignity. "What else are we going to do with these boys? We can't take many nature hikes in the heart of Manhattan. Campfires are a bad idea when you're surrounded by tenements. We teach them traditional crafts to distract them from the temptations of the street. They enjoy it. We let the boys dream."

"Hmmph," she said, unconvinced that teaching young men how to make slipknots was the best use of their talent. "Still seems like a mighty thin thread to hang an accusation on, if you will excuse the pun."

"You must understand that I am a man of some notoriety," Hampton said. He patted his chest modestly. "The police have been searching for a way to discredit me for decades. This is the perfect opportunity. Even if they can't make the charges stick, the accusations alone will hurt my credibility. I was about to announce my candidacy for city council. This will hurt me in some people's eyes. I am looking to expand my constituency beyond the traditional confines of my people."

"Well, in that case I should think that you would get a more traditional haircut and start dressing like a senator and stop backing people on causes that don't matter and concentrate on ones that do." Auntie Lil knocked back the rest of her Bloody Mary and plunked the glass down on the coffee table, unaware that not everyone appreciated her blunt approach to giving advice.

The Reverend looked startled.

"And another thing," Auntie Lil said, with no intention of stopping. "You need to agitate a little more selectively. Didn't you ever hear the story about the boy who cried wolf? And try some issues that involve more than minorities, perhaps all poor people."

Hamilton Prescott turned to the fire to hide his smile.

"Is that all?" the Reverend asked with pulpitlike patience.

"No," Auntie Lil admitted. "You need to shout less now that people know who you are. People expect it from you. They don't even hear what you are saying anymore. Try being reasonable, a little more low-key. You'll be that much more interesting, seem as if you have matured. And appeal to a lot more people. People want to believe in someone," Auntie Lil explained. "You must give them a reason to believe, not frighten them into believing."

"I'll keep that in mind," the Reverend promised with a smile.

"Good," Auntie Lil said. "Now that I'm done lecturing you, what more can you tell me?"

"I think I saw the killer," the Reverend admitted.

Auntie Lil leaned forward.

"I was returning from my stroll with the, uh, young lady," the Reverend explained. "She had taken leave of my company for a prior engagement and I was alone. I was walking along the sidewalk that borders the bandstand area at the rear of Lincoln Center."

"I know the spot," Auntie Lil said. It was heavily manicured with bushes and trees in order to soundproof the bandstand area from the many theaters in the complex.

"I had just concealed myself in the bushes," Hampton explained. "Nature called, you see, and the public facilities were not convenient. As I turned my back to the walk, I heard footsteps behind me. Someone was running down the alleyway in a hurry. The footsteps sounded like a machine gun almost, just tap, tap, tap, tap down that brick path right by where I was standing. I couldn't turn around until I finished my business, but I was curious. I popped my head out and I could see a man at the far end of the alleyway where it reaches the main sidewalk. He took a left there and headed toward Broadway."

"What did he look like?" Auntie Lil asked eagerly.

"I couldn't see clearly," the Reverend admitted. "There's a string of bright streetlights in the alley on account of it being a prime mugging spot. The glare was in my eyes and the man was in the shadows when he reached the end."

"Was he tall? Was he short?" Auntie Lil asked. "How was he dressed?"

"He was tall and wearing dark clothes," the Reverend offered hopefully. "Couldn't get more specific than that."

"Was he black or white?" Auntie Lil demanded.

Ben Hampton looked offended. "He was most definitely white. That much I can tell you."

Auntie Lil was silent. It could have been the killer. It could have been a man fleeing a mugger. But still . . . it was a start. And the man had dashed past close to 9:30, so the timing was right.

"What did the police say to all this?" she asked.

The Reverend shrugged. "Didn't believe me."

Auntie Lil bristled. She considered every scrap of information valuable, regardless of the source. Preconceived notions were dangerous. His story was important—and should have been given the consideration it deserved.

"There's more than one way to skin that cat," she promised. "I have a friend. Margo McGregor. I am sure you know of her."

The Reverend nodded. "She covers my activities often."

"I can arrange for you to talk to her. She'd probably do a column on your side of the story. But you'd have to work it out with her about what you were doing in the park alone at night. It might be better to focus on an entirely different subject and not bring up the park at all. At any rate, I am sure Margo will work with you. Would that help?"

Ben Hampton looked at Auntie Lil in keen admiration. "I couldn't have come up with a better solution myself."

CHAPTER SEVEN

1. "Do you believe him?" T.S. asked. They were sitting in a coffee shop near Lincoln Center, discussing Auntie Lil's visit with Reverend Hampton and deciding on their next move. T.S. had been surprisingly calm about foundation money going to help Hampton. The truth was, he had never wanted the money in the family in first place and didn't care where it went.

Auntie Lil nodded. "Why would Ben Hampton jeopardize his career by killing Morgan? Fatima Jones is just one cause in a long line of causes," she said. "Unless a better motive comes up, I don't think he's our man. I'd like to go over to the Metro this afternoon and question some other people. Feel up to the trip?"

T.S. calculated his schedule for the day. He was supposed to meet Herbert at four o'clock to learn the fox-trot and after that both he and Auntie Lil were meeting with Gene Levitt, the producer who had lost millions when Mikey Morgan backed out of his movie contract. Auntie Lil had arranged the meeting with her usual tact: she had called up and demanded it. If T.S. could come up with a plausible cover story to get away for a few hours for the dance lesson with Herbert, he might be able to pull it off.

"What?" Auntie Lil demanded. "I can hear your wheels turning, Theodore."

"I can do it," T.S. said quickly. "Will anyone be there?"

Auntie Lil nodded. "They have classes and rehearsals all afternoon. We'll be able to find someone."

The first someone they found turned out to be Lisette Martinez, wife of the artistic director and long the Metro's prima ballerina. She was a self-conscious exotic beauty as she sat in the sunshine on outside steps near a side door to the theater, smoking a forbidden cigarette. She was wearing rust-colored leotards and a black sweatshirt. Her legs were wound with strips of white cloth as if she were a Thorough-bred preparing for a race. Her hair whipped loosely in the wind. She was in her midthirties, but the physical toll of her profession had aged her beyond her years. Up close, her artificially low weight accentuated every wrinkle.

Auntie Lil perched on the steps below her and smiled. T.S. hovered behind his aunt. Lisette stared at the two of them without expression, her eyes flat and dark. She took a long drag of her cigarette and looked up at the sky.

"Should you be smoking?" Auntie Lil asked, trying to establish rapport.

"Who are you? My mother?" The ballerina blew a smoke ring that was instantly dispersed by the breeze.

"No. I'm a member of the Metro's board, looking into the recent death of Bobby Morgan."

The dancer's eyes flickered. "Raoul told me about you. So did Lane Rogers. She doesn't want me to talk to you. So naturally, I will." She stretched her legs in the sunlight and admired them, flexing them with feline grace. "Who's he?" she asked, nodding at T.S. as she cataloged his charms.

"My nephew Theodore."

The ballerina raised her eyebrows at T.S. in amusement, but he was too besotted to notice. She was a little haughty for his usual tastes, but Lisette Martinez had something all right. Fire seemed to flash from her eyes, her lips were incredibly expressive, and she had a way of holding her head and abandoning her hair to the wind that made T.S. think of silky strands spread across a bed pillow. She represented all things forbidden and exotic—and he was fascinated.

"We're here to ask questions in an official capacity," Auntie Lil explained.

"Raoul will be thrilled," the ballerina said, her sarcasm elegant in its subtlety. "He's rehearsing the brats inside.

Parents keep pulling their kids from the show and he's helping Pork Chop Puccinni train the new beasts."

T.S. ignored the appropriate but nasty reference to the Metro's ballet master. "The parents are afraid their children are in danger?" he asked.

Lisette smiled enigmatically. "They are in danger. I've thought of killing a few of them myself over this past week."

"Did you know Bobby Morgan?" Auntie Lil asked, watching in disapproval as Lisette lit up a fresh cigarette.

"Sure, I knew the late great Bobby Morgan. He put the moves on me pretty hard when we first met about six weeks ago."

"Put the moves on you?" Auntie Lil asked.

"He's the type," Lisette explained. "I was the most famous woman in the room. He had a biological urge to try to impress me."

"What form did his efforts take?" Auntie Lil asked.

"Ambushing me in the hall between classes. Asking me to lunch. As if I ever actually get to eat. Bringing me flowers. Cheap ones. Telling me how much money he made. The usual."

"Wasn't your husband offended?" T.S. asked.

"Raoul wouldn't have noticed if we'd fallen on him from the rafters," she said. "Which, come to think of it, Bobby almost did." She took another deep drag of her cigarette. "Raoul is not exactly Old Faithful, if you know what I mean. He's too busy to care what I do."

"Yes, but ..." Auntie Lil began. Her voice trailed off. She was routinely tactless, but not even she could decide how to charge in on what was a very delicate topic.

"My aunt is inquiring about all the press stories," T.S. explained, correctly guessing Auntie Lil's thoughts. "We often read that your husband has a jealous temperament."

"That's just show," she explained. "Good publicity. Supports his reputation as a fiery artist. Raoul could care less who I see or what I do with them when I see them." A strand of hair blew into her mouth and clung to one side of her generously made-up lips. T.S. watched in fascination as Lisette carefully picked the hairs free with a long fingernail.

Auntie Lil didn't know who she wanted to slap more: Lisette or Raoul Martinez. In fact, she became so lost in a fantasy about the lecture she would give them both that T.S. had to take over the questioning.

"How did Morgan act when you rebuffed him?" he asked.

Lisette shrugged. "He didn't care. By that time, there were a dozen younger dancers hanging on him. Gold chains and lots of money look good when you're too young to know better." She glanced at her watch. "I have to get back in."

The door behind her opened abruptly and Raoul Martinez stuck his leonine head outside. The sunlight momentarily blinded him, but when his eyes focused on his wife—and the cigarette dangling from her fingertips—his face flushed in rage. "How many times must I tell you!" he roared. He burst through the door, snatched the butt from her hand, and ground it out beneath his foot. "You must conserve every ounce of your energy," he thundered. "Why will you not listen to me? Do you want to continue to be a star or are you going to give it up for the sake of this poison?" Lisette sat calmly throughout the tirade, but both Auntie Lil and T.S. inched as far away from the bellowing artistic director as possible.

"Who are you?" Martinez demanded, staring at T.S.

"My nephew," Auntie Lil said, wedging herself firmly between the two men. "He is helping me with my inquiries."

"And who are you?" Martinez demanded of Auntie Lil, his anger blinding him nearly as much as the bright sunlight.

"A board member," she said indignantly. "Good heavens, I sit next to you every month."

Martinez peered at Auntie Lil, his eyes blinking in the bright sunlight. "So you are. But don't bother my wife. She has work to do."

He grasped Lisette firmly by the elbow and pulled her

inside, letting the wind blow the metal door shut in Auntie Lil's face with a bang.

"A charming sort of fellow," T.S. said.

"With a charming sort of temper," Auntie Lil added. "Come on."

"Where are we going?" T.S. asked, following her around the building toward the southwest side of the complex.

"I want to check out the Reverend's story," she explained. "I need your help."

Auntie Lil's idea of his help was to command T.S. to stand in the bushes at the rear of the complex, back turned to the pathway so he could simulate heeding the call of nature while she briskly walked past in varying degrees of hurry. Feeling like a complete ass, T.S. complied and was acutely embarrassed to find himself the object of eagerly fearful scrutiny by a group of gray-haired female tourists sunning themselves by the bandstand.

"Hurry up!" he whispered fiercely as Auntie Lil jogged past for the third time.

"Did that sound like a machine gun?" she asked breathlessly, returning to his hiding place.

"No, it did not," he told her, irritated. "Though a machine gun is starting to sound awfully good to me." She missed the significance of his stare. "What is the point of this?" he demanded.

She gaze thoughtfully at the rear exit of the Metro's theater. "I'm just trying to see if Reverend Hampton's story makes sense. Can you see over your shoulder and up the path while turned like that?"

"Yes," he said wearily. "Please don't make me go through this again. Those ladies already think I have the largest bladder in the history of mankind and all twenty of them are hoping I'll expose myself next."

"But I haven't yet sounded like a machine gun, have I?" she asked.

"You're wearing soft-sole shoes," he pointed out. "If you weighed five hundred pounds, you wouldn't make a tapping sound."

"Good point," she said, her forehead furrowed in concentration.

"Better hurry!" a breathless voice interjected. A small blond woman scurried past with a hasty wave at Auntie Lil. She was a member of the Metro's board, one of the silent majority. "You'll be late."

"Late?" Auntie Lil asked after her.

The woman checked her diamond-encrusted watch. "The meeting starts at three-thirty today," she explained, hurrying around the corner toward the executive offices.

"A board meeting!" Auntie Lil's anger was instant. "They're trying to hold a meeting without me!"

"Maybe they tried to leave you a message," T.S. pointed out. "If you'd just get an answering machine like the rest of the world, these things wouldn't happen."

"Nonsense. They are deliberately trying to exclude me and I intend to find out why." She started down the path before he could protest. "You'll have to meet that producer on your own," she called back. "Call me later and let me know what you think." She disappeared around the corner.

At least he wouldn't have to think up an excuse to cover up meeting Herbert, T.S. thought to himself as he hurried toward his clandestine dance lesson. The fox-trot? Hah! If a fox could trot, so could he.

2. Herbert was not afflicted with T.S.'s lack of self-esteem about romantic matters. When T.S. had confided that Lilah seemed too busy to notice him recently, Herbert's take on the situation had been more objective and, most probably, more accurate: Lilah was working too hard. She needed a hobby. Women in her social class were taking up ballroom dancing again. If T.S. would learn to dance, then he and Lilah would have a hobby they could enjoy together, he pointed out. And T.S. might be able to lure her away from board meetings for an evening or two each week.

Put that way, it was hard to argue, which was why T.S. was meeting Herbert nearly every day in a small rented studio on upper Broadway. Herbert had long been a ballroom dancer extaordinaire and often stepped out with Auntie Lil. "Your aunt attempts to lead at all times," he had once confided. "But she is otherwise a fine and skilled partner."

They finished the lesson early so T.S. would be on time for his meeting with Gene Levitt. He hated being late for anything, a trait Auntie Lil did not share.

"Do you think this producer has anything to do with the murder?" Herbert asked as they changed into fresh clothes with a masculine camaraderie that T.S. always felt was more like the movies than real life.

"He has the best motive of anyone," T.S. explained. "Morgan ruined him professionally and financially. But I don't know if he was even there that night. Do you want to come along? Auntie Lil can't make it."

Herbert's normally golden glow flushed slightly as he patted a knapsack full of neatly packed clothing on the bench beside him. "No. I have a ballet lesson to attend. I have caught the bug, it seems."

"I salute you," T.S. admitted. "I suppose you're wearing tights?"

Herbert bowed his head modestly. "When in Rome, as they say."

3. Gene Levitt had fallen on hard times with the cruel swiftness that only a career in the entertainment business offers. His company had been reduced to a small but clean cubicle in a shared office complex run by a desperate real-estate management firm out to turn a buck on an underoccupied skyscraper in midtown. The other cubicles were rented out monthly by accountants, public-relations consultants, money managers, and other entrepreneurs seeking success. Since it was after regular working hours, the shared receptionist had long since departed. Many of the offices remained well lit, however, as self-employed hopefuls struggled to make ends meet.

Gene Levitt was clearly a soul on the way down. T.S. knew that he had, until recently, headed up a successful independent production company out of a studio in Hollywood. Now his kingdom had dwindled to eighty rented square feet of not so prime Manhattan real estate.

"It's not much, I know," Levitt said. "What can I say?" He was a small man, trim and deeply tanned with receding black hair cut short and brushed back from a rounded forehead. He had babyish features that looked out of place on such a serious face. His button nose and pursed lips belonged on a cherub, not a Hollywood executive facing disaster. He held his energy close to his body, seeming to hover above surfaces rather than sitting and standing like everyone else. His suit was custom-tailored and obviously expensive. T.S. guessed that his wardrobe would survive the bankruptcy better than most other aspects of his life.

"Have a seat." Levitt nodded toward a small plastic chair pulled up near his plain wooden desk. "I don't suppose you have money?"

"I beg your pardon?" T.S. asked. He felt uncomfortable in his sweater and casual slacks. It made him feel disadvantaged to face a man in a suit without similar corporate armor.

Levitt waved a hand nervously in the air. "Don't worry. I know you're here to ask me questions about that bastard Morgan. The old lady was pretty explicit about what she wanted on the phone. But I can't help myself. Reflex action. I'm here on the East Coast trying to raise money for a new venture. Thought I'd give it a try. So *do* you? Have money?"

"No money," T.S. said quickly. "At least none I can get my hands on."

"Join the rest of the world," Levitt said with a grimace. Smiling had long since disappeared from his repertoire. "That's why I'm in New York."

"Having much luck?" T.S. asked politely. "Raising funds, I mean."

Levitt shrugged. "Movies are glamorous," he explained. "And I have a pretty good track record. Two successful independent features, nothing to write home about but they made a fair piece of change. A line of cheapo horror pics.

They turned a good profit, too. Plus a couple of okay made-for-television ventures. I make my people money."

"Or did, until the last time around," T.S. said.

Levitt sighed and the energy drained from him like a deflating beach ball. His compact frame slumped and he stared at the desk top glumly. "Until recently," he admitted. "There's no way around it. It was a disaster."

"What happened?" T.S. asked, wondering if he should take notes. Sam Spade wouldn't be caught dead taking notes. But then, Sam Spade didn't have to report to Auntie Lil. . . .

"We'd signed Mikey Morgan to star in a big-budget feature. Our biggest yet," Levitt explained. He picked up a fountain pen and jabbed joylessly at a blotter as he spoke. "We were lucky. We signed him before his back-to-back hits and got him on the cheap. Shooting was supposed to start last month out in Hollywood on soundstages, followed by Seattle this month. We'd already contracted for the stages, put down a deposit, and invested a lot of money on location in Seattle when we got the bad news."

"The news that Mikey Morgan was pulling out of the picture?"

Levitt nodded. "That bastard father of his left me a message on my answering machine. Can you believe that? The guy is costing me nine million dollars and he can't even tell me to my face."

"Wasn't there a contract?" T.S. asked. "How could he break it?"

"Sure there was a contract." Levitt rummaged around in a lower drawer and withdrew a thick sheaf of paper, tossing it across the desk at T.S. "Here. Maybe you can find a use for it. It's worthless to me."

"Why?" T.S. asked. He paged curiously through the document, amazed at the complexity of the terms and the petty conditions attached as riders. "Jellybeans?" he asked. "In five specified flavors at all times?"

Levitt shrugged. "I hope the kid's teeth rot. Soon."

"What excuse did Morgan use to pull his kid out?" T.S. asked.

"Claims he had a prior legally binding arrangement elsewhere that was running over schedule. It was a lie, of course. He was stalling for time so he could stonewall the film. He knew I put my investors together project by project and that they aren't the most patient backers in the world. If he could have held out long enough, I would have had to fold the flick and go on to something else. If I took him to court, the kid would have been so old by the time the case came to trial that no one would have wanted him when we were through. Face it. He has another year or two of being cute and then it's good-bye time. It's already too late for me, of course. I'm ruined. I don't know if Morgan knew how far we had extended ourselves with pre-production expenses, but I wouldn't be surprised if he had. He had a reputation of costing people money."

"You sound resigned to losing your shirt," T.S. said.

"I'm not." Levitt patted down his pockets and located a pack of cigarettes. "But I'm prepared for the inevitable. Want one?" He offered the pack to T.S.

T.S. declined but did not have the heart to ask him to hold off. The guy needed a smoke pretty badly if his shaking hands were any indication.

"Morgan could have pulled his kid out a hell of a lot earlier," Levitt admitted. "Before I'd put all that money on the line. Waiting until he did is what put me under. I gotta wonder if maybe it wasn't deliberate."

"Deliberate?" T.S. asked. "Why would he do that?"

Levitt shook his head. "I've been asking myself the same thing. I never met the guy before this project, never worked with the kid either. Best thing I can think of is that he didn't like one of my investors. Or he just didn't care. Or maybe he likes ruining people. Maybe it was some kind of weird revenge for his own failures. He didn't like to be reminded of his own days as a kid actor, I can tell you that."

T.S. was silent for a moment, considering the possibilities. "Did you ever work with Bobby Morgan when he was an actor?" he asked Levitt.

Levitt frowned. "Hey, do I look old enough for that to you? I'm forty-one, for chrissakes. He and I were about the same age. No, I didn't work with him way back when. I just wanted to work with his kid."

"Maybe he was afraid the salary you were offering Mikey would pull down his fees for other films?"

Levitt shrugged. "Look, the kid was already lined up to get a fortune on two other flicks once he finished my film. He gets more than any other kid in the history of Hollywood and more than most leading men I know. He could have knocked out my picture and then moved on, raking it in while he could. I don't think it was the money, but maybe it was. Maybe the father planned to wait a couple weeks then start the kid on one of the high-priced flicks instead of mine to cash in quick while the kid was still cute. I don't know." He finished his cigarette and went back to playing with the fountain pen.

"Who were your investors?" T.S. asked.

Levitt shrugged. "Some financial guys, representing a group of limited partners. Some old money attracted by the glamour. Plus a handful of industry old-timers, mostly producers out in L.A. and some aging film stars hoping to make money on the other end for once."

"And they all lost their money?"

"I'll say. But at least they kept their day jobs. Me, I'm ruined. I'll be lucky if I can raise enough money for my nephew's Christmas pageant after this." He threw the pen down and ran his hands over his head. "Sorry. I'm kind of nervous right now."

"Nervous?" T.S. said. "Over the future?"

"Over right now." He glanced at the door anxiously. "They're going to arrest me. I know it. They've already called twice. The cops."

"Arrest you?" T.S. said. "What for?"

"What do you think?" Levitt stared at T.S. "Come on, who has a better motive than me? The guy ruined me. I can't say I'm sorry he's dead. And I was there."

"You were there?" T.S. asked.

"I was there," Levitt explained defensively. "I came to opening night. I thought maybe if I could get Morgan alone at the party afterward, I could talk to him, get him to change his mind. Figured he'd be in a good mood. Instead, he decided to hang around backstage for a while." He grimaced again. "They're coming to take me away. I can feel it."

"Nonsense," T.S. said. "The police don't arrest people for nothing."

"Sure they do," Levitt said. "Don't you ever go to the movies?"

At that exact moment a man and a woman dressed in nearly identical gray suits stuck their heads into Levitt's office. "Gene Levitt?" the female half of the duo asked, shifting her gaze from T.S. to Levitt.

"That's me," Levitt said wearily, raising his hands above his head as if he were about to be shot.

"You don't need to put your hands above your head, sir," the detective explained as she flipped open a small leather case and flashed a gold badge. "We're just here to bring you downtown for questioning. I assume you're willing to cooperate?"

"Here," Levitt said, tossing a scrap of paper at a startled T.S. "Call this guy for me, will ya? He's my lawyer. Make it sound like I got money, okay? Otherwise, he'll never come."

T.S. took the crumpled note and watched in bewilderment as Levitt was led from the office wedged between the silent detectives. His figure disappeared into the darkness of the deserted reception area, leaving T.S. feeling vulnerable in the sudden silence. He felt very lucky to be who he was. Here was a man without hope, without friends, without even a lawyer who could be counted on unless big money was on the table. You could take your celluloid dreams and Malibu beach homes, T.S. thought. He'd stay right here in New York where friends were friends and fortunes took a little bit longer to slide downhill.

He stared at the contract before him. Where had Levitt stored it? His eyes wandered to the double drawers anchoring the right side of the desk. If there was a contract, there was a file. If there was a file, it had the names of his investors in it. Looking around carefully to make sure he was not being observed, T.S. crept to the front of Levitt's desk and tried both drawers. The bottom one was filled with contracts and schedules for the aborted Mikey Morgan movie. Paging through quickly, T.S. removed all of the documents pertaining to financial matters. He stuffed them under his sweater and guiltily fled the lonely office.

Why not take the papers? T.S. thought to himself as he hurried out to the street to find a cab. By tomorrow, they'll just be sitting in a box in a precinct somewhere.

CHAPTER EIGHT

1. "I would like to know why I was not informed of this meeting," Auntie Lil demanded. Lilah Cheswick was not present, leaving her without an ally. "And was Mrs. Cheswick notified?"

"We attempted to call you," Lane Rogers said stiffly. "I assume you were too busy pursuing your investigative activities. As for Mrs. Cheswick, she seems a bit too busy to concern herself with our affairs these days."

Lane still looked pale and drawn, no better than she had at Bobby Morgan's funeral two days before. Her hair was pulled stiffly back from her face in an untidy bun and her makeup was unevenly applied.

"We did try to call you," Ruth Beretsky began, but she was a timid woman and immediately withered under Auntie Lil's steady gaze. "At least, Lane says she tried to call you."

"Ruth!" It was a bark more than a command, but it had its effect. Ruth fell silent. "It is a moot point, anyway," Lane said smoothly. "As we are all well aware that you are here, Miss Hubbert, this emergency meeting of the board will now come to order."

"What is the point of this meeting?" Hans Glick demanded. His usually impeccable grooming was marred by a crooked tie. On him, it looked as out of place as a dog wearing a hat.

"The point of this meeting is to ask you what financial standing the Metro currently holds," Lane replied. "Specifically regarding our insurance coverage."

"Why is that relevant?" Glick asked, his voice faltering.

"I will submit my usual monthly financial review next week."

"It is relevant because we are being sued," Lane announced. A gasp ran through the room. "On behalf of his minor children, Bobby Morgan's ex-wife has filed a multimillion-dollar lawsuit against the Metropolitan Ballet for insufficient security and other safety violations which contributed to the death of her ex-husband. I was served the papers at the Plaza in front of half of New York. You can imagine my mortification. I fired my maid for telling the process server where I was."

On cue, Ruth produced a thick document from her briefcase and stacked it on the table for all to see.

"Are we insured?" a timid voice asked from the rear. All eyes turned to Glick.

"I believe so," he said uneasily.

"You *believe* so?" Auntie Lil repeated loudly.

Glick cleared his throat. "I was investigating a more economical source of liability insurance, but I believe the old policy is still in effect."

"You better do more than believe," Lane ordered. "You better find out right now." Her face flushed red. "Someone must pay for Bobby Morgan's death and I would prefer that it not be the Metro."

"I suggest you remain calm," Glick said, hoping to deflect attention from himself. "It would be a mistake to let your personal feelings interfere with your role as board chairman."

"My *personal* feelings?" Lane locked eyes with Glick and a dangerous glint flared in her gaze. "What do you mean by that?"

Glick cleared his throat again. "I mean that perhaps you are too close to the situation to be able to effectively govern. Perhaps someone more experienced in crisis management should take over. Someone who is not involved quite so personally. Someone like myself."

"What personal feelings are you referring to?" Lane asked, her voice quivering with incipient anger.

Glick straightened his tie and dropped his voice to a

professionally soothing tone. "Now, now, Lane. No one is questioning your ability. It is just that we were all aware of your personal relationship with the deceased. Perhaps it is clouding your judgment here today."

Before Lane could react, the standoff was interrupted by a knock at the door. The room froze. Who would dare interrupt an emergency meeting?

The door opened and a beautiful woman in her late thirties entered. Her long brown hair rippled around her face in gentle Pre-Raphaelite waves, softening the effect of her sharp features and triangular chin. Her brown eyes were large and heavily rimmed with dramatic liner. She moved gracefully, her skirt swishing against long legs. She was—or had been—a dancer.

"I am Emili Vladimir," she announced to the startled board. Clearly, she was not cowed by the prospect of speaking before a group of strangers. She marched to the head of the table, her self-confidence obvious. Lane Rogers automatically sat down, then looked startled at her own reaction.

"My son, Rudy, is now dancing the parts of Drosselmeyer and the Prince," the stranger explained to the group.

"Of course," Raoul Martinez interrupted, his deep voice filling the room. "I am charmed, madam. A pity we have never met before." He slipped from his chair and hurried to kiss Emili Vladimir's hand. "I saw you dance in Paris, madam," he added. "*The Dying Swan* when you were with the Kirov. You were magnificent."

Emili Vladimir dipped in a practiced half curtsy, acknowledging the compliment. "I am no longer a performer," she explained modestly to her waiting audience. "My grand days are over now. I come before you today as a mother." Martinez took an empty seat nearby and gazed at her as if he were a disciple awaiting instructions. She looked around the room carefully, making eye contact with everyone present. "I wish to personally thank all of you for giving my son the opportunity to dance in these roles." A slight Russian accent lent steel to her otherwise softly husky voice. "It is a great step forward for him. He has worked very hard to get here. We have come many miles to be here in America and sacrificed a great deal for his studies, as I am sure you know. There have been many obstacles along the way, but we did not let anything stop us. We have worked hard to attain this dream. I am here today to assure you that Rudy will make the Metropolitan Ballet proud, not only now but for many years to come. If his father were here, I am sure he would be deeply grateful for your generosity."

The board sat, stunned into silence. Her appearance was so unexpected and her gracious words so at odds with the board's bickering that no one knew how to react. Some of the members felt unfamiliar patriotic pride stirring within them at her words of praise for America, land of opportunity. Auntie Lil was more pragmatic. She was wondering where Emili Vladimir had been the night Bobby Morgan died and how she had known of the board meeting today.

Martinez broke the silence. "Your son is a most talented dancer," he cried suddenly, leaping to his feet and bowing again. "Most talented. I am proud to say he is a student of mine."

"Yes." Her smile was beatific. "When he was a child, I taught him myself. But, of course, I cannot claim credit for his talent. It is God we must thank for that."

She had pointedly not thanked Martinez, Auntie Lil noted with amusement. She suspected Emili could dance rings around the artistic director, both inside the classroom and out.

Lane Rogers looked up from her notes at the slender creature standing beside her. Tight lines of authority appeared grimly at the corners of her mouth. But before she could speak, Hans Glick interrupted. "We are most pleased with your son," Glick told Emili. "Ticket sales are overwhelming and the reviews in today's papers were glowing. I received word just a few hours ago that we are sold out throughout the run."

"That is not my son's doing," Emili said modestly. "I am

sure it is due to the epic scope of your production and to the talents of the young ballerina Fatima Jones."

Martinez took the adjective *epic* as a compliment and moved even closer to their visitor. She smiled prettily, but nonetheless stepped back out of panting range.

Lane Rogers had had enough of the interruption, particularly the spectacle of men melting in front of her eyes. "Thank you for stopping by," she said briskly. "We are delighted that you are pleased. Good day."

Emili turned her placid eyes to Lane. Her smile did not waver. "You must forgive my interruption," she said sweetly as she floated toward the exit with trained grace. "It is just that we are not used to such opportunity, to having the doors opened in this way. Life has been so very hard for Rudy and me. America is truly a wonderful place. I just wanted to thank you all personally." She smiled and bobbed her head before slipping out, leaving most board members wondering uneasily just how terrible things had been for the Vladimirs in Russia.

"A charming lady," Martinez announced in the silence.

"Pick your jaw up off the floor," Lane snapped. "We have work to do." She glared at Glick. "I suggest you check on that insurance policy *now*. Ruth will accompany you to the files and make photocopies of the current policy for everyone."

"Oh, shut up, Lane!" Ruth cried out unexpectedly. The entire room stared in astonishment. "I'm tired of you telling me what to do all the time. Go make the damn photocopies yourself."

2.   "The idiot let our liability insurance lapse," Auntie Lil explained over a belated dinner in a brick-and-hanging-plant-heavy restaurant across from Lincoln Center. "If we don't prove that the Metro is not responsible for what happened—and find out who is—we could lose everything."

"We?" T.S. asked uncomfortably.

"Not our foundation, but the Metro. I'd like to strangle

Glick. He was pursuing some sort of scheme designed to involve his company in supplying the Metro's insurance." Auntie Lil was enthusiastically demolishing a grilled steak and a pile of mashed potatoes that rivaled Mount McKinley. "He said it would have saved us a lot of money. Now, of course, we could lose millions. I thought the board was going to turn on him and strangle him with his tie. So did Glick. He announced a prior appointment and left."

"What does this mean for us?" T.S. asked, savoring his more modest meal of lamb chops and rice.

Auntie Lil shook her head. "We have to try even harder, Theodore. And for God sakes, pray the killer has nothing to do with the Metro."

"Maybe it was someone connected to Gene Levitt," T.S. said hopefully. He summarized what he had learned in his meeting and produced the list of investors in the failed Mikey Morgan movie.

"You don't think it was Levitt himself?" Auntie Lil asked.

T.S. shrugged. "He's so nervous. I just can't see him holding still long enough to conk someone over the head and string him up."

"Theodore!" Auntie Lil stared at him, wide-eyed.

"What?" He dabbed self-consciously at his chin with a napkin, thinking she had spotted stray food. For someone with such creative table manners, Auntie Lil was awfully picky about his own.

"You're absolutely right. Bobby Morgan had to have been conked out first and then strung up," she said. "He would have put up too big of a fight any other way." She leaned forward, her bright orange scarf trailing across a mound of baby carrots. "This means the struggle could have occurred at any time prior to or during the performance—and the body could have been stored somewhere for a while. I couldn't figure out why no one noticed the struggle, but that explains it. And it gives us hope. Perhaps it wasn't someone in the company after all. Anyone could have had access to the backstage area." She drummed her fingers on the tabletop. "Let me see that list of investors."

T.S. pulled out the pertinent papers and they scanned the materials while they ate. "I don't really see any names I recognize," Auntie Lil admitted. "I think this woman was on some television show a few years back and I thought this fellow had died years ago. Hmmm . . . here's a name that looks familiar. Know him?"

T.S. shook his head. "No. But I've heard of him. He must be one of the Hollywood types Levitt spoke about. Here are a couple of guys I recognize. But they're well-respected money managers. Wall Street leaders. I can't imagine them killing Bobby Morgan over an investment."

Auntie Lil stared out the window of the restaurant and across Ninth Avenue toward Lincoln Center. "I wonder what Levitt's telling the police," she said. "Do you think he told you everything?"

T.S. shrugged. "I'm surprised at how much he did tell me. I don't know him from Adam and he freely admitted anything I wanted to know. I think I would have heard his whole life story if the detectives hadn't arrived to take him away."

"Isn't that Herbert?" Auntie Lil asked suddenly, peering across the traffic at the subway entrance. She could have put her reading glasses on to make sure, but hesitated in front of her nephew. She disliked admitting any sort of physical weakness.

T.S. stared out the window. "I don't see him. What would he be doing up here anyway?" he asked innocently, knowing full well that Herbert was hiding his ballet lessons from Auntie Lil in the hopes of sparing her feelings about her own ineptitude.

"Maybe not," Auntie Lil said slowly. "But *that's* definitely Jerry Vanderbilt. Rehearsals must be over." She waved her handkerchief in the window like a seaman semiphoring for help.

"Not now," T.S. said, staring balefully at his remaining lamb chop. "I'm tired of talking to suspects."

"Too late. Here he comes!" Auntie Lil declared gaily, her spirits buoyed by the prospect of more information.

"Thank God!" the Metro's accompanist cried as he burst through the restaurant's swinging doors. Several New Yorkers at the bar froze but returned to their wine spritzers after satisfying themselves that he wasn't waving a weapon. "I've been looking for you everywhere. I heard you were at a board meeting, but when I got there, it had already been adjourned."

"News travels fast." Auntie Lil moved over to make room for him. "I suppose you heard about the lapse in liability insurance as well?"

The pianist flapped a long hand, dismissing the topic. "Who cares? That's only money. You've got to help Gene."

"I beg your pardon?" Auntie Lil asked.

"Gene Levitt?" T.S. interrupted.

"He didn't do anything wrong. You must help him."

"You know Gene Levitt?" T.S. asked.

The flush that spread over Jerry Vanderbilt's craggily masculine face was remarkable. T.S. looked tactfully away, but Auntie Lil scrutinized him with frank curiosity. "What's going on?" she demanded.

"I met him at a party last month," Jerry explained.

"This is very important," Auntie Lil said, suddenly alert. "Did he introduce himself to you or was it the other way around?"

"It wasn't like that," Jerry said. He stared down at the table. "It was a tree-trimming party in the Village. My friends John and Grant were hosting. They knew Gene from when they lived in Los Angeles. They invited him because he had just moved to New York and didn't know anybody. They were the ones to introduce me to him."

"Did he know you were a pianist for the Metro?" T.S. asked.

"Of course." Jerry was offended. "They couldn't just introduce me and not say what I did. I'm lucky enough to be gainfully employed doing something I love. Why should I hide it?"

Auntie Lil and T.S. exchanged a glance that did not

escape Jerry. "I know what you're thinking," he said. "It wasn't like that at all. He was very honest from the start. We hit it off right away. He told me how Bobby Morgan had ruined him the very first time we went out to dinner together. He didn't try to hide anything. He said he'd been ruined and explained why. I wasn't his spy or anything."

"But he asked you lots of questions about Bobby and Mikey Morgan," T.S. guessed.

"I *offered* him the information. But nothing that could have hurt anyone. I just told him the kid couldn't dance and that his performance would be a disaster. It wasn't like it was a state secret or something."

"Gene did not kill Bobby Morgan," Jerry continued. "You have to help him. I heard that you helped that big-mouth Reverend guy."

"I arranged for his bail," Auntie Lil admitted. "I can't go arranging bail for everyone the police haul in."

"Besides, Gene wasn't arrested," T.S. said. "He was just brought in for questioning. He went willingly."

"I know, but he's scared. He called me. He said his lawyer hadn't shown up yet and he was afraid it was because he was out of money."

The blood drained from T.S.'s face. "Oh my God," he said, stricken. "I was supposed to call his lawyer for him."

"See!" Jerry cried. "You've abandoned him. Now you simply must help."

"Theodore." Auntie Lil frowned in disapproval. "Give me the name and phone number." She scanned the piece of paper. "How could you have forgotten?"

He was too ashamed to explain. He had forgotten because he had gotten caught up in the romance of sitting at a bar sipping Dewar's and soda while perusing the financial files, searching for clues.

"He's been languishing for hours," Jerry declared. "You must help. It's all your fault!"

Auntie Lil lowered the piece of paper and gazed coolly at the accompanist. "Young man," she said, despite the fact that Jerry was well past fifty, "Gene Levitt has been brought in for questioning, not for torture. And he is not our responsibility. However, if you can prove to my satisfaction that he is not involved in the death of Bobby Morgan, then we may help. Perhaps."

"I *can* prove it," Jerry whispered loudly. As if attracted by some magnetic force, they leaned forward until their foreheads nearly touched over the dinner table. "Come with me back across the street to the theater," he said softly. "I want to show you something."

Auntie Lil glanced across the avenue. "I thought the theater was dark tonight."

"It is," Jerry explained. "But they're blocking *Apollo*. Man does not live by *Nutcracker* alone. There's something I want to show you. Not even the police have seen it yet."

"Okay," Auntie Lil agreed. "As soon as *you* call your friend's lawyer"—she thrust the paper at him—"and I finish my mashed potatoes, we'll go."

3. The Metro's theater was eerily deserted. As Jerry ushered them in a side door toward the backstage area, Auntie Lil stopped to peek through a crack in the curtains at the empty auditorium. The stage was well lit with a utilitarian glare and Martinez stood at its center, demonstrating a series of steps to an attentive male dancer. Martinez's wife, Lisette, waited patiently to one side for her partner to receive his instructions. Four other ballerinas clustered stage right, watching the proceedings with little interest. They had long since learned their parts and were ready to go home. It was nearly nine o'clock at night and they had been rehearsing since before noon. Paulette Puccinni sat in the front row, taking notes and charting the choreography for future reference. It seemed odd to have dancers without music, but the only sounds that broke the silence were the authoritative commands of Martinez. His voice was not unpleasant, however. Indeed, it softened perceptibly as he explained his vision of the dance, transforming his personality from forbidding to compelling. His body seemed to grow in length and agility, taking on a lightness as he demonstrated moves.

"Come on," Jerry whispered. "He hates outsiders at rehearsals. Let's go upstairs before he sees us."

The Metro theater included three stories of administrative and rehearsal floors built in behind the stage and auditorium. To access each floor, they had to walk up a set of steps then traverse the floor to reach the next stairwell and floor. Auntie Lil had visited these work areas of the Metropolitan Ballet on several occasions and knew that the layout made sneaking around difficult indeed. She also knew that the first floor housed rehearsal rooms where classes were held each morning. The second floor stored the locker rooms, scenery, sets, costumes, and complicated electrical equipment necessary to sustain a varied repertoire. The third floor provided room for the all-important toe-shoe room, sheet-music shelves, and more storage areas. Jerry led them to this top floor, switching on lights as they made their way through the otherwise deserted building.

"This is a madhouse during the day," Jerry explained. "Everyone went home a couple of hours ago."

Auntie Lil and T.S. stopped to read a prominent notice posted on the door of the locked shoe room. ATTENTION! the top of the poster proclaimed in bold red letters, followed by a neatly printed warning: *It has come to management's attention that members of the corps are reselling pointe shoes in violation of company policy. May we remind you that the Metropolitan spends more than $400,000 per year on shoes alone. All used, ill-fitting, or otherwise outdated pairs should be turned into the wardrobe mistress and remain the property of the Metropolitan Ballet. In addition, lockers are subject to search by the wardrobe mistress at any time. Anyone caught violating this policy will be subject to fines, suspension, and possible discharge.*

"Good grief," said T.S. "What are the shoes made of? Gold?"

"Layers of canvas and satin," Auntie Lil explained. "With cotton wool stuffed into the toe area. But it's not what they're made of that makes them so valuable, it's how they are made. It takes a master cobbler hours to create each shoe, and even after he is done, the girls work with the shoes on their own, attaching ribbon, embroidering the tip, wetting the vamp, softening the pleats. You wouldn't believe the trouble and care that go into a pair that may only last three or four performances. That's why no one is allowed to touch pointe shoes but the owner. It's a long and expensive process to supply the corps with them. If a girl could get her hands on a usable pair that she doesn't need, she could get fifty or more dollars for them."

T.S. looked down at his plain old Hush Puppies with new appreciation.

"This way," Jerry Vanderbilt hissed from around a corner. "Hurry up." They followed him down the hall and stopped in front of a storage room. A smaller door marked the end of the corridor to their right.

"Where does that door lead?" T.S. asked uneasily.

"Catwalk above the stage," Jerry explained. "This floor is level with the top of the main stage. Electricians and technicians work on the rafter areas from here." He turned his back on the door to the catwalk and led them into a small but cluttered room that obviously provided storage space. An unused upright piano was shoved against one side, huge stage lights were stacked at random at one end, excess rope was coiled in a massive mound on the floor, and sealed lockers rimmed the walls.

"This is a general dumping ground," Jerry explained. "I'm surprised there aren't a bunch of over-the-hill dancers living in here."

A large bump from outside the room startled them. Auntie Lil moved closer to the door.

"I thought we were the only ones up here," T.S. said uneasily.

"We are." Jerry frowned. "Might be the crew working on lighting angles or something."

"Let's get this over with," T.S. demanded suddenly. "I keep expecting the Phantom of the Opera to appear."

"Don't say that," Jerry warned. "You're tempting fate. That's what the girls call the murderer that never got caught."

"What murderer?" T.S. asked uneasily.

"A violinist was strangled here at Lincoln Center about ten years ago," Jerry said. "Don't you remember? They never caught the killer. The police thought it might have been a member of one of the Lincoln Center crews since she was so pretty. Maybe a spurned lover. But no one was ever charged. Hey, maybe he's the one who murdered Bobby Morgan."

"Speaking of which," Auntie Lil said firmly, "what did you want us to see?"

"This is it," Jerry said, holding out his hands.

"This is what?" T.S. asked.

"This room," Jerry said. "It's where it was done. It's where he was killed. I'm almost certain."

"Why do you say that?" T.S. asked, keeping an eye on Auntie Lil. She was on her hands and knees, lifting up debris and searching for evidence. All she lacked was a magnifying glass and a hunting cap.

"I was in here the day before the premiere," Jerry explained. "I came to check on the piano."

"Why?" Auntie Lil demanded, moving a heavy light to one side so she could check the corner behind it.

"I don't have one at home," he explained, his tone growing indignant. "Here I am, one of the best rehearsal pianists in New York City, maybe the world, and I don't even have my own piano at home. They pay me far less than I am worth. Someone mentioned there was an extra one stored in here. I came by to check and see if it was in good enough shape to salvage. If it was, I was going to ask Raoul if I could buy it from the Metropolitan."

"Buy it or steal it?" Auntie Lil asked.

"Buy it," he protested. "Paying for it out of my salary a little at a time. I came to check it out first. I wasn't sure if it was worth it. It was badly out of tune and you know what that does to my ears. I have perfect pitch."

"And you saw something suspicious then?" T.S. asked.

"No. Later. I returned to this room two days after Bobby Morgan was killed, this time with Mario. He's the Metro's piano tuner. He was going to look at the piano and give me his opinion. As it turns out, the piano is hopeless. I shall have to find other means of keeping up my skills."

"Try working," Auntie Lil suggested. "Play more and gossip with Miss Puccinni less."

"Yes, well, thank you very much for the advice." He glared briefly at Auntie Lil, but she was too busy examining the rope to notice. "Anyway," he continued. "I saw at once that everything in the room had been disturbed. The rope had been moved, the lights were knocked over, some of the locker doors were hanging open, even the piano was sticking out from the wall like someone had bumped into it."

"Perhaps the stagehands needed props?" T.S. suggested.

Jerry shook his head. "At that time *The Nutcracker* was the only production we were even considering. The sets had long ago been pulled together and were being stored on the first-floor level. Likewise with the lights. They had been in place for weeks by that point. Hardly anyone even knows this room exists. I can't figure out why someone was in here."

"I can," Auntie Lil said. She held up a length of dirty white ribbon that had been torn off at one end and neatly clipped at the other. Small shreds of a white substance clung to a portion of its fabric. "See these white bits of material?" she asked. "I saw them before. Clinging to the heavy rope around Bobby Morgan's neck. I think you're right. I think he was killed in here sometime during the first act and then tied to the stage rope and maybe even tossed from the catwalk at the right time."

"That makes sense," Jerry agreed. "I saw Bobby Morgan alive just a few minutes before the show so he can't have been killed any earlier than the first act. But during the show would be hard without being seen," he added. "During a performance, a crew member usually stays up here. Anyhow, the point is that Gene was with me the entire time and can't have done it. He was sitting next to me in the audience, which tells you how much I care for him." He paused. "I do not willingly sit through *The Nutcracker* for just anyone. It had to have been someone else. Maybe a crew member saw something."

"Indeed. Where would I find this crew member?" Auntie Lil asked.

Jerry thought for a moment. "I think you need to talk to Ricky Lee Harris. He's our lighting supervisor. He'd know. Or he might even have been the one up here that evening, since it was opening night."

"I want to see the catwalk," Auntie Lil said, carefully replacing the ribbon where she had found it. "I also suggest you call the police, young man. Immediately. No need to mention our presence here, of course."

"It's this way," Jerry said, leading them back out into the hall and toward the smaller door set against the end of the passageway. He pushed on it and a sliver of stage light leaked through. Auntie Lil and T.S. followed him through the door onto a narrow steel walkway that hugged the back of the stage, far above the sight lines formed by the curtain. Below them, the four female members of the corps were practicing their steps, moving in unison, stopping, backing up and moving forward again. Raoul Martinez had disappeared, as had his wife and the principal male dancer. But they could hear the faint hum of voices talking further back in the auditorium.

"This is incredibly high," Auntie Lil said, peering over the edge. "If Morgan wasn't killed first, his neck would certainly have broken on the way down." She looked at the thick cords of rope dangling near the far end of the catwalk. "Those are there during a performance?" she asked.

Jerry shook his head. "There might be a few loose ends around, but mostly the ropes are used to hoist backdrops or anchor counterweights. During a show, they wouldn't be here on the catwalk."

Auntie Lil crept farther out onto the walkway and T.S followed reluctantly. Though the floor was steel, he imagined it swayed beneath his feet. It made him dizzy.

"Listen!" Auntie Lil commanded, grabbing his elbow with a surprisingly firm grip. "We know that voice."

Beneath them, concealed behind the side curtains, a man

was speaking to the corps de ballet. His brisk, no-nonsense accent floated up to where they stood high above the stage.

"Forgive me for interrupting," the clipped voice said. "But I have seen *Apollo* several times, including one magnificent performance in Zurich. I cannot help but see that you are moving the wrong way on the stage during this most crucial of scenes. You will conceal the most interesting part of the choreography if you do. May I suggest that you sweep right, then veer just a touch to the left so that the principal dancers are revealed. I will show you how to do it." Hans Glick stepped from the shadows and took the stage, prancing in the direction he had indicated and sweeping his arms out in an oddly feminine gesture.

"What does he think he's doing?" Jerry Vanderbilt whispered. He had joined them on the catwalk and was staring down at the action below. "Martinez will break his neck if he catches him interfering."

The four ballerinas were huddled together, giggling. They had no intention of following Glick's advice. But since they would not be the ones getting roared at by the artistic director, they considered Glick potential entertainment and made no move to stop him.

"Is that Julie Perkins?" Auntie Lil whispered. "The one on the right?"

T.S. squinted through the bright lights. "I think you're right," he said.

"What in God's name are you doing on my stage!" a voice roared from the auditorium. Pounding footsteps followed and the massive figure of Raoul Martinez dashed into view. He scurried around the orchestra pit and, without bothering to take the steps, swung himself up onto the stage with the deftness of a panther. He waved his arms and screamed at Glick, *"How dare you presume to instruct my dancers? How dare you presume to interfere on my stage? Get out! Get out or I will break your neck now!"* He advanced on the suddenly frozen Glick, arms outstretched as if he intended to follow through on his threat.

Glick swayed to one side, eyes wide, as he calculated his exit routes. "I apologize," he said in a less than steady voice. "I was merely waiting for the rehearsal to end so that I could speak with you in private about a certain matter. I suppose now is a bad time?"

"*Get out!*" Martinez roared again. He took another step forward and a frightened Glick retreated, catching his foot in the sunken pit that housed the prompter for operatic productions. He tumbled backward, falling over the small metal hood of the pit. His arms flailed and his slender body did a full turn as he slid down the curve of its roof and tumbled over the edge of the stage into the orchestra pit, crashing on top of several music stands and tipping over an entire row of metal chairs in a dominolike effect. The din was unending. It sounded like a parody of a cartoon sound effect. Yet neither Auntie Lil nor T.S. dared laugh for fear of being discovered.

Martinez marched to the edge of the stage and peered into the pit. "See what happens when you interfere with my authority," he yelled down at Glick.

Paulette Puccinni had crept to the edge of the pit and was gazing fearfully down at Glick. "I think he's hurt," she stage-whispered.

"I am hurt!" a voice wailed from the pit. "I've broken my foot."

"*Good!*" Martinez thundered back. "Now get out of my theater before I break your head!"

Glick needed no further convincing. He crawled past the fallen chairs and clawed his way over the lip of the orchestra pit, hauling his body into the seating area. Glancing nervously at Martinez, he hobbled up the center aisle, dragging one leg behind him like a character from a horror movie. The dancers began to laugh and Paulette turned her head to hide her smile.

Martinez was not amused. "If I catch you in here again without authorization," he shouted after Glick, "I'll throw you out personally. Maybe next time from a window!"

Auntie Lil and T.S. exchanged a glance. "We'll just slip quietly out," Auntie Lil whispered. "There's been enough excitement for the night."

Jerry Vanderbilt had gone pale. "I'll go with you," he whispered back. "Don't make a sound."

They tiptoed single file from the catwalk, taking exaggerated care not to make any noise. As the elevator bore them down to street level and away from the artistic director's furious temper, Auntie Lil suggested that they wait outside the auditorium for Julie Perkins to emerge after rehearsal.

"Are you serious?" T.S. asked. "What if Martinez comes out first?"

"We'll hide in the bushes," Auntie Lil suggested. "I hear you know a good spot."

"Hide away," Jerry Vanderbilt told them as he scurried toward the subway. "But I'm getting the hell away from Martinez."

4. Most any girl would have screamed in fright had two figures emerged from the shadows and flanked her in the middle of the night. Julie Perkins was not like most girls. She seemed to regard T.S. and Auntie Lil's sudden presence as nothing more than a stage cue well met.

"Who are you and what do you want?" she asked, her dancer's bag held slightly behind her, ready for a swing if need be. Although only sixteen, Julie Perkins had the bearing of a confident woman. Her delicate face had been hardened by fatigue and glowed with a dull ashen sheen in the reflected light of the street lamp. Her blond hair was still pulled back in a tight dancer's knot, although thin wisps of it had escaped at each temple and waved prettily down the sides of her high cheekbones. She wore jeans and a light turtleneck underneath a leather jacket embroidered with the logo of a recent Broadway hit show. Her makeup lay heavy against the paleness of her gaunt face.

Auntie Lil explained who they were and why they were there. Julie got right to the point. "Why do you want to talk to me?" she asked, staring down the side street as if searching for a cab. "Lane Rogers told one of my friends we were not to talk to you."

"The board has empowered me to talk to anyone who

may have been backstage the night Bobby Morgan was killed," Auntie Lil explained. "That includes you. I think he was killed just before or during the performance. What do you think?"

Julie made a face. "I'm trying to forget about it all, if you don't mind."

"But did you see anything unusual?" Auntie Lil persisted. "Anything that might point to the killer?"

The young girl reached for a pack of cigarettes stored in a back jeans pocket. Auntie Lil and T.S. watched in silent disapproval as she lit the cigarette with an expensive gold lighter shaped like a flat oval and began to puff away. Smoking was an occupational hazard, they were beginning to realize, a necessary evil relied upon by ballerinas desperate to keep their weight down. T.S. saw that Julie smoked the same brand as her father and with the same intense nonenjoyment.

"Well?" Auntie Lil prompted.

The girl blew smoke out her nostrils, sending tendrils curling in T.S.'s face. He suspected it was deliberate, but remained silent. She was stalling for time and he did not want to give in to her distractions.

"Look," Julie finally said, "I was in over my head, okay? I was being sent out center stage in front of a full audience dancing a part that I really wasn't ready for, okay?" She looked defiant in the moonlight, hard and otherworldly, like someone whose cynicism was not shaped by age or circumstances but somehow innate. "I didn't want to dance the part. I told Paulette I couldn't. She insisted. My father insisted. Raoul insisted. Everyone insisted. I knew if I failed, I wouldn't get another chance at a lead for a long time. I didn't want to, but I did it. I did it knowing that everyone would compare me with Fatima and that I would end up looking bad." She sucked deeply on the last of her cigarette then dropped it to the sidewalk, letting the butt smolder. "So in answer to your question, I noticed absolutely no one and nothing the night of the performance. I was too scared to notice anything but my cues."

Auntie Lil appraised her silently. "How do you feel about being replaced?" she finally asked.

"Relieved," Julie answered. "I'm no fool. I could probably never dance that part. Perky is not in my repertoire."

It certainly was not, T.S. thought to himself. He had never run across a more depressingly mature teenager. It was as if Julie Perkins had been born old, made weary at birth by the weight of expectations.

"Why don't you live with your father anymore?" Auntie Lil asked abruptly.

The girl looked up in surprise. "He told you that?" she said.

"No, we went to see him and I looked in your room. I could tell you had moved out. Where are you staying?"

"With a friend," she said. "And I'm not telling you who because then you'll tell my father and he'll come and get me and try to make me come home. He sent you, didn't he?"

"No, he did not. Why don't you want to go home?" Auntie Lil asked.

"Because my father lives at home," Julie said simply. "And I hate my father."

She slipped her dancer's bag up on one shoulder and stepped between them, walking away as naturally as if she had just bid them a loving farewell. Two cabs screeched to a halt on Ninth Avenue when they saw her and she hopped into one nimbly, zooming away without a backward glance. Her silhouette was framed in the back window of the cab and looked as regally unmovable as the bust of an ancient Egyptian queen.

CHAPTER NINE

1. The next day Auntie Lil wasted no time in moving forward. The lawsuit had piqued her interest in Bobby Morgan's ex-wife, Nikki. And she knew a way to get to her. As Auntie Lil suspected, her lawyer, Hamilton Prescott, knew the partners of the firm representing Bobby Morgan's children. He arranged a meeting between Auntie Lil and Nikki Morgan for the next evening, but balked when told he could not attend.

"That is most unwise," he warned Auntie Lil. "I cannot allow it."

"I'm not going to talk about the lawsuit," she said. "Just her ex-husband."

"Her lawyers will be there," he warned her. "I can't let you go alone."

"I'll tape the entire conversation and bring Theodore," she told him. "But I cannot go in looking like I have litigation on my mind. I want to talk to her about everything but the lawsuit, don't you see?"

Prescott sighed. He knew there was no arguing with Auntie Lil. When she had her mind set, she was more immovable than a hound dog intent on sleep. "What about *her* lawyers?" he asked.

"You let me handle them," Auntie Lil said. "Don't worry. I won't make any promises. I'll hear no evil, see no evil, speak no evil."

Yes, the lawyer thought to himself, and you'll end up making monkeys out of us all. "Good luck," he told her. "And tape it."

"I will," she said, though she had no intention of bringing a tape recorder. She knew that Nikki Morgan would be reluctant enough to talk as it was. The newspapers had carried few comments from her on Bobby Morgan's death.

T.S. needed little convincing to attend the meeting. "Sure," he said. "The evening is fine." He'd be done with his dance lesson by then.

But when he returned from his lesson with Herbert, he found a most surprising individual waiting for him in the lobby of his high-rise. Mahmoud the doorman had allowed the visitor to wait for T.S. and was maddeningly nonchalant about the fact. "But he is an injured man," Mahmoud explained with feigned peasantlike simplicity when T.S. complained. "How could I turn him away into the streets?"

T.S. glanced at the forlorn figure of Hans Glick slumped on an upholstered love seat near the elevators, his right foot encased in a heavy cast. Crutches were propped against the wall behind him. "Did I leave instructions to admit any visitors?" he asked the doorman, teeth gritted.

"But Mr. Hubbert," Mahmoud protested, spreading his arms wide. "You live such an exciting life. I am but a humble doorman. I cannot resist the impulse to participate in your adventures. Please forgive me." His dazzling smile did little to lessen T.S.'s suspicion that Mahmoud lived to torment him. Still, there was nothing to be done.

"How do you do," he said, extending a hand to Hans Glick.

Glick struggled to stand. "You must forgive the intrusion," he said in his clipped accent. "I took the liberty of looking your address up in the phone book. I hope you do not mind."

Despite his apology, T.S. noticed, Glick did not hesitate to hobble after him into the elevators. "How can I help you?" T.S. asked as the elevator doors shut. He reminded himself to get an unlisted phone number and address as soon as possible.

"I must speak to you," Glick explained. "Businessman to businessman. I know your aunt relies on your good judgment. I have seen you with her often, and I have heard from my business colleagues that you are a most meticulous man. Like myself. That is why I have come to you and not to her."

"My aunt doesn't rely on anything except her own common sense," T.S. said firmly. Asking Glick in was redundant, he realized. The man had no intention of going anywhere else.

Glick glanced about T.S.'s immaculate apartment with approval. Modern chrome furniture gleamed immaculately atop spotless white area rugs and a highly polished wooden floor. The built-in shelves, understated sculpture, and open space appealed to his spartan sensibilities. "I see we are alike in our living tastes," he said.

But his look of approval turned to one of apprehension when Brenda and Eddie crept from their favorite hiding spot behind the couch. Tails switching, they slunk in unison toward the stranger, sniffing cautiously. Glick sat down on the couch abruptly, as if the weight of the cast had suddenly proved too much. He held the crutches in front of him and eyed the cats. "Why do they twitch their tails in that manner?" he asked faintly.

"Habit," T.S. replied. "Relax. They're big for house cats, I admit. But they *are* house cats."

Brenda and Eddie reached out their paws to scratch at the smooth surface of Glick's cast. Glick endured the contact with stoic dignity. "As I was saying," he said. "I have come to appeal to your good sense."

"In what way?" T.S. asked. He would not offer Glick a drink. The man's smooth exterior irritated him. T.S. had worked for decades with such men and had learned long ago not to trust them.

"Two things," Glick explained. "Your aunt seems convinced that I am to blame for this misunderstanding about the liability insurance."

"Oh?" T.S. asked. "If you are not to blame, who is?"

Glick frowned. "It appears one of my assistants failed to send in the quarterly premium, believing that the other policy would take effect sooner than it did." He paused. "I will have to fire her, of course."

"Why not just cut off her head?" T.S. suggested. "In the

middle of Lincoln Center would be nice. We could invite all the board members and maybe Reverend Hampton could arrange for a few protesters." He wasn't usually so sarcastic, but Glick's attempt to blame some poor hapless subordinate offended his personnel manager soul.

"I beg your pardon?" Glick's eyes widened. Humor was not in his repertoire—particularly humor directed at him.

"Never mind," T.S. said, sighing wearily. The day's dance lesson had exacerbated his sore right knee and he hated reminders that he was growing inescapably old. "What else did you want to discuss?"

"You haven't asked about my foot," Glick said. "I presume you have heard how it happened?"

T.S. knew, of course, but was not eager to admit that he had been lurking in the wings and seen everything. "I heard," he offered.

Glick's expression was grim. "I was not interfering," he explained. "I was merely correcting a glaring error. Martinez had no right to threaten me. I may well sue him over his actions. They led directly to my injury."

"Good idea," T.S. said absentmindedly, gazing longingly at his liquor cabinet. There was a fresh bottle of Dewar's inside.

T.S.'s wandering eye escaped Glick. "That is not important, however. What is important is that I have had an epiphany." Glick held a hand in the air and pointed toward heaven.

"An epiphany?" T.S. asked. Out of the corner of his eye, he saw Eddie's tail begin to switch more rapidly.

"Yes." Glick leaned forward breathlessly, staring intently at T.S. "As I was falling off the stage and into the orchestra pit, it suddenly occurred to me. I know how Morgan was killed." He let a dramatic silence fill the apartment, though it was marred by the scratching of Eddie's paw on Glick's cast. The cat had discovered that fine dust could be created by clawing the plaster and was busily making his mark on the unsuspecting guest.

"Tell me your theory," T.S. said, his Dewar's forgotten as a new thought intruded. He wished Auntie Lil was there to help him evaluate Glick's manner. Was he being too smooth? A little too enthusiastic? Had he seen them at the theater after all, up in the catwalk? Did he know they had already figured out how Morgan was killed? Was he trying to join their team, as it were, before he was suspected himself?

"Morgan was killed *before* the rope went around his neck," Glick explained. "Not strangled during the performance. Otherwise someone backstage would have seen him. I would have seen it." He stared intently at T.S. "Very little escapes my attention," he added. "I have wondered ever since the murder why I did not see the killer myself. I was backstage watching everything. I felt it my duty to ensure a smooth production. My honor was on the line as a member of the board."

Yes, and you are constitutionally incapable of letting well enough alone, T.S. thought to himself.

"I was all over that stage area," Glick explained. "The entire first act. I didn't see anyone unusual at all. Where then had the killer hidden? Where had the struggle taken place? Who had done the killing?" Glick's eyes gleamed and T.S. wondered if they had given him pain pills for his broken foot. He seemed stimulated well beyond his usual Swiss reserve.

"Go on," T.S. said, hoping the man might reveal more.

"As I was falling off the stage, I realized that Morgan must have been killed in much the same way." Glick continued. "I believe the struggle occurred prior to the performance, or perhaps quite early on. In a deserted area of the stage far from witnesses. Then Morgan was tied to the rope to make it look as if he were strangled and pushed to create the momentum that sent him swinging across the stage." He finished triumphantly, eyes still gleaming, and waited for T.S.'s reaction.

Glick was correct, T.S. felt sure. Auntie Lil had reached the same conclusion. But he was not about to give away their own theory. Instead, he forced himself to be enthusiastic. "I think you're right," he told Glick. "This is vital." He noticed Eddie's intense scratching for the first time and shooed his pet away from Glick. Eddie went sullenly, Brenda beside him, their ample rumps leisurely and defiantly strolling from the room. Once again their fun had been ruined. "You must tell the police what you have told me," T.S. said. "Immediately." That would get him out of his hair.

"Yes," Glick agreed. "I must tell them. Perhaps I can assist them in fleshing out this theory. Your aunt has been very stubborn in resisting my efforts to help her. The police may be more welcoming."

"Absolutely," T.S. agreed, bobbing his head so hard that he felt like one of those purple cows in the back window of cars. "Go to them at once and tell them all that you have told me here today."

T.S.'s enthusiastically biblical-sounding suggestion worked. It propelled Glick off the couch and onto his crutches. To T.S.'s intense relief, Glick made a beeline for the front door, stopping on his way out to ask a final question. "Is my theory consistent with yours?" he asked, once again in command.

"Our theory?" T.S. repeated, his laughter convincingly casual. "We don't have a theory. I'm just doing this to humor my aunt."

"Of course," Glick said, joining in the laughter. "Those old ladies. They have nothing else to do. We must do our best to keep them amused." He waited for T.S. to open the front door, then crutched his way to the elevator, his manner suddenly jaunty. "Onward and upward, eh?" he called back to T.S. as the elevator arrived. "I'm sure the police will be delighted to be enlightened," he said as the doors closed on him.

Sure they will, T.S. thought to himself.

2. "Glick said *what*?" Auntie Lil asked as their cab approached Nikki Morgan's apartment on Manhattan's Upper West Side. "How could he arrive at such a theory just from falling off the stage? I don't trust that man."

"Well, we can let the police decide for themselves." T.S.

paid the driver and endured Auntie Lil's usual unsolicited advice about what constitutes a proper tip. She was a notoriously generous tipper.

They approached the front door of the apartment building with awe. It was a magnificent ten-story stone structure on Riverside Drive overlooking a park that ran alongside the Hudson River. The neighborhood was a favorite of professional families who could not bring themselves to flee to the suburbs but nonetheless craved greenery along with their urban blight. Rents were astronomical, but the quiet more than paid for itself. Available apartments in the area were always scarce.

"She's not doing too badly for herself," T.S. observed. "I bet she got a ton of alimony."

"I bet she deserved it," Auntie Lil replied.

Nikki Morgan's attire at the funeral had been elegant and sparse. Her sprawling and crowded apartment was at odds with this image, but since it was home to four children, its chaotic atmosphere was easily explained. Even when quiet, as it was that evening, the scattered toys and clothes of four young lives filled every corner. In the living room, wedged between a pile of hockey equipment and a stack of computer-game cartridges, sat a beefy man with red hair.

"This is Harry," Nikki explained. "One of my lawyers. He insists on being here. He's afraid you've come to twist my arm into a settlement. He's going to tell me what to say and I am going to ignore him. He's promised not to make a peep unless you mention the lawsuit." When she smiled, her austere face was transformed into one of singular beauty. T.S. wondered what she had ever seen in Bobby Morgan. Auntie Lil wondered the same. Nikki seemed remarkably friendly and willing to talk. Either she had remained silent to the press out of some particular quirk of her own or the nearly empty bottle of red wine that sat on a sideboard had only been recently opened.

"I don't want to talk about the lawsuit at all," Auntie Lil explained. She scooped a pile of freshly folded laundry off a chair and plopped it on top of a radiator with the practiced ease of one who wholeheartedly endorses the pile method of organization in her own life. "I think that's best kept between the lawyers. I only wanted to get a chance to meet you, to talk to you a bit about your husband. I believe you know about my role as the board's official representative investigating your husband's murder."

"Ex-husband," Nikki reminded her as she perched on the edge of a small French antique chair that had miraculously escaped annihilation in the child-oriented household. T.S. chose a chair across from their hostess in hopes of seeing her smile once again.

"Ex-husband," Auntie Lil agreed. "We are not trying to solve the case per se. We leave that to the police. But we do want to aid them in their efforts and we do have access to so many more people. . . ." Her voice trailed off as she sought the right approach. "So without interfering, we are pursuing our own path. Just to reassure ourselves that the board is doing everything humanly possible to find the killer."

"I see," their hostess said cheerfully. "You want to cover your butts. Perhaps some of you even have a conscience."

"Exactly," Auntie Lil conceded. "I suppose all of us are motivated by the desire to cover one end or the other. How is Mikey, by the way?"

"Mikey?" She looked surprised. "You know, you are the very first person to ask how my son is doing." She glanced around as if to assure herself that they were alone. "I sent them out to the movies. All four of them. It's not easy for Mikey to be living back at home. He's more of a stranger to his brothers and sister than anything else at this point. Bobby taking him to L.A. was the fastest way he could possibly have alienated him from his siblings. But there was nothing I could do. He's doing quite well right now, I think, though it's hard to say. Mikey has always shown emotion only on cue. Even as a baby, he rarely cried or smiled. He usually just watched everyone else as if trying to figure out exactly what was in any situation for him." Her bright smile faltered. "He's a lot like his father, actually."

"You sound as if you didn't approve of what your ex-husband did for your son's career," Auntie Lil said.

"Approve of it?" Nikki Morgan stared at Auntie Lil. "Don't you ever watch television?" she asked. She popped up suddenly and strode to the sideboard, where she poured herself a healthy glass of red wine. "Drink?" she asked, but all three guests declined.

Auntie Lil looked apologetic. "I'm afraid I don't watch television."

"How wonderful!" Nikki looked at Auntie Lil with new admiration. "I try so hard to keep the kids from rotting their brains watching too much T.V., but it's impossible. I'm surprised you missed the tabloid reports. Bobby and I broke up specifically because we disagreed on how he should handle Mikey's career. He wanted to milk him for every dollar while he could. I didn't see the point. We already had more money than we could possibly need. I thought Mikey deserved what was left of his childhood instead. But Bobby always wanted more money and more fame. I accused him of violating his parental duties. He accused me of trying to steal money from Mikey. Our fight over Mikey's career was the basis of our whole divorce."

"He sacrificed the marriage over money?" Auntie Lil asked.

"Not over money. Over fame," Nikki explained. "Bobby never stopped trying to make up for being bumped out of the spotlight. When I first met him, it was about four years after his show had been canceled. He was only twenty and in despair. I thought I could help him. I loved him. I got him to go back to school, to study business. We started a family right away. I was very young when Mikey was born. I wanted to show Bobby that life held a lot more than the chance to be on the cover of *TV Guide*. At first I thought he agreed. But as the children grew older, I realized that I was nothing more than a broodmare to him and that he looked at our children as potential clients more than anything else."

"That's ghastly!" T.S. burst out. His own mother had

been less than affectionate, but she had never gone so far as that.

Nikki shrugged. "At the time it was happening, it wasn't so horrible. I didn't see it. It took nine years of therapy for me to figure it out. I just thought he wanted the best for his kids. When he insisted on getting their teeth straightened right away, the dance lessons, the modeling schools, the speech training, I just thought he wanted to make sure they were well prepared for a capricious world. He really wanted to make sure they looked and acted like professionals on camera."

"Are your other children in show business?" Auntie Lil asked.

Nikki shook her head firmly. "Not for lack of trying. They see what their brother gets—the money, the attention, the letters, the absurd spectacle of adults falling all over themselves to get near him—and they want it, too. But I'm not letting them get near it. Period. When they are out of college and away from the house, it will be their choice. Until then, the only camera any of them will get in front of is my Instamatic on their birthdays."

"That must be a very difficult policy to maintain," T.S. said.

Her eyes flashed with resolve. "It is, but I feel quite strongly about it. Bobby took Mikey's childhood away from him. I am not going to let it happen to the others."

"Surely that drives a wedge between Mikey and his brothers and sister," Auntie Lil said.

"I'm not sure we should discuss—" the red-headed lawyer began.

"Oh, shut up, Harry. Who cares?" Nikki took a healthy gulp of wine. "It does divide them, but the damage is done. Can you imagine being a child and worshiping your father? Then one day he announces that he's moving to the other side of the country and taking someone with him—only that someone isn't you. It's your older brother, who is special enough to go with him. I spent the last two years trying to repair the fallout from that stunt. I'm almost there. They have their own circle of friends, school activities, something they do better than the others. I try to see them as individuals and I'm succeeding." She leaned against the sideboard as she spoke, her small chin pointed out defiantly as if daring anyone to disagree.

"Does Mikey have any friends?" Auntie Lil asked.

Nikki's smile was bitter. "Not many, if you mean friends his own age. He moves around too much for that. And it's hard to be sure who really likes him and who is just trying to use him. That's always what bothered me the most—the piranhas that swam around Bobby, hoping to feed: the producers, studio execs, rock stars, groupies, you name it. Bobby always acted like those people were the greatest, the warmest, the most loyal of friends. I knew they were slime." She stared out the window thoughtfully. "Children are quite resilient, you know. I'm amazed at how much faster they can bounce back from trouble than I can. So when Bobby called to say that Mikey was taking the role in *The Nutcracker* and that they would be in New York for a couple of months, I hoped that maybe it would give him enough time to make some friends here and to get to know his brothers and sister again."

"Is that why your ex-husband wanted Mikey to dance in *The Nutcracker*?" Auntie Lil asked. "Mikey was doing so well in the movies. Why take a step backward?"

Nikki's eyes were unnaturally bright as she stared at Auntie Lil. "I don't know why Bobby wanted Mikey to return to New York," she said softly. "Maybe Bobby wanted to be near our family, too. I like to think that. You have to know how my husband grew up to understand why he became who he was. Bobby's mother pushed him constantly as a child. She was frantic to get them out of Bensonhurst. It worked. She became a legendary stage mother. He took them out of Queens and into the Promised Land of Los Angeles. But Bobby never learned to love anyone just for who they were. He was always looking for what they could do for him. And he never thought anyone could love him back just for being himself, either. He kept wanting to know what I wanted of him." Her eyes filled with tears. "All I

while the blonde continued her well-rehearsed monologue without taking the slightest notice of the commotion behind her. She began to recap the known facts about Bobby Morgan's death.

"Gene Levitt is just getting released?" Auntie Lil said. "Two days seems a long time just for questioning."

"And why do I think that isn't his usual lawyer?" T.S. asked. Levitt's regular lawyer, T.S. knew, would be wearing a suit that fit. Word must have reached everywhere that the producer was flat broke.

The blonde had finally worked her way up to her late-breaking tidbit. "Prior rumors proved unfounded this evening as a producer embroiled in questionable business deals with the deceased was released after nearly two days of questioning. Apparently, attention was deflected from the suspect when a previously unknown associate of Bobby Morgan's called the crime team in charge of the case and revealed details of Morgan's death until now known only to the coroner's office and detectives assigned to the case. One delighted detective on the case termed the unexpected event as akin to 'the bad apple falling right out of the tree and into our laps.' "

"So much for confidentiality," T.S. muttered. "And similes."

"Although the name of the new suspect is not yet known, I have been assured that a plainclothes team is bringing him in right now and we are on the spot to bring you this important development live." The blonde's eyes sparkled with the prospect of barging in on the bust. T.S. could practically see her calculating the resulting rise in her ratings.

"Oh, dear," Auntie Lil said. What sounded suspiciously like a giggle erupted from her lips. She pointed to the television.

T.S. stared in disbelief as a crippled Hans Glick was hustled into camera range by two huge plainclothes detectives. There was no need for his crutches as each massive detective was gripping him firmly by an arm and practically lifting him off his feet. Glick's wire-rim glasses were askew, his normally impeccable hair stood on end, and his self-assured face had dissolved into a flushed and panicked study in frustration.

"Here comes the suspect now!" the newscaster cried, pouncing on Glick with the swiftness of a cat on a baby sparrow. She thrust the microphone in Glick's face, bumping it on the tip of his nose. "What is your name, sir?" she shouted above the commotion.

"Come on, Sally. Knock it off," one of the detectives growled, trying to elbow the newscaster away. She held her place and the detectives were forced to stop and figure out a way around her.

"Sir! What is your name?" The microphone knocked Glick on his top lip and he jerked upright, perhaps realizing for the first time that hundreds, maybe even thousands, of his clients and coworkers were likely watching the late-night news and witnessing his humiliating march into po-lice custody. He ducked his head with the unerring instincts of a thrice-convicted felon, hiding his face from the prying camera. Twisting, he attempted to turn his back and his bro-ken foot bumped the newscaster in the shins. She looked down and spied the cast. New headline-making theories zigzagged through her brain before tumbling from her lips. "Sir! Did you have that cast before you were taken into custody? Have you been brutalized by the police?"

"Oh for chrissakes, Sally," the detective nearest her shouted. "Get the hell out of the way! We didn't touch the guy. Now beat it." Lifting Glick up in the air, his two escorts bore him over the tangle of camera and microphone wires. One of the detectives hip-checked the newscaster solidly as they passed. She bounced against a bystander and right back into the trio, catching Glick's plaster-encased foot in her stomach. She skidded sideways from the impact, but recov-ered and started after them. Suddenly new prey caught her at-tention and she froze like a pointer spotting a duck. "Follow me!" she whispered at the camera and viewers were swept along again, rushing past sleeping junkies and unknown drunks being hustled up the precinct stairs. "Reverend Hamp-ton!" the newscaster called out. "Ben! Just for a minute."

The figure dominating the archway into the precinct

stopped and turned to the cameras with a graceful and effective sweep. Ben Hampton smiled broadly, at home in all his cinematic glory. Lights blazed and the cameraman scrambled to adjust the lighting for this well-known media icon.

"He looks different," T.S. said. "What happened to his hair?"

Indeed, the Reverend Ben Hampton was a changed man. In place of his electrified hairdo was a well-cropped buzz cut that accentuated the kingly shape of his head. He had ditched his trademark bright tie for a subdued navy one that complemented his tasteful charcoal-gray suit. As he held out his hands for quiet, the entire sidewalk fell silent as if awed by his personal magnetism. When he spoke, his voice was softer than usual, more authoritative and less strident. It swept his listeners along like a mighty current, pulling them toward his conclusions.

"I am here voluntarily this evening," he explained into the camera. "I have put the unfortunate incident of my misguided arrest behind me and have taken it upon myself to report back to the police with additional information I may have on the true murderer of Bobby Morgan—father, agent, Hollywood man extraordinaire."

"Are you kidding?" T.S. asked the television out loud. Talking to inanimate objects was another Hubbert trait.

Hampton bowed his head as if he were wilting under the weight of many sorrows. "It is a sad day in this city's history when no one is safe from crime. When no one—not even those of us fortunate enough to live in the crystal palaces of Lincoln Center—can escape random death." He looked out at the cameras with blazing eyes. "I am taking it upon myself to fight crime in this city starting right here and now. In every way and by every means possible. Tomorrow, I urge you to look for a column in *New York Newsday* outlining my twenty-point plan for preventing crime. A column by our city's most talented award-winning reporter, Margo McGregor." The newscaster's mouth puckered at this and her microphone wavered. She wasn't keen on plugging a competitor on air. Sensing her displeasure, Ben Hampton grabbed the microphone and began talking into it as he paced the steps. He looked like the lead minister at a gospel revival. "Join me in my fight against crime on all fronts!" he exhorted. "We will fight crime from our homes and on the streets." He paused and flashed a bright smile. "My allies in this fight are many. For example, I am proud to announce that the Metropolitan Ballet has named me to their board and agreed to increase its scholarships to minorities as a way to enable our children to leave the streets and take to the stage in the search for normal lives, where dreams are reachable and crime unthinkable."

"What?" Auntie Lil shrieked, rising from the sofa. "I never said he could be a board member."

"What exactly *did* you say?" T.S. asked, alarmed.

"I can't remember! I can't think." She sat down abruptly. "Oh, dear. No one is going to like this."

Within minutes, T.S.'s phone began to ring.

"Don't get it," Auntie Lil warned.

"Don't worry," he replied.

"How do they know my number?" he asked grimly as the fourth frantic message from a board member was recorded for posterity on his answering machine. It had been preceded by three from local television stations and newspapers.

"I put you down in case of emergency. I guess Lane Rogers considers this an emergency," she said glumly. "She probably got rid of the press by sending them to me."

"You mean to *me*," he corrected her. By midnight, his entire supply of answering-machine tape had been used and still no word yet from Lane Rogers or, worse for T.S., from Lilah Cheswick.

"Lane's probably waiting in a car outside my apartment," Auntie Lil said. "Hoping to run me down."

"Anything's possible," T.S. said as he finally unplugged the telephone.

"I don't know if I can sleep," Auntie Lil admitted, staring at a now blank television screen.

"Then spend the time thinking of what you're going to do to get out of this mess," T.S. suggested as he swept out of the living room intent on sleep. There were some problems she'd have to solve on her own.

CHAPTER TEN

1. "You can't be serious," T.S. said as he watched Auntie Lil use most of a tub of cream cheese on a single half of bagel. "They'll lynch you if they see you."

"Unfortunate choice of words, Theodore. I must go. I want to talk to the boy. And I haven't time to deal with this Reverend Hampton mess. They'll have to figure it out on their own." She scraped the last of his sour cherry jam from the jar and eyed it with disapproval. "Can't you buy bigger jars?" she asked.

He removed the sticky spoon she had dropped on the bare surface of his treasured oak dining table and carefully sponged the spot clean. He put down yet another place mat, which she promptly ignored. There was no point in chastising her. She simply did not notice.

"What can Mikey Morgan tell you?" T.S. asked.

"That's what I want to find out. But I better go in disguise. The board will be out to tan my hide." She thought for a moment. "Do you still have that fedora I gave you in 1964?"

"Still in the original box," he said grimly. "As if you didn't remind me of it constantly."

"Perfect. And I'll need to borrow your black jacket. I'm sorry but I must insist you sit this round out. We would simply be too conspicuous together."

If Auntie Lil's aim was to avoid being conspicuous, she failed miserably. Her idea of a disguise was to look like an elderly and chubby Marlene Dietrich. She tucked her wiry white hair up under T.S.'s black fedora and smoothed out its brilliant scarlet band. She wore her black crepe trousers from the day before with one of his oversized white T-shirts and his black tuxedo jacket. The odd thing was, she looked wonderful. Even odder, hardly anyone gave her a second glance when she boarded the crosstown bus that would take her to Lincoln Center for a matinee of *The Nutcracker*. Of course, this was New York City—and most of the attention went to a well-dressed man at the rear of the bus who was eating sunflower seeds, mumbling to himself and wearing a pair of boxer shorts upside down on his head.

To Auntie Lil's chagrin, the Metro's rear fire-exit doors had been locked, against all regulations she knew. She hovered near a tree for cover and scouted around for errant board members. She had neither the energy nor inclination to tangle with anyone over the Reverend Hampton. Fortunately, the maintenance man, Calvin Swanson, appeared before any board members did.

"Pssst!" Auntie Lil hissed from her spot behind a tree. She stepped out into the sunlight and adjusted the brim of the hat low over her eyes.

"Why are you dressed up like that, Miss Hubbert?" Calvin said. "You look real sharp, but seems to me that's evening wear."

She placed a finger to her lips. "Avoiding the board," she explained.

"Can't blame you." He raised his eyebrows. "They got another one of them emergency meetings scheduled for today. I had to clean the room. There's an agenda printed on the chalkboard. You're on it."

"Me?" Auntie Lil asked. "What did it say?"

Calvin shrugged. "Just your name. 'Lillian Hubbert,' it said, right at the top under a heading called 'New Business.' "

"Oh, dear," she said absently. "They believe I'm responsible for Reverend Hampton thinking he's on the board." She didn't add that she *was* responsible.

"Yeah," Calvin said, drawing the word out into four syllables. "I saw him on television last night. I was a bit surprised myself. Didn't think the board had the gumption to let a man like that sit among them. I must say I've gained some new respect for the board. And what about that Swiss fellow? Think he did it? He sure did look guilty, didn't he? Ducking his head and all." He stroked his chin thoughtfully as he contemplated the possibility that Hans Glick would be sent up the river for life. "I'd like to see him try and get along with a warden, the way he keeps trying to tell folks what to do."

One of the exit doors opened and a pair of nervous parents scurried out to take their seats in front for the matinee. Auntie Lil stared at the door, then at Calvin. Calvin shook his head.

"Please, Calvin," she said.

"I've got orders to keep them locked," he explained. "From the top. That chairman lady."

"She's breaking the law," Auntie Lil explained. "Those are fire doors. They are supposed to be kept unlocked at all times. You could get in trouble if anything should happen."

Calvin shrugged and produced a huge ring of keys from his pocket. "Sorry, Miss Hubbert. Can't help you. But I do need to unlock that door, come to think of it. Seems I can't find my mop." He fiddled with the lock and tried a couple of keys until he found the right one. The door opened with a metallic bang and he propped it ajar with a pail of soapy water he was carrying. He poked his head inside then stared across the courtyard. "Must have left my mop in the main building. Guess it will take me a good ten minutes to get the dang thing." He headed off slowly without looking back. She was no idiot. The moment Calvin was far enough out of sight to be able to claim a clean conscience, she slipped inside the theater and hid behind the first flat of scenery she found.

It was quiet backstage. The show would begin in half an hour. She could hear the distant murmur of voices and an occasional thump, but the area was so immense that most of the action was taking place much closer to the stage. She stepped cautiously from her hiding place and inched along the wall to stage right. She wanted to see the spot where Bobby Morgan had been cut down.

A group of dancers had beat her to it. As she drew near

she saw a circle of figures bent over the spot where Bobby
Morgan's body had lain. The dancers were already in cos-
tume, making it impossible for her to tell who they might
be. She detected five toy soldiers, several mice, and a
number of young boys in nineteenth-century garb. One of
the mice was using his tail as an impromptu noose and
demonstrating an apparent theory on a willing toy soldier.
Auntie Lil watched this charade then realized with sicken-
ing clarity that one of the toy soldiers might be Mikey Morgan. How could he reenact his own father's murder? One of
the boys spoke, eliciting laughter, and as he pointed overhead, the others followed his gaze and stared up at the catwalk. Several heads nodded in agreement. Their meeting
was interrupted, however, by the stout figure of Paulette
Puccinni. She wore a peacock-blue caftan embroidered with
hot-pink flowers. As she shooed them away from the spot
and into place on various sides of the stage, Auntie Lil
stepped behind the oversized grandfather clock used in the
show to watch the dancers take their places.

   Young Rudy Vladimir padded by on soundless feet, his
innate grace obvious even when he was merely walking. He
was dressed as Drosselmeyer and wore a large top hat. A
big black cloak flapped behind his slender figure. He scurried across the passageway and waited quietly in the wings,
stage left. A burly man clad in blue jeans and a plaid shirt
walked past Rudy, stopped, leaned forward to check out
Rudy's face, then walked on. The man had black hair that
was thinning on top and a permanent scowl. He was wearing headphones and held a clipboard in one hand so he
could check off items on a list as he walked. He headed directly toward Auntie Lil's hiding place but stopped abruptly
to open a fuse box in the wall. He examined the fuses carefully, made a few check marks on his list and continued on
his rounds. When he was a few feet in front of her, Auntie
Lil stepped from her hiding place and called out to him.

   "Yoo-hoo. Young man."

   If a woman well into her eighties dressed as a man surprised him, the crew member did not show it. He squinted
and stepped closer to get her in better focus. He was either

nearsighted, drunk, or quite possibly both. "Who are you?" he asked. He looked down at his list. "You're not in the show."

"I'm on the board," she explained.

"No board members backstage," he said firmly in a voice that was just slurred enough around the edges to confirm that he had been drinking. "New rule. Who can blame them?"

"I just want a quick word with you," she explained, tilting the fedora back so he could see her face. "You're part of the technical crew, aren't you?"

"I'm Ricky Lee Harris, the lighting director," he said slowly.

"Were you working the night Bobby Morgan was killed?"

He stared for a moment without speaking, as if waiting for a signal to be sent from his brain to his mouth. "Yes," he finally said. "I work every opening night. Most nights, in fact. And most matinees, too. I need the overtime. What's it to you?"

"I wondered if you noticed anything unusual that night," she said.

"Unusual like how?" he demanded, shifting impatiently from foot to foot. "I went over this with the cops, you know."

Auntie Lil glanced up at the rafters. "Unusual like someone up on the catwalk where they don't belong."

"Hey," he said, holding up a palm and backing away. "I was the only one up on the catwalk, okay? Me, myself, and I. Are you saying that makes me the killer?" His tone grew instantly belligerent as he changed moods with the mercurial swiftness of the drunk.

"Not at all," Auntie Lil replied sharply. She had no patience with people who could not control their liquor intake. "I just need the benefit of your eyes. You were here. I was not. Did you see anyone unusual near the catwalk, even just on the third floor near its entrance perhaps?"

He shook his head but opened his mouth at the same time, froze for a second, then snapped it shut.

"You did," Auntie Lil stated matter-of-factly. "You saw something, didn't you?"

The man stared at Auntie Lil as if debating whether to try to fool her or not. "Maybe," he finally admitted.

"Please tell me," Auntie Lil said evenly. "You may be in danger if the killer believes you know something. It might be better if you tell."

Harris shifted the clipboard and slipped his right hand into a rear pocket. Rocking back and forth on his heels, he studied Auntie Lil. "No one saw me," he said quietly. "I saw someone, but I can guarantee you they didn't see me. I was hidden behind that side curtain over there." He nodded toward a series of short curtainways stored at stage right. "I saw a guy who was sort of out of place."

"What did he look like?" Auntie Lil asked.

"I couldn't tell," Harris replied. "It was just a guy in a cape."

"Why didn't you step forward earlier?"

He laughed and the sound was bitter. "They'd think I was hallucinating. Puccinni's out to get me. Says I drink on the job. You think I'm stupid enough to come forward and say that I saw some tall dude in a big black cape all wrapped around him so I couldn't see his face?"

"A cape?" Auntie Lil asked. "Maybe it was just Mikey Morgan playing Drosselmeyer?"

Harris shrugged. "Could have been," he acknowledged. "Except his cue is on the opposite side of the stage. It's hard to say."

Auntie Lil nodded. "Did you notice anything else unusual about him?"

He chewed on the end of his pencil. "He wasn't wearing the right kind of shoes. They were shiny and black. Dress shoes. That's all."

"What size?" Auntie Lil asked.

He stared at her like she was daft. "Do I look like a shoe salesman to you?" he asked, before turning and walking away.

She was disappointed he couldn't tell her more, but her thoughts were distracted by the scene unfolding onstage. In the final moments before curtain, Fatima Jones was practicing the timing of a difficult passage. It was the first time that Auntie Lil had seen the young ballerina dance outside the confines of a rehearsal room. The girl was impossibly lithe and as delicate as a gazelle, an impression enhanced by her creamy tan color. Her arms flowed through the air as if made of fluid, not flesh, and her long neck curved up to cradle an oval head. Her features were delicate and uniformly slender, from her thin curving nose to an exquisite mouth and perfect almond-shaped eyes. As she moved about the stage she seemed to float from spot to spot, propelled by long legs unfettered by gravity. As she executed a series of graceful jumps, a pair of young dancers scurried across the set, anxious to take their places in time for curtain. Fatima missed crashing into them by inches and drew back angrily, her eyes flashing fire. Her body rose in height as her long neck seemed to grow even longer, like a snake advancing on its prey. Her nostrils flared as she advanced on the two boys and her dark eyes pinned them in a haughty glare. Before she could scold them, they dashed away in fear.

Fatima Jones had more than the physical requirements for a prima ballerina. She also had the attitude.

Auntie Lil's thoughts were interrupted by the sound of applause. The orchestra was taking its place. Should she wait around and see the first act from backstage, trying to find out more about when Bobby Morgan could have been killed? Or should she take the information she had learned from Ricky Lee Harris and call it a day?

Her decision was made for her. A tall blond man hurried toward her and gripped her elbow. "How nice to see you again," Andrew Perkins said between clenched teeth. "But I believe we are both trespassing."

"Get your hands off me," Auntie Lil whispered, shaking her hand free.

"You're strong for an old lady," he said, rubbing his hand where she had pried it free. "Don't get excited. It's just that I saw Martinez heading this way. I assume you know him and are as eager to avoid him as I am."

Being discovered by Martinez *was* a very good reason to hurry. Auntie Lil slipped silently along the back wall toward the exit door, followed by Perkins. "What are you doing here?" she asked.

He hesitated as if he were about to lie, but changed his mind. "Looking for my daughter," he said. "She hasn't been home in over a week."

"I know," Auntie Lil said as they emerged into the bright light of the afternoon sun. "Want to tell me why?"

"No," Perkins said, turning on his heels and hurrying down the pathway to Ninth Avenue.

She was about to follow when the unmistakable hulking figure of Lane Rogers turned the corner and headed down the walkway toward her. A smaller figure shouted at Lane from behind, and when she turned to see who it was, Auntie Lil took the opportunity to slip into the familiar bower of bushes so prized by Ben Hampton. She waited in the cool darkness, protected by overhanging leaves, as Lane Rogers and Ruth Beretsky walked past.

"But you can't have a meeting about getting rid of her without inviting her," Ruth was saying. "It isn't fair. You don't even know if she promised him the seat."

"What do you know?" Lane said angrily. "Just shut up and do what I tell you."

"I know plenty," the smaller woman cried, stopping to glare at her companion. "I know a lot more than you think."

"What does that mean?" Lane asked calmly.

"I heard you talking to Bobby Morgan," Ruth said angrily. "I heard every word you said."

"That was nothing," Lane reassured her. "I didn't mean any of it."

"Yes, you did," Ruth hissed back. Her voice caught in her throat—she was close to tears. "You meant every word."

"Oh, Ruth," Lane said, putting an arm protectively around her friend's shoulders. "You make too much of the little things. Sometimes we say stuff we don't really mean. Come on. We're going to be late for the meeting." They hurried down the pathway, leaving Auntie Lil to contemplate just exactly what had been said to whom.

2. "Why do you want to talk to Mikey?" Nikki Morgan asked. She was dressed in a black linen dress and wore a matching hat decorated with tiny red roses. She looked quite Italian and very beautiful. More than one man passing across the plaza slowed to admire her.

"I've talked to some people who were backstage the night that your ex-husband was murdered," Auntie Lil explained. "They may have seen an extra person. Someone who didn't belong. I want to ask Mikey what he remembers."

Nikki checked her wristwatch, then squinted through the sunlight at the door of the theater. "He'll be out in about five minutes. He meets me away from the crowd so no one will know who he is. But I have to pick up the other kids from the YMCA in half an hour after their swim lessons. It's about five blocks down Broadway." She tapped a delicate foot against the pavement, her high heels making a firm *tap*, *tap*, *tap* as she thought things over. "I'll let you talk to him for the hour it takes me to get the other kids dry and dressed. Then we'll meet back here. You can take him to a coffee shop or something. Buy him an ice-cream soda."

"Ice-cream soda?" asked Auntie Lil. "That sounds like a normal kid to me."

Nikki Morgan looked at Auntie Lil from over her sunglasses. "Don't be too sure. You'll find that he eats only brand-name ice cream and *real* whipped cream. And he knows the difference."

3. Auntie Lil was in agreement with Mikey Morgan on the subject of real whipped cream. Perhaps that was why she felt so instantly at home nestled with him in a booth at Rumpelmeyer's, the ridiculously overpriced café on Central Park South. It was famous for its ice-cream treats and solicitous nature toward the children of rich tourists. At that particular moment, late on a Saturday afternoon, the joint was quite literally jumping as screaming children crawled over leather-back chairs, raced through the dining room, careened around scowling waiters, and knocked seven-dollar-a-scoop ice cream into their parents' laps.

"More sugar all around," Auntie Lil murmured, but nonetheless did not hesitate to slurp the bottom of her ice-cream soda out with a straw. "Let's get another one," she told a surprised Mikey Morgan.

He had been very quiet throughout his first course of plain ice cream, ordered so he could vouch for its freshness and designer label. He perked up at her suggestion of more and decided on a banana split. Auntie Lil told the waiter to make it two. The waiter agreed readily since, at Rumpelmeyer's prices, two more orders of dessert would come close to pushing the bill into high tip territory. He had decided that Auntie Lil was an aging film star who no doubt lived in a nearby hotel. He was not quite sure if Greta Garbo was dead or not, but he knew enough to be certain that confident old women in black fedoras were forces to be reckoned with—and might even be able to get him a part in a movie or two.

"Know why I want to talk to you?" Auntie Lil asked Mikey when the overly helpful waiter had left and they were alone again. They had exhausted their supply of small talk, which had chiefly consisted of making fun of Paulette Puccinni. Both Mikey and Auntie Lil had suffered humiliation at her hands in ballet class and this had helped establish common ground between them.

"Yes. About Dad's murder." The boy's expression was hidden behind the oversized sunglasses he wore. They were an effective means of disguise. His face was so small that the lenses obscured most of his distinguishing features. The only recognizable components of Mikey Morgan, child star, were his ears and his generous mouth. So long as he refrained from his trademark grin and stifled his well-known war whoop, they had a chance of remaining undetected.

Auntie Lil got right to the point. "You entered from stage left when you danced Drosselmeyer, didn't you?"

"Yeah," he said. "So what?"

"So you weren't hanging around onstage right the night your father was killed? Near the spot where his body was cut down?"

The boy stared at her, but his eyes were hidden from her return scrutiny by the sunglasses. "No. Not until afterward."

"I saw you with your friends today before the performance," Auntie Lil said. "Examining the spot where they cut him down."

"So?" he said defensively, squirming in his seat.

"What were you doing?" she asked gently. "I heard some of the boys laughing."

"I wasn't laughing," he said.

"But what were you doing?" she persisted.

"We were just trying to figure out how he had been hung up that way," Mikey explained. "Why we didn't see him fighting back or hear him or anything." He might have been talking about a scene in a movie for all the emotion he displayed. Auntie Lil wondered how long he would be able to keep it bottled up inside him.

"And the laughter?" she prompted.

Mikey sighed. "Just kid stuff. We were nervous. We were talking about hanging Pork Chop Puccini next time around. We thought she'd go good early on when Drosselmeyer first enters the party. It would make the scene so much more interesting. Drosselmeyer could reach out his boney old fingers for Clara and *whap*! Pork Chop's fat body would come flying across the stage and smack him in the face." He stretched out his hands to demonstrate. "I hated playing that part," he added. "Dad made me."

"Why?" Auntie Lil asked.

Mikey shrugged. His banana split arrived and he dug in with gusto, eating each section precisely in neat bites before proceeding to the next one. Auntie Lil watched the whipped cream disappear and one half of a banana before she spoke again. "Did he say why he wanted you to dance the part?" she asked.

"He wanted us to be in New York," Mikey explained. "And he thought it would do me good to sit a couple of months out, make people a little anxious that maybe I wasn't coming back. Might drive my price up. Do you know how much I get per movie now?" He raised his eyebrows expectantly.

"Yes," Auntie Lil said firmly, hoping to stop him before he could slip into his movie-star role. "Are you aware that your father pulled you out of a movie and broke a contract for you to do this?"

Mikey shrugged again. "It happens all the time. It was a dumb movie anyway. The story line treated me like a kid. Dad explained it all. It would have been bad for my image."

"Did you always do everything your dad said?" Auntie Lil asked.

He had finished the other half of the banana and was carefully spooning hot fudge into his mouth. The lower half of his lip was smeared brown with the goo and this typical display of childishness was reassuring to Auntie Lil. "I tried to," he finally said. "Dad knew what he was doing."

A young girl walked by dressed in seductive clothing far too old for her tender preadolescent years. Her blond hair was coiled on top of her head and she wore plenty of makeup, though Auntie Lil doubted she was even a teenager yet. Mikey watched her walk by with obvious appreciation. "Her skirt is up her butt," he said, giggling, then eyed Auntie Lil for a reaction.

It reminded Auntie Lil of something: like father, like son. "Did your dad have many girlfriends?" she asked. "Did you meet any of them?"

Mikey wiggled his eyebrows theatrically. On the movie screen, it was cute. In person, it bordered on the obnoxious. "Dad was a stud. He had tons of girlfriends."

"How lovely for your mother," Auntie Lil murmured.

"They were divorced," he explained patiently, as if she were particularly dim-witted. "Guys are supposed to be studs," he added. "Besides, Dad said Mom was seeing someone new anyway. Except I can't figure out who it is."

Auntie Lil mumbled something under her breath and

Mikey looked at her with new interest. "What did you say?" he asked.

"Nothing," she replied. What she had said was that she hoped Nikki Morgan was dating a marine so he could help whip Mikey into shape.

"You don't like kids, do you?" Mikey asked as he scraped the last of the crushed pineapple from one end of his dish.

"No," Auntie Lil admitted. "I don't like children. Not that you seem like much of one to me."

"I'm very mature for my age," he explained matter-of-factly. "Most adults love me. Why don't you?"

"I don't like your attitude," Auntie Lil replied. "You strike me as being a bit on the flippant side. Considering your father has been killed."

He sat back and stared at Auntie Lil. "Everyone thinks I should be boohooing," he said angrily. "I'm not going to cry unless I really feel like it." Auntie Lil shrugged, which only made him madder. "Why should I cry just because he got himself killed?" Mikey demanded. "It was his own fault. He was screwing people right and left, everyone told me so. He was a shark, they would say, like it was such a great thing. I was the one who made all the money, but he was the one who got all the credit and he was the one who got to spend it. It wasn't fair. I didn't even like him very much." He thumped the backs of his heels against the seat with vicious energy and several people turned to stare.

"You didn't like your own father?" Auntie Lil asked quietly. "Are you sure that's true?"

"I know what I like and don't like," Mikey said belligerently. "Dad didn't care about me. He just thought I could make him rich. He never spent any time with me. He was always running off to dinner with some producer or taking some bimbo out for lunch or attending some reception where he knew there would be lots of girls with their boobs hanging out of their dresses. He was always out having fun while I had to sit alone in some dumb hotel room watching movies on television. He wouldn't even let me go home and visit Mom and the others last Christmas. Said I had to stay and finish this stupid, stupid movie in Toronto. I hated him."

"No wonder," Auntie Lil said quietly.

"He just wanted to come to New York for some dumb old woman," Mikey said suddenly. "He acted like it was for my own good, but I heard him talking to her every night." His voice rose as he mocked his father, his eyes rolling up in his head as if he were in the throes of ecstatic love. "Don't worry, beautiful. I'll be there soon! We'll have hours together. He'll be too busy. He'll never notice. I have the perfect cover." Mikey finished his imitation and pushed his empty dish away grumpily. "What a jerk."

Auntie Lil stared at the young boy. His lower lip was pulled in tightly and his face was rigid. He was determined that no emotions escape. "Mikey," she said. "If you are ever in trouble, you can come to me for help."

"What do you mean by that?" he asked sullenly.

Auntie Lil shrugged. "If you ever want to talk to me about anything, or if you find yourself in trouble, just call me or come by my apartment. I'll help you if I can." She wrote her phone number and address down on a napkin and slid it across the table toward him. It was insurance against all the things she was sure he had not told her.

He stared at the napkin for a moment, then crumpled it up and stuffed it in a back pocket. At least he hadn't thrown it on the floor—or blown his nose with it, as she had first feared.

Auntie Lil reached across the table and took his hands in hers, ignoring his attempts to pull away. "Mikey," she said, "your mother loves you very much. And she is angry and sorry for what happened to you over these past few years. She missed you while you were gone and now she's happy that you're back with the family where you belong. Why don't you let her help you right now? If you feel bad, she can make you feel better."

He tugged his hand away but could not stop the flush spreading up his face. "Of course I'll let her make me feel better," he said in a mocking tone. His voice dropped, growing serious. "She is my mother, you know. I'd do anything for her."

CHAPTER ELEVEN

1. It had been a maddening week of missed phone calls for T.S. and Lilah. When he returned her call about the Metro-board mess, he got her answering machine. When she returned *his* return call, he had just stepped out with Auntie Lil. In his opinion, modern technology only meant modern frustration. Thus, when Monday rolled around, T.S. made the decision to stay put. "I'm not going anywhere today," he told Auntie Lil. "I'm tired of traipsing all over Manhattan. I want to stay home with my cats and, yes, turn my brain to jelly watching television. Maybe I'll order in a deli sandwich for lunch. I may even put on a torn T-shirt and watch some more football."

"Nonsense, Theodore. You're just waiting for Lilah to call." Auntie Lil's disapproval seemed to snake through the telephone wires. "Really, Theodore—sitting around mooning and waiting for a phone call like some lovesick teenager. I thought you were more in control of your life."

"You're joking, aren't you?" T.S. replied. "What in the world makes you think I'm in control of my life?" He replaced the receiver firmly and turned his attention to the first soap opera of the day.

With T.S. unwilling and Herbert suspiciously missing in action, Auntie Lil was forced to tackle the day's agenda on her own. She had slept little the night before, wondering just what the board had discussed about her. Surely they would have called if she had been voted off the board. Or would they? And if she had been voted off, who had decided that she was responsible for the Reverend Hampton misunderstanding? Okay, maybe she *was* responsible, but she still wanted to know who the tattletale had been. She contemplated the possibilities as she drank her four cups of black coffee and nibbled on an Entenmann's cherry cheese strudel. The strudel was not as good as her mother used to bake—it had tasted straight out of Vienna—but it was good enough that she polished off an entire pound of it in a single morning.

She would just have to confront Lane Rogers on her own. There was no other way around it. That was how you dealt with slugs anyway, she reasoned. You dragged them into the sunlight and watched them writhe. Lane would hate public exposure of her sneaky tactics. Auntie Lil would go right to where she worked and demand a conference and do her best to embarrass Lane into being up-front for once. Auntie Lil hated people who ruled through innuendo. Why had she fought Lane on her terms until now? It was time, Auntie Lil decided, to take a direct approach.

Lane worked in the corporate communications department of Bartlett Brothers International, a global investment bank. As the official arbitrator of corporate identity, her job was to ensure that the company's logo and adopted colors appeared on every scrap of paper, coffee cup, T-shirt, trinket, and publication offered under the Bartlett Brothers name. It was the perfect job for Lane. It had little real importance to the bottom line, yet yielded her frequent opportunities to meddle in other people's plans. She had no real power except the power to compromise someone else's deadline. And she could squelch creativity at every turn, imposing a drab universe—so comforting to her—on anyone foolish enough to request official approval of their project. She also frequently sat in on meetings to review the design and copy of corporate brochures. Her favorite trick was to say nothing during the meeting—her enigmatic smile, she felt, was her best attribute—but shortly afterward, she would fire off a lengthy memo pointing out exactly where and why the writing or graphics were once again inadequate and why the writer or designer must be replaced. To say she was hated was an overstatement. She was not important enough to hate. She was, instead, loathed

by all Bartlett Brothers employees with spines and pitied by
all those with better things to do with their lives.

The opinions of Lane's coworkers mattered little to
Auntie Lil, however. The time had come to express her
opinion about Lane. When she entered the gilded and mirrored tower in midtown that housed the posh offices of
Bartlett Brothers, her resolve had built to the point where
not even a tank could have stopped her. She steamrolled the
lobby receptionist, shanghaied the elevator guard, talked her
way past a dim-witted secretary on the public-relations
floor, and confused Lane's personal secretary so thoroughly
("Did you say you were related?") that she gained entrance
into a private conference room within seven minutes of setting foot in the front door. Lane was meeting with a junior
copywriter who had made the colossal mistake of asking
her to approve a two-page circular they hoped to provide
large clients with each week. Auntie Lil burst into the room
wearing a lavender pant suit and matching hat just as the
copywriter sputtered, "But how can you say that? You
haven't even read it yet!"

Lane's mouth shut abruptly when she recognized Auntie
Lil.

"Surprise," Auntie Lil said gaily.

Lane's face reddened and her coworker stared. Who in
the world was this old woman? he clearly wanted to know.
Lane's mother? Lane's lover? Lane's boss? The young
copywriter took a chance. "She says the copy isn't corporate enough, not subdued enough," he whined. "But she
hasn't even read it yet." He thrust the pages toward Auntie
Lil.

"The copy is just fine," Auntie Lil said absently, pushing
the manuscript back across the table. "What lovely headlines. Now run along and write something else."

"Thanks!" the kid said, rising from the chair and fleeing
with this mysterious approval in hand before his luck
changed.

"Terrorizing babies now?" Auntie Lil asked.

"What do you want?" Lane demanded, but her voice was
curiously weak. She was wearing a bright red A-line dress

from an expensive department store. Auntie Lil knew the manufacturer well. The dresses went for four times their actual value to people attracted by labels and too stupid to recognize poor workmanship. A matching scarf had been tightly wound into submission and was anchored at Lane's neck with a large gold pin. Her hair was still anchored in a severe bun and no offending tendrils dared escape during office hours. Despite her careful grooming, however, her inner spite still sat upon her face with a heavy dourness. Her eyes were puffy and red.

"What do you want?" Lane demanded again. "Tell me before I call a security guard."

"Why did you hold a meeting yesterday and not inform me?" Auntie Lil asked.

"That is board business and it is inappropriate to discuss it while I am under the employ of someone else."

"You tell me right now," Auntie Lil said, "or I will pick up the phone and call my nice banker at Sterling & Sterling, the one who is best friends with your chairman. I can have you selling hot dogs on a street corner by the end of the week."

"How dare you?" Lane said, rising to her feet.

"How dare I?" Auntie Lil repeated. "Let me tell you something. I have sat back and let you rule that board like a petty demagogue for far too long. You have successfully blocked any attempt at bringing the Metro into the twentieth century thus far and Lord knows what you'll do when faced with the twenty-first. But you have made it personal by going behind my back and I do not intend to roll over and play dead while you interfere with my life. You tried your best to block my appointment as the board's representative into Bobby Morgan's death. I want to know why. I want to know what you are hiding. And you called a meeting yesterday with my name on the agenda. You tell me why right now."

"This is my office," Lane said angrily.

"This is my life," Auntie Lil replied.

"It's your fault, promising that awful Reverend a seat on the board."

"I did no such thing. Whoever told you that is misinformed."

"*He* told me that," Lane shot back.

That made things a bit more difficult. "He misunderstood me," Auntie Lil said smoothly. "I don't consider it a very big deal. Simply tell him he is mistaken."

"Apparently no one else considers it a big deal either," Lane said bitterly. She stared out the window. "The board refused to remove you."

"Isn't loyalty wonderful?" Auntie Lil said.

Lane glanced at her sharply. "You don't know a thing about loyalty," she said.

"I think I do," Auntie Lil replied. "More than you will ever know. Now tell me why you're blocking my inquiries into Bobby Morgan's death."

"I believe the dead should be left to rest in peace," she said piously, folding her hands together and shifting her gaze to the door of the conference room as if praying for an interruption.

"Nonsense," Auntie Lil said. "That man is not resting in peace. He was strung up like a prize turkey and put on display. Humiliated in front of an enormous audience. Quite a fate for a former actor, don't you think?"

"He deserved exactly what he got," Lane burst out.

"Oh?" Auntie Lil leaned across the conference table and scrutinized her foe. "If you don't explain that remark, I will be forced to form my own conclusions."

"Form whatever you like," Lane said abruptly. She rose and marched toward the door, plodding forward as gracelessly as an all-terrain vehicle. "I have an important luncheon engagement. This interview is terminated."

Auntie Lil watched her go, then heard the slam of an office door farther down the hall. Lane had chosen to barricade herself behind her corporate walls, where she felt safest. So let her, Auntie Lil thought to herself. She had found out the two things she needed to know most. One, she was still on the board, and two, Lane had taken a most definitely personal interest in Bobby Morgan and had been rebuffed. Hell truly hath no fury like a woman scorned,

Auntie Lil reflected. Especially a divorced, proud, and lonely woman like Lane, who seldom put her heart on the line.

She rode the express elevator back down to the lobby and reminded herself not to feel sorry for the woman. Lane wallowed in her own unhappiness, and this self-indulgence robbed her of the joy everyday life had to offer. Auntie Lil loathed professional victims. There were too many unwilling victims in this world more worthy of her sympathy. She would not waste her time on the self-involved.

But she would waste her time on a cappuccino, she decided, especially if it allowed her to determine who Lane planned to meet for lunch.

The lobby of Bartlett Brothers had been an architectural wonder when first built. An entire wall was taken up by an artificial waterfall. Auntie Lil loved the sound of the water gurgling downward and the feel of the fine spray on her face. She ordered a large cappuccino and settled in at a small table to spy on the entrance. Half an hour later she saw Ruth Beretsky enter the lobby and start toward the elevators before hesitating as if deciding whether or not to turn back. Auntie Lil was out of her chair with the agility of a woman several decades younger. Abandoning her cappuccino, she waylaid Ruth before she could choose a final path.

"What are you doing here?" Ruth asked in alarm as Auntie Lil grabbed her elbow.

"I visited Lane and tried to talk to her," Auntie Lil said. "She's not talking."

Ruth removed her arm from Auntie Lil's grip and rubbed petulantly at her elbow. "What's there to talk about?" she said.

Auntie Lil sighed, then seemed to change the subject entirely. "How often has Lane stood you up for lunch?" she asked a startled Ruth.

"What? Why do you want to know?" she answered.

Auntie Lil shrugged. "I just wondered. A relationship is an interesting exercise in power, don't you think? The way the power shifts so subtly, from one person to the other, according to the tiniest of events. Like how one person is always treating a friend worse than they expect to be treated themselves. And doing things like standing up their friends for lunch. It's a way of showing that you are the superior person, I think—and that your friend is someone who can be pushed around."

Ruth stared at her suspiciously. "So what?"

"Ruth." Auntie Lil put an arm around her shoulders and guided her away from the elevators toward the outer doors. "How long have you been Lane's friend? How long have you endured being bossed around by her? Stood up for lunch? Kept waiting? Poked fun of to amuse her other friends?" As Auntie Lil talked Ruth's back tightened, telling her she was on the mark. "I don't want to tell you what to do, dear, but I will say that I do not treat my friends the way Lane treats you."

"She's my mentor," Ruth insisted. "She got me on the board. It was a coveted spot. And she has helped me quite a lot in my career."

"She has helped her own career quite a lot, thanks to you," Auntie Lil pointed out. "Who gets credit for those neatly typed agendas, for the comprehensive board reports, for the meticulous planning of all the meetings and functions?"

Ruth was silent.

"Come, dear," Auntie Lil prodded her. "I know you're the one doing the work. But she's the one getting the credit."

"She made fun of me!" Ruth suddenly cried out, her hands clenching into fists at her side. She wore her trademark big bow at the base of her neck and it drooped forlornly, as if sensing its owner's sorrow.

They had reached the outer door. The sun shone brightly, forbidding unhappiness on such a fine day. "I know a wonderful outdoor café," Auntie Lil said. "Do something different with your life. Stand Lane up for a change. Let me treat you to lunch. Here comes a cab now."

Ruth stared at the approaching taxi with the wide, grateful eyes of a maiden being rescued. Her glance darted to the elevators, then returned to the cab. "I will," she said, waving the taxi to a halt with an extravagant gesture. "It will serve her right."

Fifteen minutes later they were seated at a prime sidewalk front table where Auntie Lil could watch the foot traffic in Greenwich Village go by. She had known the restaurant's owner for years and had been a regular patron ever since it first opened its doors. That, combined with her overtipping, made her a favored customer.

"They sure like you here," Ruth observed as a waiter rushed to fill their water glasses. "Whenever I go out to eat with Lane, she bosses everyone around and pretty soon you can't find a waiter anywhere."

"You are going to eat a lot today," Auntie Lil decided, casting a disapproving eye on Ruth's skinny frame. "You're far too thin."

"I have a nervous stomach," Ruth confessed. "I have a nervous everything, in fact." She laughed in an uncertain manner as if she was trying on a sense of humor and wasn't quite sure it fit.

Auntie Lil smiled. "In that case, we'll begin with black-bean soup." The restaurant specialized in Cuban food, and before Ruth could fathom what had happened, Auntie Lil had ordered a three-course lunch for them both, complete with roast pork, avocado soup, fried plantains, and beans and rice. The sheer excess of this order made Ruth's eyes widen; the bottled beer that quickly arrived made her relax.

"I feel like I'm playing hooky from school," Ruth admitted. "Look at me. I look ridiculous compared to the rest of the world." She glanced down at her unflattering brown business suit, comparing it with the colorful dress of the Greenwich Village natives parading by. Though the air was cool, many still wore their brightly hued summer clothes and matching sandals.

"What did you mean when you said Lane made fun of you?" Auntie Lil asked once most of Ruth's first beer was gone. Given her weight and inexperience at drinking, it was probably enough to start her talking.

Ruth blushed. "My mother and sister tell me she's no

good for me," she admitted. "They don't like Lane at all. They say she thinks she's too good for the rest of the world. But Bobby Morgan, he didn't think she was good enough."

"He rejected her?" Auntie Lil guessed.

Ruth nodded happily and Auntie Lil wondered if, in some deep recess of her lonely heart, Ruth had harbored a flame for Bobby Morgan as well. "She was always throwing herself at him," Ruth explained. "It was embarrassing in a way. But I liked seeing Lane embarrass herself," she added defiantly. "All the other women on the board whispered about it. I overheard them talking about it sometimes."

"This was during *Nutcracker* rehearsals?" Auntie Lil asked. "It went on for over a month?"

"Oh no," Ruth said, gulping the last of her beer. Auntie Lil signaled for more. "Much longer than that. Lane met Bobby Morgan at a charity ball that the Metro held in Los Angeles last year. She made a fool of herself that night. First of all, she had on a Grecian gown, one of those flowing white things, you know?" She draped a napkin over her shoulder to demonstrate. "I know I'm not Miss Fashion Sense, but Lane is kind of big and, well, hulking, to be wearing curtains draped over her body."

"Quite," Auntie Lil said grimly.

"Anyway, we went to the fund-raiser together. It was very exciting for me. I had never been on the West Coast before. But when we got there, Lane kept trying to pretend that she wasn't with me. I don't know why." Her face flushed slightly. "I thought my dress was much more appropriate than hers. It was a long blue gown covered with these little bows that—"

"I'm sure it was lovely," Auntie Lil interrupted. "Now, about Bobby Morgan?"

"Lane met him at the fund-raiser and went crazy over him. I could tell you the exact moment it happened. Being her slave has its advantages, you know." She gave a half grin. "I see everything she does. He kissed her hand when he first met her and she almost went through the floor. But he was just kissing her butt because she was chairman." Ruth looked up in alarm. "Please excuse my language."

Auntie Lil dismissed it with a wave. "It paints an accurate picture. Do continue."

"He was sucking up to everyone he thought was important and people were sucking up to him right back. The celebrity turnout was sort of low. Bobby Morgan was about the biggest thing there. I guess no one is really into ballet out in Los Angeles. Not snappy enough, I suspect."

"No doubt," Auntie Lil agreed.

Ruth sighed. "I could tell he was just flattering all the women, but Lane took her compliments seriously. On the plane home, he was all she talked about. I got quite bored with it, you know. I wanted to sleep. Six months later, when Lane found out that Mikey Morgan wanted to dance in *The Nutcracker*, she got it into her head that it was all because his father wanted to be near her." She gave a bitter laugh. "For once, I wasn't the pitiful one!"

"What happened during rehearsals?" Auntie Lil prodded.

"Lane made a regular fool of herself. Always hanging around the halls, trying to talk to him. It was easy because he was hanging around, too. She thought he was waiting for her. But one day I saw him with his arm around another woman, way at the other end of the hall."

"What did she look like?" Auntie Lil asked.

Ruth shrugged and gulped at her fresh beer. "I couldn't tell. She was tall and had long dark hair pulled into a bun. I only saw her from behind."

"Straight or curly hair?" Auntie Lil asked.

"I don't know," Ruth admitted. "It was pulled back too tight. But she was a dancer, I think. She was tall and thin."

It didn't narrow things down much. Of course she'd been a dancer. It was a ballet company. "Were they an item?" Auntie Lil asked.

Ruth shrugged again. "I didn't hear if they were. But I did know then for sure that Bobby Morgan didn't even care who Lane was, much less have a thing for her. It made me happy, to tell you the truth." She looked at Auntie Lil as if daring her to protest her ill will. "I was sick of Lane and her theories about why they weren't together yet. She was like a lovesick teenage girl. Only meaner."

"Meaner?" Auntie Lil asked.

Ruth nodded miserably. Her soup arrived and she eyed it suspiciously.

"That's just avocado in a chicken broth," Auntie Lil explained.

Ruth took a sip and seemed pleasantly surprised. "Could I have another beer?" she asked.

Auntie Lil signaled for more beer, wondering if she would have to pour the woman into a cab when they were done. "How was Lane mean?" Auntie Lil reminded her.

"A couple of days before the opening night of *The Nutcracker*, I overheard her talking to Bobby Morgan in the hall," Ruth explained. "They were at one end of the third-floor hallway, near the shoe room, and I was coming up the connecting steps from the second floor. I heard my name, so I stopped and listened." Her voice dropped to a lower pitch and grew pompous as she imitated Lane. "She was saying, 'Bobby! How nice to run into you again. We seem to be on the same wavelength, don't you think?' He mumbled something and she gave this phony laugh and said, 'That silly Ruth, you know, the ghost of a girl who follows me everywhere, poor thing. She doesn't have a life and just worships me. I try to help her, but you know how it is. If you haven't got it, you just haven't got it.' " Ruth's face threatened to crumple and Auntie Lil hastily pushed the fried plantains her way in an attempt to distract her. Ruth bit her lower lip and recovered. "She went on to tell him that I had seen him at the end of the hall with someone in the company and then she reminded him that fraternizing with corps members was a bad idea."

"What did Bobby say to that?" Auntie Lil asked.

"He gave this really mean laugh—and I was glad—and said something like, 'Unless, of course, I'm fraternizing with a board member, is that it, Ms. Rogers?' He would never call her Lane, you know. He didn't even want to be that familiar with her."

"What did Lane say to that?" Auntie Lil asked.

"She got all stiff and offended and said something like, 'I have no idea what you're implying, Mister Morgan. No idea at all.' Then she huffed off. I would have felt sorry for her except for the nasty things she said about me. She was making fun of me, her only real friend, just to try to look better for some sleazy, oily old agent from Los Angeles who was getting fat and wearing too much gold jewelry. And then she expected me to be loyal and follow her every command—even after I told her I had heard everything!"

Auntie Lil recalled the conversation she had overheard between Ruth and Lane at Lincoln Center. "You were at the meeting yesterday, weren't you?" she asked Ruth. "When Lane tried to vote me off the board?"

"How did you know about that?" Ruth asked. Her plate of food arrived and she dug in with gusto. Two and a half beers had stripped her of all assumed defenses and she was acting like a young girl.

"I have my sources," Auntie Lil said.

"I didn't think it was fair and I told her so," Ruth said angrily. "She wants to ruin people's lives, everyone's lives, just because she hates her own. But it didn't matter in the end. The board voted to keep you on. No one knew if you had anything to do with that Reverend Hampton mess. Most of the people said that without any proof, it was silly to even call a vote. Boy, was Lane mad. She wanted to replace you on the board with someone else."

"Who?" Auntie Lil asked curiously.

"Emili Vladimir," Ruth explained. "Rudy Vladimir's mother."

"Emili Vladimir?" Auntie Lil repeated. "It seemed to me that Lane didn't like her when she interrupted the board meeting the other day."

"That was before Lane found out that Emili had been a famous ballerina in Russia," Ruth explained. "They'd never met before. Now that Lane knows who Emili was, she wants to suck up to her. Which shows you how little Lane really knows about ballet. If she knew anything at all, she would have known who Emili was from the start."

"When did she come up with the idea to replace me with Emili Vladimir?" Auntie Lil asked.

"She said something like it would be better to have Emili as a friend than as an enemy. I was sort of surprised that Emili even wanted a seat on the board. I thought she was too busy with the Freedom Ballet Company to care about us."

"Freedom?" Auntie Lil asked. "I've seen them at the Joyce Dance Theater. But they border on modern dance. Emili Vladimir is associated with them?"

Ruth nodded. "She helped found it about six years ago, but she mostly choreographs and teaches. She doesn't like the limelight. It was sort of a big deal, that the great Emili Vladimir would turn her back on classical ballet. One of those nuances dance people get all excited about. Hey, these are pretty good." Ruth gobbled down two more fried plantains.

Auntie Lil watched in alarm, wondering if she would have to order another plate to satisfy her own preferred quota. "I think I donate money to Freedom," she said thoughtfully.

"Sounds like you donate money to everything," Ruth observed. "That's another reason they wouldn't throw you off the board."

"Money can be useful," Auntie Lil admitted. "Very useful, indeed."

2. If Ruth had needed help returning to her office, Auntie Lil might have gone straight home to ponder the inner workings of Lane Rogers's weaselly mind. But since Ruth slammed the cab door shut and zoomed away in that singularly intent manner of drunks trying very hard to appear sober, Auntie Lil was left with most of the afternoon still at her disposal. What better way to spend it than taking a nice stroll up Hudson Avenue, which just happened to turn into Eighth Avenue, which, in turn, just happened to take Auntie Lil right by the Joyce Dance Theater?

The woman at the box office knew her well, since it

could be argued that Auntie Lil paid her salary in a round-about fashion. She directed Auntie Lil to a rehearsal space in a warehouse building on Twentieth Street. She would probably find Emili Vladimir there.

Many people have tried to articulate the difference between classical ballet and modern dance over the years, particularly the exact categorization of modern ballet—which often seemed neither here nor there. But Auntie Lil had no problem defining what set one apart from the other: it was the attitude. And it was a relaxed attitude that greeted her when she stepped out of the groaning freight elevator onto the main floor of the Freedom Ballet Company's headquarters. The Metropolitan Ballet would never have tolerated the heaps of gym bags stacked in one corner, or the group of huddled dancers sitting cross-legged near the window, chatting while others worked out. Nor would the Metro ever have allowed the thumping bass beat that filled the room to contaminate its speakers.

Emili Vladimir stood in the center of the immense floor. She was dressed in plain black leotards, legs bent out to the side and pelvis thrust forward as she instructed a muscular black male dancer on the proper technique to use when flinging his redheaded partner high into the air. Unlike ballet, which allowed for only the most carefully prescribed movements, Emili's choreography apparently called for wild twirling and an abandoned tossing of the female into the air by her partner. Each time the dancers rehearsed their series of steps, it looked—and felt—quite different. This immediacy was one reason why Auntie Lil preferred the more spontaneous modern style to classical ballet.

After about fifteen minutes of practice, the pair had the athletics down to perfection and retired to a far corner of the room to practice timing and ancillary gestures. Emili Vladimir watched them go, then ran a hand through her wavy hair and retied it loosely with a scarf. She was drenched in sweat but still breathing easily. "Natasha!" she called out, snapping her fingers sharply. "Bruce, Marianne, Ralph, Trevor, and Sylvia: start from the top of the second movement. All the way through. Watch the pacing. You're dragging. Remember the half beat." She clapped her hands to illustrate as dancers obediently scurried into position and the music segued into a New Age conglomeration of waterfall-and-bell sounds. Satisfied with their initial efforts, Emili turned her back on her dancers and strode toward Auntie Lil with confident grace.

"How do you do, Miss Hubbert," she said, extending a hand. It was dry and cool, despite her recent exertion. "How can I help you?"

"You remember my name," Auntie Lil said.

"I remember everyone's name," Emili answered, managing to make it sound somewhat ominous. "Habit." She had a mournful voice that dragged at the ends of words, imparting all she said with an air of regret.

"Are you aware of my role in looking into Bobby Morgan's death?" Auntie Lil asked.

"Yes, of course I am," Emili answered, guiding Auntie Lil to an empty corner of the floor where they could not be overheard. "You're dragging, Bruce!" she shouted across the room, and a tall dancer with thinning hair instantly picked up the pace of his rapidly pattering feet in response.

"So you're aware of what I'm trying to do?" Auntie Lil asked.

Emili picked up a towel that was draped over a heating pipe and wiped the sweat from her neck and shoulders. "Let's not beat around the bush, as you Americans say," she said slowly. "You and I both know that the board must find his killer or the Metro will be finished."

"You'd make a skilled board member," Auntie Lil murmured, hoping to learn more about Lane's attempt to put Emili on the board.

"Perhaps. I have my doubts, however, as to whether I'd want a seat on the board. I have had enough politics to last a lifetime."

"Would you be effective on the board?" Auntie Lil wondered aloud, hoping to provoke a reaction. "I have heard that you and Paulette Puccinni are enemies. And she is ballet mistress."

Emili sighed. "I am not her enemy. I am her excuse. She

gave up a good, perhaps great, career to indulge a broken heart and a wounded ego. She blames me for her break with the American Ballet Theater. I had nothing to do with it. I have no emotion toward her except for pity. If she needs to blame me, so be it. Perhaps she could not live with herself knowing that she did not have the courage it takes to continue performing when you begin to grow old. I could tell you much sadder stories than hers."

Auntie Lil suspected that this last statement was an offer to digress and refused to take the bait. She had visited Russia in the early fifties on a fur-buying mission and had learned to spot the Russian tendency of laying a trail of red herrings as a way to deflect unwanted attention from personal topics. "Did you know Bobby Morgan?" she asked instead.

Emili froze, the towel extended like wings on either side of her shoulders. She stared at Auntie Lil. "Of course I knew who he was," she finally answered. "He was the man responsible for blocking my Rudy from dancing the parts he deserved. Fortunately, talent triumphed."

"Did you ever talk to him?" Auntie Lil asked.

"I am in the habit of knowing my enemies," Emili replied. "Not consorting with them."

"Did he ever speak to you?" Auntie Lil persisted.

"I do not recall," Emili said. "If so, I have forgotten." She raised her eyebrows at Auntie Lil. "Your method of questioning is rather reminiscent of the KGB. You make me feel quite guilty and here I have done nothing to arouse suspicion."

In truth, she had not. But Auntie Lil could not shake the feeling that Emili was the key to some part of the mystery. Perhaps it was only her bearing, her obvious mistrust of others, or more simply, her foreign accent. It was nothing she could articulate, but she wanted to know more about the woman.

"You think I had something to do with his death," Emili stated. "Which proves you do not understand me at all. Come home with me tonight. I will show you something. And then you will understand."

"Home with you?" Auntie Lil asked.

"Yes. Have you ever been to Brighton Beach? I will feed you stuffed cabbage. You can meet Rudy. And I will show you something that will prove that I could not have participated in the death of another human being." She turned her back on Auntie Lil to gauge her dancers' progress.

Auntie Lil thought the invitation over. It was singularly foolish to go rushing off in the middle of a murder investigation to an unknown abode. Herbert and T.S. would be frantic with worry, she hoped. It would serve them right for abandoning her just when she needed them the most. Besides, she adored stuffed cabbage and she hadn't lived life to its fullest for more than eighty years by being timid.

"I'd love to come," she said.

CHAPTER TWELVE

1.   Waiting for a phone call was juvenile, but sometimes it worked. Besides, it gave T.S. the opportunity to reach his friend Victor in the personnel department of Salomon Brothers. Despite their friendship, he was evasive. Andrew Perkins had not exactly quit voluntarily, but then he hadn't been fired either. In these days of lawsuits on every corner, it was the best T.S. would be able to get out of his former colleague.

"You're not thinking of hiring him, are you?" Victor asked. "I thought you were retired?"

"I am," T.S. admitted. "I'm just checking his references for some volunteer work with the Metropolitan Ballet." That much was true, at least.

There was a silence on the other end of the phone and T.S. could feel his friend's professional facade cracking. "Well, he's honest," Victor finally said. "But he probably wouldn't perform well under a lot of pressure. He had trouble coping with everyday stress during his final months here on the job."

T.S. thanked his friend and hung up grateful that he had left the fast-paced world of investment markets and changing fortunes far behind. A translation of Victor's words from personnel lingo pointed to a probability that Andrew Perkins had suffered a nervous breakdown. He would not have been the first superstar bond salesman to have bailed out from the gut-wrenching career in such a fashion.

When the phone rang around three, T.S. knew instantly that it was Lilah. Despite his inexperience with matters romantic, he had learned in the past few months to trust those unfamiliar tingles that his heart produced long before his brain kicked in.

"Theodore? I can't believe I got you in person." Her voice caused a pleasant flame to ignite in his belly. He grinned idiotically at his cats.

"I've had the machine on for days," T.S. admitted. "That business with Reverend Hampton has the board up in arms. Everyone has been calling here looking for Auntie Lil."

"Did she have anything to do with it?" Lilah asked.

"Of course she did," T.S. admitted. "But she says it's all a misunderstanding. Where have you been?" He had not intended to be so direct, but her familiar voice, full of delight at talking to him, gave him courage.

"Very busy," Lilah said. "I can't tell you the details right now. I'm sorry I'm being so mysterious. It's business and it wouldn't be ethical to talk about things before they're completed. Please forgive me. One day I will explain."

T.S. was the king of keeping private matters close to his chest. But that didn't make him any less annoyed when others tried the same trick. "Agreed," he said with false cheerfulness. "Will this keep us apart forever?"

"It better not!" Her laugh was rich. "In fact, I was calling to see if you wanted to meet me for dinner tonight. Just you and me. It will have to be midtown, I'm afraid. I have a meeting with my lawyers before then."

T.S. suggested Michael's Pub since it was a Monday and Woody Allen would be leading a jazz and Dixieland band on his clarinet. Lilah agreed to meet him there at nine o'clock and T.S. hung up feeling like the winner of a particularly grueling Olympic event. He was exhausted and elated at the same time. He realized with surprise that a great band of tension had relaxed in some unexplored part of his psyche. Lilah wanted to see him after all. Her absence had nothing to do with her feelings about him. He thought.

There was no point in taking a shower. He was still so clean from his morning ablutions that he squeaked when he walked. Yet he was so nervous that he could not stand to sit in his apartment, watching the hands of the clock move.

He decided he would go insane if he didn't leave the apartment. Perhaps a tour of the Museum of Modern Art would help. At least it would give him something to talk about with Lilah later.

He selected a cashmere sweater from the pastel drawer of his light coverings bureau, then chose a navy jacket from among the depths of his meticulously organized closet. He looked rather spiffy, he thought, surveying himself in the mirror.

T.S. was a handsome man, but his immersion in his career had occupied him so totally that he had never been aware of his physical attractiveness. His lack of vanity was appealing, and because of this, he was twice blessed: he was neither hard on the eyes nor hard on the ego. His abundant head of thick gray hair was, he felt, becoming more distinguished every day thanks to growing silver highlights. He wore it fuller each year as others his age fell by the thinning wayside. It was a tribute of sorts to the great genetic god who had spared him the male-baldness-pattern gene. His features were nearly identical to those of Auntie Lil. He had high, round cheekbones, a solid nose, and a widely generous mouth. His large eyes had a habit of growing dark when he was angry, a trait that many an employee had noticed with alarm before he retired.

"What do you think?" he asked Brenda and Eddie, modeling his attire. The cats yawned in boredom, took a swipe at his trousers, and wisely scurried beneath the bed to avoid counterattack.

T.S. was feeling incredible by the time the elevator reached the lobby floor. He looked good, he had money in the bank and Lilah lined up for dinner later on. Thus, all his elation shattered in a thousand shards when he spotted a distraught and disheveled Jerry Vanderbilt steaming toward him across the lobby like a determined process server. Mahmoud the doorman scurried behind him, shouting in a combination of Arabic and English.

"Mr. Hubbert! Mr. Hubbert!" Mahmoud pleaded, his black-and-gold cap askew. "I told him you didn't live here! But he did not believe me!"

"Good thing, too," Jerry said angrily, glaring at Mahmoud with indignation. "As we can both see that you were lying."

"You call me a liar!" Mahmoud cried. He took off his cap and threw it to the floor as if signaling for a duel. T.S. stepped quickly between the two men.

"Mahmoud was just acting on my orders," T.S. explained. "I was waylaid in the lobby by a distraught person this weekend."

"Well, you're being waylaid by another distraught person today," Jerry cried, grabbing T.S.'s sleeve like a beggar desperate for alms. "I was picked up by the police. The police! Right on the corner next to my apartment building. My newsstand man saw the whole thing. How can I ever face him again?"

"Picked up?" T.S. asked, prying the man's strong fingers from the arm of one of his best jackets. Pianists sure have strong grips, he thought to himself.

"The police?" Mahmoud interrupted, his eyes narrowing. "You are a fugitive?"

"Get this man out of here!" Jerry demanded, stomping his foot.

"He works here," T.S. explained tersely. "Why don't I get you out of here instead." He fixed Mahmoud with what he hoped was a no-nonsense gaze. "If anyone else comes looking for me," he warned softly, "I don't live here. Understand? Anyone at all!" He hustled the accompanist out the door, enduring the stares of several building residents entering. No telling what the neighbors thought now that distraught gentlemen were accosting him with regularity in the otherwise tranquil lobby of the exclusive building.

"I had no one else to turn to," Jerry apologized as T.S. marched him down the block to a coffee shop he frequented nearby.

"Where's your pal Miss Puccinni?" T.S. asked grumpily. He hoped Jerry didn't start sniffling or make a scene. He had to live in this neighborhood and his continued dignity was most important to him.

"She's turned on me," Jerry said miserably. "Stabbed me

in the back. Revealed her true colors. She's nothing but a perfidious liar, a two-timing Judas. No telling what she's saying about me right now."

"Let's hope it's nothing like you're saying about her," T.S. said. He steered the distraught pianist to a corner booth where he had a hope of avoiding his regular waitress. Ordering coffee for them both, he turned to Jerry with resignation. "Tell me what happened," he said.

"I'm a little hungry from all the excitement," Jerry hinted.

T.S. sighed. "What do you want?"

"I'll take a jumbo cheeseburger, medium rare. With fries," he told the waitress as she hurried away. "You're paying, right?"

T.S. nodded, thinking to himself that Auntie Lil would be the one to pay—with interest.

"Artist's salary," Jerry apologized mechanically. "I haven't eaten in six hours. Can you imagine? They picked me up early this morning and dragged me into a grimy precinct somewhere in the heart of Hell's Kitchen and began grilling me like a common criminal. I had to sit across a desk from two detectives who were positively brutal in their questioning."

"What did they want to know?" T.S. asked.

"You would not believe the extent of Puccinni's betrayal," Jerry confided. He leaned forward and dropped his voice to a near whisper. "When she heard that Gene had been detained by the police, she called them up and said that we were lovers. She intimated that I might have information on that odious Bobby Morgan's death. I know what they wanted. They were looking to hang an accessory-to-murder rap on me."

T.S. suppressed a groan. The recent popularity of true-crime and law-enforcement shows on television made every man and his brother think he was F. Lee Bailey. "*Are* you his lover?" T.S. asked sensibly.

"Maybe I am," Jerry answered, offended. "In this day and age, reliable suitors of my age are hard to find. I will not deny that there was a certain emotional attachment between us, but the possibility of my having gained information via pillow talk is absurd. We had better things to do than chat in bed."

His burger arrived. T.S. felt queasy just smelling it. He had given up consuming mass quantities of partially cooked animal flesh several years before. He might nibble on a discreet sliver of veal every now and then, but mountains of ground meat were out. Jerry had no such reservations. He bit into his burger and munched with the hearty enthusiasm that perpetually thin people alone can afford to show.

"Why did the police think you were involved?" T.S. asked.

"They believe that someone who knew the ballet must have been involved," Jerry explained. "They didn't come right out and say it, but I got the impression that Morgan was killed at a very specific time during the first act. Probably during that over-the-top crescendo the orchestra pulls out in the dance of the brats."

"Dance of the brats?" T.S. asked.

"You know. That melee in Act One when all the little boys leap around with imaginary guns shooting each other and the girls swoon with their imaginary dolls and the adults jostle each other along the edges and everyone is vying for the audience's attention. God, more people than you see at Lourdes each Easter cram the stage at that point. It would mean two things: hardly anyone was left backstage and the sounds of a struggle would be masked. But how would a person know to wait until then unless they knew the ballet—and unless they knew Raoul's vision of it? The police naturally suspected me, thanks to Paulette's filthy mind and the fact that I am the most well-known of the Metro's pianists. Fortunately, I convinced them otherwise."

T.S. was silent, absorbing this information. "It sounds like you think the police have a point," T.S. finally said.

"It makes sense," Jerry explained, cramming several french fries into his mouth. "But it certainly wasn't me and I told them that. If they want suspects, I can give them suspects."

T.S. eyed him carefully. "Who exactly did you give them?" he asked.

"For one thing, Paulette. It serves her right for betraying me. Like she admitted to your aunt, she and Morgan fought all the time because he thought she was pushing his son too hard in classes. I just casually mentioned their mutual animosity. That, and the fact that she's under suspicion of reselling the company's pointe shoes for her own personal profit."

"How helpful of you," T.S. muttered.

"That's nothing," Jerry said defensively. "I'm sure they didn't take it seriously once I told them that the person they really should be looking at was Ricky Lee Harris, that ghastly lighting director. He had a knock-down-drag-out fight with Morgan the day before he was killed. And the man drinks. I can smell it. I figure he strangled him with an extension cord or something then tossed him off the catwalk."

"The catwalk isn't much of a secret anymore, is it?" T.S. asked.

Jerry shrugged. "Can I help it if people talk?"

"You better hope no one tells Ricky Lee Harris you turned him in," T.S. pointed out sensibly. "If he's the brute you seem to feel he is."

Jerry looked startled at the idea. "I hadn't thought of that," he said. "I have a class with Paulette at the Dance Center this afternoon, but after that, maybe I should lie low."

"Maybe you should," T.S. agreed. "When your options are getting strangled with an extension cord or being beaten to death with a pointe shoe, I'd say that now is a good time for you to develop a bad case of the flu."

2. Auntie Lil had him hooked. T.S. had to admit it. How else to explain why he was heading for Lincoln Center to talk with Ricky Lee Harris and Paulette Puccinni instead of spending a quiet few hours at a civilized museum? He was intrigued by this Harris fellow, though. Auntie Lil had described her encounter with him and the lighting director had assumed a Heathcliff-like stature in T.S.'s mind.

A harried-looking prop mistress directed T.S. around a corner and up to the second floor, where he discovered Ricky Lee Harris bent over a lighting board in a workshop room, muttering to himself.

"Excuse me," T.S. said. He had been right: the man was dark, large, and brooding. The bushy eyebrows lent him a nineteenth-century look.

"Who are you?" Harris growled. He removed a tiny fuse from the back of the lighting board and held it up in the air, scowling.

"T. S. Hubbert. My aunt talked to you Sunday just before the matinee."

Harris glanced at him. "I think your aunt has a few loose screws."

"A lot of people think that," T.S. admitted. "It's a common mistake."

"A mistake?" Harris repeated. He bent back over his work. "How much of a mistake could that be?"

"I wouldn't underestimate my aunt," T.S. said, wondering how the conversation had wandered onto this strange path. "She's pretty hard to fool. There are a couple of people behind bars who would agree."

"You're kidding." Harris ran a hand through his thinning hair and shifted from foot to foot. "What do you want? Are you her cleanup batter?"

Pleasantries and small talk would only be wasted on this character and as T.S. stepped closer he realized why: Harris smelled of stale beer. "I came to ask you a couple more questions," he said.

"You an undercover agent or something?" Harris asked. "Why should I answer any question you ask?"

"You don't have to, but my aunt represents the Metro board. Your employers."

"I don't need reminding about who signs my paychecks. Small as they are." He began fiddling with dials of the lighting board. "Hurry up and ask your questions and leave. I have work to do."

T.S. ignored his rudeness. "I heard you had an argument with Bobby Morgan the day before he died."

"So. I suspect half the company had an argument with him that day."

"Maybe. But why did *you*?"

The big man shrugged. "He was being a Class-A jerk. Accused me of not lighting his precious human money machine properly. Hinted that I wasn't sober enough to handle the light changes. As if I didn't have a computer to do that for me. If you ask me, he was in the mood to climb down someone's throat and I was the one nominated."

"How ugly did it get?"

"Pretty ugly," Harris admitted. His eyes narrowed. "If I don't like someone, I don't bother hiding it. Know what I mean?"

T.S. could nearly feel the heat of his glare. "Did you threaten him?"

Harris laughed. It was an ugly, mocking sound. "I was the one being threatened, not him. He said he'd make sure I lost my job. And let me tell you—if he was able to force that no-talent son of his onto the Metro stage, then I can guarantee you that he had the power to get me fired."

"Which made you pretty mad," T.S. pointed out.

"Not mad enough to kill him." Harris folded his arms and spoke more slowly. "Let me spell it out for you. I was not the only one to have a fight with Morgan on that day. He was in a foul mood. He was biting people's heads off left and right. Maybe he was nervous for his son. Maybe he'd gotten a call from the IRS that morning. Maybe his girlfriend left him high and dry. I don't know. But I do know that he created havoc backstage the day before the premiere. So I didn't take it personally when it was my turn, okay? I have enough real enemies to worry about."

He returned to the lighting board as if the matter had been settled. T.S. stared at him for a moment, then checked the time. Paulette Puccinni would be getting out of her dance class soon. His time would be better spent with her than with this lout. He left without bothering to say goodbye.

3. T.S. heard Paulette Puccinni approaching long before he saw her. Her piercing voice rang through the stairwell of the Dance Center building in shrill indignation, directed, he suspected, at a cowering Jerry Vanderbilt.

"How dare you inform the police of those ill-founded accusations?" she was screaming. "And how dare you sneak into class late just so I can't tell you exactly what I think of you—you piano-playing worm."

"Unfounded?" Jerry shouted back, his figure unseen but his deep voice easily recognizable. "Who's kidding who? You know as well as I do that you've been selling old toe shoes and pocketing the cash for years and blaming the corps. Now you're about to get caught, so you plaster warnings all around to throw everyone off your trail."

If the pair thought that arguing in the stairwell afforded them privacy, they were very much mistaken. The empty space amplified their voices for anyone within fifty yards to hear.

"You are despicable. I ought to slug you," Paulette screamed in very unartistic terms. "Don't you talk to me about stealing. You tried to heist a piano! Wait until I tell them all about that!"

"Go ahead. They won't believe you. You already told them about me and Gene and you were dead wrong," Jerry countered angrily. "You're just jealous I have a friend."

"That's exactly right, Jerry," Paulette shot back. "A friend as in *one* friend. Because you and I are through!" She burst out the double exit doors at the base of the stairs, flinging them open with such enthusiastic force that T.S. was flattened against the concrete wall. His head reverberated with a terrific *boing* as the hollow metal met his skull.

"Now see what you've done," Jerry cried. "You've killed him!"

"My God," Paulette fluttered, rushing to T.S.'s side.

T.S. slumped against the wall, somewhat dazed, but coherent enough to know that he did not want this overblown, overperfumed, and overgauzed woman fussing over him in front of dozens of strangers. He had never met the ballet mistress up close and was starting to wish he had kept it that way. "I'm fine," he groaned, holding a hand over his nose. Was it broken?

"I'm so sorry," she repeated over and over as a small crowd gathered. She loosened his collar as he tried to swat her away, but she sat on the floor next to him and pulled his head into her lap as if he had the vapors instead of a bloody nose. Oblivious to most people's desire for privacy in such matters, she stared at T.S. with eager eyes. "Why, I recognize you now by your hair. *Such* a distinguished silver mane. I've seen you at the ballet with that Hubbert woman. You're her bachelor nephew, aren't you? You live in a fabulous apartment on York Avenue, but you have no one to share it with. I heard you retired early from some Wall Street job with scads of money." She peered at him more closely and he could smell peppermint on her breath. "You *are* still her *bachelor* nephew, aren't you?"

Dazed, he stared at her without comment, struck dumb at hearing his entire life tumble from her lips so unexpectedly.

"Don't you remember me?" she asked breathlessly. "We met across the lobby at intermission during *Giselle* last year. At least our eyes met. I had on a midnight-blue caftan sprinkled with silver moons and stars. Very cosmic. I felt a spark of electricity leap between us. I know you remember."

T.S. touched his nose and cringed. "You've disfigured me," he said.

"Well, what were you doing lurking behind the door, then?" Paulette demanded, her sympathetic demeanor disappearing as fast as it had arrived.

"I wasn't lurking, I was waiting for you," T.S. said angrily, sitting up and glaring at the gathered crowd. He felt something sticky on his fingers and realized his nose was bleeding. Thank God he always carried a handkerchief. He balled it up and tilted his head back, pressing the linen firmly over his nostrils. He couldn't bleed on his jacket or sweater. He had that dinner date with Lilah.

"You are a dangerous woman," Jerry declared from his

prime viewing spot at the head of the pack. "How many men have fallen at your touch?"

"Get out of here before you're next!" Paulette warned him. The pianist took her at her word and scurried away, head held high as if he, for one, were above this low-class fracas.

"I'm so terribly, terribly sorry," Paulette told T.S., her fluttery persona returning as she realized that a lobby full of people were watching her closely. She stood and grabbed T.S.'s free arm, jerking him upright. "Is there any permanent damage?"

"No, no. I'm fine," T.S. said, pulling his arm away. But Paulette could not be dissuaded. Every time he drew free, she clamped back on, securing herself as efficiently as a lamprey eel to his side. In the end, he staggered out the lobby with Paulette adhered to his side like an overblown goiter.

"I can't walk with you hanging on me like that," he complained through the bloody handkerchief.

"Let me help you walk, then," she suggested, looping her second arm over his. His entire right side was losing feeling thanks to her tourniquetlike support. "I'm so terribly sorry this had to happen," she said. Her eyes lit up as a new thought occurred to her. "You said you were waiting for me?" she asked in a teasing tone. "I thought I felt a spark between us back there. I have quite an instinct for such things."

A spark between them? T.S. wished there was a blow-torch between them. He could use the breathing room. Pre-occupied with his nose, he allowed himself to be led out into the chaos of Broadway during rush hour.

"A woman can sense these things so much better than a man, don't you think?" Paulette asked in a conspiratorial tone as she pressed her body against his. The sleeve of her giant caftan was caught in a sudden updraft and the corner lashed out, whipping in the wind and narrowly missing his eyes.

Not content with maiming him, she was now intent on blinding him, he thought. The multipronged assault was confusing. "Yes, I did come to see you," he admitted, unaware that this confession invited gross misinterpretation.

"You're attracted by artistic women, aren't you?" she asked. "The fiery temperament is sexy, don't you think?"

His sanity returned in a rush. He realized with horror that Paulette thought he had romance on his mind. Panic flooded through him and he blurted out, "Where are you taking me?"

She stopped in the middle of the sidewalk, causing a ten person pileup behind her. "What do you mean, where am I taking you? I thought you were taking me somewhere."

"I came to talk to you about Bobby Morgan," he explained, still pressing the handkerchief cautiously against his nose. He thought the bleeding had stopped.

Paulette patted his arm reassuringly. "Of course you did," she said. "It's as good an excuse as any. Shall we avail ourselves of the dancers' lounge at the Metro? It's only a few blocks away and we'll have some privacy."

She wanted to dangle him in front of the other members of the corps, T.S. realized with a rare flash of insight into the female mind. She wants to parade me as her beau, like I was some sort of prize tuna catch, he thought. But at the same time that he was grasping her intent, another part of him—probably the one genetically linked to Auntie Lil—also surmised that allowing her to do so would mean he could get more information out of her. He made a decision to go along.

"Sure you're not stunned?" she asked.

He had failed to answer. Better act quick. T.S. stashed his handkerchief away and pulled out his personnel-manager smile and agreed to the dancers' lounge. At least he wouldn't have to watch her eat. But as they neared Lincoln Center—and Paulette insisted on taking a tour of the plaza first—he realized his error. Suppose Lilah happened past and saw them? The thought made his stomach flip. Or suppose another board member recognized him and then told Lilah? That was even more likely. He ducked his head lower and lower, putting his nose in danger of bleeding again, as he attempted to maintain a discreet profile. Never again, he swore to himself. He'd leave the flirtatious approach to others.

Mercifully, they reached the dancers' lounge without being recognized by anyone he knew. It was a small room tucked between two rehearsal rooms on the first floor, just off the long hallway. Paulette plopped herself down on the worn couch and arranged her caftan around her like she was a queen receiving homage. "Right here, love," she directed, patting a cushion beside her. "This talk is probably pretty confidential. Am I right?"

Shelley Winters in *Night of the Hunter.* That's who she reminded him of, T.S. decided grimly. He suppressed a gulp and obediently perched beside her, his rump so close to the edge that he'd tumble to the floor if he so much as sneezed.

"What is it you wanted to say?" she prompted brightly. "Go on. You aren't the first, you know. Others before you have found difficulty finding the right words. I quite understand. It's important to express feelings like we're having in just the right words."

What in the world was she talking about? T.S. had to end this debacle quickly before he found himself in front of a Las Vegas judge dressed as Elvis, exchanging *I do's* with a white lace caftan-clad Paulette. "I understand that you and Bobby Morgan had words," he said quickly.

Her face fell. "Are we going to talk about *that* again?" she said. "I thought I had exhausted the subject at lunch with your aunt last week. Are you sure that's what's on your mind?"

"Quite sure," T.S. said emphatically. "I heard that you and Bobby Morgan fought quite often over the subject of his son's dancing skills."

Paulette sighed, a prolonged and dramatic offering of breath that any martyr would have envied. "Jerry is so obvious sometimes. I suppose he's been blabbing to you. Of course Bobby Morgan and I fought. His son had no talent. He didn't when he was first a student here six years ago and he doesn't now."

"But you agreed to his dancing the role," T.S. pointed out.

Paulette was indignant. "I most certainly did not. No one asked my opinion. I would never, never have agreed to Mikey Morgan being put in that role." Her anger was genuine. "I was appalled at the board's interference. Performing roles should be awarded based on talent alone. Not politics. Not ticket sales. Not pity. Just talent. If we are to allow other influences to interfere, then what is ballet? Ballet should remain pure, a living, growing entity apart from such concerns. Attach strings to the ballet and what do you have? You have puppets!" She mimed a marionette and the effect was not the least bit comical. She believed passionately in her point. "Worse than allowing that abomination to dance was removing Fatima Jones from the role of Clara. That child is the finest ballerina I have ever trained. The absolute finest. I don't care if she is green, purple, brown, blue, or black. She should have danced that role from the start."

"She's in it now," T.S. pointed out, taken aback by her fury.

"She most certainly is. And I have never seen a finer Clara."

"What did you think of Julie Perkins?" T.S. asked.

"She's a competent student. Perhaps the next best to Fatima. But nowhere close. And we did not do her a favor by thrusting the role of Clara onto her. I believe it has undermined her confidence to an irreparable degree."

"She is dancing badly now?" T.S. asked.

Paulette waved a hand impatiently. "Not badly. With disinterest. She never had enough emotion. Now she is a robot. She simply goes through the motions. Perhaps she is burned out. I have seen it happen before at that young an age. She was brought en pointe too early, I suspect. Though not by me. I see her massaging her feet when she thinks no one is looking. I intend to give her a few more days and then confront her. She may be hiding some serious physical problem. Or her problem may be emotional."

T.S. remembered something that Nikki Morgan had revealed. "If you think Mikey Morgan is such a horrible dancer," T.S. asked, "why are you letting him dance as one of the toy soldiers?"

"How do you know about that?" Paulette asked coolly, her gaze turning suspicious for the first time.

"His mother told me," T.S. explained.

The ballet mistress relaxed. "I told her I would keep it quiet."

"But why?" T.S. asked.

"You wouldn't understand," Paulette said, smoothing the skirt of her caftan out primly over her knees.

"Try me," T.S. suggested.

Paulette sighed again, this time wistfully. "I know what it's like to be a child star," she said slowly. "It seems incredible looking at me now, I know. But I was something of a prodigy in my time. And I paid a heavy price. I had no friends my own age. Not one. I deeply regret that now that I am older. I find I don't know how to have a friend." She wiped one eye and T.S. fervently hoped the memory would not trigger a flood of tears. "When Nikki Morgan approached me about her son, I understood his desire to be with his friends. After all, his father had just died. So I agreed to teach him a small toy soldier role. He handles it fine."

"What happened to not polluting the art with outside influences?" T.S. asked.

"Oh, who cares," Paulette snapped back. "We're talking about one crummy toy soldier out of twenty, thanks to the hordes that Raoul pours on stage each night. You call that art?"

Her rapid lapse back into acerbic observation was comforting to T.S. He much preferred the sarcastic version of Paulette Puccinni to the coquettish and sentimental versions.

"Is that it?" she suddenly demanded. "You only wanted to ask me more questions about that infernal murder?"

"That's it," T.S. admitted, resisting the urge to apologize. He had not misrepresented himself. It was her fault for misreading his intentions.

"Have it your way," she announced, standing up and

assuming her regal carriage. "You don't know what you're missing." She strode from the room in a billow of brightly colored cloth, leaving behind the sweet stench of floral perfume.

T.S. was struck with a sudden pang. There was something oddly sad about her parting shot. He had been boorish. And he *had* led her on a bit. How could he have stooped so low?

He dashed out the door to apologize and nearly collided with an agitated Andrew Perkins. The man did not even recognize T.S. He simply mumbled an apology and continued past.

T.S. did not hesitate. He followed Perkins automatically, keeping him in sight as they both hurried down the hall. Perkins pushed through the exit doors. T.S. waited a few seconds before following. Perkins paused for a moment in the sunlight, looked around, then immediately relaxed. He leaned against the corner of the theater and began to smoke a cigarette as he watched the street carefully. T.S. casually removed the bloody handkerchief from his pocket and placed it back over his nose. It wasn't bad for an impromptu disguise. After a few minutes a cab came roaring up the inner roadway that provided an easy drop-off point for patrons attending Lincoln Center shows. The taxi glided to a halt and the back door opened. T.S. caught a glimpse of a slender arm as someone beckoned Andrew Perkins inside. Perkins ground out his cigarette and hurried to obey. He folded his lanky frame inside the cab and slammed the door shut just as the enthusiastic driver gunned the engine.

As the taxi shot past, T.S. darted toward the driveway, shamelessly stooping for a better view. Despite the handkerchief still over his nose, he had a clear look at the woman's face and was absolutely positive. Dark glasses and a scarf could not hide all of her features, nor the trademark haircut he had seen at Morgan's funeral.

Andrew Perkins had just hopped into the backseat of a cab with Nikki Morgan.

CHAPTER THIRTEEN

1. "You're what?" Herbert asked, straining to hear Auntie Lil over the backdrop of street noise. "I never thought I'd say this, but I can't hear you."

"I'm whispering!" she explained. "I'm in the lobby of a warehouse on Twentieth Street. I'm going home with Emili Vladimir. In case anything happens to me, I wanted you to know."

Herbert Wong was no fool. He was well aware that his time spent with Auntie Lil had been severely curtailed in recent weeks by his dance interests. She would never admit that she missed him. It was not her way. But he knew what this phone call really meant. "I have let you look into this too much on your own," he told her. "Wait for me now. I will go with you."

"No," Auntie Lil said. "There isn't time. She'll be downstairs in a minute. I'm only going to Brighton Beach. I'll be fine. I just wanted someone to know."

"Lillian," Herbert said in a businesslike tone, "I do not approve. Your voice tells me that you may be in danger. You must call me tonight when you get home and let me know that you are okay. And starting tomorrow, I will stick to you like paste."

"Glue," Auntie Lil said. "Stick to me like glue."

"Glue," Herbert conceded. Had he detected a note of relief in her voice? That pleased him. Auntie Lil was so capable that one seldom had the opportunity to be of assistance. Of course, when she finally did need his help, it was usually a pretty lively affair. "Do not forget to phone," he warned her. "Or I will come over and check on your safety for myself."

"I won't," Auntie Lil promised, ringing off as Emili Vladimir emerged from the building's elevator. Her imperious manner had disappeared, along with her black leotard. She was wearing jeans and a carefully ironed man's shirt. Her face had relaxed, softening her features, and her wide smile was framed beautifully by the dark waves of her unbound hair. She was, Auntie Lil realized, a stunning woman. "I hope you're hungry," Emili warned her.

"I'm always hungry," Auntie Lil admitted.

"Good. I made stuffed cabbage last night and it's always better reheated. I'm starved myself. I usually forget to eat all day when I'm creating." Emili stepped back nimbly to avoid Auntie Lil's huge pocketbook as she tried to get a cab. Auntie Lil's cab-hailing methods were spectacular and had been known to harm innocent bystanders. They also worked. As a taxi screeched to a halt Emili climbed inside with a sigh. "This is a luxury. I can't afford to take a taxi on my own."

"It does beat the subway," Auntie Lil agreed.

Auntie Lil had not been to Brighton Beach since the early 1960s when she had visited a favorite fit model who had recently given birth to twins (and given up her career as a perfect size eight). The Brooklyn neighborhood had changed in the ensuing years from a comfortable middle-class enclave into a neighborhood in flux, caught between the old world and the new. The main avenue was lined with four-to-ten-story brick buildings in various states of repair. In each case, the ground floor was given over to small businesses, ranging from grocery stores to shoe-repair shops to dry cleaners and apparel shops. A few blocks over, a grimy waterfront served as home for a community of noisy seagulls and the homeless, who had made themselves comfortable amidst the industrial decay.

What set Brighton Beach apart from other New York City neighborhoods was that most of the store signs appeared in the ornate Cyrillic letters of the Russian alphabet as well as in English. The area was referred to as "Little

Odessa" by many people, including a number of detectives assigned to its precinct. Beginning in the seventies, wave after wave of Russian, Polish, Balkan, and Czechoslovakian immigrants had fled their homelands under relaxed travel laws and settled down in Brighton Beach to pursue the American dream. Most were hardworking, newly God-fearing, and relatively honest. Some were not. Auntie Lil knew that a branch of Russia's largest organized crime organization controlled illegal gambling, loan sharking, prostitution, and extortion in the area. Behind the windows thick with Polish sausage and Russian caviar lurked illegal betting parlors, currency smuggling operations, and access to a dark underworld.

All Auntie Lil could think of as she passed through the bustling streets was whether Emili Vladimir belonged in the hardworking category or in the dark underworld. It would be easy to find a hired killer in Brighton Beach. And the price would be a bargain compared with many other sections of New York. But why would Emili kill Bobby Morgan? Unless she had been the woman that Ruth Beretsky had spotted him with. And even then, what had been her motive? Did it somehow involve a seat on the board?

"This is it," Emili told the driver as the taxi pulled up in front of a two-story brownstone nestled between larger buildings. A black wrought-iron fence rimmed a small concrete yard barely big enough to house a pair of garbage cans and one lawn chair. Someone had placed tubs of begonias in each corner of the fence, lending the yard a festive air.

"Are you the gardener?" Auntie Lil asked.

"My upstairs neighbor," Emili explained. She waved to a stout woman staring out of a second-story window, then led Auntie Lil inside.

The Vladimirs' apartment consisted of four narrow rooms that opened off opposite sides of a central hallway. The small kitchen was jammed with ceramic canisters, storage jars, and rows of spice bottles. The outdated appliances were spotlessly maintained and looked at home with the flowered linoleum and lace panel curtains. The lingering odor of a recently cooked meal made Auntie Lil's stomach grumble.

"Let me put this in the oven right away," Emili said, removing a foil-covered pan from the refrigerator. "Rudy will be home soon and he only has an hour before he has to get back for curtain."

"He comes all the way home to eat dinner?" Auntie Lil asked.

Emili nodded. "It's one of the few times we get to spend together."

They toured the rest of the apartment, Auntie Lil admiring the overstuffed furniture with heavy brocade upholstery in the living room. Lace doilies covered the chair arms and the walls were decorated with colorful impressionistic paintings of the Russian countryside. "You're the artist?" Auntie Lil asked, admiring a scene that showed a hay wagon stopped beside a mountain lake.

"My father," Emili explained. "He was a painter, an aberration in our otherwise dance-mad family."

It was obvious which bedroom was Rudy's and which belonged to Emili. Rudy's was crammed with sweatpants, athletic and flat dance shoes, posters of popular sports figures, cassette tapes, and schoolbooks. Emili's was a feminine lair, crowded with satin pillows, lace, lingerie, perfume bottles, tiny pairs of delicate shoes, and a large canopied oak bed.

The wall on the other side of the bed intrigued Auntie Lil. She stared at the portrait of a handsome man dressed in formal evening wear posed against a red velvet curtain. He had an elongated face, high cheekbones, a narrow nose, and thin lips. His dark eyes were wide and almond-shaped, giving him a slightly Asian look. His hair was light brown and carefully brushed back from his forehead, lending the oil portrait a 1920s air. A small maple table—a genuine antique to Auntie Lil's practiced eye—had been placed in front of the painting. Its surface was filled with votive candles in red glass cups. Emili strode to the table and lit the candles, cupping each glass jar until the flame had stabilized. She knelt in front of the table and stared up at the portrait. Auntie Lil waited in the doorway until she had finished praying and used the time to scrutinize the man in the painting. Was this a self-portrait of Emili's father? Was it her husband? If so, he didn't look much like Rudy. Rudy was rounder, less ethereal looking, and much more robust. If this man resembled anyone Auntie Lil knew, he looked like Andrew Perkins, the young ballerina's father. She studied the man's face more closely. How very odd. Was there a connection?

Emili finished her silent ceremony. She rose and stroked the portrait with graceful fingers. "This is what I wanted you to see," she said.

"I don't understand," Auntie Lil admitted.

"This is my husband," Emili explained. "Rudy's father. He was a great dancer, a star of the Kirov Ballet. An untouchable. Or so everyone thought. He's been gone now for fifteen years. They killed him."

"Who killed him?" Auntie Lil asked, bewildered.

Emili shrugged. "Them. The Soviet authorities. Perhaps some organization I never knew existed. It doesn't matter. What matters is that Erik is gone and I am the cause."

"How could that be?" Auntie Lil asked.

Emili sat on the edge of her bed and stared at the portrait. "Do you know how I first came to the States?" she asked.

Auntie Lil shook her head. "Only that you defected."

Emili nodded. "In 1980. Six years after Baryshnikov. The same way. The authorities had finally relaxed enough to allow us to travel again. Or rather, they needed the money a world tour would bring in. I was with the Kirov doing a production of *The Dying Swan* in Toronto. One morning I woke up and walked away from it all. It was easy. First I took a bus to the border. I went into a bar and an American woman there sold me her driver's license for fifty dollars. When you're from Russia, you learn how to spot people who will agree to such things. I crossed the border by bus into New York State that night and no one even bothered to look at the license. I just waved it and they let me through. It was a crowded bus. I took another bus from Buffalo here to New York City and presented my-self to a branch of the U.S. Embassy at Rockefeller Center. No one but my husband knew I was going to do it. I wasn't even sure myself."

"Why did you do it?" Auntie Lil asked.

"I was pregnant with Rudy. Only two months. No one in the company knew. I wasn't going to raise my child in Rus-sia." Emili laughed bitterly. "If it had been today, it wouldn't have been so important to get out. Things have changed so much. Now there is no more U.S.S.R. There is not even an enemy to blame for my husband's death. All of that has disappeared, along with my Erik."

"But why would they kill him?"

"He couldn't get out fast enough and joining me was something they could hold over him to try to make him talk. But he didn't know enough to please them. Many of our friends were on their dissident lists. They probably threatened Erik or offered to let him join me if he would only turn in some of our friends. He would never have agreed to that. Maybe that is why he died."

"How could that have been your fault?" Auntie Lil asked.

Emili stared down at her hands. "They picked him up while he was waiting near the border at Urkutsk for a sig-nal from me. As soon as he heard I had defected, he was going to cross over. But they fooled us. They kept the news very quiet. They were embarrassed about it happening again. Then a friend of mine betrayed me. A man in the company. I called him from New York and he promised to call Erik and tell him I had been granted asylum. It was a backup plan to make sure Erik got the news. Instead, the government representative traveling with us on tour got to my friend first. They were watching him from the moment I disappeared and knew that I had called. He told them where Erik was waiting. They convinced him to phone Erik and say that I had been detained, that all plans were off. So Erik did not cross over the border. They came to get him the next day. For questioning only, they told the manager of the Urkutsk hotel. No one ever saw him again."

"Then he may be alive," Auntie Lil said.

Emili shook her head. "No. Erik is dead. I can feel it." Tears welled from her eyes and trickled down her face. She made a move to wipe them away. "So you see, that is why I could not have harmed that Morgan man. I have already had a hand in one man's death. Because of me, a man's life has been cut short before his time. I would not be a party to such a thing again."

Before Auntie Lil could reply, a clatter in the front hall signaled the arrival of Rudy. Books tumbled to the floor in the distance, a chair was bumped and light footsteps padded rapidly down the hallway toward them. He shouted a question in Russian, his voice cracking as it struggled to escape that elusive mixture of child and man.

"Another fifteen minutes," Emili answered in English. "I'm heating it up now. Come into my bedroom, Rudy. We have a visitor." She stood and wiped the tears from her face, replacing her grief with a smile. Rudy dashed into the room but stopped short when he saw Auntie Lil. He was tall and well muscled yet graceful. He had a thick mop of blond hair that fell into his eyes and was cut short on the sides in the current style of New York City teenagers. His eyes traveled from Auntie Lil's face to the portrait of his father on the wall. He studied the lit candles flickering beneath the image, then his eyes lingered on his mother's face.

"This is Lillian Hubbert," Emili explained, gesturing toward Auntie Lil. "She's on the Metro's board."

"I know who you are," Rudy said, extending his hand politely. "All of Mikey's friends do."

2. Although the stuffed cabbage was excellent—and Auntie Lil had astonished her hostess with her appetite—she had not learned anything new that might help her in identifying Bobby Morgan's murderer. She felt that Emili and Rudy Vladimir were exactly what they appeared to be: a small family made stronger by trouble, devoted to dance, poor but talented, and at least in the case of Emili, grateful for the freedom they enjoyed in their lives. Rudy had been a typical American teenager, eating noisily, boisterously recalling events of the day, answering Auntie Lil's questions with one- or two-syllable replies and generally remaining unconcerned about anything except whether Auntie Lil would leave enough stuffed cabbage rolls for him to have seconds. After dinner, he had raced to his room, changed into fresh clothes, and dashed out the door for the subway with a hurried good-bye. Auntie Lil left soon after and had the distinct feeling that Emili would be in bed and fast asleep before she got halfway home. There had been no sign of a man in Emili's life, other than the oil portrait on the wall. There were no photographs of her with anyone on display, no mementos, fresh or dried flowers, and certainly no men's toiletries hidden in the bathroom cabinet. Auntie Lil knew because she had given it a thorough search.

All together, the evening had been a draw. She had gotten an excellent dinner but little else. Well, perhaps a new friend. She could do worse, Auntie Lil reflected, settling back against the seat of her cab with a sigh. The taxi was one of the newer models, painted a vibrant yellow that bordered on orange. She admired its cleanliness then spotted the telephone mounted on the divider between the front and back seats. It was absurd, she reflected, how modern man could not leave that abominable contraption behind for even a few minutes. It probably did not even work, the reception no doubt horrific. Telling herself that she was simply testing the new technology, she searched through her cavernous purse for a credit card and slid it through the magnetic reader. She contemplated which of her many acquaintances she might call. Of course—Herbert. He answered immediately and sounded relieved that she was safe. As they chatted and made plans to meet in the morning, the taxi emerged from a cluster of industrial buildings onto a main thoroughfare with a stunning view of the Manhattan skyline. Auntie Lil stared at the magnificent outline of brightly lit buildings etched against the twilight, the electric glow seeming to be fed by the slow-moving line of car headlights that inched toward the great city. She felt the wonderful sense of security that talking to a friend in a cozy cab in the midst of such chaos provided and suddenly understood quite clearly why car phones were so popular.

By the time the taxi reached her apartment building in Flushing, she had left a message on T.S.'s answering machine, rung up Lilah Cheswick without success, checked on whether her dry cleaning was ready for pickup, and ordered her groceries for the next week. If the driver had not known a clever shortcut, she would also have called an old friend in Tacoma.

"Better be careful, ma'am," the driver warned as he pulled up to her building. "It looks like someone is waiting in the shadows there beside your front door. Want me to walk you inside?" Her customarily generous tip had ensured his gallantry.

Auntie Lil peered out into the darkness. A small figure stepped into view. "It's just a child," she told the driver.

"The kids around here can get pretty rough," he warned.

"I know him," she said. "What are you doing here?" she asked the figure as she opened the door to get out.

Mikey Morgan darted from his spot near the stoop and crouched by her taxi door, looking to the left and right as if he were being followed. "You told me to come and see you if I ever needed help," he said. His eyes were wide with fear and he was breathing heavily. Either he was a better actor than his movies indicated or he really was in danger. "I didn't have anywhere else to go so I came here."

"What about home?" Auntie Lil asked. "Does your mother know you're gone?"

"She's out," Mikey explained. "Anyway, I can't stay there. Last night I saw a man outside my window, looking up at me. He knew where I lived. He was in the shadows of a street lamp in the park outside. And today, at the theater, someone was following me in the hallways. I know they were. I took the steps upstairs and heard footsteps behind me. But the footsteps stopped when mine did. If you make me go home, I'll just run away. I have noplace else to go."

"Are you being followed now?" Auntie Lil asked.

"I think so. I don't know." He looked around again. "Maybe."

"We must go to the police," Auntie Lil said firmly. "Get inside."

"No," Mikey shouted. He rubbed his mouth with his hands then stuck them in his jeans pockets and hunched his shoulders in misery. "You can't go to the cops. I won't let you. I'll run away," he threatened again.

Auntie Lil made a quick decision. She pulled him inside the taxi. "Come with me," she said. "I'll take you somewhere safe. You may have been followed here. Driver, can you take us to Manhattan?"

The driver flipped on the meter, visions of another gigantic tip dancing in his head. "Lady, I'll take you anywhere you want to go."

3.   "What do you mean he doesn't live here?" Auntie Lil asked, her voice rising in disbelief. "Are you daft? He's my nephew. I know where he lives. I just left him a message on the answering machine. Do you mean that he's not home yet?"

"No." Mahmoud shook his head vigorously. "I mean he does not live here. Not anymore. He is gone. You are mistaken."

"Mahmoud, that is preposterous. Let me upstairs immediately." Auntie Lil smacked her pocketbook against the front desk in exasperation. Mikey stood beside her, one eye on the door.

"Mr. Hubbert does not live here," Mahmoud insisted firmly. "I will say no more." He crossed his arms across his chest and planted his feet wide as if daring Auntie Lil to push past him.

"We shall just see about that," Auntie Lil warned. She marched past Mahmoud, Mikey Morgan in tow, and took a seat on the bench near the elevator. Mikey sat beside her meekly, slouching so that he was hidden behind her stout frame.

Mikey had insisted again during the cab ride that he was

being followed by a man but had not yet gotten a clear look at him. Auntie Lil had believed him enough to take him to the place she considered safer than her own: T.S.'s apartment. She knew T.S. was out to dinner with Lilah, but he had to come home sometime, never mind what his obviously disturbed doorman said. Perhaps Mahmoud had taken to drink. She remembered her tour of the Arab countries well. Though they swore it was against their religion, she had observed many of her hosts weaving suspiciously following the frequent banquets given in her honor to celebrate her large purchases of fabric from them.

Half an hour later T.S. arrived home. He strode through the doorway—still glowing with the pleasure of his dinner with Lilah—and called out a cheery hello to Mahmoud. The doorman ducked his head guiltily and stared at his shoes, certain that his Christmas tip was in danger again.

T.S. spotted Auntie Lil and Mikey and stopped short in surprise. "Why didn't you wait for me upstairs?" he asked, his eyes scrutinizing her companion without comment. Nothing Auntie Lil did would surprise him.

"I would have, but he insisted you no longer lived here!" She pointed an accusatory finger at Mahmoud.

The doorman scurried over, ready to defend his honor. "I told her again and again that you did not live here, but she refused to believe me!" He cowered as fearfully as an ill-treated dog awaiting the lash of his master's whip.

T.S. stared at him in complete exasperation. He had no recourse. He'd never have the nerve to cut his Christmas tip. Mahmoud was simply the price he paid for his beloved apartment. He settled for being magnanimous. "Aunt Lil, may I escort you upstairs?" he said with exaggerated politeness, offering her his arm.

The politeness did not last long. "What is going on?" T.S. demanded as soon as the three of them were alone in the elevator. "What is he doing here?"

"I'll explain in a minute," Auntie Lil said, checking the elevator control panel for a microphone.

Mikey had yet to say a word. But his demeanor changed dramatically once they were inside T.S.'s apartment. He

took off his blue-jean jacket and tossed it over the back of
the couch, causing T.S. to wince. Then his eyes spotted the
large-screen television against one wall—it had been T.S.'s
one extravagant retirement purchase—and his eyes lit up
with enthusiasm. "Cool!" he said. "Mom won't let me get
one even though I could afford a thousand of them." He
switched on the set and began rapidly changing channels
with the remote control, a habit that T.S. loathed in others
and ignored in himself. Brenda and Eddie ventured out
from behind the couch, eyed the teenager suspiciously, and
slunk back out of view.

"Explain," T.S. said tersely to Auntie Lil.

She explained the situation as briefly as she could.

"So why are you here?" he demanded.

"I can't keep him at my house," she insisted. "He may
have been followed. And I'm getting old, you know. I don't
know if I could keep up with a teenager."

T.S. stared at her in amazement. "Don't hand me that
line," he warned. "You aren't too old for tracking down
killers or rumbaing twice a week or hiking through the
Alps," he said. "I cannot believe you expect me to swallow
that excuse."

"Please, Theodore," Auntie Lil pleaded. "Just for a few
days. We're getting close. I can feel it."

Mikey had plopped down on the couch and propped his
feet up on the glass coffee table, destroying the precise
alignment of T.S.'s magazines in the process. "Got anything
to drink?" he yelled out.

"You hear that?" T.S. said, dropping his voice to a whisper. "He thinks I'm his butler."

"I'll make it up to you," Auntie Lil promised. "Why
don't we have a drink and talk it over?"

"Don't try to soften me up by getting me drunk," T.S.
warned. "If I wanted teenagers in my house, I'd have decorated it in early rumpus room."

"Can we order in Chinese or something?" Mikey asked,
flipping the channel and lingering on a local cable show
that featured a transvestite chef dressed in tacky suburban
clothes who specialized in Southern favorites and wore his

wig askew while reciting recipes in a thick drawl. "I'm starving."

"That's a good idea," Auntie Lil said brightly. "We can discuss things over a snack."

"Food?" T.S. said. "I just got back from dinner. And it's after eleven o'clock. We order in Chinese and we may as well lie down on the couch right now and wait for the heartburn to begin." He sighed, knowing defeat was near. "Does his mother even know where he is?" he finally demanded, seeking refuge in assuming the outrage of a responsible adult.

"She doesn't care," Mikey announced, flipping channels to a highly improbable wrestling match between two gaudily clad thugs. "She likes my brothers and sister better than me."

"Your mother," Auntie Lil said. "Of course. We must call her and let her know you're okay."

"She's probably not even there," Mikey insisted. "I think she has a new boyfriend or something."

"We are most certainly calling her immediately," T.S. informed him. He marched over to the phone on the table next to his couch and made a great show of calling information for Nikki Morgan's number, then carefully dialed each digit with great indignation. He was so startled when Nikki actually answered the phone—and so caught up in his zeal to appear in command—that he forgot to introduce himself.

"Mrs. Morgan," T.S. began. "I have your son. He's right here beside me and if you want to—"

Suddenly Mikey reached over and pressed the disconnect button. "No!" the boy shouted. "Don't tell her where I am. I don't want her to know. If you tell her, I'll run away!" He jumped up from the couch and grabbed his jacket as if preparing to flee.

"It's okay," Auntie Lil said quickly, leading the young boy back to the couch. "We won't tell her where you are. We'll just say that you're safe with us."

"No!" Mikey said. "I'll run away. I will!"

Auntie Lil was silent for a moment. "We'll work something out," she finally announced. "In the meantime you watch television and we'll order you in some nice Chinese food to eat." She stared at T.S. pointedly and gestured for him to follow her into the small kitchenette.

"Are you crazy?" T.S. whispered furiously. "Do you know what I just said to his mother? Let me recap for you: 'I have your son. He's right here beside me and if you want to—' Do you know what that sounds like?" He stared at her for emphasis. "You and I may know that I was going to say 'and if you want to talk to him,' but the police are most definitely going to assume that I'm a kidnapper. Think about it—I sounded just like a kidnapper, Aunt Lil. One that didn't get a chance to ask for ransom. We can't just let him stay here. This is serious."

"You make such a big deal out of everything," Auntie Lil complained.

"*One* of us is going to call his mother," T.S. insisted. "Either you or me. Your choice. And, by the way, I saw her meeting Andrew Perkins earlier tonight." He described what he had seen.

"I'll go visit her myself," Auntie Lil decided. "Right now. She'll have to let me in if I have news of her son. I'll ask her why she was with Perkins."

"You will not," T.S. said flatly. "It may be dangerous."

"Theodore, her other children will be right there in the apartment with me," Auntie Lil said. "What can she do?"

"Force you to baby-sit?" he suggested.

"I'm hungry!" Mikey shouted at them from the living room.

T.S.'s expression was eloquent. Auntie Lil ignored it anyway. "You stay here with him," she said. "Just let him stay here for twenty-four hours. That's all I ask. I'll phone you when I'm through talking to his mother."

T.S. was silent, wrestling with his conscience. Finally he spoke. "The only reason I am agreeing to this," he told Auntie Lil slowly, "is because I don't think Nikki Morgan had anything to do with her ex-husband's death. I had dinner with Lilah tonight and she told me something that makes me think Hans Glick may be involved. I wasn't supposed to say anything until she was sure, but maybe you should know about it now before you go rushing off to accuse Nikki Morgan of anything."

"What did she find?" Auntie Lil whispered furiously.

T.S. put a finger to his lips and glanced back toward the living room, then led Auntie Lil down the hallway toward his bedroom. He closed the door carefully, then leaned against it and told her what he knew. Lilah was very active in fund-raising for a number of charities. When she received the report on the Metropolitan's charity ball held in Los Angeles last spring, she had grown suspicious about some of the expenses listed and the small percentage of profit the Metro had cleared. For the past week she'd had her own accountants looking into the matter, examining the books from the event and double-checking listed expenses with the purported vendors.

"It's all a lie," T.S. told Auntie Lil. "Glick listed last-minute first-class airline tickets for Raoul and Lisette Martinez, when they really flew coach and booked weeks in advance. That's a discrepancy of thousands of dollars when you're talking about an East to West Coast flight. Plus, he overbilled the flowers by three thousand, the food by nearly twenty, padded the list of waiters to justify paying out more salaries, and made payments to two decorating firms, including one that doesn't even exist. He's stealing money from the Metro!"

"Raoul and Lisette Martinez attended the L.A. benefit?" Auntie Lil asked. "Is that what you're saying?"

T.S. was exasperated. "That's not my point. Of course they attended. He's the artistic director. She's the star. Did you hear what I said about Glick?"

"She lied to me," Auntie Lil said. "Remember when we asked her about Bobby Morgan while she was taking a break on the steps? She said she just met him this season. She had to have met him at the L.A. party. Ruth Beretsky said he was there and flirting with all the women. She would have been the first one he was attracted to. Like you said, she's the star."

T.S. was annoyed. "So Glick doesn't even count?"

"Of course he counts, Theodore," Auntie Lil said fondly, patting his arm in a patronizing gesture. "I thought something was making him behave strangely. But all of his actions have been consistent. Consistent with someone who has something to hide, but consistent nonetheless. Lisette Martinez is another story. So friendly. So helpful. So big a liar . . ." Her voice trailed off as she considered various ways to deal with this new bit of information. "I know," she decided. "Tomorrow morning, you call Margo McGregor. Ask her to pull any photos her paper may have taken at the charity ball. I know they covered it. Get the outtakes and everything. Wire photos, too. I want to be sure before I confront Lisette."

"What are we looking for?" T.S. asked.

"Photos of Lisette and Bobby Morgan together," Auntie Lil explained. "If she lied to me, maybe she's the woman Ruth saw with Morgan. Maybe she's the reason why he suddenly pulled his son from Hollywood and flew back to New York to dance in a minor production of *The Nutcracker*. It's never made sense to me that he would do that."

"And maybe she's the reason he was killed," T.S. added.

Scrambling sounds in the hallway alerted them that someone was near. T.S. opened the door to find Brenda and Eddie tumbling around Mikey Morgan's feet.

"I was just looking for the bathroom," the boy explained. "Are we gonna order in food or not?"

Auntie Lil's gaze was steady. "Theodore will order you something now."

4. It was just after midnight and Riverside Drive was deserted. The huge trees lining the park cast eerie shadows underneath the infrequent streetlights. Had Mikey really seen a man lurking beneath his windows or was his already overactive imagination simply reacting to his father's death? Auntie Lil hopped from the taxi and examined the street beneath the Morgans' apartment. It was brightly illuminated. It would be hard to mistake a tree for a man. But it would be easy for a man to hide on the edge of the light, blending in with the sudden darkness.

Auntie Lil pressed the bell firmly and Nikki Morgan immediately answered, as if she had been waiting by the door.

"Who is it?" she asked, the fear in her voice apparent even through the intercom's static.

"Lillian Hubbert. Mikey is perfectly safe. I want to talk to you about it."

Nikki buzzed Auntie Lil upstairs without comment and met her at the elevator door wearing a bathrobe. She had been home for some time, Auntie Lil was sure.

"Where is Mikey?" Nikki asked at once. "Is he okay? I was just about to call the police. I don't want any more publicity and he left me a note saying not to but the note doesn't make any sense." She clutched the top of her bathrobe anxiously around the base of her throat. "I should have called the police hours ago, but you never know with Mikey. I thought maybe he'd just gone to the movies or Rollerblading at some rink with friends or some other normal activity like he's always saying he doesn't get to do."

"He's very safe," Auntie Lil said, interrupting her slightly tipsy speech before she could begin more apologies. "But I promised Mikey I would tell no one where he is."

"I'm his mother," Nikki protested. "How dare you make such a promise?"

"I'm sorry," Auntie Lil apologized, following Nikki into the Morgans' apartment. Her voice lowered. "He seems to feel he's in danger and said he would run away if I told anyone where he was, even you."

"What kind of danger?" Nikki led Auntie Lil past a row of closed bedroom doors and into the living room. It was as chaotic as ever. She unceremoniously dumped a pile of schoolbooks on the rug to make room for Auntie Lil to sit on the sofa. She reached into her coat pocket and pulled out a crumpled piece of notebook paper to hand to Auntie Lil. "This makes no sense," she said.

Auntie Lil examined the note. *See you later,* it read in a

childish scrawl. *I'm lying low for a few days. Don't call the police. —Mikey.*

"He says he's being followed by some man," Auntie Lil explained. "He doesn't know who the man is."

"Some man? That's nonsense." Nikki perched on the arm of the sofa and swung a leg anxiously. "Mikey is very imaginative. His father let him watch too many movies. Do you really think anyone would bother to follow a child?"

"Did you ever think anyone would ever bother to kill your ex-husband?" Auntie Lil pointed out.

Nikki was silent for a moment. "I got a call a little while ago. The man sounded very sinister. He said he had Mikey with him."

Auntie Lil looked away. "I know who that was. He was just trying to let you know Mikey was safe. Mikey disconnected him before he could tell you where he was. Your son is very serious about running away if anyone knows where he is."

Nikki frowned and brushed a lock of dark hair off her forehead. "Why would anyone want to harm Mikey?" she asked. "He doesn't have an enemy in the world. Unlike his father."

"I thought maybe you could tell me that," Auntie Lil replied.

"I've told you everything I know," Nikki said. "I thought I was very cooperative considering the circumstances."

"Did you tell me everything? You never told me that you knew Andrew Perkins."

Nikki's expression was blank. "You never asked," she answered.

Auntie Lil had to admit this was true, but still wanted to know more. "But you do know him?" she asked.

"Of course I know him. His daughter has been in the Metro's School for the past six years. Two of my other children besides Mikey have attended classes there. And his daughter danced the lead with Mikey the night that . . ." She paused. "The night that Bobby was killed."

"And you're aware of his history with your ex-husband? That they acted together as children?"

"Of course I am." She looked around as if searching for something. Her eyes lingered on the row of liquor bottles atop the sideboard before she quickly looked away. "I thought at first that Andrew was only interested in me because I was Bobby's wife. Especially since he became really friendly following my divorce. I thought maybe he wanted to try to hurt Bobby by, well, I don't know the word to use—by romancing me, maybe. I knew they had been rivals. I also knew Andrew's wife had left him and he was alone. I thought maybe he had something to prove to Bobby by sleeping with me. But I squelched that idea pretty quickly and Andrew backed off without giving me any trouble about it. We're just good friends now."

"How good?" Auntie Lil asked without apology.

"We have dinner occasionally," Nikki explained. "We've taken the kids out together. Not all of them. That would be a zoo. Andrew brings Julie and I bring Mikey." She smiled. "I get the impression that Mikey may have a little crush on Julie. She's a few years older, but from the way he acts I can tell he thinks he's in love. It's cute."

"It's not cute if Julie doesn't feel the same way back," Auntie Lil pointed out. "Children that age are easily hurt."

"She likes him fine," Nikki said. "After all, he is a star. Although she does act like she thinks he's a little young. But I think that's good for Mikey. It's the most normal I've ever seen him behave. Or be treated. It's just puppy love. He'll survive."

"But you meet Andrew without the children also," Auntie Lil said, without explaining how she knew.

Nikki shrugged. "I help him out by giving him advice on Julie," she explained. "She's been without a mother for almost four years now. He doesn't know how to handle her. Julie is difficult." She paused, struggling to explain. "She grew up very quickly. Young dancers do. Then, when her mother left, she had to grow up even faster. Andrew doesn't know what to do with her now that she's a grown woman at age sixteen. He's had problems."

"What kind of problems?" Auntie Lil asked.

Nikki hesitated. "They're private problems, really."

"Nikki," Auntie Lil said. "I understand that you promised Andrew you would be discreet. But there has been a murder and Mikey may be in danger and I don't think it's appropriate to hold back any secrets at this point."

Nikki thought it over and continued. "Julie's been smoking. But so what? So does Andrew, like a chimney. Which makes it hard for him to lecture her on that particular subject. Besides, it's an occupational hazard for dancers trying to keep their weight down. But she's also been rebellious. Staying out late at night. Skipping her gym workouts. Not eating. Her weight is dangerously low now and she's losing strength. It's affecting her dancing. I told Andrew to send her to an eating-disorder specialist, but she refused." She stopped, her voice hesitating as if she had more to say but was not quite sure if she should bring it up.

"What is it?" Auntie Lil asked. "If you don't want to tell me, it's probably the most important thing of all."

Nikki shook her head. "I remember when I was Julie's age," she said. "I wanted so badly to be grown up and for people to take me seriously as an adult. Now I would give anything to be sixteen again." She smiled sadly. "She started staying out all night occasionally. It was during *Nutcracker* rehearsals and Andrew was furious. It was Julie's first big role and she was having trouble handling it. Staying out all night didn't help. He confronted her about it and they fought. She began coming in late after that, but she did come home at least."

"When did she move out?" Auntie Lil asked.

Nikki looked at her in surprise. "How did you know that?" she asked.

"I saw her room. It was obvious."

"She left right after Bobby died," Nikki explained. "I think Julie knew they were going to take the role away from her after Mikey pulled out and the door was opened for Fatima Jones to take over. She didn't want to deal with her father about it. Andrew pushed her too hard. He was just like Bobby in that respect. He wanted his child to make up for all he'd never achieved himself. I told him to back off but he wouldn't listen."

"Where is she staying?" Auntie Lil asked.

Nikki shrugged. "I have no idea. I see her at the Metro between classes and sometimes Andrew tries to talk to her, but she just walks away. But at least we know she's okay. I assume she's with a friend." Nikki sighed. "Andrew raised her to skip right over childhood. Now she's operating like an adult. That's what happens."

"Why did you see Andrew tonight?" Auntie Lil asked.

Nikki raised her eyebrows. "We had dinner. Am I to assume that I'm being followed, too?" Her tone was dry.

"An acquaintance saw you picking him up at Lincoln Center," Auntie Lil explained. "I would never have you followed without permission."

"That's a relief," she said sarcastically. She stared down the hallway. "One day your life is perfectly normal. You get your kids up in the morning, dressed, and off to school. You wait for them to come home at night. The next day you're surrounded by murder, your son runs away from you in fear, and the entire world is asking you questions."

"You think Mikey is running from you in fear?" Auntie Lil asked.

Nikki's voice was steady. "I believe my son no longer thinks of me as his mother, so he has not even considered turning to me in his fear. I also believe Bobby did this entire family irreparable damage when he took Mikey away with him to Los Angeles. I don't think I will ever be able to make up for it now. Besides, Mikey is angry at me right now."

"Why?" Auntie Lil asked.

"He wants to continue his movie career and I think it's time for him to take a break. He can wait out a few years, make the leap from boy to young man, and then maybe try again. God knows we have enough money."

"But it's not what Mikey wants," Auntie Lil said.

"I'm his mother," Nikki replied firmly.

Auntie Lil sighed. "Mikey is already a star," she pointed out. "He's learned how to throw his weight around and get what he wants. Take my advice. Compromise. Let Mikey be in one more movie, then he can take a break." She thought for a moment. "Kill two birds with one stone. Save yourself years of litigation. Let Mikey do the movie for Gene Levitt after all, if it's not too late. Everyone will be better off."

Nikki stood. "Maybe. I'll talk to my lawyers about it." She yawned involuntarily and shrugged an apology. "If you'll excuse me, I have to get up at six o'clock to marshal the troops. Do I have your personal assurance that Mikey is perfectly safe? Or do I need to lie in bed awake and worry?"

"You have my word," Auntie Lil promised. "He's in no danger whatsoever."

CHAPTER FOURTEEN

1. His coffee table was heaped with empty Chinese food containers. Hot mustard was smeared across one edge. A pair of dirty tennis shoes marred the pristine nap of his living-room rug and the dining-room table was littered with white paper bags and empty take-out plates from a nearby diner. Brenda and Eddie were crouched in the center of the table, snarling at each other over a leftover chunk of bagel and lox. Syrup from a double serving of pecan waffles had left a trail like a snail across the polished oak surface of his beloved heirloom.

T.S. surveyed the mess and sighed. Mikey Morgan looked upon the telephone as his umbilical cord. In the past twelve hours, the boy had ordered in both a late-night dinner and his breakfast—never in his life had T.S. been so decadent as to order breakfast delivered—and had then spent an inordinate amount of time talking to a woman named "Candy." Once T.S. discovered that Mikey was watching a soft-porn cable channel consisting chiefly of phone-sex ads, he put a stop to the Candy business. But he was dreading the day his phone bill arrived. Mikey was now napping on the sofa with his stockinged feet propped up on a raw silk pillow. T.S. had no intention of waking him to tell him to remove his feet. So long as Mikey was silent, he would endure any indignity.

He tiptoed to the telephone and called Margo McGregor to request the photographs of last spring's Metro Los Angeles ball. The columnist was persistent in demanding why he needed them, but after T.S. assured her Auntie Lil would keep her promise to break any news through her first,

Margo agreed to the request. She promised to put a rush on the order and would messenger them over in early evening, if possible.

T.S. hung up feeling the first small flush of satisfaction that day. Unfortunately, Brenda and Eddie had finished their tussle over the salmon and, before they could be stopped, pattered over to the couch to leap on Mikey's stomach. They landed with a solid thud, waking the boy at once. "What time is it?" Mikey asked, swatting the cats to the floor. "I'm hungry. Let's order something in."

"It's only eleven o'clock," T.S. protested, suddenly realizing that he was missing his favorite talk show. "You just had breakfast." The child had slept disgracefully late, not rising until nine o'clock.

"Oh, yeah." Mikey swung his feet around until he was in a sitting position, knocking a take-out carton off the table as he did so. A dried-up dumpling tumbled to the carpet and lay there like some sort of alien egg. "I'm bored. There's nothing good on TV." As if to illustrate his point, Mikey proceeded to click through all seventy-seven channels.

T.S. sought refuge in the kitchen and sipped his fifth cup of coffee of the day. Auntie Lil would pay for this, he vowed. He'd think of a way.

"I'm bored," Mikey announced again, appearing at the kitchen door. "Let's go buy some computer games. With your big screen, it will be cool."

"Computer games?" T.S. repeated, his mind leaping with optimistic fervor to one key thought: if he could plug the boy into electronic pastimes, maybe he'd get some peace and quiet. "What kind of games?"

"Let's get Sega Genesis *and* Nintendo. I can afford it." Mikey produced a platinum American Express card from a jeans pocket and held it up. "My treat. Mom never lets me buy Sega games anyway. She says they're too violent. But you'll love them."

T.S. did not hear. He was too busy staring at the credit card. Fourteen years old and the kid probably earned a hundred times more per year than any annual salary T.S. had ever pulled down.

"Where can we buy the games?" Mikey asked.

"There are a couple of electronics stores over on Third Avenue," T.S. said. "But I thought you were afraid to go outside."

"No problem." Mikey tucked his credit card back in place. "I can disguise myself in *your* clothes."

2. Auntie Lil hurried down the pathway toward the Metro's back entrance. She had overslept, then taken longer than usual to go through her morning routine. She should never have used growing old as an excuse to T.S. the night before. It was a jinx. Her bones had woken up tired. At least the glorious sun revived her. She breathed in the fresh air and admired the day. Behind her, she heard a *tap, tap, tap* approaching—it sounded almost like a machine gun—and turned to find Herbert hurrying after her.

"Lillian!" he called out. "I'm so sorry. I was delayed."

Auntie Lil stared at his feet. He wore black shiny shoes that did not fit his casual attire.

"I know they don't match," Herbert apologized. "I've just had a ballroom dancing lesson."

"What kind of shoes are those?" Auntie Lil demanded.

Herbert looked perplexed. "Ordinary men's dress shoes. The kind one would wear with a tuxedo. I wear them to ballroom dancing since I dance most often at formal events."

"That's it," Auntie Lil decided. "The Reverend Hampton heard a man wearing dress shoes running down this path. That's the tapping sound he was talking about."

"Does that narrow it down?" Herbert said.

"Not on opening night, it doesn't," Auntie Lil conceded. "But it does rule out anyone wearing dance shoes. They would be softer and less likely to make a sound."

"What is the purpose of our visit this afternoon?" Herbert asked, falling easily into step beside her.

"To catch a liar," Auntie Lil replied.

The Metro's backstage halls were deserted. Most of the dancers were in class. Classical tunes mingled and overlapped as they passed by each door. Auntie Lil peeked in a few windows and saw solemn rows of Metro dancers bending and stretching to the steady beat of piano music. Lisette Martinez was not among them.

"Maybe she doesn't need to practice?" Herbert suggested.

"Everyone takes classes at the Metro," Auntie Lil said. "She's here somewhere." They passed by the dancers' lounge and Auntie Lil stuck her head inside. Lisette Martinez sat on the lumpy couch, her feet tucked beneath her, holding an unlit cigarette and gazing at it with longing. She did not seem to recognize Auntie Lil when she entered the room.

"You don't remember me?" Auntie Lil said. Herbert stood at the doorway quietly, saying nothing.

Lisette looked up at her. "I remember you now," she said flatly.

"May I sit down?" Auntie Lil asked.

"Can I stop you?" the dancer replied.

Auntie Lil took a seat at the opposite end of the couch. "The first time we talked, you said you didn't meet Bobby Morgan until *Nutcracker* rehearsals began," Auntie Lil said.

"That's right. What of it?" Lisette raised the cigarette absently to her lips, realized it was not lit, and dropped it back down in her lap.

"But you attended the Metro's charity ball in Los Angeles last spring," Auntie Lil said. "And Bobby Morgan was there."

"So were six hundred other people and I didn't meet all of them."

"You're the prima ballerina of the Metro," Auntie Lil pointed out. "And you yourself told me that he always flirts with the most famous women around. You said he had a need to do so."

Lisette yawned. "I can't remember every man I meet. It would be impossible. I am frequently approached."

"Bobby Morgan did not strike me as a man who was easy to forget."

Lisette shrugged. "Why is it so important when I met him?"

"Someone's coming," Herbert announced from the door. "And I do not think that you will like who—" He stopped abruptly as Raoul Martinez charged into the room.

"Why aren't you in class?" he demanded of his wife. He saw Auntie Lil and his face flushed with anger. "I told you to stay away from her."

"I was just passing by," Auntie Lil explained innocently.

The artistic director stepped close to Auntie Lil and towered over her as he spoke, trying to intimidate her with his size. He was a powerful man and his muscles quivered against his tight-fitting leotard top as he struggled to maintain his temper. "I am going to tell you this one more time," he said. "The board may have given you the right to poke around and stick your nose where it doesn't belong, but I have absolute power when it comes to what goes on backstage or onstage here at the Metro. If you ever come near my wife again, I will have to see that you—"

"See that she what?" Herbert asked, sliding in between the larger man and Auntie Lil. Herbert was small, but his power seemed all the greater for being so compact. He waited quietly for an answer and his body was still and calm. His breathing was slow, but his eyes never left Martinez's face.

The artistic director looked away and his gaze settled on his wife. "Get to class now," he ordered. "I won't have you evading classes when the others must be there."

Lisette stood and stretched elaborately, knocking the unlit cigarette to the floor. She glanced down at it then deliberately ground it into the carpet as she strode by her husband and glided gracefully from the room. Martinez glared at Auntie Lil as if it were her fault.

"I have a right to be here," Auntie Lil said, more calmly than she felt.

"Stay away from my wife," Martinez ordered again. "And stay away from me." He turned abruptly and stomped from the room, but the effect was spoiled by the shoes he wore. It's hard to stomp in soft leather slippers.

3. As Herbert and Auntie Lil approached the door of T.S.'s apartment, strange noises emanated from inside. They heard a series of beeps, then a boing, a squawk, and the sound of a gunshot followed by a plop. "What in the world?" Auntie Lil asked, knocking on the door.

"Who is it?" T.S. yelled, not bothering to come to the door.

"Me," Auntie Lil said firmly. "Let me in now."

"Go let her in," T.S. ordered Mikey, his voice muffled by the door.

The door opened to reveal the back of Mikey Morgan's head. He was turned to T.S. and complaining loudly. "Come on, that's a dumb game. It's for babies. Let's play Sega. The one where you hang cheerleaders from meat hooks."

"Just let me have one more round," T.S. said, not bothering to greet his guests.

Auntie Lil and Herbert stepped inside the chaos of T.S.'s apartment. The floor was littered with plastic bags, clear wrappings, fast-food sacks, and articles of T.S.'s clothing that Mikey had discarded once they returned home from their shopping expedition. Brenda and Eddie had knocked the top bun from a leftover hamburger littering the floor of the foyer and were busily licking the meat patty. Every surface in the room was covered with video-movie and game boxes, comic books, bags of snacks, and half-eaten cookies. T.S was oblivious to the mess. He stood mesmerized in front of his large-screen television set, holding a green plastic device up in front of his eyes like a visor. As an animated duck flew out of the bushes depicted on the screen before him, T.S. bent his legs slightly and pressed a button on the control device. The duck squawked, flapped its wings, and tumbled from the video sky to the sounds of T.S.'s triumphant yell. "Got 'im!" he shouted. Another duck flew out of the bushes and he fired again, sending it plummeting to earth with a plop.

"What in God's name is going on here?" Auntie Lil demanded. "It looks like a tornado hit."

"He won't let me play Sega Genesis," Mikey whined. "He's been playing that dumb duck-blind game for hours. He's obsessed."

"Bring me a cookie," T.S. shouted over his shoulder before steadying his aim for the upcoming duck.

Auntie Lil picked up a bag of cookies, marched over to T.S., and conked him over the head with it before switching off the television set. "You have obviously lost your mind," she said.

T.S. looked around as if he were coming out of a trance. "What time is it?" he asked.

"It's time to ask this young man a few more questions," Auntie Lil said grimly. "Sit down." Her natural authority was so great that both T.S. and Mikey sat obediently on the couch. "Not you," she told T.S. "For God's sakes, go comb your hair and straighten up this place. You're both a mess."

T.S.'s eyes were glazed; he was having trouble focusing at close range.

"Go wash your face," Auntie Lil instructed him firmly. She sighed and sat next to Mikey. "This is my friend Herbert Wong," she said, nodding toward the door where her friend stood. "He's helping me out, and if you want a bodyguard, he might be of assistance."

Mikey looked the small Asian man over with scorn. "If I need a grandpa, I have my own."

Auntie Lil sighed. "We will both ignore that comment. I went back to the Metro today and I met a very angry man. Angry enough to do something like follow you, perhaps. I began to wonder why he might follow you, if indeed he is the man. So I have a question for you."

Mikey squirmed uncomfortably and evaded her eyes.

"I asked you if you saw anything suspicious backstage," Auntie Lil reminded him. "You said no."

"I didn't see anything," Mikey insisted, his eyes sliding to the blank television. "I was busy getting ready to go on."

"I think you did see something," Auntie Lil said. "I think you saw someone who had been wearing your Drosselmeyer cloak try to replace it before you came looking for it. Did you?"

Mikey stared out the window for a moment then turned to Auntie Lil, widening his eyes and holding her gaze with an innocent expression. "No," he said. "I would have told you. Why do you think that?"

"Because if you are being followed, there's a reason. And I think that reason may be that either you saw the killer or the murderer *thinks* you saw him. If you know more, you must tell me now."

Mikey shrugged. "I can't tell you something I don't know."

"Fine. I've talked to your mother. You can go home tonight."

"No!" Mikey shouted. "I'm not going home."

"But you are going to tell me what I want to know," Auntie Lil said. She waited, hands folded in her lap. She'd seen the gleam in his eye. He would tell her sooner or later.

"It was dark backstage. I can't be sure." His lower lip stuck out in a pout.

"What do you *think* you saw?" she asked slowly.

Mikey shrugged. "Nothing much. A man putting my cloak back in place on a hook by the big fuse box."

"What did the man look like?" Auntie Lil asked patiently.

Mikey's face scrunched up in concentration. "He had dark hair."

"How tall was he?" Auntie Lil said.

Mikey bit his lower lip with his teeth while he thought the question over. "Average height," he finally said. "He wasn't tall, if that's what you mean."

"Did you recognize him?" Auntie Lil asked again.

Mikey shook his head emphatically. "You won't make me go home, will you?" he asked just as T.S. reentered the living room, a thick envelope in his hand. The boy turned to T.S. "Can I stay? Please?"

"I don't see why he can't stay another day just to be safe," T.S. conceded. "We were going to order in Indian food tonight and we already have two movies picked out. Here—this came an hour or so ago. From Margo McGregor." He handed the envelope to Auntie Lil and picked up an unopened video-game box, reading the description with interest. "Two people can play this one," he told Mikey. "Want to give it a try?"

Auntie Lil gave up. She took the envelope to the dining-room table and shoved aside a stack of video movies with titles that favored the words *Kung Fu*. Herbert joined her, scooping a bag of potato chips off the chair before he sat down. She opened the envelope and spread out several dozen black-and-white oversized photographs.

"What are we looking for?" Herbert asked.

"This woman," Auntie Lil said, holding up a photo of Lisette Martinez entering the party on the arm of her husband, Raoul. "With this man." She held up another photo, this time showing a bored Bobby Morgan being cornered by a determined Lane Rogers. Lane's sweeping Grecian gown made her look like the patio window in a badly decorated suburban home.

"You mean a photo like this one?" Herbert asked. He held up a glossy print of Lisette Martinez and Bobby Morgan laughing together.

Auntie Lil grabbed the photograph and examined it. Morgan's face was far more animated than in the first shot. His grin was wide and he was holding his champagne glass aloft with one hand while he held out an oval gold cigarette lighter in the other. Lisette's head was thrown back and her long hair rippled behind her like a dark waterfall. One elegant arm was extended in front of her and a cigarette dangled from between her graceful fingers. Unlike the other more crowded photos, this shot showed only the two of them alone in a corner of the room. The table beside them held four bottles of champagne. "Just like this one," Auntie Lil said.

4. "What do you expect to find?" Herbert whispered. They were crouched in a darkened storage room on the third floor of the Metro, the one where Auntie suspected Bobby Morgan had been killed. Despite the murder, security at the Metropolitan was still dismally poor. Auntie Lil and Herbert had simply waited until that night's performance of *The Nutcracker* was over, then slipped in the side door when a distracted group of dancers exited. They were able to make their way upstairs without being noticed and had waited in the darkness ever since.

"I don't know what we're going to find," Auntie Lil admitted. "Do you think everyone has left yet?"

Herbert shrugged. "Is this wise?" he asked. "We could be caught."

"I gave her a chance to tell me the truth. Now I'm going to find out why she's lying."

"How?"

"By searching her locker and her husband's office and every other room of this place if I have to." Auntie Lil's fingers worked over the thick rope coiled on the floor. If Jerry Vanderbilt had called the police as she had advised, they had left the scene exactly as it was before. Perhaps they had dismissed the bits of cotton and dirty ribbon as leftover refuse from an earlier use for the room. And maybe they were right.

"Where are we going to look first?" Herbert asked, his voice low.

"Her locker. I'm going to pry it open and see what's inside. Those two are hiding something."

"Why didn't you tell me we'd be breaking and entering? I could have brought tools," Herbert said.

Auntie Lil patted her enormous handbag in the darkness. "Don't worry. I've got us covered. I raided Theodore's toolbox. I could have stolen the furniture right out from under his nose. Those two will be in exactly the same position when we return, mark my words. They'll be sitting on the couch, slack-jawed and glassy-eyed, with drool running down their chins."

"At least he is not protesting having to baby-sit," Herbert pointed out.

"Did you hear that?" Auntie Lil whispered. They fell silent as footsteps approached the room. The doorknob rattled as if someone had bumped into it. Auntie Lil's heart was pounding so loudly in her chest that she was sure Herbert could hear it. A few seconds later the door to the catwalk slammed shut with a bang, causing them both to flinch. The footsteps returned past their room, and a minute later the sliver of light leaking in under the door of their room disappeared. The upper floor was now in total darkness.

"Ricky Lee Harris," Auntie Lil whispered. "The lighting director. He'd be one of the last to leave."

They waited fifteen minutes to be safe, then crept cautiously from their hiding spot and out to the third-floor hallway. There were no windows in the cavernous backstage building, so they had to find their way around in the darkness. Auntie Lil kept her hand on the wall and carefully followed it back toward the inner stairs. Two floors below, they heard a door slam. Auntie Lil froze; Herbert bumped into her and took a silent step backward. They waited, ears straining for unfamiliar sounds, but heard nothing. Auntie Lil put her mouth close to Herbert's ear. "Someone was just leaving," she barely sighed. "Shall we go on?"

Herbert touched her arm in assent and they began to descend the stairs. The lockers were on the second floor at the far end of the hall, well beyond the other rooms and closer to the first-floor steps. It was a long walk given the need to maintain absolute silence. Auntie Lil's legs began to ache with tension long before they reached their destination. But the door to the dressing area opened easily to her touch and they slipped inside without trouble. She fished a navy scarf out of her pocketbook and carefully taped it over the small window in the door with strips from a roll of cellophane tape she also produced from the depths of her bag. Herbert was well acquainted with the endless contents of her purse and not the least surprised. Next out of her carryall was a small penlight. She handed it to Herbert and he lit her way to the first locker on the right. It was the most spacious of the lockers and its name tag confirmed that it belonged to Lisette Martinez. A small metal lock barred entry, but it was easily jimmied apart with the shaft of a screwdriver. It flew open so suddenly that the tool banged against the metal door of the locker with a clang. They froze, their breath loud in the silence. But no footsteps approached and they continued with their task. Auntie Lil opened the door, holding her breath as she lifted the latch. The metal door opened quietly and she crouched before it, examining the contents inside using the narrow illumination emanating from the tiny flashlight. The top shelf of the locker held a stack of neatly folded T-shirts. She searched between and beneath them but found nothing unusual. Several pairs of toe shoes were stored behind the clothing and she pulled them out for inspection. They were delicate in appearance but sturdy in construction. Soft satin pleats covered canvas sidewalls the consistency of cardboard. The soles were heavy canvas and the hardened tips reinforced inside with carefully sculpted wads of cotton batting. She examined the cotton under the light. It was impossible to tell if it matched the shreds found by Bobby Morgan's body. But one thing was certain: the ribbon that Auntie Lil had found on the floor of the storage room had been a grimy white. And while Lisette Martinez probably wore white shoes in many ballets, she did not store those shoes in her locker. All three pairs were a pale pink and the ribbons matched the shoes exactly. Auntie Lil was disappointed but undeterred. She replaced the shoes carefully and searched the pockets of several pairs of sweatpants hanging from hooks on each side of the locker. She discovered bits of tobacco in each pocket and a few sticky breath mints, but nothing more. The floor of the locker proved more promising. Amidst a heap of clean cotton socks, Auntie Lil uncovered a small leather-bound date book.

"Why would she keep this in her locker instead of with her?" Auntie Lil whispered to Herbert, holding the date book aloft for his inspection.

Herbert opened it and examined a few pages. "Maybe to hide it from her husband?" he suggested.

"Exactly," Auntie Lil agreed. They searched through the book's calendar pages carefully. Last spring, Lisette had marked approximately three days a week with the initial *L* and nothing more. By summer, the initial *C* had taken *L*'s place, though an occasional *B* appeared. In September, the *B* was followed by an arrow blocking out an entire week.

After that, *C* disappeared from the calendar, and except for the initial *S*—which appeared no more than two times a month—the days were blank. Beginning in mid-October, *B* began appearing again almost every other day before disappearing abruptly one month later. After that, the pages were completely blank.

"No wonder she needed a calendar," Auntie Lil whispered. "She had to have some way to keep all these men straight."

"You think those are dates with men?" Herbert asked.

"They can't be anything else," Auntie Lil decided. She slipped the date book into her purse. "Let's compare this to her husband's calendar, shall we? I think we're going to find that Raoul Martinez was not in New York last September during the time when *B* was blocked off for an entire week."

"*B* as in Bobby Morgan?" Herbert asked.

"That's my bet," Auntie Lil agreed. She checked the floor of the locker a final time but found nothing more of interest. Carefully shutting the door, she replaced the lock. It hung open crookedly. "She'll know someone has been in her locker anyway when she sees the date book is missing," Auntie Lil decided. "It may be better to spook her and see what she does next."

After removing the scarf from the window, they silently inched their way back toward the first-floor steps. When they reached the stairwell, they caught the tail end of an echo. The sound was elusive. A scrambling? Rats? Or someone sliding past below? Auntie Lil touched Herbert's arm lightly, not daring to speak. He patted her hand reassuringly. They waited in the darkness, straining to hear more. The night was silent. Slowly they began to move down the steps, making it to the first floor without incident. Raoul Martinez kept a cluttered office toward the back of the building, near the rear exit doors. Auntie Lil was prepared to slip the lock with her Macy's credit card. Indeed, she used it more to gain illegal entry than she did to charge purchases. But to her surprise, the office door opened easily. She hurried inside with Herbert right behind her. They shut the solid wooden door behind them and Herbert flicked on the penlight.

Lisette Martinez stood crouched over an open drawer of her husband's desk, a sheaf of papers in one hand.

"What are you doing here?" she and Auntie Lil asked simultaneously.

Before anyone could react, the door of the office flew open and the overhead lights blazed on. Auntie Lil shielded her eyes. In the seconds that it took for her vision to clear she realized that they were trapped: Raoul Martinez blocked the doorway and he held a heavy cane in one hand—a prop from *The Nutcracker*.

"Raoul!" Lisette cried, dropping the papers.

"What are you doing in here?" Martinez asked his wife. "You said you were going home to bed early."

"What are *you* doing here?" she asked him back, the color draining from her face.

Herbert Wong did not hesitate. He took advantage of their inattention to dart past Martinez, knocking the cane away with one hand while grabbing the bigger man's shirt collar with the other. He shoved a surprised Martinez against the door and sent him sprawling. "Run!" he shouted to Auntie Lil.

Auntie Lil sprinted from the room, the ache in her legs forgotten. She barreled toward the outer exit doors, flinging her weight against them. The doors were illegally locked from the inside. She whirled around and saw that the nearest side door was blocked by a recovered Martinez. The artistic director had leaped back to his feet and was struggling with Herbert for the cane. Lisette stood in the background as if frozen by fear, watching her husband tussle.

"Go, Lillian!" Herbert shouted, aiming a kick and catching Martinez solidly on a shin.

Auntie Lil began to run through the darkness of the backstage area, crashing into scenery and props as she did so. Scrims fell to the floor with a crash and props tumbled from tables. Her progress was easily charted by the tremendous din that marked her passage. She could hear Martinez moving after her. She began to fling objects out of her way, clearing a path toward stage right, pushing heavy curtains away from her face, and for one terrifying moment, becoming lost in a series of overlapping side curtains before finding her way free again. She reached stage right and hesitated. How could she leave Herbert alone with Martinez? She turned to go back and discovered her friend right behind her.

"Go, Lillian!" Herbert shouted again. "The side door. Try the side door up ahead." But as they scurried toward the door, they heard the heavy thud of Martinez cutting across the stage to block their exit. Auntie Lil stopped uncertainly, her hands reaching out in the darkness. She touched the metal of a permanent ladder embedded into the backstage brick walls. It probably led to an upper floor. Perhaps she could find a place to hide, a telephone, or a way out from there. "Come on," she whispered to Herbert, pulling herself onto the bottom rung. With Herbert pushing her from beneath, she climbed steadily upward, breathing hard, her shoulders aching from the effort. The ladder jiggled beneath her and she felt dizzy. She stopped to catch her breath.

"He's following us!" Herbert whispered frantically. "I can feel his weight on the rungs beneath us!"

Suddenly the backstage lights blazed on, illuminating the brick wall and scattered scenery with a blinding glare.

"Leave them alone!" Lisette Martinez screamed at her husband. The back curtains of the stage opened with a jerk, creating a gap of several yards. The ballerina dashed into view from stage left, breathing hard. Her husband was only a dozen rungs up the ladder. She jumped in the air, grabbing at his legs as if to stop him. He climbed up out of her reach then paused to stare down at his wife.

"Let them alone!" Lisette shouted again. "Enough people have been hurt. Leave it, Raoul. It's time to let it go." She stepped back and looked up at Auntie Lil. "I did it!" she shouted. "Is that what you want to hear? I killed him. I killed him because he left me and no one leaves me. He left me for someone younger. Just like him." She pointed a finger at her husband and he stared back at her, his face crumpling in despair.

"No," he yelled. His deep voice reverberated across the empty stage and rolled up into the rafters. "It won't work, Lisette. We must tell them the truth." He leaned back and dangled from the ladder so he could see Herbert and Auntie Lil better. "I did it," he said. "I killed him because he was flaunting his affair with my wife. No one does that to Raoul Martinez."

"He's lying," Lisette shouted. "I'm the one. He's only saying that to protect me."

"No, it won't work," Raoul yelled at his wife. "They know you haven't the strength."

"I have the strength," Lisette screamed back, and as if to prove it, leaped onto the bottom rung and climbed up to her husband. She grabbed one of his legs and attempted to pull him from the ladder. "Let it go, Raoul," she ordered. "I'm going to the police right now and turn myself in."

Auntie Lil stared at the battling couple in confusion. She had spent weeks trying to track down a killer and now these two were arguing for the right to claim the title for themselves. "What should we do now?" she asked Herbert.

Herbert glanced down at Raoul Martinez. He was only a few yards below but was making no move to climb higher. Instead he had grabbed his wife's hand and was staring into her eyes, murmuring her name over and over as if it were a spell he could cast upon her. "Lisette, Lisette, Lisette," he murmured. "You must not do this, my darling Lisette."

"Which one of them did it?" Auntie Lil asked loudly.

"I don't think either one of them did," Herbert replied.

5.   Raoul and Lisette Martinez sat in the front row of the Metropolitan Ballet's magnificent theater separated from each other by three red velvet seats. They stared at one another in incomprehension, their faces reflecting a combination of joy and relief. Auntie Lil and Herbert waited cautiously a few feet away, watching the strange scene unfolding before them.

"You didn't do it after all, did you?" Raoul asked his wife. His eyes filled with tears of happiness.

Lisette shook her head. "I thought you did it," she said softly. "I thought they would take you away from me forever. I knew that you had found out about us. . . ." Her voice trailed off.

"How could I ever have thought you could do such a thing, my precious angel," her husband replied. He moved to the seat next to her and encircled her with his arms. "I didn't blame you for seeing that man, you know. I have flaunted my affairs. I knew when you were . . . doing the same."

"Oh, Raoul," Lisette said, turning her face to the side so her expression was hidden from all but her husband. "None of them meant anything to me, you must know that."

"My beautiful ballerina, I do know," he replied. The couple began to kiss, their bodies melding together until they sat in the same seat.

Auntie Lil cleared her throat loudly. When that did not work, she coughed as if she were in imminent danger of dying from tuberculosis. Not only was she annoyed at their mutual stupidity, she was feeling queasy at this display of dramatic affection. And she was determined to wring whatever information she could from the situation. "Now you two listen to me," she finally announced firmly, marching over and planting herself beside them until they were forced to turn their attention to her. "You are both grossly guilty of obstructing justice, and thanks to you two, a killer has gone free for far longer than he should."

They stared at her as if she were speaking Swahili.

"You owe me," Auntie Lil told them. "If you tell me what I need to know, then I promise I will walk away from this nonsense, never breathe a word of it to the board, and leave the two of you to find your way through your most peculiar marriage all on your own."

Martinez looked as if he might put up a fight, so Auntie Lil continued. "Don't tempt me," she warned them. "The board would be most interested to learn of your extracurricular behavior if, as I suspect, your hobbies happen to involve students at the Metro School."

"They were all of age!" Martinez protested.

"No matter. It's tacky at the very least." Auntie Lil shifted her gaze to Lisette. "Why did Bobby Morgan dump you?" she said. "I'm sorry to be so blunt, but that is exactly what happened, isn't it? He came back to New York and insisted his son be in *The Nutcracker* just to be near you, didn't he? But then he grew bored."

The ballerina nodded slowly. "He was a pig."

"Nonetheless, why did this pig dump you?" Auntie Lil asked firmly.

"He began seeing someone else, someone younger. I'm sure of it."

"Who?" Auntie Lil demanded.

"I don't know," Lisette shouted, her anger real. The fire in her eyes told Auntie Lil that she was telling the truth. Lisette did not know who her rival had been and her lack of knowledge rankled.

"Then why do you think it was someone younger?" Auntie Lil asked.

"Something he said to me," she said bitterly. "I will not repeat it here."

"You have no idea who it was?" Auntie Lil said.

Lisette shook her head. "I assumed it was one of the other dancers. He was always surrounded by them. It could have been anyone."

"Do *you* know who it was?" Auntie Lil asked Martinez. "Since you seem so well-informed about the dancers." Her sarcasm was so subtle it slipped right by Martinez. He merely blinked and shook his head.

"I watched him closely when I knew he was seeing my wife," Martinez admitted. "But I didn't care about him once I knew they had broken up."

"How did you know they had broken up?" Auntie Lil asked.

"My wife's behavior. She was desolate. Angry at me for every little thing. Tearing me apart for such small transgressions. That is how she always acts when her affairs fizzle."

He made a hissing sound like a firecracker being dipped in water.

"Such small transgressions?" Lisette cried, moving away from her husband. She perched two seats away and glared. "I suppose you consider your four affairs in six months small transgressions?" she asked. "I suppose you think it's perfectly acceptable for me to have to take a mental audit every time I enter a class. 'Who in this room has slept with my husband? You? You? What about you?' How dare you dismiss your despicable behavior as acceptable? You do not deserve to be married to me."

Raoul began to protest.

Auntie Lil and Herbert exchanged a glance. Herbert nodded and the two of them marched up the short set of stairs at stage right without bothering to look back. As they pushed through the side exit door and breathed in the fresh night air, they could still hear the couple battling, their passionate shouts echoing in the emptiness of the magnificent auditorium.

CHAPTER FIFTEEN

1. Auntie Lil woke out of a sleep so deep it was like swimming up from the depths of a heavy sea. Her dreams had been ominous and exhausting: she was being chased by small creatures dressed in black cloaks and forced to climb ladder after ladder to flee them. The pursuit felt so real that she woke grateful for the respite that awakening offered. She rose and touched her toes in front of the mirror. At least the ache in her shoulders had subsided somewhat. She had slept for over ten hours and her body had welcomed the rest.

As she brewed her morning pot of coffee Auntie Lil reflected on the events of the night before. She had followed a trail, but when it ended, she felt little closer to a solution than when she began. Neither of the Martinezes was guilty, she was sure. Worse, they had no idea who was. She could try to find out who had usurped Lisette Martinez in Bobby Morgan's affections, but that, too, could prove to be a fruitless path. The possibilities were limited only by the size of the Metro's corps and school. His new lover could have been one of over sixty girls. Perhaps it was better to pursue another direction. She could try to identify the man that Mikey Morgan claimed to have seen backstage replacing Drosselmeyer's cloak. A man of average height with dark hair. That could be several people, even with Raoul Martinez ruled out. Jerry Vanderbilt, Gene Levitt—he was the most likely prospect—or he and Jerry could be in it together. But something about the description Mikey gave just didn't make sense.

She took her second cup of coffee to a window and

stared out at the street below. Mikey said the man replacing the cloak had been of average height, but then he had claimed that the man following him was tall. Either there were two people involved or Mikey was mistaken. But hadn't Reverend Hampton said it was a tall man running down the path behind the Metro just a few minutes after Morgan's body swung across the stage? She felt more comfortable with Hampton's assessment. He was an adult and both shrewd and observant. Perhaps she should call the Reverend and ask him again just to be sure.

The phone line was dead. She remembered disconnecting it the night before so she could sleep late without interruption. No wonder no one had rung her up yet. She reconnected the jack and dialed Reverend Hampton's home. As usual a polite voice answered and, when she gave her name and said it was an emergency, promised to track down the Reverend as soon as possible. No more than four sips of coffee later, Ben Hampton called back.

"You aren't going to yell at me about the seat-on-the-board comment, are you?" he thundered into the phone in lieu of saying hello. "It's just politics. Although I wouldn't turn one down."

"Any other time I'd have to differ with your handling of that," Auntie Lil said. "But I've got far more important things on my mind."

"So have I," the Reverend replied. "Have you seen my latest opinion polls?"

"I've been too busy," Auntie Lil admitted.

"My support among whites has shot up thirty percent and I've gained more than a dozen points on my opponent. I owe you my thanks."

"Don't thank me," Auntie Lil said. "I only suggested a few surface modifications. You're the genuine article."

"Did you read my Twenty-Point Plan Against Crime yet?" he asked. "It was in Margo McGregor's column a few days ago."

"No," she admitted. "Anything new? Many have tried before you."

"Sure," he said with a chuckle. "I suggested we make

you police commissioner." His laugh made her smile. "I have a meeting with the mayor in fifteen minutes to discuss the plan, in fact. You said it was an emergency?"

Auntie Lil asked him to again describe the man he had seen running down the path. He did so with immediate consistency: the man had been white, tall, and slender with an unknown color of hair. "He was a regular beanpole," Reverend Hampton added.

"You're positive?" Auntie Lil asked.

"More positive every time I tell it," he said. "Though the police still don't believe my story."

"Could a child have thought he was of average height?" she asked.

"I would think a child would be more likely to see him as even taller," the Reverend said. "Sorry I can't be more specific about this guy."

"You've been helpful enough as it is," Auntie Lil said. "Thank you."

"The same to you," Reverend Hampton answered. "You'll have to dance with me at my inauguration ball in ten years when I become the governor of this great state of New York."

She had no doubt he was serious. She rang off and wondered if Mikey Morgan was lying and, if so, about which man. Perhaps about both. Perhaps about neither. If only she could see inside that infernal child's head. He'd been play-acting for so long that she wondered if he even knew how he really felt—or what he really saw—at this point.

Her thoughts were interrupted by the shrill ring of her telephone. When she answered, the husky voice of Emili Vladimir greeted her. She sounded in a hurry. "I've been trying to call you all morning," the former ballerina said. "I was just trying one more time before I head downtown to my studio."

"I had the phone off the hook," Auntie Lil admitted. "What has happened? Why are you calling?"

"I must speak to you," Emili said. "Alone. Today. Immediately. Now, if possible. I will postpone my next appointment until the afternoon. Please, it is very important."

Auntie Lil was silent. "Why alone?"

"It is about my son," Emili explained. "I must talk to you as one mother to another."

"I'm not a mother," Auntie Lil pointed out.

"I must talk to you woman to woman, then. Please. You will not be in any danger," Emili promised, her voice thickening with a Russian accent as she grew more agitated. "I will meet you in a public place. You may choose."

"The dancers' lounge at the Metro," Auntie Lil said at once. There would be many people passing by. "I will meet you there in an hour."

"Come alone," Emili pleaded, hanging up without another word.

2. Auntie Lil had no choice but to meet with Emili alone. Herbert did not answer his phone and T.S. was no doubt lost to the waking world as he bathed in video stimulation with his temporary charge. Fortunately, it was the middle of the day and the Metro was a bustling center of activity. Classes were being held in all of the rooms and the hallway was full of dancers, musicians, and support staff hurrying to their next destinations. The dancers' lounge was an oasis of calm amidst the frantic scurrying: no one would have time to relax for several hours and the room was deserted. Auntie Lil waited a few minutes for Emili to arrive, carefully situating herself at the end of the couch closest to the door. Her dash from Martinez the night before was still fresh in her memory. From now on, she'd keep a getaway in mind at all times.

Emili entered the lounge flushed and out of breath. She wore her dancing clothes under a leather jacket, which she immediately threw on a nearby chair. "I must shut the door," she said, and did so without waiting for Auntie Lil to agree.

"What is it?" Auntie Lil asked, relaxing a bit after Emili sat on the far end of the couch.

"I know you don't trust me," Emili began. "I have talked to my friend Ruth and she tells me that you know all about that Lane woman's attempts to replace you on the board. You may think I am involved, but I am not."

"You are a friend of Ruth Beretsky's?" Auntie Lil asked skeptically.

"Yes. Why not?" Emili said. "She called me several months ago and asked if I needed help in setting up a foundation to support my ballet company." Emili tapped her heart with a fist. "She is a plain woman, perhaps, with little spark in her life. But she has fire in her heart for the dance. She has no talent herself, but she receives great joy from watching others dance and she is very much committed to seeing new art forms flourish. I admire that in her and I don't mind that she wears those silly bows and creeps around like a mouse."

"What did Ruth say she had told me?" Auntie Lil asked.

"The truth," Emili explained. "That Lane had called me about a seat on the board. I was very surprised at first. I knew she didn't like me. I have met her many times and always she pretends not to know who I am. But then she learns that I have founded my own company. She reads a review of my work in *The New York Times* and thinks, 'Aha! This woman will be famous again. I must collect her now.' I have met many people like her here in New York City. I am no fool. I know how those types of people are." Emili leaned forward, speaking earnestly. "She was the one who called me about a seat on the board. I did not know she meant your seat. I apologize. I would have said no. I have no real desire to be involved with the Metro. The ballets are so rigid, the style excessive and stuffy. That Martinez man does not understand the beauty of an isolated movement. He cannot grasp that ballet should be like poetry. The fewer the lines, the greater the impact." She sat back and sighed. "I tell you all of this only so you can understand that I am telling you the truth here today. I have nothing to hide."

Auntie Lil did not know whether to believe her or not. But she also conceded that cultural differences could be at the root of her skepticism. "Go on," she told Emili.

"You must understand something else first," Emili said.

"So you can be certain that I am telling the truth. When *The Nutcracker* was first cast, the students in the classes knew who had been originally picked for the leading roles. One of the boys broke into Martinez's office and found the scores from the tryouts. It was common knowledge among the students that Fatima Jones would be dancing the role of Clara and my Rudy would be Drosselmeyer and the Prince. He came home and told me, very proud that he had gained such a part." She paused for breath. "You can imagine our disappointment when we learned that the parts would be going to that child actor and Julie Perkins instead." She shrugged. "Rudy was disappointed, but I was not surprised. In Russia, it was always this way. What surprised me was that later, the board returned the parts to their rightful owners. When I thanked the board I was truly grateful for that decision."

"What does this have to do with Morgan's murder?" Auntie Lil asked.

"I am coming to that," Emili promised. "I want you to know that I was the one who told Ruth Beretsky about the tryout scores. And she was the one who called that columnist woman and told her the truth."

"Ruth Beretsky was Margo McGregor's source for her article starting the whole Fatima Jones protest?"

Emili nodded. "Ruth did not think that what had happened to Fatima was fair. And, of course, it was not. But if Lane Rogers finds out, Ruth will be off the board. Perhaps this is why she wishes to work with my company now. But I tell you all this so that you understand that I knew and had accepted all along what had happened. I held no grudge against this Bobby Morgan man. In fact, I want to help you find the killer so that we may all return to our normal lives."

"How can you help me?" Auntie Lil asked.

"Rudy knows more than he told you the other night," Emili said quickly, as if wanting to get the words out of her mouth before she changed her mind. "I knew it the moment he met you. Do you remember what he said?"

Auntie Lil shook her head.

" 'I know you,' " Emili repeated. " 'All of Mikey's friends do'." She shook her head as if thinking it over. "I thought it was a funny thing to say, as if he had been talking about you with his friends. Yet he had never mentioned you to me and he usually tells me every detail of his day. I knew then that he was hiding something from me. It made me unhappy, you must understand." She smiled sadly. "He is growing up and becoming his own person, moving away from me, and I must learn to accept that. But this is different. This is murder, and if Rudy knows something about it, then he must tell you."

"And not the police?" Auntie Lil asked.

Emili's eyes flashed. "Never the police," she said in a flat voice. "I am sure you understand why. I will have Rudy tell you what he knows firsthand. Now. It may not be important. But you must be the one to decide that." Impulsively, she moved closer to Auntie Lil and grabbed her hands, holding them as if they were old friends. "You are an honest woman. I can feel it clearly. You are not always discreet, but you are always yourself. That is a rare thing to find in anyone."

Auntie Lil nodded, unsure of how to treat the compliment. "Thank you," she finally said. "But I am more interested in hearing what Rudy has to tell me about the murder."

Emili stood. "Yes. I will go get him now."

"But he's in class," Auntie Lil protested.

"That will not stop me," Emili promised. She strode from the room with a resolve that would have no trouble overruling any instructor the Metro might employ. She returned a few minutes later with a pale-looking Rudy in tow. "Sit," she commanded her son. He moved obediently to a chair across from Auntie Lil and perched on the edge of it. He was wearing leotards and breathing heavily. His mother had probably plucked him from class in midjeté. "Tell her what you told me," Emili ordered in a voice that would have made a KGB agent proud.

Rudy looked mutely at Auntie Lil and then back at his mother, his eyes pleading.

"Tell her," Emili said firmly. *"Now."*

"But Mikey will be mad," Rudy protested. "And the other boys will call me a snitch."

"We do not have time for such nonsense," Emili said crisply. "This is not a matter of protecting friends. It is not honorable to protect a person who would kill another like that. You must tell her the truth right now."

Rudy stared miserably at his feet. They were splayed to the side in an automatic and perfect first position.

"Rudolph Erik Vladimir, you tell this woman what you told me last night," Emili ordered for the last time in a voice that held every ounce of the discipline and strength that had brought her to where she was today. "You tell her this very instant or you shall have me to deal with from this day forward. Do you want that?"

Rudy sighed. "Mikey had a big fight with his dad that afternoon."

"The afternoon before his father was killed?" Auntie Lil asked.

Rudy nodded. "They were yelling and screaming at each other on the third floor. They thought that no one could hear them, but the door to the catwalk was open and their voices carried down onstage. I was onstage with the wooden soldiers and mice waiting to rehearse my Nutcracker part. Just the guys who were standing on stage left could hear them."

"What were they saying?" Auntie Lil asked.

"Mikey screamed that he hated his father, that he wished he was dead, that he always took everything away from him, and it wasn't fair."

"What did Mikey's father say back?"

"He yelled back that Mikey was nothing without him, that he had been the one to create his career and talent had nothing to do with it. Then he yelled that Mikey couldn't even dance very well because he was too lazy. Mikey really got mad then. He said that he never wanted to be in *The Nutcracker* to begin with and he was only doing it because his dad made him. Then it sounded like he was going to cry."

"Mikey was going to cry?" Auntie Lil asked.

Rudy nodded guiltily. "We kind of sneaked off the stage and went up the stairs to listen," he admitted. "Me and a couple of other boys."

"What did you hear when you got closer?"

"Mikey's dad was trying to whisper, but Mikey was too mad to keep his voice down. He kept saying, 'It's not fair. You don't care about her. You'll just get rid of her like all the rest.' Then Mikey's dad started making fun of him, reminding him of how young he was and asking him how could he know what was fair and what wasn't. He told Mikey that when he was a man he'd understand everything."

"Everything about what?" Auntie Lil asked.

Rudy looked miserable.

"Tell her," Emili ordered.

"I think Mikey's dad stole his girlfriend."

Auntie Lil's stomach twinged. She was a long, long way from the age of fourteen, but she knew how emotional teenagers were. They felt everything a hundred times more than adults. If what Rudy was saying proved to be true, then Mikey Morgan probably had really hated his father at that instant—and been capable of murder. At least mentally.

"Who was Mikey's girlfriend?" Auntie Lil asked.

Rudy shrugged. "He wouldn't tell us. I guess he thought we would tease him," he explained. "We're his friends, but Mikey's been around a lot more, you know? He thinks we're babies about some things. We didn't even know he had a girlfriend until we overheard the argument."

Auntie Lil was quiet, mulling over the information. She thought she knew who the girlfriend was. "I have some very important questions for you, Rudy," she aid. "And you must tell me the truth."

Rudy nodded solemnly.

"Why were you and your friends talking about me?" she asked. "Why did you say that all of Mikey's friends knew who I was?"

"He said you were trying to find the killer but . . ." His voice trailed off.

"But what?" Auntie Lil prompted.

"I don't think Mikey really wants you to find out who it is," he whispered. "He said you were way off base and he sounded glad about it."

"When did he say that?" Auntie Lil asked.

"Last week," the young boy replied.

"My next question is this: Did anyone else overhear what Mikey and his father were arguing about? Think carefully."

Rudy's face scrunched up as he concentrated. "We were on the steps," he finally said. "So I don't really know. They had dropped their voices and I don't think anyone else onstage could hear them anymore. But maybe someone on the third floor might have been able to hear. I didn't see anyone."

"Was anyone on the catwalk?"

Rudy thought hard. "I don't think so. Sometimes parents go up there to watch their kids because Mr. Martinez never notices them when they're on the catwalk. When he sees them watching backstage, he yells, so they sneak up there."

"But the door to the catwalk was open, so someone may have been there?"

Rudy shrugged. "I don't know. It's hard to see if there's anyone on the catwalk when you're standing right below it."

"My final question is the most serious," Auntie Lil said. "Did you or any of your friends help Mikey hurt his father?"

"No," Rudy said, shaking his head emphatically. "I would never do anything like that."

"But would any of the other boys? Maybe some who wanted to prove to Mikey that they really were his friends?"

Rudy's voice was less emphatic. "I don't think so," he said.

Auntie Lil thought of the day she had seen a cluster of boys gathered around a rope near the spot on the stage where Mikey's father had died. They had been pointing and laughing. "Are you absolutely sure that you are telling me the truth?" she asked again.

"Rudy is telling you the truth," Emili said firmly. "I would not allow my son to lie."

3.   Auntie Lil sat alone in the dancers' lounge, her spirits low. Emili Vladimir had returned to her studio, escorting Rudy back to class along the way, satisfied that her moral obligation had been fulfilled.

Was Emili being genuine about her motives? Auntie Lil did not know. But she did believe what Rudy had to say.

And if Rudy were telling the truth, then there was something so careless about this case that her soul hung heavy at the thought. Did no one think about the impact of their actions on others anymore? Was she just too old for the way the world had evolved? When had the search for self-fulfillment turned into a lifestyle of sanctioned selfishness? Mikey Morgan was a boy; he should never have had to face certain truths about his father, at least not quite so soon. Bobby Morgan owed his son respect, if not his love. And Julie Perkins, despite her seeming maturity, was still a young girl. Bobby Morgan should have had more class.

She rose, distressed and anxious to bring the matter to an end. It would be an easy matter to find out the truth now. Julie Perkins would tell her the truth, if not in words then in other ways. She walked slowly down the hallway, peering in windows until she found the young girl. Julie was in a room at the end of the hall, moving gracefully in tandem with three other girls. She was pale and skinny, perceptibly thinner than she had been last week. Her bony shoulders protruded from her loose leotard. Paulette Puccinni stood careful watch nearby, clapping her hands while Jerry Vanderbilt filled the room with music. Rudy Vladimir waited with three other boys at the barre behind the ballerinas, awaiting his turn. Every person in the room was lost in effort, faces frozen in concentration, all thoughts focused on nothing but movement and music.

Now would be a good time.

Auntie Lil hurried down the hallway, passing no one. She reached the back stairwell and paused before going upstairs. The door to Raoul Martinez's office was shut. She wondered what today had been like for the couple, if knowing that they had been prepared to go to jail to protect one another had made any difference to either of them. She doubted it; Raoul and Lisette thrived on hurting one another.

The second-floor dressing rooms were empty. The benches were littered with discarded towels and bits of wrapping tape. Auntie Lil noticed that Lisette Martinez's locker remained undisturbed from the night before. The lock still hung crookedly from its hinge.

She found the locker for Julie Perkins near the end of the fourth row, well into the room. No one could see her from the doorway. She removed the screwdriver from her purse and inserted the tip between the small lock's metal arch. Using the locker door as a fulcrum, she pried the lock until it snapped open.

Julie's locker was the mess she had expected of a teenage girl. Clothes were jammed into the upper compartment with no regard for whether they were clean or not. Auntie Lil went through them carefully: cotton leotards, leggings, and pastel T-shirts. None had pockets and the shelf beneath the heap of clothing was bare. A pair of jeans and a thin turtleneck sweater hung from one of the side hooks. She found a few dollars in one pants pocket and a subway token in another, but nothing more. Julie's tapestry handbag dangled from the other hook. Auntie Lil undid the macramé handles and searched inside, taking each item out so she could examine it in the light. She discovered a makeup bag crammed full of powders, lipsticks, and three tubes of heavy mascara; loose change; a paperback romance novel, and a small photo album with only two photos inside it. One was of a pretty, slender woman posed against the backdrop of New York Harbor. The woman had long brown hair that fluttered in the wind and her thin features resembled Julie's. She looked to be in her late thirties, but her face was tired and grim. She stared into the camera without smiling, her eyes vacant, as if focused on something far away. The other photo showed a younger, plumper version of the woman sitting on a lawn chair with a grill behind her and a tendril of smoke silhouetting her head. She was laughing and holding a fat pink baby immaculately dressed in a ruffly blue jumper and a matching hat that topped blond curls. In this photo, the woman's eyes were bright and lively. The two photos showed two very different views of Julie Perkins's mother—for Auntie Lil was sure that was who she must be. She knew she had left her family four years ago. Did she ever write to her daughter? The next few items in the purse confirmed that she did. A small stack of postcards bound with a rubber band had been carefully tucked into a zippered side pocket. Each postcard showed a different scene, most of them from towns along the coast of California or Oregon. Each message was brief and a slightly different version of the first one: "I'm thinking of you my darling, my precious girl—every day. One day you will understand. Don't give up the dancing, you are too good to quit. Do it for yourself, if for no one else, my darling. Love, Mom." Auntie Lil held the stack in her hand, thinking of her own long-dead mother, of a stiff cold woman whose rigid bearing had masked any emotion beneath it. And yet Auntie Lil had felt loved. Had Julie?

The last object of importance in the purse was a small gold lighter crafted in an unusual flat oval shape. Auntie Lil turned it over in her palm. No engraved initials or dedication marred the surface, but that didn't matter. She remembered it well. She had seen Julie Perkins use it to light a cigarette on the path outside the Metro's theater a few days after Bobby Morgan had died—and she had seen it in Morgan's hand in the photograph from the Los Angeles charity ball. Had he given it to Julie as a token of whatever emotion he'd felt for the girl? Had she stolen it when he wasn't looking as a reminder that her lover was real? It was the kind of thing a young girl might do.

Or—and the thought disturbed Auntie Lil because it should have occurred to her before—had Julie taken it after Bobby Morgan's death as a souvenir of a different kind?

She returned the purse and turned her attention to the bottom of the locker. Toe shoes were heaped on the floor, along with a pair of leather street flats. Auntie Lil examined the dance shoes. Two pair were white. She held them up to the light. One set was new, the canvas still stiff and in need of breaking in. Auntie Lil had seen the dancers struggle to soften new pairs before: they bent the sheath, slammed the shoes in doors, stomped on them, rubbed them with oils, even put them in plastic bags and pounded them with hammers until they achieved the consistency they preferred. The other pair of white toe shoes was softer and worn at the ends. The ribbons that wrapped around the dancer's ankles were soiled. The right shoe of this pair had shorter ribbons than the left, with ends that were ragged and torn.

She examined the thin strips carefully. The ribbon clearly matched the scraps she had found on the floor of the third-floor storage room. Either Bobby Morgan had been strangled with a similar ribbon before he was strung up on the bigger rope, or someone had killed him in another manner and used such a ribbon as part of a revenge fantasy that Auntie Lil could only imagine. But who?

There were dozens of white shoes in the company, of course. But this pair belonged to Julie Perkins. And Julie Perkins had been Bobby Morgan's lover. Someone close to Julie, if not Julie, had done the deed.

Auntie Lil held the slipper in her hands and examined the outer covering more closely. Toe shoes were notoriously disposable; she doubted this pair would last another performance. It was not the pair Julie had worn during *The Nutcracker*. Those had been blue, Auntie Lil recalled. That meant these shoes could have been used during the murder of Bobby Morgan if he had been killed just before or after the curtain went up. But how could she be sure? She compared the shoes again and noticed that the toe of the right shoe was scruffed and torn, far more so than the left. She pulled her reading glasses from her purse and scrutinized the square, reinforced tip. Small, evenly spaced indentations marred the satin.

Auntie Lil realized with sudden clarity—and equally sudden horror—that the indentations were teeth marks.

Bobby Morgan's teeth marks, she was sure. Who could have accomplished such a task? Had several boys held Morgan down while Mikey stuffed the shoe in his mouth, suffocating him? Or had a larger person been the murderer and the shoe been used only as a prop? It was such a stylized form of revenge; would it have been one that a boy would choose?

"I had to put it back," a deep voice said from the other side of the room.

Auntie Lil dropped the shoes in surprise and looked up to find Andrew Perkins blocking the end of her row on the door side of the room. "I knew Julie needed those shoes the next day for rehearsal," he explained. "She'd miss them if they were gone and figure out what I had done. So I had to put them back. I was going to take them as soon as they wore out and throw them away. I don't like to leave loose ends lying around." He stared at Auntie Lil, his gaze steady and determined. He looked exhausted. His lean frame had grown gaunter in only a week, puffy pouches hung beneath his eyes, and age lines had appeared from the sides of his nose in deep grooves to his mouth. His hair was unkempt and he needed a shave. His clothes looked as if he had slept in them. A nearly empty pack of cigarettes poked from his front shirt pocket and he held a lit one in his hand.

Auntie Lil tried to remain calm, but her voice quavered when she spoke. "I think your daughter already figured out what happened," she said. "That's why she moved out, isn't it? The day after the funeral she realized that you had killed Bobby Morgan—and why."

"My daughter would never be able to understand why I killed Bobby Morgan," Perkins explained with a voice as emotionless as if he were describing a boring vacation. "No one can understand what it was like to live on the same planet as that man. He had to go."

"I can imagine what it was like," Auntie Lil disagreed. She had to keep talking, she needed to buy time. "Always having him there, competing with you. Always winning." If she could keep him occupied, someone would come along. It was nearly three o'clock in the afternoon. Classes would break soon. Her eyes slid to the wall, searching for a clock.

"He didn't always win," Perkins said sharply. "I was the one that carried the show in the early days. He was just an amateur. I had the experience. I got twice as much mail as him the first year."

"But not later," Auntie Lil said. "Not after that."

"I grew older," Perkins said angrily. "That's what happens when you outgrow your usefulness as a child star. I expected it to happen. I welcomed it when it happened. I was ready to move on."

She opened the clasp on her pocketbook under the cover of her other hand. If she could keep eye contact with him, perhaps she could slip her hand inside. The screwdriver was still there—and its shaft was long. She might be able to fend him off with a weapon long enough to keep him at bay until someone came along. "I don't believe you," she said, locking her eyes on his. "I think you lived for that attention. I think you never got over being fired from the show. I think you've always blamed Bobby Morgan for it and hated him because of it. I think you've been waiting to murder him for twenty years."

"That's a lie," Perkins said quickly, his eyes blazing. "I have far more important things in my life. Bobby Morgan was a loser. He was a bloodsucker. He couldn't earn a living on his own. He had to earn it off his own kid's back. At least I was good at something when I grew up. I could make money. All he could do was spend it."

"But you lost your job," Auntie Lil pointed out. Her hand slipped inside the purse, but she was having trouble finding the screwdriver among the cluttered contents. Her fingers touched a pocket calculator, a small nylon wallet, and a roll of mints. Where was the screwdriver?

"I left my job willingly," Andrew Perkins corrected her. "The money was gone. The eighties were over."

"You were fired," Auntie Lil said flatly. Her fingers brushed against hard metal and she closed her hand on the screwdriver handle. "I have sources. My nephew told me you were fired."

"Your nephew is a liar," Perkins said angrily. "The world is full of liars. Liars like Bobby Morgan." Suddenly he laughed, his head thrown back in delight. Auntie Lil took the opportunity to pull the screwdriver from her purse. She held it behind her back, out of sight. "He always had to be center stage," Perkins said, his shoulders shaking as if he had just heard a hilarious joke. "He was center stage all right. Did you see him? I'd have given anything to have been in the audience to see it instead of stage-managing." He laughed again. "He sure made a hell of a grand exit."

Auntie Lil stepped back toward the far end of her row. She had found the clock. There was still four minutes to go before the hour. She would never be able to stall him long enough. He blocked one end of the row, but if she took him by surprise, she might be able to run toward the door on the far side of the room and get through it before he could react.

No, it was impossible. She was too old.

But if she was running fast enough and he was preoccupied enough, she might reach it in time to frighten him away with her weapon and get into the hall. He would have to be following her for it to work. She had to try it. She had no other choice.

"You find it funny that Bobby Morgan's dead body was displayed like that for an entire theater of children to see?" Auntie Lil asked, her mouth a grim line of disapproval.

"I find it hilarious," Perkins admitted, nodding his head happily. "Bobby Morgan, L.A. swinger. Swinging for the very last time."

"I would say you didn't kill him soon enough, then," Auntie Lil pointed out. "You should have stopped Bobby Morgan the swinger before he met your daughter." She took another step back toward the far end of the room, closer to the back passageway that led to the first row of lockers.

Perkins's face flushed. "That isn't true," he said. "I stopped him before he could do anything."

"Really?" Auntie Lil asked, forcing herself to smirk, though she hated the words coming out of her mouth. "Do you really believe that? Nikki Morgan told me that your daughter had been staying out all night. Who do you think she was staying with? What do you think she was doing? Do you really believe Bobby Morgan would leave her alone? She's a beautiful young woman. And she is your daughter. He was doing it to get back at you, you know. He was using your daughter just to show you he could."

"Bobby Morgan was a pig," Perkins yelled. "Julie was too smart not to see it. She would never have had anything to do with him." He darted toward Auntie Lil, but stopped abruptly. She would have to taunt him further until he gave chase. If he stayed at his end of the row, he'd be able to simply turn back toward the door and cut her off. She had to bait him further.

"Don't kid yourself," she said quietly. "Bobby Morgan loved young girls. He probably came back to New York City just to get his hands on Julie. Let me guess. You met him at the Los Angeles charity ball for the first time in years. You mentioned you had a daughter now, one dancing with the Metro. You were eager to let him know that he wasn't the only one who had a star for a child. But he had to one-up you again, didn't he? He had to go on and on about how much money he was making off his son's career. And then he had to take it one step further. Because he never could let well enough alone. He came here to start an affair with Lisette Martinez, but once here, he met Julie and Lisette was history. Julie may even have been the one to initiate their affair. He was famous and successful. Everything she wanted in a man." Auntie Lil did not really *believe* this, but she had to goad him.

"Shut up," Perkins said, taking another step forward. "Julie wouldn't have looked at him twice. He's the one who pursued her. I heard the phone ringing every evening while he begged her to see him. I could hear her tone of voice. I saw the flowers, read the unsigned notes. He did it all. He drew her into it. If I had known it was him, I would have killed him earlier. I thought it was Mikey instead. I thought it was cute." His voice faltered. "I would have killed him the first night if I'd known."

"If you'd known that he was going to take your little girl away from you forever, you mean?" Auntie Lil said. "If you'd known about him before he did all those things to Julie that you can't seem to forget? If you'd known enough to plan the murder better, to hide it from your daughter? Because now she will never forgive you for what you've done."

This time her taunts were enough.

"My daughter is glad he's dead and she will never tell anyone that I did it," Perkins shouted. "And once you're dead, no one else will ever know it was me." He darted toward her angrily, his arms outstretched. She turned on her heels, dropped her heavy purse in his way, and ran around the far end of her row of lockers, dashing back toward the front of the room. Perkins followed, his long legs quickly making up the space between them. She could hear his footsteps against the tile floor, the sharp tap of his businessman's shoes as he drew closer. Her body was too old to sustain the chase, and she was tired and beat-up from the day before. She faltered, her will slipping, then forced herself to move faster. She pushed her body to the limit, reaching the doorway just as she heard several doors slam on the floor below. Three o'clock, she thought, it was three o'clock. Classes were letting out now. Help was near.

"Help me!" she screamed, but the sounds of lingering music floating up from the first-floor space masked her cry. The accompanists were still winding down and Jerry Vanderbilt was thumping away at his usual deafening level of sound. Could anyone hear her cries? She whirled around and jabbed at Perkins with the screwdriver, hoping to slow him down. It caught him on the wrist, sinking into the flesh no more than a quarter of an inch. It was enough to draw blood. He cursed and grabbed at his wrist, screaming. Auntie Lil turned toward the first-floor stairs, but he stepped forward and blocked her way, his wrist clamped to his mouth as he sucked on his wound.

"You must be kidding," he said almost calmly, droplets

of blood trickling from his lips. "By the time anyone gets up here, you'll be dead. And I will be long gone." He began to run toward her again. She had no choice but to flee toward the far end of the hall and the stairs to the third-floor storage spaces. She threw the screwdriver at him, but it bounced harmlessly off his chest and clattered to the floor, rolling in front of him down the passageway. In his haste, he stepped on the handle and the round barrel turned beneath one foot, sending him off balance. He scrambled to regain his footing. Auntie Lil took the time to dash down the hall and run up the stairs to the third floor. Surely someone would be there, a technical person perhaps. Someone who could intimidate Perkins into giving up.

The third floor was empty. "Help me!" Auntie Lil screamed as she moved down the hall, trying each doorway she passed. She could hear Perkins's footsteps clattering up the stairs. He was angrier and moving faster now. "Someone help me!" she shouted, her voice echoing across the empty space.

"What's going on?" she heard a deep voice yell from the far end of the hallway near the abandoned storage room. She fled toward the sound as if it were a beacon of light in the darkness.

"Help me," she shouted again as she ran. Perkins was moving rapidly down the hall toward her, his bloody wrist forgotten as he sprinted to make up his lost time. She reached the end of the long hallway and turned the corner. No one was there. Where was the voice coming from? She tried the empty storage room. Perhaps she could lock herself inside. The door would not budge. Perkins rounded the corner and started toward her. She backed up, hands reaching out behind her. There was no place to go but through the smaller door at the end of the shorter hall and onto the catwalk. Flinging open the door, she ran out onto the swinging metal ramp, slamming the door behind her, yet knowing it would not stop him for long. The catwalk was heavy steel, but it swayed as she ran down the center of its length, searching for escape. Did the metal ladder she had climbed the night before reach up this high or was she trapped? The walls were bare except for thick stage ropes. She would never be able to climb down them without falling.

"Help me!" she screamed over the edge of the catwalk just as the door opened. Perkins spotted her and smiled.

Where was the man that belonged to the voice she had heard in the hall, she thought frantically. "Help me!" she screamed again.

Ricky Lee Harris poked his head out from a storage area built into the sidewall of the stage one story below. He peered up at the catwalk but was too directly beneath it to get a clear view. "What's going on up there?" he shouted.

Perkins stopped at the other end of the walk when he heard the lighting director's voice. He froze, peering over the side to his right, wondering if he could be seen.

Auntie Lil had run almost to the far end of the catwalk, ignoring the movement beneath her feet that her frantic scrambling produced. "It's Andrew Perkins!" she screamed. "He's the one who killed Bobby Morgan. He's got me trapped up here on the catwalk. He's trying to kill me!" If she was going to die, she decided, she was going to make sure everyone knew who had killed her.

"Now, Miss Hubbert," Perkins said loudly in a soothing voice, "you're overexcited. Don't be silly. You shouldn't be out here. It's dangerous. You might slip and fall. Let me help you off." He leaned over the edge of the catwalk and smiled at a puzzled Ricky Lee Harris. "It's okay, Rick. She's just a little excited. I found her going through my daughter's locker, and when I got angry, she flipped out on me. I can handle it."

"Don't believe him!" Auntie Lil screamed angrily, alarmed when Perkins took several more steps toward her. She began to rock the catwalk, holding on to the metal sides as she shifted her weight from left to right. As it swung more wildly she caught glimpses of Ricky Lee's quizzical face staring up at the catwalk, his eyes unfocused and bleary. He was going to believe Perkins, she realized with despair. He was probably so drunk he didn't even know if what he was hearing was real. She would have to get help from someone else. "Help me!" she screamed over the edge of the catwalk in the loudest voice she had ever summoned from her considerable lungs. "Help me! Help me!" She took off her shoes and threw them to the stage below. There were people moving about on the stage. Someone had to notice. "Help me!" she screamed over and over.

Her cries had no effect on Perkins. He advanced on her faster, holding on to the metal railings, stumbling slightly from side to side as the catwalk rocked beneath her vigorous movements. It was harder for him to keep his balance because he was moving; if she kept rocking it, she might slow him down. She could hear voices beneath her. Someone shouted up toward them. "Help!" she screamed back, not hearing what had been said, unable to focus on anything but keeping Perkins off balance.

Perkins was only a few yards away when she threw herself against the sides of the catwalk, desperate to slow him down. He stumbled and lost his footing, teetered against the metal railings, cursed, and then regained his foothold.

"What the hell?" Ricky Lee Harris shouted a story below. "What are you doing on that ladder? Get off there. It's dangerous."

Who was he talking to? "Help me!" Auntie Lil screamed again. "He's trying to kill me! For God sakes, help me!"

"Get off of there!" Ricky Lee bellowed again. Why was he shouting at her? She began to panic. Not only wouldn't he help her, he was shouting at her and making it even harder to think.

But Ricky Lee Harris wasn't shouting at Auntie Lil. He was yelling across the stage at the lithe figure of the young dancer climbing steadily up the metal ladder embedded into the back brick wall of the stage. Rudy Vladimir had heard Auntie Lil's cries from below and believed her. He climbed rapidly, his strong young body surmounting the rungs with the ease of a practiced sailor. He passed the second-story level and shouted at Harris, "Get help! She's telling the truth."

But Auntie Lil was trapped on top of the catwalk without a view of below. She had no way of knowing Rudy was on his way to her. She rocked the catwalk furiously, feeling tears coming, angry at herself for not holding on to her calm. She would not die in this manner, tumbling to the stage below, disposed of by a man who thought only of himself. "Stay away from me!" she screamed as Perkins moved even closer. Just a few feet of swaying catwalk now separated them.

Rudy scrambled up the remaining rungs. The ladder didn't reach all the way to the catwalk. He couldn't catch hold of the railing or reach the pathway. Besides, it was swaying too much to chance a jump. He spotted the clump of heavy ropes hanging down from the rafters. Grabbing the nearest cord, he shimmied up the remaining distance until he was above the catwalk, flush against the wall behind Auntie Lil. He leaped lightly onto its surface and stepped in front of her, pushing her down on the floor to protect her from Perkins. He faced her assailant. Andrew Perkins stood frozen in surprise as with one beautiful, soaring, and perfect leap, Rudy launched himself from the swaying surface of the catwalk. He flew through the air, his right foot held straight out in front of him as unyielding as a steel pillar. The weight of his entire body was focused on that single, muscled leg and it slammed into Andrew Perkins's groin with the force of a locomotive. Perkins crumpled to the ground, his face a mute mask of agony as he writhed on the narrow steel ramp. Rudy reached for Auntie Lil and helped her to her feet.

Perkins tried to sit up, his body rocking violently as the full impact of the blow sank in. He rolled to the right and tried to scramble toward them in his rage. His body swayed and he rolled toward the edge of the catwalk, part of his upper body slipping between the two thick wire ropes that served as the railings. His torso disappeared over the edge and he arched desperately, trying to grab the lower railing to pull himself back up. But his sudden movement only tipped the catwalk even more steeply. The lower half of his body slid almost gracefully from the steel floor, slithering over the side until one foot caught on the lower railing. The catwalk jumped and Rudy grabbed Auntie Lil to steady her.

They heard the scream as Andrew Perkins's foot pulled clear and he began to fall. It sounded as if it went on for moments: a deep, agonized scream that faded in sound as he tumbled three stories to the stage below. It rang in their ears, echoing and echoing in its madness. There was a thump—and the theater fell silent.

Rudy pulled Auntie Lil to him and patted her head. His arms were so strong and reassuring that she began to cry at a single thought: another boy had, too soon, been forced to become a man.

CHAPTER SIXTEEN

1. The boardroom was packed. Calvin Swanson brought in two loads of folding chairs and still some members had to stand. Faces that hadn't been seen since the hula hoop appeared to hear the inside dirt. Everyone knew this was one board meeting of the Metro Ballet that should not be missed.

"What will happen to the girl?" someone asked from among the crowd as Lane opened the floor for business. Andrew Perkins had died two days after his fall from the catwalk. A young girl was now fatherless. Finally, it seemed, people were catching on that this tragedy extended beyond the lurid headlines: many people had been hurt.

"Julie Perkins has accepted a position in the corps of the San Francisco Ballet," Raoul Martinez announced. "She intends to take a hiatus from dancing until next fall before joining their company."

"Her mother will be living with her," Lilah explained. "My private investigator tracked her down in Sacramento."

"Why didn't you just have *her* do it," one of the socialites on the board asked, nodding at Auntie Lil.

The room burst into laughter and applause as Auntie Lil accepted their accolades with unconvincing modesty. Lane Rogers endured the scene, her lips clamped in an unhappy line. Ruth Beretsky rather defiantly took great pains to record the comment and subsequent outburst in her meeting notes.

When Auntie Lil did not offer any details, however, one of the many curious among the crowd finally broke protocol in favor of satisfying her curiosity. "How did he do it?"

a thin woman with gold bracelets the size of handcuffs asked eagerly.

The room fell silent. This was why they had come.

"Andrew Perkins killed Bobby Morgan early in the first act," Auntie Lil explained. "We're not exactly sure what happened because only Julie is left to tell us and she herself does not know everything. She thinks that her father found out about her and Bobby Morgan in this manner: the day before the premiere, she couldn't find the white toe shoes she wanted to wear for *The Nutcracker* dress rehearsal and complained to her father about losing them. Later she realized she had left them at Morgan's apartment earlier that afternoon. The next day, right after the performance started, Bobby Morgan walked past Perkins toward the locker room, holding Julie's shoes. Perkins may have been smoking a cigarette in a doorway, hidden from Morgan's view. Perkins confronted Morgan when he realized that the shoes belonged to his daughter—and that the flowers and phone calls she had been receiving were coming from Morgan and not his son, as he had thought. The two men went upstairs to argue in private to avoid being heard during the performance. They ended up in the storage room and there was a scuffle. Somehow Morgan went down. There were bruises on one side of his head, a fact the police kept from the papers but that Hans Glick inadvertently guessed—which is one reason why the police arrested him when he came to them. Either Morgan died from a blow or a fall, or he was knocked unconscious and suffocated later when Perkins wrapped the ribbons from his daughter's white toe shoes around his neck and strangled him, then stuffed the shoe down his throat for good measure."

An appreciative murmur ran through the crowd. This would make excellent cocktail conversation indeed.

"So he was already dead when he came swinging across the stage?" a board member asked eagerly, sweeping an arm across the table for emphasis.

Auntie Lil nodded. "Perkins wanted to shame and mock Morgan. The length of the first act gave him time to plan just how. Perkins disguised himself in Drosselmeyer's cape and made a quick tour of the backstage area, finding out what he needed to know. Replacing the cape, he returned to the third-floor storage room and dragged Morgan's body out onto the catwalk. He then tied a noose around Morgan's neck using the spare end of the counter rope that anchored the huge Christmas tree. Morgan was left securely hanging against the bricks way up in the shadows of the rafters, where no one could possibly see him. Perkins planned to cut the rope holding the heavy weight on the other end of the noose when he was safely downstairs and could quickly leave the scene. He expected the body to plummet to center stage. It would have been the perfect gesture. Not only did it mimic in many ways a scene from a recent Mikey Morgan movie, it stripped Morgan of all dignity in front of as large an audience as possible. But Perkins had not accounted for the fact that the Christmas tree had unevenly distributed weight. Without the counterbalance, it tipped as it fell and Morgan's body was jerked to where it got caught behind the scrim instead of dropping to center stage. Perkins needed to humiliate Morgan so badly that he took a chance and actually dashed to where the body hung and grabbed it. Repositioning the body, he sent it swinging to center stage. In the confusion afterward, it was easy for him to slip out an exit door. He ran around the back pathway and into the lobby. By the time the lights went up, he was standing at the back of the auditorium and blending in with the audience. He looked just as confused as the rest of us. We know that because the Reverend Ben Hampton saw Perkins in his tuxedo or, more literally, heard him in his dress shoes running down the back path."

"How much do you think the girl knew?" someone asked, and a lively debate arose. It halted only when Lane Rogers thumped the table vigorously with her gavel.

"I will stop this discussion if it does not remain civilized," she announced, but she, too, was burning with curiosity. So long as her own embarrassing fixation with Bobby Morgan did not come up, she wanted to hear the dirt as badly as the next person.

"Julie Perkins actually tried to break things off with

Morgan the day of his death," Auntie Lil explained. "That is the irony of it. And it was also why Morgan was in such a bad mood that day. Julie was afraid her father knew or suspected and realized what it might do to him if he found out. He was the only parent she had left, in her eyes. That's why she never turned her father in, though she couldn't bear to live with him after she discovered what he had done. But more important, Julie had grown tired of Morgan. She thought he was 'old and boring.' For once, I believe Morgan was about to get the boot instead of the other way around."

A small blonde woman coughed discreetly in the crowd. Many eyes glanced toward then looked conspicuously away from Raoul Martinez.

Lilah Cheswick took charge. She believed that discretion was the mark of a civilized society and was determined to reintroduce the concept to this crowd. "As you may be aware, I was never comfortable with Mr. Morgan's stated reasons for having his son dance in *The Nutcracker*," she said. "A desire to give Mikey more stage experience did not seem plausible to me. It turns out that Mr. Morgan devised the plan so that he would have a good reason to come back to New York City and frequent these premises as often as he needed to in order to conduct a romance with an unnamed but very married member of the Metro company. A woman older than Julie who was perfectly capable of making an informed decision on becoming involved with Mr. Morgan. I do not believe it necessary to divulge her name."

Raoul Martinez stared stonily ahead as Lilah continued. "The affair began a few weeks before auditions while Morgan was conducting preliminary negotiations with Hans Glick. However, during this period, Morgan met Julie Perkins in the hallway of the Metro. Eventually, this led to his last-minute demand that Fatima Jones be dropped from the role of Clara before Mikey would agree to join the company. He knew the role would pass to Julie Perkins and he wanted to surprise her with the lead. His scheme worked. He overlapped his affairs with the two women, if it is fair to refer to a sixteen-year-old as a woman, for several weeks before he called a halt to the affair with the older one. Through sheer exhaustion, I presume."

"You say the unnamed woman was a member of the dance *company*?" someone asked while Lane Rogers fidgeted in discomfort and ignored the slightly smug stares of her compatriots.

"In other words, this was a *dancer*, right?" a blonde dressed in a designer suit clarified. "Not a board member?"

"I believe we have discussed this topic long enough," Lane interrupted grimly, banging the gavel for emphasis. "Let's move on to new business."

2.   "Do you think we look out of place?" T.S. asked Herbert. They were sitting on stools in a slightly seedy bar at Broadway and Seventy-second Street, dressed in tuxedos and waiting for the Metro meeting to adjourn.

"I prefer to think of it as raising the caliber of the establishment," Herbert replied. He could not bring himself to admit that what had really attracted him to the bar was the old-fashioned neon sign in the shape of a giant martini glass that blinked on and off outside. It had evoked the emotions of an earlier era within his soul. It seemed a fitting beginning for the evening they had planned.

The bartender planted himself between them and admired their finery. "Nice suits, gents," he said in a heavy Bronx accent. "How may I be of service tonight?" Just seconds earlier he had flung a mug of beer down the bar toward a toothless patron like a surly saloon keeper in a cheesy Western movie but their tuxedos had called out the gentleman in him. If these two patrons could aspire to something better, then, by God, so could he.

"Dewar's and soda," T.S. said automatically, his eyes sliding to a bank of video machines arranged in a far corner. Two drunken construction workers were busy abusing the nearest one. The far-off pinging of electronic bells was calling to T.S. as surely as the singing of sirens, stirring deep desires within his immaculately clad bosom.

"I'll have a martini," Herbert decided with uncharacteristically reckless abandon. "Tonight we are tripping the light fantastic."

T.S. tore his eyes from the lure of the flashing lights and back toward the bar. "I've changed my mind," he told the barkeep. "I'll have a martini, too." He had sworn to himself—as well as to Auntie Lil—that he would give up video games cold turkey. This was not a task easily accomplished sober. A martini was most definitely in order.

"You made the reservations?" Herbert asked, his martini glass hovering on the edge of his lower lip as if he would not allow himself to drink until business had been taken care of.

"A table for four at the Rainbow Room," T.S. confirmed. "Near the orchestra but with a spectacular view of the city skyline."

"Nervous?" Herbert asked.

T.S. sipped his martini and nodded. "But only about the fox-trot," he lied. "I think I've got the rest of the steps down pretty well."

The man next to them got up with a belch and patted his enormous belly in satisfaction. A squadron of empty beer bottles had been neatly lined up in front of his seat beside the decimated remains of a double cheeseburger platter. He had efficiently polished off close to a six-pack while perusing the day's newspaper and enjoying his dinner. As he rumbled contentedly out the door T.S.'s eyes slid to the open paper. "Is that *Newsday*?" he asked Herbert.

Herbert checked the front page. "Yes. Shall I?" he said.

T.S. closed his eyes and took a gulp of martini. "Yes," he decided. "May as well." All week long Margo McGregor had been uncovering every secret that the Metropolitan Ballet had ever concealed. Thus far, T.S. had managed to avoid mention in her column but was sure that one day soon some ugly and forgotten tidbit of his private life would be revealed.

"It's about Glick, mostly," Herbert announced after a quick scan of the column's contents.

T.S. relaxed. Thank God. This called for another drink.

He flagged down the bartender and ordered a new round, though his first martini still had a few healthy gulps to go. "Anything new?" he asked.

Herbert reread the information more slowly. "Glick's been transferred back to Zurich by his company and they have promised to make restitution."

"Does it say why he did it?" T.S. asked. "It was a most un-Swisslike thing to do. Imagine, embezzling money from the coffers of the poor." Whenever T.S. drank, he had a tendency to slip into jargon more worthy of the Scarlet Pimpernel than a lifelong resident of New York City.

Herbert absently sipped his martini and scrutinized the newspaper. "It sounds like he invested the Metro's cash in some risky ventures and lost almost everything. It would have disgraced him. Or showed that he didn't know what he was doing and that, apparently, was anathema to him. He was trying to make up for the loss by skimming cash off the Los Angeles benefit receipts. That way he could juggle a few numbers and fake a few entries and maybe no one would notice."

"Stealing from the Metro to pay the Metro?" T.S. mused, downing the last of his first martini and taking an inaugural gulp of the second. "A sort of reverse, postmodern, but not quite organized Swiss Robin Hood."

He lifted his martini glass in homage and Herbert looked up at him sharply. What in the world was T.S. talking about?

3.   "Where *is* Glick?" a board member demanded. "Am I the only one to notice that he was at the root of this entire mess? Negotiating with Bobby Morgan and not telling us. Cooking the books . . ." Her voice trailed off indignantly.

"Glick is in Switzerland. He's been 'promoted' to director of corporate car rentals for his bank," someone offered. "I read it in the paper today."

"There is no need to panic," Lilah explained. "Glick's company had insurance against malfeasance caused by his actions while an officer of the company. And that includes his serving on the Metro's board."

"So the insurance on the insurance pays our insurance?" one confused board member asked as Ruth Beretsky dutifully noted the comment for the record.

"Sort of," Lilah conceded, giving up on explaining the concept. "The point is this: Even if Nikki Morgan continues with her lawsuit and wins, we won't have to pay. Glick's insurance company will pay because he failed to pay our premium on time, violating his fiduciary duty."

"But we don't think it will even get that far," Lane Rogers interrupted as if she personally had arranged to sweep the entire matter under the carpet. "Nikki has indicated that she will be too busy overseeing her son's new movie role on location in Vancouver to pursue legal matters. She will let the lawsuit drop. I intervened personally on behalf of the board."

So now it was "Nikki," Auntie Lil thought to herself. If you can't land one famous person, then, by gum, make a beeline for the warmest body who can claim to have known that famous person.

"Mikey Morgan is back to making movies?" Raoul Martinez asked. He rubbed his chin thoughtfully. "Good thing. I always said he couldn't dance. I was against his ever taking part in *The Nutcracker* in the first place, if you will recall."

They all recalled, all right. But no one bothered to call him on it.

"He's making one more movie, the one for Gene Levitt," Auntie Lil explained. "Then retiring from show biz to finish high school and college."

"He must have a fortune," a short brunette commented.

"Look here!" Ruth Beretsky cried out suddenly. "Is money the only thing that any of you ever think about? I have asked twice now whether the board intends to send a representative to Andrew Perkins's funeral and everyone ignores me. I am tired of being ignored. I want to know what the board is going to do."

Most people in the room were shocked into silence by

her unexpected outburst. The others stared at her blankly, wondering whether they had ever even seen her before.

Lane recovered first and, bristling at her assistant's rather roundabout accusation, was the first to respond. "I hardly think it is appropriate for the Metro to send an official representative to a murderer's funeral," she said.

"He was a *man*," Ruth cried out angrily, her voice wavering as she fought to regain control. "He should never have murdered Bobby Morgan, but we can all lose control if we are pushed far enough." Her eyes blazed and Lane looked away. "Besides, Andrew Perkins helped the Metro for more than eight years—and he was a nice man once. Before . . . before *things* happened to him. And what about his daughter? We should go to support Julie, if nothing else. We're the only people she knows. She's spent her whole life here."

Lane's rebuttal was swift. "As I said before, I hardly think that this should be our concern."

"Shut up, Lane," a voice suggested from the back of the room. Other voices murmured their assent. It was not the first time that day that board members had called for the chairman to button her lip. Mutiny hung in the air.

"I'm not going to turn my back on a sixteen-year-old girl just because it may be embarrassing to the board," Ruth declared. "Good grief, what's left to be embarrassed about? We're already the laughingstock of Manhattan."

"I vote we appoint Ruth Beretsky the official board representative to Andrew Perkins's funeral," Auntie Lil suggested quickly. "And that we appropriate a modest sum for flowers." She paused. "But make the card out to his daughter."

"I'll go with you," Lilah said quietly, patting Ruth's hand. "My driver can take us. That is, if you'd like the company."

Ruth nodded mutely and the subsequent vote was swift and overwhelming. For the first time in her quiet life, Ruth Beretsky had been singled out by her peers to represent them.

4. "Are you sure you're not nervous?" Herbert asked again, one eye on the nearly empty martini glass by T.S.'s elbow. It was his third.

"Absolutely not," T.S. declared. "My toes are positively twinkling." He caught Herbert's glance. "But don't worry. I have no intention of having another drink."

A groan went up from the crowd at the far end of the bar as the bartender resolutely changed the channel on the television set, switching off a basketball game in favor of a local cable station. "Sorry, guys," he announced. "This is my favorite talk show. Is this dame hot or what?" He turned up the sound and the canned applause of a prerecorded intro rolled down the bar. Dozens of images of a blond woman's face merged and moved on the screen. Her smile was so wide T.S. could count the cavities in her molars.

"I can't stand this woman," T.S. announced loudly as the opening credits segued into a shot of the talk-show host bouncing perkily onto the set. "She's had more parts replaced than my aunt Minnie's Audi and her taste in guests deserves excoriation." He slurred the final word a bit, but thought it unlikely that anyone had noticed. Who ever used *excoriation* anyway?

Herbert checked his watch. "How much longer for the meeting, do you think?"

T.S. shrugged. "I'd give it another half an hour. Bottoms up." He drained the rest of his martini.

The studio audience broke into obedient applause as the hyperkinetic hostess introduced her first two guests. To the utter disbelief of both T.S. and Herbert, Paulette Puccinni and Jerry Vanderbilt bounded onto stage, holding hands like the coziest of couples.

"Today," the talk-show hostess announced breathlessly into her microphone, "we have two very special guests from right here in Manhattan. Two very talented artists who endured a conspiracy of murder and mayhem at the Metropolitan Ballet, facing death each day yet bolstered by the deep and enduring friendship that exists between them."

"If not for Jerry, I would never have survived the experience," Paulette gushed as she settled her ample caftan-clad rear into the guest chair. "I would have gone mad with fear. But we had each other, and while we faced unknown danger daily, at least with one another we knew we were safe." She beamed at Jerry, who held his hand up in the air while the audience broke into thunderous applause.

"Bartender!" T.S. bellowed down the bar. "Bring us another round!"

5.   "Why not?" Auntie Lil asked Lane. "It's time for the Metro to make a change. If we offer Ben Hampton a seat on the board, we can only win. He will never attend the meetings. Believe me, he's far too busy and has more important items on his agenda. But we will look serious about our desire to right past wrongs, and most important of all, we will have found a way to differentiate ourselves from the City Ballet and ABT."

"She has a point," one of the socialites on the board said, although her sentiment was rather more self-centered than Auntie Lil's. "I'm tired of having to apologize for the Metro to my friends. We're always not quite good enough. Why do we keep chasing the other ballet companies? Let's take a chance and do something different."

"Exactly," Auntie Lil said, warming up to a topic that had been percolating in her mind for a week now. "Let the Metro Ballet become the real ballet of New York City, open to people of all shapes and colors. Let our ranks reflect the true nature and glory of this great international city of ours. Let people years from now look back and say—"

"I quite agree," Lilah interrupted smoothly before Auntie Lil launched into an updated version of Shakespeare's St. Crispin's Day speech. "There's no point in trying to be ABT or the City. Let's just be ourselves."

"If you elect that man to this board, I will resign!" Lane Rogers declared. She stood and glared around the room. "He will make a mockery of us. I tell you—I will resign!"

The room fell silent. A board member in the back

coughed nervously and a handful of chairs scraped against the wooden floor. Raoul Martinez studied the clock on the wall intently, ignoring Lane's gaze. Auntie Lil sat with her chin cupped in her hand, content to let others do the dirty work on this one.

Lane waited, standing alone at the top of the table, for her usual coterie of supporters to come to her rescue. She waited in vain.

"Well, Lane," one of them finally said with an apologetic smile. "You *have* been chairman for three years now. Perhaps it is time to take a rest."

"Yes," another agreed eagerly. "We can't possibly ask you to do more."

"Ruth?" Lane said, turning to her faithful friend. She opened her mouth to speak, but shut it when she couldn't find the right words.

Ruth shrugged. "They're right, you know," she said. "Everyone's tired of you. I nominate Lilah Cheswick to be the new chairman of the Metropolitan Ballet. She was smart enough to find out what Glick is doing and she knows everybody in the world."

"Oh, no. I'm far too busy," Lilah protested as dozens of heads nodded agreement and turned expectantly to her.

Ignored, Lane sat abruptly at her end of the table, staring in shock at the faces around her.

"Quit some of those other boards," someone suggested. "We need you more."

"Perhaps you should," Auntie Lil agreed. "Being chairman of the Metro would allow you to focus your energies. You might have more time for fun." She nodded ever so slightly toward the clock to remind Lilah that fun awaited them that very evening if only they could wrap up all their business and move on.

"Yes, Lilah—do it," other voices echoed, eager for the board to be ruled with grace and tact after years of dissension and spite.

"I suppose I could . . ." Lilah began doubtfully, and before the words were out of her mouth, a vote had been called.

Five minutes later Lilah Cheswick was duly installed as the new chairman of the board of the Metropolitan Ballet. Her first action was to call for a vote on the issue of the Reverend Ben Hampton. Auntie Lil's bid to offer him a seat on the board was narrowly defeated, but she took the matter philosophically. By now, she knew, the Reverend had probably forgotten all about the Metro and was moving on to more important things. Besides, Lane Rogers was in no danger of being suddenly reelected and that was a most cheering thought.

"Before we adjourn," Lilah announced with admirable aplomb given her short tenure, "I would like to announce that it is my intention to block any attempt to mount a production of *The Nutcracker* next holiday season. This city is awash in *Nutcrackers* and I for one have had enough. I don't see our city's orchestras mounting dueling versions of the 1812 Overture year after year." The room burst into spontaneous applause. When it had died down, she continued, "I propose we vote now to commission Emili Vladimir to create a new ballet for next holiday season. If we act now, we will have months and months to perfect it."

"How do you know she'll agree?" someone asked.

"She will agree," Lilah explained, "because this ballet will star her son Rudy."

"Yes," Auntie Lil agreed emphatically. "Right now, Fatima Jones and Rudy Vladimir are our biggest weapons in establishing a new identity for the Metro."

"Beautiful!" thundered Raoul Martinez without warning, causing his entire row of board members to jump. "We'll do something Russian. Something cold, with sweeping tundra vistas and gales of snow and sleighs being drawn across the stage."

"No!" a small bald man interrupted hastily in a pipsqueak voice. He seldom spoke at meetings. As the Metro's orchestra conductor, he was far more comfortable communicating through music than words. "No more fake snow. I must insist. You are giving my horn players pleurisy."

"He's right," a socialite agreed. "I'm sick of your fake

snow. It's bad enough we have the real stuff. Let's do something romantic and Russian, something that Fatima and Rudy can really get into. Like *Romeo and Juliet*."

"Your geography is off, but the idea is sound," Auntie Lil agreed.

"Romanoff and Juliet!" Raoul Martinez cried.

"Let's leave it to Emili," Lilah countered calmly. Before anything more could be said, she banged the gavel and announced that the meeting was adjourned.

Board members scrambled for the door, eager to be the first to phone their friends with the inside news on Bobby Morgan's death. They burst into the hallway, only to find a tipsy T.S. blocking the door with help from a barely more sober Herbert Wong.

"Sorry," T.S. said, stepping back with the flair of Gene Kelly in his prime. "We are here to escort the two loveliest ladies in New York City to the Rainbow Room for a bit of dancing." He demonstrated his intentions by holding an imaginary partner in front of him and fox-trotting down the hall a few feet.

"This is easy," he thought to himself. "It just takes a little practice." And what better way to practice than by grabbing a partner, he decided, taking a surprised board member in his arms and leading her back to the doorway just as Auntie Lil and Lilah appeared in it to see what was causing all the excitement.

"Theodore," Auntie Lil said in amazement as her nephew swept past in a cloud of gin and vermouth.

T.S. thrust his current partner at Herbert then highstepped it nimbly back toward Auntie Lil. He bowed low as he passed her then grabbed Lilah around her waist. "Let's switch now to the Latin dances, class!" T.S. cried as he executed a few mamba steps, swayed to a samba, and followed with a lively rumba shake.

Herbert Wong was never one to leave his friends to suffer singular embarrassment. He collected Auntie Lil and followed T.S. down the hall, his firm grip on her elbow making it plain that she was not to attempt to lead.

"Theodore," Lilah exclaimed, admiring his tuxedo, "I

love to dance. But I haven't danced in years. Whenever did you find the time to learn?"

"Wouldn't you like to know, my sweet," T.S. said, dipping her over his knee to the admiring gasps of the crowd. "Now everybody cha-cha!"

When there's a murderer loose, you can bet senior sleuths Angela Benbow and Caledonia Wingate will let neither age—nor a love of food—slow them down when they search for the killer.

Cozy up to some exciting adventures by Corinne Holt Sawyer.